50p

D0130217

This book should be returned/renewed by the latest date shown above. Overdue items incur charges which prevent self-service renewals. Please contact the library.

Wandsworth Libraries
24 hour Renewal Hotline
01159 293388
www.wandsworth.gov.uk

Wandsworth

"A narrative full of invention and surprises . . . Iczkovits mixes real history, fable and the products of his imagination into an intoxicating, thoroughly enjoyable brew"   NICK RENNISON, *Sunday Times*

9030 00007 5837 8

"Echoes of Russian and Yiddish literature resound in this delightful picaresque, but you need not hear them to enjoy it . . . Technicolour characters, pathos and humour are all wonderfully captured in a nimble translation from the Hebrew" *Economist*

"A born storyteller . . . Iczkovits is clearly a talent to watch and *The Slaughterman's Daughter* is the place to start"

DAVID HERMAN, *Jewish Chronicle*

"Ever entertaining, Iczkovits' lively, transportive picaresque takes readers on a memorable ride" *Publishers Weekly*

"Occasionally a book comes along so fresh, strange, and original that it seems peerless, utterly unprecedented. This is one of those books. Iczkovits is a superb talent, and this novel is a resounding success" *Kirkus Reviews*

Yaniv Iczkovits

THE SLAUGHTERMAN'S DAUGHTER

The Avenging of Mende Speismann
By the Hand of Her Sister Fanny

Translated from the Hebrew by
Orr Scharf

MACLEHOSE PRESS
QUERCUS · LONDON

First published in the Hebrew language as תיקון אחר חצות by Keter Books,
Jerusalem, in 2015
First published in Great Britain in 2020 by MacLehose Press
This paperback edition first published in 2021 by

MacLehose Press
an imprint of Quercus
Carmelite House
50, Victoria Embankment
London EC4Y 0DZ

Copyright © 2015 by Yaniv Iczkovits
English translation copyright © 2020 by Orr Scharf
Map and illustrations © 2020 by Halley Docherty

The moral right of Yaniv Iczkovits to be
identified as the author of this work has been
asserted in accordance with the Copyright,
Designs and Patents Act, 1988.

Orr Scharf asserts his moral right to be identified as the translator of the work.

All rights reserved. No part of this publication may be reproduced or transmitted
in any form or by any means, electronic or mechanical, including photocopy, recording,
or any information storage and retrieval system, without permission in writing
from the publisher.

A CIP catalogue record for this book is available from the British Library.

ISBN (MMP) 978 0 85705 830 0
ISBN (eBook) 978 0 85705 826 3

This book is a work of fiction. Names, characters,
businesses, organisations, places and events are
either the product of the author's imagination
or are used fictitiously. Any resemblance to
actual persons, living or dead, events or
locales is entirely coincidental.

10 9 8 7 6 5 4 3 2 1

Designed and typeset in Miller by Libanus Press Ltd, Marlborough
Printed and bound in Great Britain by Clays Ltd, Elcograf S.p.A.

Papers used by MacLehose Press are from well-managed forests and
other responsible sources.

CONTENTS

LONDON BOROUGH OF WANDSWORTH	
9030 00007 5837 8	
Askews & Holts	
AF HIS	
	WW21006561

For my daughters, Daria and Alona

The author would like to extend a special thanks to Professor David Assaf from the Department of Jewish History at Tel Aviv University for his generous and illuminating comments.

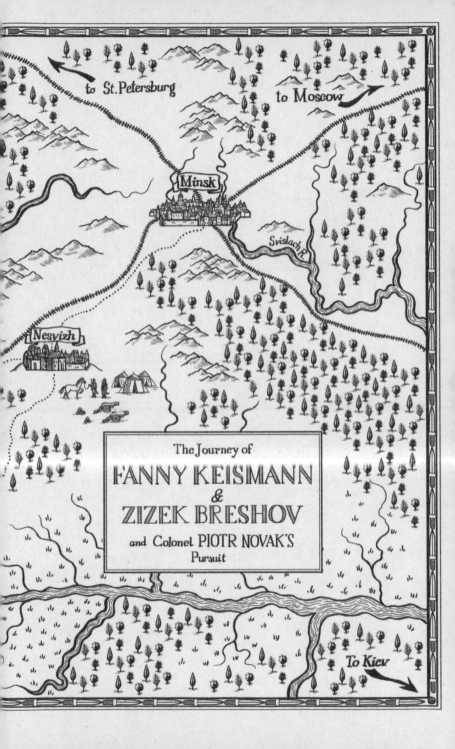

to St.Petersburg

to Moscow

Minsk

Svislach R.

Nesvizh

The Journey of

FANNY KEISMANN
&
ZIZEK BRESHOV

and Colonel PIOTR NOVAK'S
Pursuit

To Kiev

THE YASELDA RIVER

From *Hamagid*

Issue No. 6, Thursday Adar 2, 5654   (February 8, 1894)

THE CRY OF A MISERABLE WOMAN

I implore the honourable readers to pity me, a lonely and despondent woman, because my husband has left me and our three healthy children during Passover, just five years after our marriage. As he was making his way to Pinsk to earn our bread, he sent for me and I followed him until Sukkot. Now he has vanished without a trace, and I was told that he was seen in a hotel in Minsk, and later he was spotted in a railway carriage bound for Kiev, whereas I am left with nothing, dispirited and beleaguered, stripped of my possessions, penniless, with no-one to come to my aid. Therefore, honourable readers, I ask if perhaps one of you knows of my husband's whereabouts? Have mercy upon me and at least obtain from him a duly signed writ of divorce. I am prepared to give money, up to one hundred and fifty roubles, to whoever releases me from my husband's yoke. These are his details: his name is Meir-Yankel Hirsch of the town of Drahichyn, he is now twenty-four years of age, of average height, with brown, curly hair, fair beard, green eyes, and has a mother and a brother in the town of Uzlyany. I, the complainant, am Esther Hirsch, daughter of Shlomo Weiselfisch, righteous man of blessed memory.

I

Poor Esther Hirsch, Mende Speismann thinks, as she lies on her back and tucks the wrinkled clipping from *Hamagid* under the mattress. Three healthy fledglings she's got? She said so herself. One hundred and fifty roubles in her pocket? At least! Not so shabby. Then why the rush to put an advert in the paper? Why give out her name and the name of her family so publicly? With that kind of money, one could hire a gentile investigator, a fearless brute who would pursue her Meir-Yankel and not give the man a moment's peace, even in his dreams, and knock out all his teeth, save one for toothaches.

Mende pulls out the clipping again, careful not to move the shoulder on which her son Yankele is sleeping. She stretches slightly to relieve her cramped neck, which her daughter Mirl has been jabbing with her elbows. The heavy breathing of her in-laws, may they live long, drifts in from the next room. Soon, Mende knows, she must get up, light the stove, dress her children while they are still half-asleep and serve them a bit of milk in a tin bowl with grains of spelt. They will complain about the stale taste, as they always do, and she will ask Rochaleh, her mother-in-law, for a teaspoon of sugar, just one for the children to share. And Rochaleh will look back at her with disapproval that stretches her wrinkled face and scold, "No sugar! Nit! The party is over!" But after a few moments she will sigh in resignation. Every morning, a single teaspoon of sugar is grudgingly brought out.

And what is it about this notice of the loss suffered by poor

Esther Hirsch that has made Mende check and reread it constantly for the past fortnight?

Although she would never admit it, this advertisement gives her pleasure, as do the two others that ran in a previous issue of *Hamagid* (one entitled "A Cry for Help!" and the other "Urgent Appeal!"), and the dozens of other similar notices that keep coming, day after day, from across the Pale of Settlement. Women who have been left behind, women chained to a husbandless marriage, miserable women, schlimazel women abandoned by their husbands with deceitful assurances and charades. One husband leaves for America, *die goldene medina*, with promises to bring the family over to New York; another sails for Palestine to be burned by the sun; a man tells his wife he is going into town to learn a trade, only to be swept up in the intellectual circles of Odessa; a father swears to his daughters that he will come back with a hefty dowry and, all of a sudden, one hears that he is "kissing the mezuzahs" of Kiev bordellos. Mende knows that only fools find consolation in the knowledge that others suffer the same woes as they, and yet contentment steals over her as she reads, overcoming any sentiment of feminine solidarity that she might have felt with these women. She is not like them, she will never be like them. She has not rushed off to publish advertisements, she has not complained to the leaders of the community and she has not circulated descriptions of Zvi-Meir Speismann, the man who tore her life to pieces. She will never do any of this.

Mende's limbs are aching even though she is still in bed, as if she has strained herself in her sleep. The sour odour of sweat wafts in from the room of her elderly in-laws, God bless them. Even the reek of her husband's parents is cause for thanking the Blessed Holy One. True, their house is only a dark, dilapidated old cabin of rotting wood, with two small rooms and a kitchen. But the walls are sealed against draughts, and it has a clay floor, wooden roof shingles and thick-paned windows. And sometimes, a small living space can be an advantage, particularly if the kitchen stove has to heat the entire house. True, chicken is never served here, and the Friday-night fishcakes contain little by way of fish and plenty by way of onion. But borscht and rye bread are served every lunchtime, and cholent stew without meat on Shabbat is not so terrible.

The Speismanns could easily have turned their backs on Mende. After all, they couldn't stand their son, Zvi-Meir, as it was. When he was young, they had hoped that he would make them proud, and they sent him to the illustrious Volozhin Yeshiva with the notion that he should become one of its top students. But after his first year, they heard that their son was openly declaring that the yeshiva's rabbis were all hypocrites, and that the Vilna Gaon himself would have been ashamed of them. "They are a bunch of good-for-nothing wastrels," Zvi-Meir said. "No more than dishonest schemers masquerading as *hakhamim*." So Zvi-Meir left Volozhin, declaring that he would be better off as a poor pedlar than a Torah sage, if being a sage meant that he had to be officious, greedy and aloof.

This change of career notwithstanding, Zvi-Meir still found plenty of reasons to blame and complain. He would bring his pedlar's cart to the market but never encourage passers-by to buy his wares. He would stand there like the congregation's rabbi, convinced that people would flock to his cart as they flocked to synagogue on Shabbat. But the "congregants" walked on by, thinking: if he does not behave like a vendor, why should I behave like a customer? So the Speismann household was one of the poorest in Motal. By the time Zvi-Meir abandoned his wife and children, they had already hit rock-bottom. They lit their house with oil instead of candles, and ate rye bread with unpeeled potatoes. When Mende tried to reason with her husband and give him business advice, he told her: "When the hen starts crowing like a rooster, it is time to take her to the slaughterhouse." That is: never you mind. Heaven forfend, there's nothing more to add.

Pressure on her chest is disrupting Mende's breathing. Her children cling to her on her narrow bed. She keeps her body still, lest her fledglings awake, as her soul cries out, "Why are these children my concern?", only to be immediately beset by guilt – "God Almighty! My poor babies! Heaven protect them!" – and she prays to the good God that He leave her body intact, so that she can provide for her children and offer them a place to rest their heads, and that He unburden her from the heretical thoughts that rise in her mind like the Yaselda in springtime, as it overflows and floods the plains of Polesia, turning them into black marshes.

Another indigent morning lies in wait for her and the children, begging at the gates of dawn. Yankele will go to the cheder and Mirl will help her with the housekeeping at the Goldschmidt residence on Market Street, where the rich of Motal live. Together, they will scrub the floor tiles of the jeweller's opulent stone house, and once again, they will ogle Mrs Goldschmidt's pearl necklace worth three thousand roubles, the value of an entire lifetime of only just making ends meet. From there they will go on to more of the same at the Tabaksmann household, and then they will walk to the tavern: perhaps they will need a hand there too, and perhaps Yisrael Tate, the landlord, will treat Mende to another old issue of *Hamagid* that no-one wants to read anymore.

Cloths and rags, scourers and buckets, floor tiles and ovens, tin bowls and sinks. And so their fingernails peel away the time, one house after another, the smell of detergent clinging to skin

18

and soul. Their toil ends at sundown, leaving them just enough time to regain their strength for the next day. And so the waters of the Yaselda surge on.

II

Once a week, Mende's younger sister, Fanny Keismann, comes over from the village of Upiravah, a seven-verst ride from Motal, and takes Mirl's place in the cleaning work, so that her niece can join her own daughters' Hebrew and arithmetic lessons. Working as a charwoman is disgraceful, all the more so for a wife and mother. Mende is ridden with guilt for dragging her sister into her humiliating attempts to escape poverty. What is more, Mende does not know how to thank Fanny for her help, and is unkind to her instead. Everything that Fanny does or says is met with Mende's rebuke: no-one cleans this way, and why did she forget to polish that window frame, and she must not use so much soap, lest they squander all their pay on suds.

Mende knows that her sister has no need for the meagre wage the cleaning earns her. Once, she saw Fanny slide into Mirl's pocket the coins she had earned in her niece's place. Although Mende said nothing, this infuriated her all the more. How dare she? Will she let this *yishuvnikit*, this rustic Jewess, come over from her village, flaunt her superiority, and give them handouts just to prove that she is better than they? And what will people say about Mende? That she borrows money from her younger sister? Heaven forfend!

Fanny had already gone too far when, not two months after Zvi-Meir went away, she suggested to her older sister that she come and live with her in the village. "You know that the children would love being together, sister, and we would enjoy it too." Offended, Mende replied that village life was absolutely not for her, let alone for Yankele and Mirl, muttering to herself the word "*weit*", which means remote, isolated, or even forsaken.

Fanny was silent, but Mende knew that her sister understood exactly what she meant. Why would any Jew live in a village these days? Whoever did so must be either mad or a recluse. Since when is what most Jews find agreeable not good enough for the Keismanns? What is wrong with a place like Motal, a proper town with a synagogue and a cemetery and a bathhouse and a mikveh? What could they possibly want among the goyim in the heartlands of fields and bogs? Who will protect their home from Jew-hating thugs?

"*Weit*," Mende said again, and Fanny pretended not to hear.

Then Mende added, "Sometimes I do not understand Natan-Berl. Why does he insist on living in a village?"

Throwing Natan-Berl's name into the conversation was a big mistake, an unnecessary tug on a rope that was overstretched as it was. Fanny sent back the cold, impregnable stare of a woman capable of beheading her sister without blinking. This alarmed Mende so much that she quickly glanced down to make sure that Fanny's hands were where they should be, rather than on the hilt of her knife. Underneath her skirts, Mende knew, Fanny carried the knife gifted to her by their late father, who had raised them by himself after their mother had received an urgent summons from On High.

"Natan-Berl knows what he is doing," Fanny said.

Mende had never managed to understand her younger sister's shidduch, let alone its success. Natan-Berl Keismann was a burly hulk, more of a Goliath than a David, with a silent manner that was seen as a mark of wisdom by those who loved him and as feeble-mindedness by those who did not. He had the tan of a goy and the thick flesh of a drunk; black plumes of hair descended from his nape, growing thicker on his arms and curling around his fingers. Every day at dawn, he would rise to tend his geese and his sheep, using the sheep's milk to make the fine cheeses that had earned him a reputation throughout the region. Whenever Mende and Zvi-Meir visited Upiravah, they could hardly wait for the moment when Natan-Berl would produce the triangular wooden tray with wedges of cheese that melted in the mouth and weakened the mind. Yellow, green and blue, bitter and spicy, greasy and fermented, too delicious to be of this world, too fine for a Jewish palate.

Mende does not dare tell Fanny the rumours she hears about the Keismanns. On Shabbat and holidays the Keismanns arrive at the Motal synagogue, come rain or hail or snow, and although they receive a cold welcome from the rest of the congregation, they always ask after their acquaintances with unwavering smiles on their faces. But still the rumours abound. It is said that the unfortunate Keismanns befriend goyim, and not just for commercial purposes either: they visit the gentiles with their children, feast on wine and cheese, and chat in a mixture of Yiddish, Polish and Russian. People say that their house is made of bricks and that it is only covered with wood to fool jealous eyes. People say that the Keismanns have money coming out of their ears. People say that they set up a lavatory in their courtyard, with five openings for ventilation and a barrel dug into the ground, which they take out once a year to fertilise their vegetable patch. People say that Fanny has already learned the native languages and speaks fluent Polish and Russian, and her husband, so they say, does not know a word of Hebrew, swaying at shul like a wheat stalk in the wind – a true *golem*. People say . . .

Mende militantly wards off these malicious stories about her sister: how could a Jew's soul ever mix with the soul of a gentile?

But this is what people say: the Keismanns have split loyalties, they are chameleons through and through. And had they lived in Berlin or Minsk, they would have long since followed the descendants of Moses Mendelssohn and become Christians.

Mende knows that what is said is sometimes more important than what is true, and so she politely declined Fanny's invitation to live in the village with her family.

"Zvi-Meir," she told her younger sister, with wholehearted faith, "will return to his home, sure enough. You know what he is like. He will not settle for anything less than the best. Even if he is doomed to be a trader rather than a scholar, it is only natural that he would want to expand his business. What would he say if he heard that his children had wandered off to the village and become *yishuvnikim*?"

A strange, pleasurable sensation spread through Mende's limbs as she expressed her confidence in her husband. And even now, ten months after Zvi-Meir's departure, it does not feel like such a long time has gone by. She has read in *Hamagid* of married women who had waited more than five years and lost all hope, when finally, without any warning at all, their husbands came home.

Today, with perfect timing, Mende is in for a surprise. Having been caught up in the humdrum of daily life, she has forgotten that today is the fifteenth day of the month of Sivan, in the year 5654. She will mark twenty-six springs today, and behind her back her sister and daughter have been scheming how best to celebrate. Today, Fanny is coming to replace not Mirl, but Mende, to allow her sister to take a day off and do whatever she pleases. They have already worked out all the details, these co-conspirators, and Providence has played along gamely and thrown in wonderful weather. After work, sister and daughter

22

will go to the market to buy delicacies and prepare a royal banquet for Mende. They have even obtained Reb Moishe-Lazer's promise to give her a blessing. In the meantime, Mende can rest at home, or perhaps she would like to leave the noise of the town and go for a walk in the forest across the river. Reb Moishe-Lazer bade them tell her that one's birthday is an opportunity to be reborn.

Mende is uneasy about this rebirth business. Doubt begins to gnaw at her mind: how can she rest and let them work so hard? And why did the Blessed Holy One create Heaven and Earth in six days, and not seven? After all, she already has one day of rest every week. But Fanny and Mirl counter all of her misgivings.

"Shabbat is the Queen, it is for celebrating the sacred; a birthday is for celebrating the mundane."

"But why celebrate my birthday as though it is a kind of achievement? And what is there to find in the forest?"

"Fresh air! Blackberries! Blueberries! Blackcurrants! Go out and enjoy this world a little."

Mende scoffs.

"This world? This world is . . ." She wants to say: terrible, damned, but finds herself stuttering before her daughter. "And besides," she goes on, "I have no way of crossing the river."

Fanny and Mirl giggle.

"We knew you would invent obstacles. We have already thought everything through and talked to Zizek."

"Cross the river in the same boat as a gentile rogue?"

"Zizek is not a goy."

"Poor Zizek doesn't know what he is, God help him," says Mende.

Fanny and Mirl tease her. "Everybody is poor and miserable in Mende's eyes."

Mende gives her sister a cross look and turns to scold her daughter.

"And what about your lessons?"

Mirl's eyes fill with tears, but Fanny whispers in Mende's ear, "Let her, sister, this was her idea. We will help her catch up with her study later, I'll see to it."

And Mende is annoyed that every time Fanny turns to her, she calls her "sister" – as if their relationship were not obvious and had to be underlined each time anew. In the end, she concedes that the two of them have pushed her into a corner and now she has to celebrate, not on her account, but on theirs. The matter is settled.

III

Fanny and Mirl bid her farewell at the market's entrance, next to Yoshke-Mendel's stall. Mende sees them walking away, giggling, peeking back at her and giggling again. Come what may, she will not go out picking blueberries; she is not an adventurous woman. How far might Mende venture on her festive day? From the cucumber stand to the radish stall, if she really tests her limits.

The market is a-bustle with the clamour of man and beast, wooden houses quaking on either side of the parched street. The cattle are on edge and the geese stretch their necks, ready to snap at anyone who might come near them. An east wind regurgitates a stench of foul breath. The townsfolk add weight to their words with gestures and gesticulations. Deals are struck: one earns, another pays, while envy and resentment thrive on the seething tension. Such is the way of the world.

Yoshke-Mendel watches the passers-by as he stands over his "shop", a wooden barrow offering this and that: pencil stubs and nails and toothpicks and kerchiefs and haberdashery. Everyone knows that you will find any useless item you can think of in Yoshke-Mendel's wheelbarrow. Now he is smiling at Mende, his broken teeth cradled in a tousled beard, wrapped in a worn beggar's kaftan and a wrinkled yarmulke. "Did I hear right, Mrs Speismann, a birthday? Mazel tov, then! Why not treat yourself to a hairpin from Yoshke-Mendel? Only two copecks, half-price, many thanks." People are selling linen dresses and leather boots, roosters and meat all around her, and Yoshke is smiling with rotten teeth.

Birds of a feather flock together. Mende does indeed wish to indulge herself on her birthday and has found herself at Yoshke-Mendel's wheelbarrow, and he is showering her with thanks before she has bought a thing. She winces when he calls after her, "Many thanks, come back later, I'll be here."

She walks by the *luftmenschen*, the "air men", the intellectuals, yawning by the roadside, reeking of grog and *vishniac*, each of them with a solitary bearing even though they are sitting in groups. They gather at the market, foraging for occasional work to feed their families – sawmen and porters are always in demand. When times were especially rough, Zvi-Meir used to join them, the *mujikim* he called them, gypsies. They talk about money and luxuries all day long, and there isn't a single broken copeck in their pockets. They admire the capitalists responsible for their poverty more than anyone else. Ask the "air men" if they would rather live decently without any prospect of becoming rich, or in poverty with an infinitesimal chance of making a fortune, and see what they tell you.

Now Mende senses that Zvi-Meir's friends lower their eyes as she passes, like partners in her husband's crime. Who among them is soon to join Zvi-Meir? Who will leave his home at dawn and abandon wife and children? This world is taking a turn for the worse, Mende thinks; suddenly everyone wants to revel in earthly delights and forget about the angels of destruction that await them in Sheol.

At the far end of the market, in the shadow of the church spire, stands the butcher's shop of Simcha-Zissel Resnick, which is really the kitchen of his own house. In the shop window – that is, in the house's front window – whole chickens hang from their thighs alongside cuts of meat and ribs and sausages. Mende usually hastens past this shop; the smell takes her back to her childhood in Grodno, to the days when she wanted for nothing.

Although her slaughterman father, Meir-Anschil Schechter, was never one to lavish affection on his daughters, he did make them banquets fit for kings. In recent times, however, Mende has scarcely touched meat herself, only ever sucking out the marrow of the chicken bones her children leave on their *yontev* plates on feast days. But now a terrible craving for meat has awakened within her, an uncontrollable desire for the taste of beef. A chasm opens up in her stomach and her head spins. Her mouth waters like the high seas, and she is so weak that she has to lean against the wall of the nearby synagogue. This will be her birthday present, it's a clear-cut decision. *A mechayeh*, what a treat.

But how can she be so extravagant? Has she taken leave of her senses? Whoever heard of a Jewess craving beef at this hour of the morning? And what will people say about the gluttony that possessed Mende Speismann, that made her ready to deny her own children food for a fleeting moment of pleasure? However, these objections only intensify her craving and make her all the more frantic as she scuttles home to her in-laws' house for more money.

Rochaleh sees her coming and wastes no time in venting her feelings. Doesn't she, her daughter in-law Mende Speismann, doesn't she care that her *shviger* has been scrubbing the house spotless for her birthday dinner? Who is all this effort for? Mende should come and see, she should at least notice that all the lamps have been polished and refilled with the kerosene Rochaleh has saved especially for the occasion.

"I've worked my fingers to the bone, all day long, and for what?" Mende's *shviger* laments. The usual tirade. And now, Rochaleh goes on, if Mende would be so kind and go out again, they need more firewood. Mende apologises, aims a kiss at the forehead of the sour-faced Rochaleh, and slips away to the back room to take out the savings she keeps hidden in a box beneath the mattress.

One rouble should be enough for a decent cut of meat. She takes two roubles from the wooden box, then puts one back and quickly closes the lid, and then reopens it and thinks again and counts the coins: thirty-two roubles and seventy-one copecks, her entire fortune. In short, two out of thirty-two is no small matter. But even if she spends the two roubles, she will still have more than thirty left. And suddenly, in a spate of mania and craving, she empties the entire box into the pockets of her dress and leaves the house, as Rochaleh's voice echoes after her: "All my bones are hurting, and for what?"

The eyes of the townspeople pierce Mende from every direction. Miserable beggars gawp at her. She avoids the market by taking a muddy alleyway between the wooden houses and arrives back on the main street by the churchyard fence, then she sneaks into Simcha-Zissel Resnick's shop and surprises the butcher as he dozes at the counter; he is unimpressed. Normally Mende only comes to his shop to buy chicken legs for the High Holidays, and such clientele is nothing to write home about. He straightens the cap on his head and wets his lips, taking the feather-plucking knife in his hand.

"What would you like, Mrs Speismann? Chicken?"

But Mende asks for a cut of beef, and Simcha-Zissel rubs the tassels of his *tzitzit* in a request for the Almighty's opinion on the matter. Four silver coins on the counter give him a quick answer and Simcha-Zissel disappears into the store in his courtyard and returns with a piece of beef wrapped in paper. Mende opens the wrapping, she cannot help herself. She could not have asked for a juicier cut, probably from the cow's loin. The meat is red but not shiny, just as her father had taught her it should be, dry on the outside and muscular, covered by a fine layer of fat. Simcha-Zissel Resnick pats his belly and says, "Only the best for Meir-Anschil Schechter's daughter!" She smiles back at him: four roubles have transformed her from a miserable wretch to so-and-so's daughter.

She returns to the alleyway that skirts the busy market. Hunger grips her and her limbs tremble. She holds the cold meat against her middle and feels her heart beating faster and faster. Suddenly she freezes, horrified: how will she cook the meat? She cannot return to her in-laws' home with four silver coins' worth of beef, and even if one of her friends let her into their home, how would she justify this indulgence without making them jealous? How could she dare roast her meat before pale faces and starving eyes without offering an explanation, without offering to share?

Mende leans against the churchyard fence. Her body slides down to the boggy, black ground, and the sun strikes her face. The town of Motal is bathed in a bright light that imbues the market people with a translucent pallor. Beards, hats and head scarves blend with blinds and awnings. Voices and chatter merge with the buzzing of flies. She raises the package, removes the paper wrapping and, without stopping to think, takes a bite of the raw meat. Her teeth are startled by the cold, her eyes widen as she tries to tear off a stubborn, sinewy bite. The taste of blood clouds her senses, stings her lips and tingles on her tongue.

Fortunately, Simcha-Zissel Resnick, suspecting that something is not right, has been watching her through the window, and now he leaves his wife at the shop counter and hastens to Mende's rescue. He gently pulls her to her feet, wraps the meat again, and leads her to a shed in the courtyard, a makeshift kitchen in which he stores wood, bags of grain and an old stove. He seats her before him on a stool, lights the stove and cuts the beef she bought from him into thick slices, which he brushes with oil and sprinkles with spices. Finally, he arranges the slices in a frying pan and fans the flames with the bellows, serving her the first piece a few moments later.

Mende devours the meat, which would have been enough for a family of four, or for six miserable paupers, or ten orphaned children. Simcha-Zissel watches her with some concern, urging her to slow down, to chew the meat and savour its taste. But she revels in her own lust, eyeing the door every other minute like an animal guarding its prey. And when the meat congests her stomach and travels back up her throat, she forces the masticated chunks down into the gluttonous surfeit. Simcha-Zissel watches her with a dismay mingled with barely suppressed desire. Then his wife calls him from the shop and he reluctantly leaves the shed.

In the meantime, Mende leans against a bag of wheat. The food fills her belly and its taste floods her with happiness. She bursts into laughter that keeps rolling on and on until she can hardly breathe. Never before has she laughed like this; no virtuous woman would lend herself to such frivolity, let alone a wife and mother. Indeed, for a moment, anxieties creep back into her thoughts: what has she done? What will happen if her in-laws find out? And what about the firewood she was supposed to bring home? And the money?

She feels the notes and coins in her pocket, but she does not want to go back to being Mende so soon. After all, Mende lashes out all the time, Mende is angry, Mende suffers, Mende worries,

Mende blames: where is Mirl, where is Yankele, why does Fanny, how long, why here, how could he have left, when is he coming back . . . No more! Enough! Not now! She shakes these thoughts from her mind, rises and makes her way back to the market, one stall at a time, one cart at a time, one shop at a time. Before she realises what she is doing, she has chosen new handkerchiefs at Grossman's and is sitting at Ledermann's stall to buy fine leather shoes, and then breaking a twenty-five rouble note at Schneider's to try on a turquoise tasselled dress – so bold! – and asking for a slice of plum torte at Blumenkrantz's pastry shop. And they all take her money and give its full return: it is not every day that they are blessed with a new customer in such high spirits. They ask for ten roubles, she suggests eight, they settle on nine, all without any of the usual mutterings of "I wouldn't even take it for free", or "It's not for me to pay your daughter's dowry". Mende meanders through the market like a bride on her wedding day, showering the stallholders with smiles and sprinkling compliments all around. Mordecai Schatz, the owner of the book cart, cannot help himself and asks, "What is the occasion, Mrs Speismann? Is Zvi-Meir back today?" And Mende roars with laughter and pulls from his cart a new issue of *Hamagid*, printed only twelve days ago, a true feast, and overpriced accordingly. But she could not care less, today she is buying it!

Once again, she comes across the cry of a miserable *agunah*, this time with a more understated headline: "Help". She chuckles and reads the advertisement to Mordecai Schatz in a voice thick with crocodile tears: "I implore the honourable readers of *Hamagid*, perhaps they have heard of my husband, Reb Yosef Zilberstein, who left me nine years ago when he ventured out to the city of Minsk, and not a word has been heard from him since. Perhaps he caught the coughs and, God forbid, his heart stood still; maybe he was taken captive by bandits? Surely he will not deny his charity to me and his two hunger-stricken sons? In his absence, we feed on our own tears. These are his details . . ."

Mordecai Schatz looks at her in amazement, not knowing if he should laugh or cry, and Mende says with a sly smile, "Nine years, Reb Mordecai, what do you think? Ill? Dead? Taken captive?"

Mordecai Schatz lowers his browless, defenceless eyes. Mende pats him on the shoulder: "Taken captive by *kurwas* in a bordello!"

At that moment, an idea flashes up in her mind and she asks Mordecai Schatz for a blank sheet of paper. On she goes to Yoshke-Mendel's "shop" and leaves a copeck for a quarter of a pencil. It all happens so quickly that Yoshke-Mendel doesn't even have a chance to say "many thanks". Mende slips away from the market and finds a shaded spot between the ramshackle huts where, with much excitement, she sits down to write her first letter to *Hamagid*, entitled "The Voice of a Merry and Contented Woman":

I would like to thank the Blessed Holy One for having bestowed upon me bounty and grace, granting me a roof for my head and the heads of my two darling children. I, Mrs Mende Speismann, daughter of Meir-Anschil Schechter, am not waiting for my husband Zvi-Meir. I find it hard to remember his features; I do not have an image of his face in my mind, I do not know how to describe his beard, and the colour of his eyes is long forgotten. But, as long as I live, I shall continue fulfilling my duties for the sake of the Creator, whose generosity to me is plain to see.

For a moment she hesitates, wondering whether this advert is of any public interest and whether it might become a topic of discussion, no longer so sure of what she had wanted to say or whether she has made any spelling mistakes, but then she addresses the letter, according to the details in the issue in her hand, to the Dear Editor Ya'akov Shmuel Fuchs. This public notice, she knows, marks her rebirth, and with trembling hands she gives the envelope to Mordecai Schatz, who travels with his cart between Pinsk and Baranavichy and can post the letter at the Telekhany post office. The matter is settled.

On returning to the street she adjusts her scarf. The smell of excrement rising from the latrines behind the houses jolts her awake as if from a dream, and an elderly horse standing next to her unloads its own contribution of dung, deepening the stench of the malodorous brew. Flies swarm around the mass of faeces, and Mende's full stomach is struck with nausea. She starts back to her home, but then she recalls the request to buy firewood. How time has flown by. She reaches the stall of the wood-seller Isaac Holz, and a chill washes through her body, freezing her breath. Three roubles and forty-five copecks is all that remains in her pockets. All the money she had saved for times of need, for buying a train ticket, for sending Yankele to the yeshiva, bribing an official for papers, giving Mirl something for her dowry and terms of marriage – she has squandered it all in a single fit of madness. And now she stands helpless before Isaac Holz, unable to give him her last coins in return for firewood.

In the distance, she sees two horsemen approaching the market, and Mende prays for the worst to happen. Let them be bandits, let them rob and massacre and burn everything to the ground. She recalls the horrific stories she heard as a child from her grandfather, Yankel Kriegsmann, who used to scare Fanny and her with tales of the pogroms wreaked by Bohdan Khmelnytzky. Her tears choke her, and she wishes desperately for the two riders to turn out to be Cossack brutes. But they are only Kaufmann the horse dealer, and his son, who ride by and greet her with a nod. Why must all the faces around her be so terribly familiar? Where can she find refuge and respite? The Jews have huddled so close to each other that they have not left themselves any space to breathe.

Her head bursts with pain. Cold shivers strike her back like the lashes of a whip. She must ask the vendors to take everything back. Even if they will only agree to half the original price. Or a quarter – anything. But Grossman cannot sell used handkerchiefs, and Ledermann has already hammered the nails into the soles of her new shoes, and Schneider has cut the fabric of her dress and started sewing, and they all refuse her requests and will not refund a single copeck.

IV

They will come looking for her soon. Her in-laws will wonder what has taken her so long, they will suspect that something is awry, and they will not wait idly at home for her return. The only way she'll be able to excuse her lateness is if she crosses the river and pretends that she wanted to be frugal and buy cheaper firewood on the other bank.

Obviously, she will not tell a living soul about her uncontrollable fit, not even her sister, and she will make up the loss with additional cleaning work. Deep down, Mende knows that she will pay a heavy price for the sudden savage impulse that just engulfed her, and yet she cannot quite admit that it was a mistake. Her heart had never throbbed like that before.

She makes for the Yaselda. The sun, that old heretic, shoots gleaming crosses of light over her head, but the pines and oak trees help her along with their fleeting shade. She peeks over garden fences and follows a raucous discussion between some ducks and roosters. A shiksa comes out of her house with her two children, and sweeps the entrance with a straw broom. The woman flashes Mende a black-toothed smile, and Mende wonders if this shiksa has also been left alone with her children.

From a fair distance, she can see Zizek waiting in his boat, and as he is fixing the oars in place, she thinks that he has also spotted her and guessed her intention. She approaches him hesitantly, but says nothing. There's no talking with Zizek. You board the boat, you are rowed to the other bank, and then you come back. He has no interest in discussing the past and he certainly will not subject his daily routine to scrutiny. But if one wants to share a cup of rum from the barrel in his boat, he is more than happy to oblige. He does not wear a hat, he does not wear a four-cornered undergarment with fringes like a good Jew, and he hasn't seen a page of Gemara since he was twelve. Those who want to travel in his boat can come aboard. Those who don't can walk away. And those who call him a sheigetz can try saying it to his face and see what happens to them.

Everybody knows that when he was a child, Zizek's name was Yoshke Berkovits, and that his only sin was to be born into a very poor family at a very sorrowful time for the People of Israel. In 5587, Czar Nikolai the First, the Iron Czar (may his name and memory be blotted out), issued the Cantonist Decree, by which he ordered the conscription into the Russian army of one righteous and innocent boy for every thousand Jews in the population. Every town, village and settlement was forced to tear out the flesh of its flesh and sacrifice its children to Moloch. The heads of the community announced a fast, confronted high-ranking officials, attempted bribes, all to no avail. And so every household of Israel came to realise that it must fend for itself. Parents

34

married off their sons when they were as young as twelve, because married men were exempt from service. Entire families fled the Pale of Settlement. Officials raked in bribes in return for "correcting" dates of birth and forging the number of registered household members. And whose names remained on the authorities' conscription lists? Impoverished families to whom no-one was in a rush to marry off their daughters, who lacked the means necessary to either bribe or escape.

This is how the community leaders came up with the name of twelve-year-old Yoshke Berkovits, Lame Selig's young son, and they sent the *sborchik*, the tax collector in charge of conscription, to break the news of the decision to the parents. Yoshke's mother fell to the ground, and his father stamped about on his lean legs and punched the wall until his knuckles bled. Selig and Leah Berkovits rushed to the synagogue courtyard and implored the rabbi and heads of the congregation to withdraw their decision. They shouted and wept all night long, their wails kept everyone awake, and the rabbi shut himself up in his room and cried with grief. He knew full well that conscription meant almost certain death. These children would be baptised and educated according to the customs of the goyim. They would eat *treif*, they would no longer keep Shabbat, and, if they remained alive after battle, they would pray to that madman, Yeshu'a, who had fantasised that he was the Son of God.

In any case, the Berkovits parents would not leave the courtyard, and their presence became a nuisance. The residents of Motal passed them on their way to the morning prayer and watched them sobbing after the evening prayer. Holiness seemed to desert the synagogue, and everyone walked around with their eyes fixed on the ground, not daring to raise their heads. On the appointed date, Selig and Leah refused to deposit their son with the *asesor*, the local assessor. They kept him at home, did

35

not send him to cheder and would not even let him go outside to draw water. And so the *sborchik* was forced to call in the *khapper*, Leib Stein, who made his living abducting children to fill conscription quotas. At the third watch, he broke into the Berkovits house with a band of thugs, struck Leah in the face when she tried to resist, and deposited Yoshke and two orphans in a prison cell not far from the synagogue. Leah Berkovits stood at the prison gates and wept with heart-wrenching sobs.

What escapades did Yoshke get up to in the Czarist army? No-one knows. Some people will swear they heard that Yoshke-Zizek slew two hundred Turks with his bare hands, while others believe that he was never any more than a paltry quartermaster. Either way, he was no longer a Jew. Clean-shaven, his hair parted on one side, decked out in army uniform and iron medals, and with an unmistakable air of majesty and grandeur, he suddenly reappeared in the town thirty years after he had been wrested from his home. Market pedlars were alarmed by the imposing legionnaire and hesitated before pointing out to him where his mother's house stood. None of the neighbours recognised the gentle boy they had once known, suspecting a confidence trickster in his place. Three of his brothers had married and now lived far from Motal. The brother who still lived with his mother feared Yoshke's vengeance, refused to open the door, and did not tell the old lady what was behind the commotion at the front door. Yoshke had intended to tell his father and mother that their youngest son was back, standing before them like a man raised from the dead. But then one of the neighbours yelled to him that his father had died of sorrow and that his mother avoided any contact with the outside world. And that now it would be best if he did not add to her sorrow; she would expire if she knew that he was there.

Even after this, Yoshke did not leave the residents of Motal in peace. He had acquired great wealth and many privileges as a soldier, and had even been granted a yellow card that permitted him to live anywhere outside the Pale of Settlement. No-one would let him rent a house in Motal, so he bought a parcel of land on the northern side of the river, beyond the lake. In the space of a few weeks he had built a sturdy dinghy for three passengers, with just about enough room for a fourth to squeeze in, although where the third and fourth seats should have been, he loaded a barrel of dark rum, to which he had become addicted during his service. And ever since then he had reported for duty on the Yaselda every day in his uniform, ready to effect a reconciliation between its two banks and burden the hearts of all who saw him with guilt. He began taking passengers thither and bringing those returning hither. And since he did not ask for any fee, and would even offer his customers a cup of grog as he rowed, he quickly built up a monopoly. Zizek transformed his undesirable presence into a necessity and a scourge for the guilt-ridden townsfolk.

What does Zizek want from the residents of Motal? If only he were to tell them, they might understand. At first they tried to get him to talk, offering to pay him with goods, but Yoshke Berkovits rejected all compensation. Then they suspected that he might not remember how to speak Yiddish and tried Russian and Polish instead. But he kept rowing and did not respond even when they addressed him by name. Does he blame them or is he in pain? Is he hopeful or disappointed? Has he come back to give them an eye for an eye or to turn his other cheek? One thing was clear: the name "Yoshke Berkovits" brought back forgotten memories that were best left where they were, and it was not a name fit for a man without religion or family. Therefore, when the name "Zizek Breshov", his name in the Czarist army, was first mentioned, the people of Motal were relieved.

Zizek is a popular name among the goyim and common enough among soldiers; in a way, it testified to Zizek's full transformation from Jew to gentile.

Now though, as Zizek is nodding at Mende and as she hops into the boat, she glimpses poor Yoshke Berkovits behind the soldier's uniform and feels pity for him. With an oar in each hand, he pushes away from the bank, careful not to rock the boat more than necessary. He rows with great precision and his face displays only an absolute calm. She makes the mistake of believing, like so many before her, that it is with her, of all people, that the unfortunate man will at last consent to talk, and she dares to address him by his original name: "Yoshke?" But nothing stirs in his face, his scarred lips remain sealed, his nostrils flare, and his bright-coloured eyes stay fixed on the bank. Suddenly, his serenity strikes her as apathy, his gaze seems to harbour death, like the vacant carcass of a deer, and a sharp pain pierces her heart. "What is wrong with this world?" cries out her soul, and she feels the few coins left in her pocket. A world where poor children are snatched away from their parents, where they can be torn from their faith, and the miserable wretches abandoned to lives of torment. Where is justice? God help us.

She is no longer thinking of herself, for she is not faring too badly, all in all. She has her commandments and customs, a roof over her head and her children, she earns a living and has good neighbours. But why is she in such a hurry now? To fetch firewood for the stove? To celebrate with a birthday meal? How is she any different from the goyim feasting in their homes while thugs burn down Jewish households? After all, she indulges her petty anxieties, just like them, as the truly unfortunate see their world fall apart.

"Stop," she says, "I want to go back."

But Yoshke keeps rowing across the river.

"Stop!" she begs. "I cannot go on."

The splash of Yoshke's oars continues unabated. His indifference terrifies her. She utters a prayer to the all-merciful God, and throws herself, head-first, into the waters of the Yaselda.

V

The Yaselda river does not lend itself to drowning. Its waters are shallow and its currents are restrained. In winter it freezes, in spring it floods the fields, and in summer its temperament is as moderate as that of a tzaddik, the righteous man, who never bellows his prayers until he is hoarse, never lavishes alms right and left on his trips to the market, and does not boast of his wisdom to others. The tzaddik keeps the commandments at home, gives charity in secret, and does not care whether or not he impresses the other members of the congregation.

Mende wakes up in her bed. Her eyes can barely open and her vision is blurred. She recognises her mother-in-law Rochaleh's sour smell, and the hunched back and the loud voice with which Eliyahu, her father-in-law, wages war against his deafness. It is hard not to recognise Reb Moishe-Lazer, thanks to his enormous coiffured beard, and she would know the silhouettes of her children from any distance. Out of the corner of her eye she notices a girl, or perhaps a woman, probably her younger sister Fanny, nerves wracked, beating her fist on the wooden wall. A man is sitting at Mende's bedside. She cannot turn her head to look at him and is only aware of the palm of his hand resting on her heart, when suddenly he rises and lowers his head towards her chin. Can it be? Has her plight driven Zvi-Meir to repentance?

Has he finally returned to his wife and children? She tries to catch a glimpse of his face, but her neck is too stiff.

"She has woken up," the man announces in a squeaky voice, and she needs another moment or two to realise that the voice belongs to Dr Itche-Bendet Elkana.

She flutters her eyelids and lets out a pained sigh. Everyone, apart from her younger sister, gathers around her. Her son Yankele lands heavily on her stomach and Mirl pulls him back. No, Mende wants to tell her, this is a wonderful pain, but her voice seems to choke in her throat. Rochaleh eyes her daughter-in-law long enough to conclude that the patient will live.

"Well," she says, clutching Mende's arm in an unnecessarily tight grip, "have you finished making us worry?" She plumps up the pillow under Mende's head, keeping hold of her bedridden daughter-in-law's arm.

"This is not her fault," Eliyahu says. "I've been saying it for a long time: that Zizek is nothing but trouble."

Mende thinks that this is the first time she has heard him say anything of the sort.

"Did he push you in the river?" interjects Reb Moishe-Lazer Halperin, by virtue of his responsibility for his congregants' well-being.

"How could he push and save her at the same time, Reb Halperin?" her sister Fanny calls from the back of the room. "It was Zizek who brought her back here straightaway, and sent for the doctor."

The rabbi is momentarily stymied by this reasoning, but rallies quickly. "He pushed to take revenge and saved to make amends, this is what happens to a man torn between the Jewish and Christian faiths."

Mende shakes her head, still unable to get a word out. "There is your answer," Fanny says. "She wanted to wet her face in the heat of the day and she slipped, did you not, sister? Now, stop interrogating her and send someone to thank dear Zizek for saving her life."

Mende nods, and they all seem disappointed by this simple explanation for the accident. When disaster strikes there must be culprits, even if the victim does not have the courage to name them. Eliyahu pays the rabbi for his blessings and gives Dr Elkana his fee, and then bows in gratitude. Rochaleh sends Mende a glance more painful than the firm grip on the arm, which plainly says, "We spent one rouble and then another one, and for what?"

The doctor bids them farewell with a prescription they could have devised without his expertise: Mende should rest for a few days, regain her strength with three meals a day, drink plenty of water and stay warm; and should her temperature rise or her neck become swollen, God forbid, they should send for him right away. What will he do then? Everybody knows the answer: not much. Still, it is better to hear these things from a man with credentials than from a fool.

Reb Moishe-Lazer Halperin re-enters the room to say goodbye to Mende and informs her of the extraordinary level of interest in her well-being from the people of Motal. She will not believe her ears, but Ledermann the cobbler has sent complimentary leather boots and called in Chaya-Leike to utter her incantations and drive away the Evil Eye with eggs and chamomile paste. Schneider the tailor has promised a turquoise dress as a gift – "You know how crazy Schneider can be sometimes." And Simcha-Zissel Reznick the butcher has brought over some leftover sausage, along with medicinal herbs and linden blossom. And they all want to know what else might bring her relief.

"I have never known such camaraderie in this town before," he says, exultant, before calling Yankele and Mirl to come and visit the neighbours with him so that their mother can rest.

Mirl resists leaving her mother's bedside but finally acquiesces, and once the children have gone, a loud argument ensues in the next room. Rochaleh and Eliyahu are complaining to Fanny, who is imploring them to leave her sister be.

"Leave her be?" Eliyahu shouts, this time not because of his deafness. "How can we leave her be when she is acting so foolishly? I've been saying for a long time that she is becoming unhinged."

"Where did she vanish off to?" asks Rochaleh. "Can't you explain? You are her sister!" with an accusatory emphasis on the word "sister".

"Do you know we found a fortune in the pockets of her dress?" Eliyahu says. "What can she be doing with more than three roubles?"

"You owe us an answer," Rochaleh continues, furiously. "Our lives have become a living hell, and for what?"

And Eliyahu says, "We did not take her into our home for her to ruin our reputation."

Then quiet takes over, and many *shushes* disperse in the air. On hearing someone walk into her room, Mende pretends to be asleep.

"Sister," says Fanny, "it's me."

But Mende retreats deeper into herself. Fanny's words cannot assuage her, neither "sister" nor "it's me". Mende is alone in the world, and this world is not for her.

The days go by, a few nights sneak in between, a week elapses and there is no change. While Mende's body is fully recovered, and her lungs are emptied of river water, her words remain trapped inside her and her soul remains despondent. She is barely able to get up from her bed, and as she can only nod in assent or shake her head in refusal, her carers switch to yes-or-no conversations with her: "Hungry? Thirsty? Tired? Do you want to get up? Are you comfortable? Want to go back to bed? Want us to cover you up?" Mende is actually beginning to like this form of communication. Firstly, it does not demand any effort or thinking on her part. Secondly, it focuses on corporeal matters and not so much on the soul. And thirdly, it deflects any further discussion about what happened on the river with Zizek.

But there is a downside. Mende's thoughts have also shrunk to consist merely of "yea" or "nay". Her gaze has become glazed, her lips are dry, and her company is becoming burdensome. But if she is possessed by a dybbuk, it is a strange dybbuk indeed. Her body does not convulse, her mouth does not spit curses, her faith is as strong as it has ever been, and the sages of Motal are unsure whether an exorcising ceremony to expel the dybbuk would improve her condition. The neighbours continue to bring talismans but keep their visits short: one minute in Mende's company is all it takes for boredom to set in. Her in-laws cannot scold an inanimate object, and her children are too afraid to come near her.

Only her younger sister travels over from the village every day to visit, bringing with her a bit of bread and cheese, and sometimes a slice of coffee cake or some marmalade. Fanny opens the window, airs the room, straightens the sheets and then sits by her sister's bed. She talks about the children for a while, telling Mende of Yankele's mischief and the progress that Mirl and her own daughters are making in their Hebrew and arithmetic lessons, and then relates a little of the news she hears in Motal. But Fanny has never been much of a talker either.

At the weekends, Fanny brings Natan-Berl and their five children with her, and sometimes Natan-Berl's mother, Rivkah Keismann, will tag along despite the torturous journey, and only because "they begged her to come".

Mende Speismann does not know how much money Natan-Berl secretly gives her in-laws for her keep – twenty roubles, maybe thirty, each month. From Eliyahu's obsequious tones, she knows that her in-laws' household would not be able to make ends meet without her sister's help. And yet Mende is incapable of showing her any warmth. One day, however, Fanny surprises Mende with the news that she is forced to go away for a while. Natan-Berl's uncle is on his deathbed, and the entire family is to gather in Kiev. She does not know how long they'll be away, a month, maybe two, but Mende is not to worry, because Fanny has already made all the necessary arrangements with Rochaleh and Eliyahu. Mende is robbed of her breath and choked by her tears. She half-rises from her bed and clings to her younger sister's neck.

"Do not worry, sister," Fanny whispers. "I will be back soon, definitely before the High Holidays."

"I— I—" stutters Mende and closes her eyes to hold in the tears.

"I know, sister," Fanny murmurs, relieved that Mende still remembers words other than "yes" and "no".

Fanny's absence is very much felt. The days meander, dates become meaningless and the High Holidays drift further and further away. The only significant effect the changing seasons have is that they dictate how wide they open the window for Mende, and the sounds of the vibrant world outside seem to mock the woman who is still shut away in her room. Rochaleh's and Eliyahu's resolute footsteps pound accusingly around the house. How much longer, Mende, how much longer? And her fledglings, who used to be the source of her joy and are now a source of torment, stand at her room's threshold, yearning for affection.

One day, a package is delivered to her by Yisrael Tate, the

tavern owner. A brand new issue of *Hamagid*, a rarity in god-forsaken Motal, which doesn't even have a post office. As soon as he has gone, Mende opens the paper with a mixture of excitement and shame: maybe it is her turn this time? What has become of her advertisement?

Yet she is in for a double disappointment today. Not only is there no trace of the announcement she wrote on her birthday, but she also comes across a new and oddly titled notice, "Wife Lost", in which help is sought in finding a lady – a wife? – who has disappeared. This is strange, thinks Mende, reading the first few lines, which contravene common sense and morality alike, and her heart is filled with animosity towards the spoiled women who turn their backs on their calling.

A woman went out in the second hour after midnight and has not returned since. All of our efforts to look for her in villages and towns, forests and rivers have failed. Her whereabouts are unknown and there's not a trace of her to be found. Therefore, anyone with the slightest bit of information regarding this woman should hasten to send it our way. She has left her husband, five children and miserable mother-in-law in despair in their village home.

Yishuvnikim, thinks Mende. Villagers. No wonder, the miserable wretches. Living among the goyim and imitating their manners. Black is white, bad is good, earth is sky, and woman is man. *Hamagid* is a despicable paper for consenting to run such abominable advertisements. What interest could the public have in this anomalous case, which tells them nothing about the way things ought to be? Besides, there's no way of knowing whether this story is just a fabrication; perhaps all the writer wants is attention, to shock the public with their arrogance.

She drops the newspaper on the floor by her bed. Has the world turned upside down? Is the sea on fire? Is there nothing else to write about? Has the Messiah arrived? Is she in the rebuilt Jerusalem? Have Jews reached the point where wretched women can allow themselves to abandon their poor children and husbands, Heaven forfend? She begins to cry. Master of the World, I beseech you to place an obstacle in the path of this woman leaving her home in the second hour after midnight. Bring her back to her village, to her husband and five miserable children, and do not let her lead other women astray. Some catastrophe is about to happen, Blessed Holy One, I can feel it in my bones.

Mende picks up the newspaper again, this time searching for a sign between the lines that her prayer has been answered. She is drawn back to the "Wife Lost" notice, and reads on to the end.

These are her details: young, twenty-five years of age, her face is round, her hair fair (blonde), ash-grey eyes, simple, unfriendly, has a long scar marking the bite of a beast on her left arm, she was seen leaving dressed in black with a short, reddish jacket over the top. Her name is Fanny Keismann, and I, her mother-in-law, Rivkah Keismann, ask that you help my son, Natan-Berl Keismann, and I am prepared to pay generously anyone who knows of her whereabouts.

GRODNO

I

For many nights, Fanny Keismann had been unable to sleep. Mende's sad eyes reminded her of their mother, during their Grodno childhood. Deep black eyes with bags underneath. When she was a girl, there was nothing that Fanny would not try to raise their mother's spirits. She helped with the chores, made kreplach and krupnik, learned to read the *Tzena U'Renah* and the *Teutsch Pentateuch*, and even drew water from the Neman. She would spill half of it on the way back, but she carried as much as a young girl could. But whenever she approached her mother, hoping for a hug and a kiss in return, she was always met with the same answer: "Not now, Fannychka, not now. Mamme is tired." A sigh.

Her father, Meir-Anschil Schechter, who was usually a stern man, had one joke that he liked to tell. He dismissed any theory that a dybbuk might have possessed his wife, and would never hear of exorcism and talismans. "Your mother," he explained to Fanny and her sister, "is actually quite a happy woman, and there's nothing in this world that she loves more than you two. But she can't help being the righteous woman that she is. And if it is said 'In pain shall you bear children', then she must act accordingly."

"There is no such commandment!" Fanny said with indignation.

"You are a bright child," her father replied, his countenance softening. "Very clever."

Throughout her childhood, Fanny used to tug down on her cheeks to avoid getting those same bags under her eyes that were so characteristic of her mother. And recently, having spent all those hours with Mende, she has noticed that her hands are once more pulling at her cheeks and her thoughts have been drawn, against her better judgment, back to those faraway days.

Even in the dead of night, at the second hour past midnight, as she left her home and climbed into Mikhail Andreyevich's cart, which was waiting for her as arranged on the outskirts of the village with his horse, she felt as if she was racing to her mother's final place of rest, somewhere between the fields of potatoes and the fields of wheat.

Fanny was ten when her mother's light went out, and the child had watched as her mother's dead body was laid out in the kitchen on a thin mattress covered with a white sheet. Her father explained to her that they were waiting for the lady morticians of the *chevra kadisha*, who had been delayed by a snowstorm. Her mother lay on the floor in this way all through the night, between the kitchen table and the oven, and Fanny could not sleep even for a moment. When she thought she could hear breathing and gurgling from the kitchen, she dared to leave her bed and go to her mother. She felt her mother's cold hands and crept underneath the sheet that covered her. For the first time in her life, she encountered neither her mother's broken voice saying "Not now, Fannychka, not now. Mamme is tired", nor that damned sigh. The child clung to the body and held its hand, until her father found them there at the break of dawn. These hours were among the happiest she had ever known, and her father smiled down at her without any sign of alarm.

II

Meir-Anschil Schechter was a decent man: *"in ehrlicher Yid"*, as everyone used to say. Not a scholar, not a sage and not among the tzaddikim, but he was certainly God-fearing. Descended from a well-known family of shochetim, he had continued the family tradition of strictly observing the laws of animal slaughter, scrupulously following the rules of kashrut and naming a fair price for both buyer and seller. He refused to accept coins or notes from his customers. "They are for speculators," he used to say. In return for his slaughtering services, clients would bring choice cuts of meat, bags of wheat, jugs of milk, fruit and vegetables, and even furniture and clothes. Monetary scepticism had been the hallmark of the Schechter family for many generations, and it had shielded them from worries about the depreciating impact various political situations had on the currency.

Meir-Anschil followed a strict daily routine. In the morning he would rise, wash his hands, say his benedictions, pray, eat his bread and go to sharpen his *halaf* on a stone. He took care of his daughters with punctilious devotion from the moment they awoke until they left the house, and then went his separate way to the abattoir for his day's work.

The cattle and poultry would arrive at Meir-Anschil's business tethered and crammed together, with the fear of death in their eyes. Cows and sheep and goats and calves and lambs and roosters came in, one after the other, on teetering legs, with dry tongues and broken spirits. As they were brought into the slaughtering pen, the animals smelled the blood and tried to resist with all the strength they had left in them. They kicked and bellowed until they tore their throats, letting out exactly the same cries they would have heard a few days earlier, coming from the direction of this very pen. Their owners cracked their whips, trying to crush any lingering resistance, but Meir-Anschil would take the animals from them and ask his customers to wait outside for a moment. Once he was all alone with an animal, Meir-Anschil never felt any real pity. True, he gave the cows water to drink and patted the calves, and looked into the subdued eyes of the lambs; but he did this out of a sense of necessity and respect, not sympathy. The animals registered the stern expression on his face, sniffed the blood on his apron, and knew that this final charity had been granted to them by none other than their executioner. It was his kindness, which exceeded that of their owners, that made them suspicious. Therefore, when he threw them on the ground, their feet bound and their bodies deep in the dirt, they gazed vacantly up at him, as if they already knew that their fate was sealed.

Once he had begun the job Meir-Anschil never tarried, guiding his knife in a single, smooth motion. He cut the trachea and the oesophagus, the carotid artery and the jugular in a single movement, without crushing the neck, or cutting from top to bottom. He did not insert the knife between the trachea and the oesophagus, did not point the *halaf* anywhere beyond the incision, did not tear at the flesh – either with the blade or with his hand – he did not press or crush the animal, and he never worked when he was tired. Only once he had checked and confirmed that the incisions were kosher and that the pipes of the trachea and oesophagus had been correctly severed, would he wipe his forehead and hands, give thanks to God for the commandment to "cover blood with dust" and throw some earth over the pool of blood to absorb it.

In the evening he returned home to his wife, Malka Schechter, and their two daughters, and because Malka usually confined herself to her room it was he who prepared a feast of a dinner for the four of them. Meir-Anschil and his daughters would eat heartily, dark bread and fresh vegetables and grains and noodles and meat, while his wife watched them with a preoccupied air. Meir-Anschil had built his home on the left bank of the Neman, a fair distance from the market square, and placed the slaughter-house as far away as possible from the ears of the townsfolk. He never took any interest in gossip and usually resented the pilpul of sages, and therefore few guests ever frequented their home. In the evenings, his only wish was to be left in peace so that he could smoke his pipe and go to bed early.

He loved his wife with a mad passion. His parents had agreed to the terms of his marriage when he had been a boy of ten, and for years they told him about Malka's beauty and wisdom. He fell in love with her before he had seen her even once.

They married two years after his bar mitzvah. All his life, his parents had taught him that marital relations evolve gradually, out of a sense of duty, but in Malka's presence he felt like a man caught in a downpour: his face burned, his heart danced, and his mouth uttered nonsense and lies. He found himself unworthy of her beauty, of her round face, pink cheeks, scarlet lips, unworthy even of the little dimple on her chin, and he was riddled with anxiety whenever he was with her. He knew that the only reason for their shidduch was his profession, which guaranteed a good income, but it was precisely because of his job that he could not allow himself to touch his wife. How could he approach her, with hands that had so much blood on them? In his clothes, impregnated with the stench of death? How could he eclipse her splendour with his dark world? On their wedding night, he did not dare enter her bed, and it took months of sleeping next to each another in two separate beds for her to move over to his and lie down next to him, which obliged him to defile her slender body with his clumsy flesh and animal-like grunts. In the morning, when she smiled at him with blushing cheeks, he felt that she was only pretending, out of respect for him. He did not love her the way righteous men love their wives, from a sense of duty and a wish to observe the commandments; he desired her like a hungry beast and he was in thrall to her like a slave. Every evening, he returned home, certain that he would find her gone, and was eternally grateful that she was prepared to endure, if even for just one more day, his awkward appearance, his acrid smell, his slow mind and his despicable profession.

He received his warning sign from Heaven in a dream that began to haunt him. He would be at the slaughterhouse waiting for a client, who arrived pulling along a strange animal by a rope: a beast with the body of a cow and the head of an angel – an angel with Malka's delicate face. They would be left alone, the shochet and this creature, her tongue parched and her eyes wide open. He would call out to the heavens with bitter tears, then raise the *halaf* above her neck, but in his anguish he would rip at her organs and defile the act. She would die in his arms, slowly, and he would wake from the nightmare drenched in sweat and petrified.

The image of his beloved wife's face on the body of a cow was bad enough for Meir-Anschil, and the memory of the desperation on Malka's face was indeed horrific. But something else unsettled him even more. How could his hands have behaved so clumsily and torn the creature's organs like an inept amateur? He realised that if he were to continue on this path of uncontrollable desire for Malka, he would first lose his livelihood, and then both he and his family would be lost altogether. That summer, he expanded their wooden house into their back yard, built an extra room for himself and moved into it permanently.

III

Ever since she was a young girl, Malka had been eaten up by guilt. Her father, Yankele Kriegsmann, never stopped reminding her that she was responsible for all his misfortunes. Times were hard, only the Blessed Holy One could remember better days, and Yankele Kriegsmann's livelihood hung by a thread. In his youth he had inherited vast stocks of wheat, which gradually rotted because he could not make up his mind about what to do with them. At first, he wanted to export them to the west, but was stalled by government bureaucracy. Then he learned to make beer, by which time Jews were banned from manufacturing and serving alcohol. He blamed these failures on his spoiled children, who necessitated his staying in one place and were a constant drain on his time. Consequently, he did not spare them his rod and terrorised them with stories about the angels that strike the dead with white-hot irons.

Yet even with lazy children such as his, Yankele Kriegsmann discovered that he could earn a nice income by taking in large dowries for his sons and paying out small dowries for his daughters. After all, there's nothing undignified about making a profit. He was not especially particular, therefore, when his daughters began to receive marriage proposals, and decided that Malka, the prettiest of them all, should marry the son of Isaac-Wolf Schechter, who came from a family of slaughterhouse owners – which, admittedly, was not a respectable profession, but they were the best in their trade in the entire district. Malka was twelve when she married.

For Malka, it was no wonder that her husband did not come to her bed immediately after their wedding. In her own eyes, she had been a liability before the wedding and was to remain a liability ever after, and if her father knew this, how could she expect anything different from anyone else? This is why she was not puzzled when Meir-Anschil kept himself to himself on their wedding night, and why it came as no surprise when they continued to sleep in separate beds for many months. Nevertheless, she invented a game of prophetic signs that gave her both hope and warnings: if the rooster calls fewer than three times, Meir-Anschil will smile at her; but if it calls more than thrice, her husband will keep his usual sour face. If she pours the tea without spilling any, her husband will notice her beauty; but if she spills even one drop, he will think her ugly. If their horse neighs, good fortune will come their way; but if her shoes become covered in mud, disaster will strike. Needless to say, this chain of cause and effect that she imposed on reality was refuted over and over again. Yet all it took was just one prediction to be fulfilled for Malka to feel in control and invent a new pact. And so, one stormy night, she promised herself that if the window blew open, she would enter her husband's bed – and when the wind duly opened the window, she did just that.

After that night, Meir-Anschil continued to pursue her, but she was not surprised when, several months later, he gave up and started sleeping in another room. She lay alone at night, unable to determine whether she was asleep or awake, fantasising about the baby that would need her and depend on her for solace. When Mende was born, Malka could not let her out of her sight and would not let anyone else come near her for fear of the Evil Eye. Malka tied the baby to her apron with a rope, because she knew that if the neighbours were to hold Mende she would not be able to find a husband for her daughter, and that if she ever left the house without her mother, the toddler would surely be run over by the wheels of a cart. Even the touch of Meir-Anschil on the baby seemed to Malka like the kiss of death.

A year later, with Fanny's birth, things grew even worse. Malka lost control altogether and could only predict imminent catastrophe. She had no doubt that one day the Neman would overflow and that both her daughters would be overcome by the water. She visualised the girls drowning as she tried in vain to rescue them. Her grief over their loss barely permitted her to get out of bed. She gave birth to them in hope, and watched them grow in sorrow, helpless against their sealed fate.

IV

When Malka Schechter died, Meir-Anschil had no wish to fulfil the commandment to be fruitful and multiply with another woman, despite repeated attempts to bring his lack of male heirs to his attention. He kept on with his daily routine and left his daughters with their grandfather, Yankel Kriegsmann. The old man was asked to teach them Hebrew and arithmetic, but he devoted most of their lessons to his descriptions, in minute detail, of the fate awaiting them in Hell, where women are hung by their hair and breasts.

One evening, as Meir-Anschil was sitting with his daughters, he noticed that Mende was eating with an unusual appetite. Fanny matter-of-factly explained that her sister had broken the hinge of a door in their grandfather's home and had therefore been punished. Meir-Anschil tried to understand the reasoning behind the decision to punish her by starvation, and it was only then that he discovered the grandfather's educational methods. Without further ado, he instructed the girls to continue eating, took his *halaf* and left his house in the direction of his father-in-law's. Kriegsmann was caught completely by surprise when his front door swung open, and the burly hulk of his son-in-law stood in the doorway, wearing a black cape and a fur hood, and wielding a knife. Meir-Anschil threw Kriegsmann across the kitchen table, grabbed him by the neck and pressed the *halaf* against his throat. The old man writhed in his grip and Meir-Anschil sent a fist flying into his jaw.

From that day on, Meir-Anschil left his daughters in the charge of Sondel Gordon, the tailor, so that they could learn his trade. Indeed, sewing is a low-paying profession whose practitioners risk dimming eyesight, but Meir-Anschil hoped that it would allow him to send his daughters to the Lower East Side in New York, where, rumour had it, seamstresses were in high demand and the Jews prospered. What is more, Gordon's shop was not far from the slaughterhouse, and Meir-Anschil could keep as much of an eye on his daughters as he liked.

Yet Providence, as is its custom, had other ideas. For a few days, Meir-Anschil sensed that something was not right, and found himself constantly turning his head to see if someone was following him. The animals sensed his nervousness and struggled with even greater ferocity, while the customers noticed his hesitation when he took the tethers from their hands. At times, he wondered if the Blessed Holy One was watching him at work and scrutinising his technique, which disconcerted him each time he brought the *halaf* to an animal's neck.

As it transpired, nothing of the sort was happening. In a moment of quiet concentration, as he covered blood with dirt, he heard noises coming from the roof and immediately concluded that he was indeed being scrutinised from above. But it was not the good God On High, but an unexpected voyeur who turned out to be none other than—

"—Fanny?!"

The child nearly rolled off the roof when she heard her father calling out her name; and when he carefully lowered her from the window, her first instinct was to run away. Meir-Anschil gripped her arm and felt her body tremble. Her grey eyes became impregnable and her face was quite calm.

"You should never have seen that," he said, alarmed by the expression on his daughter's face. "Now hurry back to Sondel Gordon."

They said nothing to each other at dinner that evening, but when Mende cleared away the plates, Meir-Anschil announced that he wished to speak with his younger daughter.

"What you saw today," he said, "is *parnussah*, which is how I make a living." He hesitated. "*Parnussah*, that is, the animals and the blood." He garbled his words. "Your grandfather was also a shochet," he sighed. "And his grandfather," he added. "The whole family, in fact. Anyway," he finished, "I am sorry you saw it." And he stopped talking.

"I want to learn too," Fanny said, her eyes gleaming behind her fair hair. Meir-Anschil burst out laughing, startling Mende, but then he realised that Fanny, who was not yet eleven, was deadly serious.

"Learn what?" he asked, to make quite sure that he had understood her correctly.

"I want to learn how to use the knife," she said.

Meir-Anschil's heart flooded with pride. The blood of shochetim runs through her veins, he thought, and then he recalled that morning, a year earlier, when he had found Fanny lying beneath the white sheet next to her deceased mother. The girl had held her mother's hand and had not been dissuaded by the soul's dance as it exited the body. She had felt a need to be the last person to bid farewell to the corpse, exactly the feeling that compelled Meir-Anschil to report for work at the gates of annihilation each and every morning. If there was one thing Meir-Anschil detested, it was the self-righteous who feed on meat but are disgusted by death and blood. They complain about the screams and screeches, and want to move the slaughterhouse out of the town to keep the stench of the carcasses at a distance. And then what do they serve at their tables?

It was unthinkable that a girl should learn the slaughterer's trade, let alone a future wife and mother. Nevertheless, in complete breach of her father's wishes and instructions, Fanny clung steadfastly to her plan, and Meir-Anschil began to notice worrying signs in his daughter's behaviour. Firstly, although Mende knew how to patch clothes immaculately by now, Fanny had not learned a thing from Sondel Gordon. Secondly, Meir-Anschil saw her nosing about the slaughterhouse on two further occasions. Thirdly, on rainy days the roof began to leak in several places, and when Meir-Anschil climbed up to inspect it, he discovered that some of the tiles had been moved and not replaced properly. Fourthly, the letter opener that disappeared from the kitchen table was found in Fanny's room. And fifthly, Meir-Anschil began to notice deep scratches on the furniture around the house.

Whatever Fanny could deny, she denied: the spying, the tiles, the scratches, and more. But when, one evening, he glanced into her room and saw her wielding the letter opener in her left hand and grabbing an imaginary creature in her right, Meir-Anschil knew that he was in deep trouble. However, a man like him does not give in to his distress, so he forbade that which he saw from continuing and accepted that which was hidden from his eyes, in the hope that the whim would pass. And then the rabbi came to see him on behalf of Sondel Gordon the tailor, who feared speaking with Meir-Anschil about his younger daughter, and yet was also concerned about the letter opener, which, it transpired, she had been using to dismember insects on the shop floor.

The rabbi made it clear to Meir-Anschil that he was speaking to him as one father to another. After all, Fanny had only recently lost her mother, and her refusal to learn to sew and her activities with the knife were surely indications that she was going through a difficult time. Best to pay special attention to her and perhaps even seek the help of a woman at home; the Almighty knows that a girl needs a mother. Anyway, let it be clear that he had no wish to interfere with the child's upbringing. As far as he was concerned, she could even become a female shochet, should the honourable gentleman so choose. It was only that it was best to put her on the straight and narrow path and avoid sealing her fate because of a childish caprice, and hence . . .

"What do you mean, 'she could even become a female sho-chet'?" Meir-Anschil demanded.

"I did not mean to offend," the rabbi said.

"She *can* be a female shochet?"

"Forgive me," the rabbi said, raising both his hands, "but that is not what this is about."

"Women can perform religious slaughter, they can actually perform the act?"

"Well, it is best if they don't. But never mind that. The thing is . . ."

"If that is so, then they *are* forbidden to practise it?"

"Well," the rabbi mumbled, "there is no explicit prohibition, and our law permits it in principle, but important halakhic rulers have already recommended that women had best refrain from practising the trade, due to their timidity and frailty. But, mind you, that is not why I came to see the honourable gentleman; that is not what is at stake."

The next day, Meir-Anschil invited Fanny to come to the slaughterhouse. The conditions were clear: she must watch and be silent. He gave her an old, oversized apron and seated her on a stool in the corner. This was how he himself had started at the age of ten; he remembered all too well being rushed back to his home twice on account of his vomiting and dizzy spells. In the evening, his father had come into his bedroom and said, "True, you will not have beauty in your world, but there will not be a thing that you and your family will need and not have." He had loathed his father for saying this and had always felt tortured by the profession he had inherited. Now, he felt a faint pang of remorse for having not promptly stopped his daughter from following him down the same path.

"Are you ready?" he asked Fanny, hoping that she might yet change her mind.

She nodded.

He brought a proud brown ram into the pen. Meir-Anschil pushed it to the ground and bound three of its legs. The ram struggled with its head and kicked with its free leg, but the shochet skilfully avoided the blows. He brought the *halaf* to the neck of the bleating animal and, with a sharp, masterful gesture, he slit its trachea and oesophagus.

Meir-Anschil looked over at his daughter as the ram began to convulse in a pool of blood. Instead of seeking consolation in her father's eyes, Fanny was riveted by the animal's final twitches. She appeared not to feel any emotion or fear, but to consider the job as a kind of game. When he approached her with his stained apron, she stretched out her fingers to touch the blood, and when the ram had stopped moving, Meir-Anschil held her arm to show her how to move the knife. The girl stood in the pool of blood and stared at the ram's neck, apparently ready to perform kosher slaughter herself.

"You do realise that this is an animal?" he asked her. "That was alive?"

"Yes, I realise that."

She watched her father in tense anticipation, for months on

end, waiting for the moment when she would leave the world of theory and step into the world of practice. In the meantime, she learned the procedure from her father and helped him spread earth over spilled blood. After more than a year, on her twelfth birthday, Meir-Anschil gave her a small knife for slaughtering chickens. Fanny was thrilled and sharpened it regularly, and even asked Mende to sew her a rag doll on which she could practise.

Mende flatly refused. As far as she was concerned, her father and sister had taken leave of their sanity. She concluded that she should spend more time with the family of Sondel Gordon the tailor instead. Mende knew that an increasing number of townspeople did not look favourably upon her younger sister's tomfoolery, and that the day when they would take their custom elsewhere was not far off, and then her father's business would run aground; and she, the eldest daughter, would not find a proper shidduch. She was therefore always courteous, avidly fulfilled the commandments and made sure to appear gentle and modest before any man she encountered. She knew that people had started calling her "Mende Gordon" behind her back, but she thought that this malicious nickname might work in her favour. At any rate, it was better than her sister's nickname, "*Di vilde chaya*", the wild animal.

V

Whether or not Fanny was indeed a *vilde chaya*, she certainly demonstrated a rare talent for shechitah from her first attempt. Generally, those who are inexperienced shochetim are alarmed when a frightened rooster flaps its wings. They recoil from its snapping beak, and are taken aback by the bird's indomitable will to live. Often, they end up cutting the throat with trembling hands, or even accidentally severing the rooster's head. Fanny knew that the cut had to be firm and controlled, never frenzied. She would immobilise the rooster with one arm, grab the wings with her right hand and with two movements of her left hand, back and forth, she would slit the trachea and esophagus. Then, instead of leaving the rooster to agonise in a flapping of wings and legs in a bucket of blood, as is customary, she would hold it against her chest until she felt its soul leave her arms, and only then would she cover the blood with the earth, and smile at up her father.

Meir-Anschil watched his daughter with a pride that was mixed with trepidation. For two whole years, Fanny slaughtered – roosters and lambs mostly – and lo and behold: his customers loved her work. Jews from all across the district came to see the wonder with their own eyes, and there was no solid counter-argument, such as an explicit halakhic prohibition, which her detractors could use against her. Customers were not allowed into the slaughtering pen, but the prospect of seeing the slender girl with fair curls and wolf-like eyes in the slaughterhouse yard was persuasive enough for them to take the trouble to ride all the way to Grodno. They sated their imaginations in the taverns and rested their bodies in inns, and the residents of Grodno quickly realised that Meir-Anschil's daughter was good for business. The marketplace makhers embellished the fable of the *vilde chaya* and told how she fearlessly seized the animals to produce kosher meat, and that no-one wielded the knife more skilfully than her. The Blessed Holy One guides the work of her left hand, so they said, and burnt offerings made with her meat bring a blessing upon diners and protect against the Evil Eye. Before long, there wasn't a single person in Grodno, Jew or gentile, who did not want to take their livestock to be slaughtered by the *vilde chaya*.

A man like Yankel Kriegsmann, pauper that he was, could not waste such an opportunity. He began to loiter around the abattoir, offering a blessing from the *vilde chaya*'s grandfather in return for a few copecks. Meir-Anschil decided it was time to forgive his father-in-law for his misdeeds and offered him paid work, cleaning the slaughterhouse.

Yankel Kriegsmann reported for duty in the afternoon hours and cleaned the abattoir until it was spotless. He performed his work with quiet dedication, as if seeking to mend his ways, and little by little regained his son-in-law's trust. Meir-Anschil and his daughter delegated to him the task of locking up and, after they left, he would sweep the floor, scrub down the walls and clear the waste around which the stray dogs would gather. He lingered over this last task, because he did not want to return to his lonely, empty house. He spent a long time watching the dogs feasting on leftover blood and tissue, sensing atonement for his sins and believing that he was doing good in the world.

Nevertheless, Kriegsmann became enraged by one of these stray dogs, Tzileyger was his name, a three-legged hound with crooked hips, whose weakness and timidity among the pack of dogs left him perpetually starving and emaciated. Tzileyger would stand back until all the others had finished sniffing and licking and chewing the day's catch, and only then would he permit himself to walk, hesitantly, on two front legs and one hind leg, to the mound of refuse.

Kriegsmann decided to teach Tzileyger to stand his ground, and stopped him from approaching the waste once the rest of the pack had left. Whenever he saw Tzileyger dithering nervously behind the slaughterhouse, he would ambush him, beat him with a stick and throw rocks at him. Once, a stone hit one of Tzileyger's front legs, and for weeks the dog scuttled on one front and one hind leg, which were luckily on opposite sides so he was able to keep his balance. The dog was forced to wait for Kriegsmann to leave and try his luck at a later hour, but the old man, who had nothing better to do, would always come back to surprise him in the moonlight.

Eventually, Tzileyger gave up and began searching for other sources of nourishment, but Kriegsmann did not relent. In the evening he would sneak over with leftover bones and meat and lure Tzileyger to his home with whistles and tut-tuts. He led the dog along the muddy streets of the town until they reached his home, where he would place the bowlful of bait underneath the front porch, whistling and calling out: "Tzileyger, you cheat, come and get a treat." Kriegsmann then peeped from his window and threw a stone at him each time Tzileyger approached. But the temptation was too great for the starving dog, who, in spite of the stones hitting his head, managed every now and then to snatch a bone that would sustain him for a few days, chewing it with great pleasure in a nook he found underneath the steps to Kriegsmann's house.

One morning, Yankel Kriegsmann awoke to the smell of rotting flesh, and found chicken remains and fur balls in the space between his house and the ground. He guessed that this was where the stray dog disappeared whenever he managed to pilfer a piece of bone. It was then that Kriegsmann decided to teach Tzileyger a lesson once and for all, and planned a sophisticated trap. He put out the bowl of food, as he had done every other evening, but deliberately missed the dog with the stones he threw at him. When he saw Tzileyger grab a juicy bone, he stole to the dog's hiding place with his stick. Fanny happened to walk by her grandfather's house exactly at that moment as she returned from her arithmetic lesson, and observed the incident to the very last detail. Tzileyger was caught by surprise and suffered Kriegsmann's beatings with whines and howls: a front leg was broken and his body suffered grievous wounds, but his jaws continued to tightly clamp the bone.

Fanny said nothing.

Yankel Kriegsmann roared with laughter at the dog's tenacity and tried to pull the bone out of his mouth, and Fanny saw Tzileyger expose his sharp teeth and snarl. The grandfather was so enraged by Tzileyger's insurrection that he pulled at the bone with one hand and kept beating the dog with the stick in his other hand until finally, triumphantly, he seized the loot. But his triumph proved to be his defeat. The dog's eyes sparked with wrath. Fanny watched as he mustered his courage and leaped at the old man with the last of his strength. Then, with a rage Fanny had never seen before, the dog mutilated her grandfather's face, tore his skin, bit off his ear and clawed out his eyes.

Fanny stood paralysed for a few moments. It was the first time she had ever seen an animal take revenge. When she regained her senses, she tried to scare off the dog with her knife, but Tzileyger leaped at her as well, bit her left arm and disappeared. Overwhelmed by the pain, she felt as though her arm had been severed from her body. Her grandfather lay at the entrance to his house, unconscious and bleeding. When the doctor reached Kriegsmann he managed to stop the bleeding and clean the old man's wounds, but when he returned the next day with ointments and medicines he told Meir-Anschil, "I'm afraid that he will live." Only those who saw the vision of horror that was Yankel Kriegsmann that night understood what the doctor meant. The old man never appeared in public again. He could barely see or hear, his diet now amounted to no more than tepid cucumber soup, and his final doom was set for the next winter.

Tzileyger was never seen again around Grodno, and from that day on Fanny refused to slaughter animals or eat their flesh. When her father objected to her change of heart and tried to preach along the lines of "humans having pre-eminence over beasts", she looked at him and said, "It depends which human and which beast."

Yet Fanny no longer needed to slaughter in order to evoke the memory of her mother's bosom, and a few weeks later, she asked her father to find her a proper shidduch that would be commensurate with her principles. Meir-Anschil promised the world to the matchmaker, Yehiel-Mikhl Gemeiner, who in turn suggested a few possibilities, all of which were rejected because the matchmaker failed to understand Fanny's "principles". Finally, Yehiel-Mikhl Gemeiner was forced to travel all the way to Motal, where he heard about Natan-Berl Keismann, a portly and rather slow golem who was older than Fanny by fifteen years. Natan-Berl had inherited from his father a cheese-making business in the village of Upiravah and made a name for himself as the most successful sheep farmer in the entire district.

The "principle" that guided his work, so Yehiel-Mikhl Gemeiner was secretly told, was not a special salting or curdling process, but rather maintaining herds of calm and peaceful livestock – that was all.

"Is this commensurate with her 'principles'?" the matchmaker asked Meir-Anschil, failing to hide the mockery in his voice.

"If you find a shidduch for Mende nearby," Meir-Anschil replied, "I will send them both to Motal."

VI

Before she left her house, at the second hour after midnight, Fanny caressed Natan-Berl's enormous back while he slept. She ran her fingers through the black plumes on his shoulders. How could she tear herself away from her awkward bear? How dare she torment him, how could she make her children so miserable?

To his own mind, Natan-Berl is cumbersome and uncouth, and she knows he does not trust his own thoughts. He waits for her to approve every sentence that comes out of his mouth, and formulates his ideas with her before presenting them to other people. Before turning in, once the children are fast asleep, he likes to smoke a cigarette in the kitchen and listen to her telling him about her day. Yet, in recent weeks, she has been barely able to talk. She has been sitting before him with an expressionless face, mumbling, "Natan-Berl, we must do something about Mende," and he knows all too well that there isn't much that can be done.

His wife wants to mend the entire world, but Natan-Berl tends to think that one person cannot walk down the path cut out for another. Zvi-Meir wanted to walk away from his wife, and he did. Mende wanted to be weighed down by melancholy, and she was. What can Fanny do other than console and encourage her? She should sit with her elder sister until she heals, and do her best to stop her from ever reaching Zizek's boat again. But Fanny, for her part, is relentless in her attacks: "You would think that, Natan-Berl." And he becomes defensive, because he has done nothing wrong. "Exactly," Fanny says, "you've done absolutely nothing, Natan-Berl." And he, who so loves to hear her say his name, fails to understand what more it is that he can do. Every morning, he wakes up to milk the sheep and goats, to tend and shepherd, his hands are filled with work from sunrise to sundown in order to provide for his family. A lamb falls ill, the meadows become boggy and he has to venture out to more remote pasture. Tomorrow he has to clean the pen and next week he must mend the fences. And if he has to care for Mende during the day, who will do the churning? "There's nothing but milk in your head, Natan-Berl," Fanny says as she walks away, "and this is why the world is going from bad to worse."

The world? Natan-Berl is befuddled. What's he got to do with the "world"? It is a word he finds impossible to fathom, and people use it in ways that he cannot understand. He often hears others complaining, "What world are we living in?" But as far as Natan-Berl is concerned, the world is just the way it is; it is what it is and could never be otherwise.

"Of course," Fanny teased him once. "As long as the sheep are calm in Natan-Berl's pens, they can be beaten and tortured everywhere else."

"Really, Fanny Keismann," he said, offended. "I have a family to care for."

A sudden thought occurred to Fanny. The injustice that rages in the world derives from the basic and simple fact that she and Natan-Berl have a family to care for. Because she looks after her own children, other people's children suffer. And due to her unwillingness to jeopardise the foundations of her own home, many other homes fall to pieces. Just look at those women, for example, whose primary duty is towards their children, and whose motherhood is the source of their virtue: they would accept any injustice provided their own safe haven remained unharmed. If these women stepped out of their homes to care for others, husbands like Zvi-Meir would not dare to abandon them at the drop of a hat. But injustice always has its silent agents at work, and every affliction that occurs in one place is made possible by its silent acceptance elsewhere. She is an accomplice to the crime that took place in her sister's home. No, not an accomplice. Worse than that. A perpetrator.

The world cannot be mended because rupture is what makes it go round. And there isn't a single Jewish woman who is prepared to go out of her way to fix it. Not even her.

She does not expect anything from men. Why should they

undermine their position as masters? Why should they waive the titles granted to them, in the absence of any challenge? Everybody in Motal knows that Zvi-Meir has abandoned his family, yet no envoys have been sent to Minsk. They pride themselves on being a tight-knit community with an influential rabbi, and the last thing anyone wants to do is rock the boat. They all emphatically condemn the wayward husband, but by not chasing after him, they reserve the right to do the same thing themselves. Their denouncement of Zvi-Meir consists of hollow words and no action.

"Natan-Berl, we should go to Minsk. We must bring back this rogue, Zvi-Meir."

"To Minsk?" He is confused.

"We will all go together, Natan-Berl, the children will be thrilled. People say that Minsk is a lovely city. There's not a single hungry Jew there. We'll take them to the theatre."

"The theatre?" Natan-Berl mumbles.

"Now is the time, Natan-Berl – when the swamps dry up and the roads are easy to navigate. In a few weeks, the mud and the ice will keep us here, we'll be stranded."

Natan-Berl says nothing. She can see that he has raised his protective barriers against her and she becomes filled with remorse. Why does she torment him? She takes all of her anger at Mende out on him. Instead of filling Mende's ears with empty chatter, she should talk to her about the leap into the river, and make sure that her elder sister never again loses the will to live. But instead of shaking Mende back to her senses, she sneaks underneath the white sheet and holds her limp hand, and in the evening, she vents her anger at her husband.

One day Fanny takes courage. She waits for Rochaleh to go out to draw water and shuts the door of Mende's room after her. She climbs onto Mende's bed, caresses her elder sister's head and

71

tries to find a foothold in her hollow eyes. She searches for all the authoritative words that have come to her mind countless times before, but her voice is caged because she can see that her sister does not want *tikkun*, she does not want to have her soul mended. Mende has always wanted only one thing – a husband and children, or, in a word: a family. Without even one of its components Mende does not feel whole, certainly not strong, and she refuses to rise above her grief for the sake of praise, such as "see how brave she is". To be frank, the status of *agunah*, a husbandless wife, does not suit her character, and her precarious family situation contradicts her faith. The dybbuk that possessed Mende is nothing more than sadness and outrage at being forced, against her will, into the world of sin. It is not Zvi-Meir that she is pining for; she yearns for the authority of a husband and for the life of a wife. She does not live for the sake of Yankele and Mirl but for the sake of being a mother. This is why Fanny said nothing and retreated from the bed and sat on a chair next to her sister for a few moments. Later, she left the house and walked north along the town's narrow paths, all the way to the Yaselda, where she found Zizek's boat. At her request, he let her board his craft and rowed back and forth, from one shore to the other. Why did she do that? She does not know. Perhaps she expected Zizek to say something or to stop at the spot where her sister jumped ship. But Zizek rowed steadily and calmly and did not stop, his expression detached and his rowing motion constant; it was then that Fanny realised that it was no coincidence that it had been on Zizek's boat, of all places, where Mende came to realise that her fate was sealed. She must have felt that this was how she would float through the years, how ten months of anticipation for Zvi-Meir would become one hundred, and she would end her life, just like Zizek, with a steadfast forwards motion towards meaninglessness.

Then a bold idea rose up in Fanny's mind, and she dared to say it out loud. Zizek kept his countenance and continued rowing with a blank face, but somehow Fanny knew that he had heard her and understood. All she said were two words, but at the second hour after midnight, as she left her home with a heavy heart, she hoped that Zizek would find a way to help her.

That evening she was very emotional around her children, jumping and dancing and hugging them too much.

"What is wrong with you?" asked Gavriellah, her eldest. "You are being funny."

"I trust you, Gavriellah Keismann," Fanny said, in tears, and her eldest daughter's eyes searched her with suspicion. After Fanny had put the children to sleep, she came to Natan-Berl's bed and stroked the small of his back for a long time. When the house resonated with the tender breathing of sleeping children, she went out to the kitchen and sat meditatively at the table.

Before going out into the dark, it suddenly occurred to her that she should leave a note, but her excitement drove the words out of her brain. What could she write? What explanation could justify abandoning five beloved children and one Natan-Berl? Finally, she tore off a piece of paper and scribbled down "I'll be back very soon", but immediately regretted this cryptic message and instead wrote "Take care of yourselves until I return". She wanted to change that too, but time was pressing, so she left the note on the table and stepped outside.

In the dead of night, she met the coachman Mikhail Andreyevich, as agreed, with his cart (and a rifle, to use against foul beasts), and paid him a hefty sum in order to ensure that this rendezvous would remain secret. Together they rode north to Motal, surprising barn owls in the topmost branches of pine trees and startling deer. They advanced along Motal's main road. Mad dogs chased after the cartwheels until they had left the town, but no lanterns lit up in any of its homes, thank God. When they reached the river, they found Zizek's empty boat. It was very dark.

Zizek emerged from the bushes, holding a lamp. He quickly pushed his boat into the river and helped Fanny to climb aboard, then jumped in after her and calmly rowed towards the northern bank. When they reached the other side, she did not know how to thank him: words and money meant nothing to Zizek. So she briefly touched his arm, but he nervously shook her off, which alarmed her. She stepped out of the boat onto the boggy ground, and as she walked away, she realised that he was just behind her. She walked towards the nearby village, where she knew a few locals who could arrange for her to hire a cart and horses at dawn. Zizek continued to follow her. She began to fear that she might have trusted him too much. He never leaves the Yaselda, and now he is following her footsteps away from the riverbank. Fanny began to formulate a plan to be rid of him and felt for the knife on her thigh.

Then Zizek suddenly strode past her, took the lead and had her follow him to a grove of trees, where she discovered that he had already hidden two horses and a wagon in preparation. He helped her climb onto the wagon seat, then took the reins and turned the horses. Now his steady rowing motion was replaced by his pulling on the leather straps. Nothing moved in his face. His bright eyes were fixed on the Pole Star, by which he would navigate their route to Minsk, and the two words Fanny had said to him at noon guided his way and blended with the horses' hoofbeats. *Zvi-Meir . . . Zvi-Meir . . . Zvi-Meir . . .*

TELEKHANY

I

The night tightens its grip on Fanny, sinks deep within her and expands, imbuing her with the sudden realisation that she is free. Man was endowed with five senses to perceive Creation – sight, hearing, smell, taste and touch – and only one sense, the sense of freedom, was granted to Creation in order to perceive man. The *Shechinah* uses it to examine the human heart and distinguish between servants, masters, and those who are neither one nor the other – and right now, Fanny can feel Freedom probing her bones, making her soul sing and her heart throb. She has always suspected that the good God On High is not content with having only the blindly obedient among His believers.

Then, out of nowhere, she is assailed by pangs of guilt. Natan-Berl will be devastated by what she has done, and her children will miss her terribly. Who else will whisper in their ears the first words they hear each morning? Who will cook their food? Who will clothe their delicate bodies and shoo away their bad dreams? What freedom is this, if it is bound up with betrayal and torment? Every day of their lives she has carved a path through her children's bodies, into the nooks of their souls and the crannies in their hearts. She has woken and fed and dressed and bathed and frolicked and consoled, each time etching new signs of her motherhood into their flesh. Few words were ever needed; she could register their innermost secrets simply by listening to the tone of their voices. It was enough for her to observe how they poured their tea or ate their rice, as their souls quivered. They never told her things she did not already know or reported any-thing that was news to her; all they gave her were ever-sweeter memories. Her children were ageless in her eyes, eternal souls, from baby Elisheva to her eldest, eight-year-old Gavriellah, whose courage Fanny had recognised the moment her firstborn emerged between her legs at birth. Now her sudden disappearance will mark them with an ugly scar. She has derailed their routine and demolished their stability. Her freedom is their prison. What kind of a mother is she?

And yet, from the moment the idea that she should set out on this quest first flickered in her mind, she felt that it was her duty to leave her home. Just as in the moments of giving birth to her children, when her overwhelming desire to care for them merged with her duty as their mother, she now knew full well that freedom and necessity are intertwined. When she returns, she will explain to her children that she had decided not to think of her sister's suffering as a divine decree. She had to gallop all the way to Minsk to bring Zvi-Meir to his knees.

Fanny disliked Zvi-Meir even before he married her sister. He had been thrown out of the Volozhin Yeshiva – evidently, he was no great scholar – and yet he never stopped dispensing the pearls of wisdom he had gleaned from the Gemara, and pointing out contradictions he believed he had found in the Bible. Whenever the family sat down for dinner and shared cabbage soup with noodles, pickled cucumber, kugel and rye bread, Zvi-Meir would also share his scruples: how could Adam and Eve have deserved punishment if they had received the gift of Knowledge only after eating from the Forbidden Fruit? And sure enough, the con-versation would soon become a full-blown monologue, because Zvi-Meir had no interest in listening to anyone else and would anticipate anything he thought they might say before they had a chance to say it. If he ever condescended to listen to others, his ears would only pick up the words that his mind could assemble in support of his sermon. All conversations with him ended the same way: he would tell them that they should all read a little and study a little, and that he was probably wrong to have raised the matter in the present company in the first place.

Zvi-Meir deserved to have it all, and everyone else was to blame for the fact that he had nothing. The rabbis at the Volozhin Yeshiva were to blame for not cultivating his talent as soon as he arrived. Customers were to blame for not rushing to buy his wares in the market. And Mende was to blame, because, as far as Zvi-Meir the Genius was concerned, intimacy should consist of his tête-à-têtes with himself and nobody else.

All the while, she, Fanny Keismann, witnessing Mende's embarrassment, had chosen to sit at the table and keep silent lest she heap further humiliation upon her sister, but Zvi-Meir never considered the silence that followed his sermons as a sign of hostility, rather as a victory. If only Fanny had intervened back then, perhaps she would not have had to abandon her sweet children and abscond from her home at an hour befitting brigands on the prowl.

Zizek takes off his army coat and places it over her shoulders. At first, she is alarmed by the uniform, which in her eyes represents the government's crushing might; but then she huddles into the coat's warm lining. As the wind picks up, she fastens the top two buttons and notices that Zizek is turning east, away from the first village on the riverbank. Fanny does not understand why this detour is necessary, but it does not make her in the least suspicious. Under any other circumstances she would have begun to plan how best to leap from the cart, but in his presence, she feels anything but intimidated.

With the first glimpse of sunshine, the emotion of the night fades, and glints of sobriety shimmer in the light that soon floods their eyes. The hazy mist evaporates completely. Now Fanny and Zizek are exposed. Zizek takes off his uniform, rolls it up and puts it in a large wooden box. This is the first time she has seen him without his uniform and the army cap that always shades his face. His age, she reckons, is probably close to sixty. His clothes, a peasant's jacket over threadbare trousers, ooze a smell of fish, and receive the addition of a grey, gentile-looking flat cap. A red sash that the locals wear for good luck is tied around his waist, and his feet are encased in plain bast shoes.

Without further ado, he removes the army coat from her shoulders. Fanny shrinks back in her seat and looks imploringly into his bright-coloured eyes. Even though he does not respond to her gaze, she lets him undo two buttons in the collar of her dress and remove her headscarf. He pulls out a brown woollen coat like the ones that the local babushkas wear, and hands her a white kerchief adorned with a Polish emblem. When their transformation is complete, they look at one another: they are two locals, he is no longer a soldier and she is no longer a Jew, and a hint of contentment spreads across Zizek's cracked lips, or so it seems.

II

A flock of greyish crows swoops in formation in the sky, blackbirds scavenge for worms, and a somnolent stork keeps a half-open eye on them from the top of an ancient, bare oak tree. The tributaries of the Yaselda suck the mire from the black bogs, and Zizek draws the cart to a halt when it reaches a tall pile of reeds and moss. He unharnesses the horses and tethers them by a hidden pool of stagnant water. Then he unloads a sack of hay from the cart, and Fanny follows him along the sloping, muddy stream.

She notices that the grey horse is quite old. Its hide hangs from its back like a blanket, its body is thin, its belly muddy, and its dark mane is strewn with silver hairs that give it an air of nobility, rather than submission. It discontentedly chews the hay she offers it, stretching its nose towards her, as if urging her to hurry up and finish serving its fodder. Its gaze remains unimpressed.

The chestnut horse is much younger. Its eyes are curious and it swishes its tail in circles. It sniffs at her for several moments and then goes back to snatching at the hay and chewing with urgency. Fanny returns to the cart, which Zizek has in the meantime camouflaged with reeds. Before them lie fields of wheat, oat and flax, and blueberry bushes, and in the distance she even sees ripe potatoes ready for the summer harvest. How long are they to stay here? She is not sure. Zizek is unloading pegs and canvas. His plan quickly becomes evident: they will travel only in the dark, because travelling by daylight in unfamiliar territory is too dangerous for two unarmed strangers like them, and all the more so considering that they lack the travel documents required of Jews wandering between counties.

Zizek secures the pegs in the ground but does not fasten the canvas too tightly, presumably to enable them to pack up and leave at a moment's notice. He adjusts the tent's position, keeping it low, so that they have a direct line of vision to the horses while staying hidden from passers-by on the main road. She is amazed by his meticulous preparations for her journey and by the care with which he has crafted each stage, and she feels ashamed for having brought along merely money and some cheese and bread. She had thought that she would stop off in villages and inns, pave her way with roubles, and catch the first train from Baranavichy to Minsk. But what had she been thinking?

That she could pass from one village to the next with a wad of notes in her pocket without arousing suspicion? Wouldn't she have attracted attention with her curious accent? And what business could a Jewess from Grodno County possibly have in Minsk? Wouldn't they ask her to present her passport? And now, as Zizek is unloading yet more bags of potatoes and vegetables, she understands that he has no intention of speaking to anyone until they reach Baranavichy.

The air grows oppressive. Zizek takes out a water flask and hands it to her. There is one problem, which neither of them had anticipated: the scorching sun of Polesia, where, for three weeks a year, the heat becomes unbearable. The advantage is clear: in the heat, the bogs recede and the roads become convenient for travel. On the other hand, the tent that Zizek has set up is like a furnace, and outside the sunlight is beating down ruthlessly, while the only shaded place for miles around is by a hill that is too close to the main road. How can they rest in these conditions? Sensing Fanny's distress, Zizek stretches out the canvas sheet to create more shade. But the heat and the bogs summon hordes of mosquitoes for an urgent conclave, and their sweating bodies attract flies in droves. This unbearable situation keeps them wide awake, and their appetites evaporate to nothing. Fanny knows that two more days of travel like this will end with a bout of cholera.

Zizek lies down on the black ground, turning his back and folding his body away from her. She puts her head in the stifling tent, because she can no longer bear the sun's blazing touch. Now that she does not have to care for children or maintain a farm, she can do whatever she likes, and yet she wants nothing more than to disappear altogether. If she were home right now, she would have washed clothes, cooked, urged David to eat and taught Elisheva another poem; hundreds of actions that any other person could have done instead of her, but whose particular meaning derives from the fact that it is she, Fanny Keismann, who is doing them. An onlooker would not have perceived anything unique about her life, would have failed to notice the lushness of its internal logic . . . Just look at her, the poor sod, not one day of freedom has gone by and she is already pining for her home.

The flies and insects prevent any prospect of napping. As soon as her eyes close, she feels something climbing up her leg and stinging her ankles. Not far from where she is lying a toad rustles in a bush – or is it an otter? Or a snake? Fanny leaps to her feet; there is no way of knowing. The dense heat forces even time to loiter, heavy and sweaty. How many days have they been on the road now? Not even one? Impossible. And in only a few hours they could be back on Zizek's boat, and time would regain its conventional dimensions. Her disappearance would soon be erased from the memory of her husband and children, and her journey would be quickly forgotten. Her passion for securing justice for her sister would amount to a brief attempt and nothing more. Worse things have happened.

Right in front of her, Zizek's back is heaving deeply. His arms are lax, and his cap is lying upside down on the ground next to him. She wonders whether she should share her misgivings with him, but knows that his answer will be silence. If she asked him to return to Motal, he would harness the horses and lead them back to the road from which they have come. If she chooses to go on, he will take the reins without blinking. The boat on the Yaselda has been replaced by the cart, and Zizek is at her service. But why did he, of all people, offer his help? How did he manage to detach himself from the meaningless daily routine on the banks of the Yaselda? She looks at him and knows that, the way things stand, they cannot go back. They? Yes, she and he.

As though he had read her mind, Zizek gets up, folds the tent, and leads the horses back to the road. The old horse moves hesitantly, probably exhausted by the heat just like them, and Zizek slows their pace. Fanny looks apprehensively at the massive man sitting next to her; if they continue travelling in this way, they will manage no more than twenty or thirty versts each night. The journey to Minsk will take longer than expected, and it is not even clear whether they will be able to endure another day like this one.

Zizek's face is expressionless, but he hands the reins over to her and turns to lift a few sacks from behind her seat. Before long she realises that he is preparing a headrest, so that she can catch up on her lost hours of sleep. Yet she feels compelled to stay awake next to him, appreciating her responsibility for their situation. And so she finds herself battling against the torturous fatigue that is throwing her head backwards and forwards without mercy. Suddenly she wakes, panicked, because she has almost fallen from the moving cart. Zizek winds a rope around her waist and fastens her hips to the seat with a tight knot. Conceding defeat, she accepts the sentence of being tied to her seat, realising that this journey is a far more complicated affair than she had anticipated. Heavy sleep abruptly descends, and her dreams are couched in scents of rum and mead.

III

On the second day of their journey, they stop in a more convenient spot on the shore of a small lake, shaded by a thicket of willows and bulrushes. When the sun rises, Zizek realises that they are too conspicuous. Some four versts away they spot a few wooden shacks standing in a cluster, probably built illegally by muzhiks who have had enough of the rent they have to pay elsewhere. Zizek decides to fold the tent and stand watch. Fanny tries to talk him into resting a little, but his face remains still as a rock and his determination is equally firm. His ears are open to any rustle or peep, and he is ready for any threat that may come their way.

The shade revives Fanny, and their improved position makes her more confident that they should push on. She has a hearty meal of apples and cucumbers that Zizek has packed, and she carefully lays a tomato and two plums by his side. Rumour has it in Motal that Zizek's diet consists of live eel that he catches in the river. Others believe that behind the unassuming, shabby appearance hides a millionaire, with a luxurious mansion where butlers serve his meals on fine china from Kiev and pour French wine into Viennese goblets.

Zizek looks at Fanny as though seeking her permission, and, seemingly against his better judgment, grabs one of the plums. His scarred mouth can hardly chew the fruit, and his face becomes distorted, as if he has bitten his tongue. She notices that his teeth are struggling with the fruit's flesh, takes the plum from his hand and cuts it into smaller pieces. Zizek says nothing when she hands him the slices but she can see that he already has his eye on the other plum.

He munches his food like an old goat, his chewing monotonous and diffident. Something in the incongruity between his enormous size and his gentleness reminds her of Natan-Berl. But while Natan-Berl's eyes are always filled with a tender expression, Zizek's bright-coloured eyes are devoid of any vivacity, despair or hope. The infinite placidity that stretches across his face is terrifying, like a lake without fish that reeks of fish nonetheless.

At midday, without Zizek noticing, Fanny lifts up her skirt and lets the breeze blow between her legs. Dressing as a peasant has its advantages; she knows them well, living out in the country as she does. Away from the townspeople of Motal, every now and again she allows herself to take off several layers of clothing and

85

carry on about her garden like a shiksa. Even though she knows that her immodesty does not sit well with halakhic rulings, she isn't inclined to think that it amounts to transgression. Even at this very moment she does not feel the need to pray, and yet she senses the sheer presence of the Almighty all around her.

Protected by the dark, they set off again and arrive at a major road, where they meet the carts of beggars and pedlars on their way to and from Telekhany. Most people who choose to travel at night tend to be in a great rush and rarely seek company. They are not the ones Zizek fears. There are also a few vagabonds with secrets that need hiding, just like theirs. Zizek does not fret about them either. But there are certain other types that the darkness prompts to inflict harm, and they are the ones that make Zizek afraid.

As soon as they have crossed the Oginsky Canal, a few drunks call out to them in a spate of high spirits, and Zizek shrinks back in his seat and waves at them. There is nothing that drunks detest more than being ignored, and all one has to do is acknowledge their merriment for them to let one be. One of the band waves a bottle at them and yells, "Somethin' else! This is somethin' else! You should try some too, girls!", proceeding to plead with the driver of his cart: "Stop, my friend, let's get to know these beauties!" Zizek is relieved when they pass by without stopping.

When the road becomes empty around midnight, Zizek's eyelids start to droop uncontrollably. At first he slaps his cheeks and wets his face, but when his tiredness worsens, he changes his position, gets on his knees and pounds his jaw with his fist. Fanny offers to take over the reins – she knows how to find her way at night – but Zizek stands up and urges the horses to a gallop like a wild drunk with a bottle of rum in his hand.

A wagon laden with bags of wheat comes alongside them, and Zizek immediately slows down. A middle-aged couple are sitting on the wagon waving and wishing them luck.

"Where to, good people?" the woman asks, her face hidden by a neckerchief drawn almost up to her eyes. And Fanny, knowing that Zizek will not say a word, replies in his stead, "Minsk."

"And where are you from, good people?" the woman inquires.

"From Minsk," says Fanny.

Zizek reins in the horses to let the peasants overtake them, but they slow down too and continue riding in parallel. A long moment of mutual inquisitiveness passes, and Zizek quickly evaluates all possible escape routes. If he had only been more alert, he would have taken another path already, but now, with no better option presenting itself, he takes the risk of pulling over. To their surprise, the peasants also stop their wagon, blocking their passage. The woman calls out to them: "Delivering goods?" "Yes," Fanny replies in Polish. "Potatoes." Zizek signals to Fanny to end the conversation.

"You should be careful, my dears," says the man, his clean-shaven cheeks gleaming in the moonlight, his eyes shaded by a flat cap. "We have twice been attacked on this path. I hope you're armed, this part of Telekhany is crawling with thieves."

The warning makes Zizek all the more suspicious, and he grabs his whip. The old horse tenses up.

"Your horse is tired," the woman observes.

"The other horse is alert, though," the man says. "What a horse! Have you ever seen such a horse?"

"No, I haven't, Radek, a wonderful horse indeed!"

"Magnificent!" the man says with an admiring whistle. "Is this the kind of horse one uses to haul potatoes?"

"A lovely horse alright!" the woman concurs.

"In return for the horse," the man called Radek says, chuckling, "we are prepared to leave you the potatoes."

The woman chokes with laughter.

"What do you say, good people?" She and Radek alight from

the wagon, heightening Zizek's fears. "They're not saying anything, Radek, maybe they swallowed their potatoes whole?"

"Maybe they are hiding something?"

"Do you think they might be *żyds*?" the woman says, now walking towards their cart.

"The woman's accent does sound strange to me," says Radek. "Who calls Minsk 'Miyansk'?"

"Maybe someone who doesn't come from Minsk, Radek."

"Maybe someone who doesn't speak Polish, my darling."

Zizek steps down from the cart, still wielding the whip. Under the mantle of darkness, he tries to unfasten the cart's shafts to release the horses, with the idea that he and Fanny can mount them and ride away.

"Perhaps they are not *żyds*, Radek, *żyds* don't hop off wagons that quickly. *Żyds* freeze on the spot."

Something stirs among the bags of wheat on the peasants' wagon. Two brawny thugs suddenly rise up and climb down to join the man.

"We'll make it quick," the woman says, facing Fanny and Zizek and exposing a set of crumbling teeth, "we want whatever you have in your cart."

"And the cart, too," adds Radek, now standing right behind her.

"And the horse, most of all," says one of the thugs in a dull voice. "That's quite a horse."

The three men have now positioned themselves right behind the woman. Zizek notices a club hidden behind the back of one of the thugs, and the hilt of a dagger in the hands of the other. He undoes the harness on the other side now, and gestures to Fanny to quickly mount the young steed.

"Zizek, let's give them what they want," Fanny whispers, trembling.

Zizek signals to her to mount the horse, vigorously pulling at her arm.

Fanny glances back at the bandits, and suddenly realises that one of the two thugs has disappeared. Before she can shout a warning to Zizek, a heavy blow lands on his back and he collapses flat on the ground. Fanny screams and tries to mount the horse, but the other thug charges at her, yanks the hem of her dress and drags her from its back. Zizek tries to stand, but a second blow smashes him unconscious.

The thug stamps his foot onto Fanny's right shoulder and tells her to keep still. She can't breathe. Only her eyes can move, still alert, still watchful. In the meantime, the man and woman leap onto the cart and begin emptying its sacks. They grumble and curse as they fail to find anything of value. They tear the sacks to shreds and empty the water flasks in frustration, until the woman finds the wooden box and discovers the uniform and the barrel of rum. She triumphantly brandishes the army coat, and calls out, "Radek, we've caught a soldier!", crouching to drink from the barrel's spout.

The gang cheers, and the thug who struck Zizek climbs onto the cart and puts on the coat. The trampler of Fanny's shoulder also hops onto the cart to fight over the remaining loot, finding a shirt, sash, trousers and military jacket. Once the booty is divided according to a hierarchy Fanny struggles to understand – mainly because the woman seems to be in charge of the others – they all jump down from the cart and approach Fanny.

"Do you know what is worse than a *żyd*?" the woman asks, and Fanny knows the answer.

"A filthy, treacherous Pole who goes off to serve in the Czar's army. Ugh!" spits one of the thugs and kicks Zizek, who is still unconscious, straight in the stomach.

"Enough!" the leader bawls, as if he is making it hard for her to concentrate. She bends down to Fanny and splatters in her ear, "We want the soldier to wake up. You know why?"

Fanny is shaking. The woman's fetid breath reeks of rotten teeth, kvass and salted meat.

"Before we hang him, I want him to see my sons banging his whore of a wife."

The two sons howl with laughter. "His whore of a wife . . . good one, Mama . . ."

And now, Fanny is supposed to either pray or cry or scream, but something else is bothering her: could this band of thugs really be a family? Impossible. Surely, the woman must have picked them off the street and raised them to become crooks. But then Fanny notices how alike they are, all with the same sunken eyes. And for some reason, knowing that this gang is made up of something as conventional as a family helps her to regain her wits. She is not facing the angels of death but ordinary people, flesh and blood, and therefore they must have weak points.

One of the thugs is already pulling at her hair, the other one is tearing open the collar of her dress, and she finds herself being dragged along the ground like an animal. It doesn't take her very long to picture Tzileyger, the miserable, three-legged dog, and her hand feels its way to the butcher's knife that has been tied to her right leg since she was a child.

The man and woman try to revive Zizek with slaps and water, and in the meantime one of the thugs grabs Fanny and forces her to bend over on the cart's platform. While the brothers bicker about who will pin her down and who will be the first to take her from behind, she carefully raises her right leg and with her left hand, she unsheathes the knife and holds it close to her heart. The thug who seized the army coat leers in front of her, and now she can see his face properly. Pristine, well-kept teeth shine between his dust-coated, ruddy cheeks. He has a delicate pug nose, and his sunken eyes flutter up and down like a fish out of water. She takes advantage of his agitation to carefully examine the arteries bulging from his neck and then, without further ado, slits his throat in one swift motion.

Blood gushes from his neck onto her face, his breath stands still, his mouth freezes, and his gaze fixes on hers. When he drops to the dirt with a muted thud, his brother, perhaps thinking that he has drunk himself into the ground, roars with laughter and lifts up Fanny's dress. Fanny spins to her right in a flash and slices open the other brother's neck. He feels his throat and continues laughing as if it were no more than a mosquito bite. Now she sees the remarkably close resemblance between the two brothers; they could be twins, they even convulse and collapse identically.

The sudden silence by the cart reaches the parents' ears. They leave Zizek and approach, and are faced with a gruesome sight. Their two boys are in the throes of death, lying in pools of blood, and the air is heavy with a latrine-like stench. Fanny is standing over them, wielding a knife used for slaughtering chickens in her left hand. Radek tries to pull his wife back towards their horses, but she, the leader, charges at Fanny with uncontrollable rage, flailing her arms and letting out battle cries. Fanny smashes her against the cart and slits her throat. The woman whips around, trying to tackle Fanny, but collapses. Radek takes to his heels, running away from the road as fast as he can. As he leaves his wagon and horses on the verge, the beasts are the only thing he can think about; he cannot believe the rest of what has just happened.

Strangely, even before she walks over to Zizek, Fanny bends down to check on the cleaved throats. The trachea and oesophagus are fully slit, the necks did not break and the incisions are clean. Pleased with the kosher slaughter she has just performed, she returns the knife to its sheath.

IV

Zizek wakes up to find himself lying on his jacket, his forehead bandaged and his body covered with a bloodstained army coat. Earlier, Fanny had tried to drag him over to the cart, but he was too heavy for her to lift. Instead, she cleaned his wounds with the little water they had left, tied bandages around his forehead and fastened the horses' harnesses that Zizek had undone earlier.

The old horse, though unharnessed all this time, had not taken the opportunity to run away. At its ripe old age, freedom is not what it used to be. When it was young, it longed to roam the great outdoors; but at this point in its life, it will certainly settle for a nice stable and a mound of hay. Fanny pats its uneven back and looks at it with gratitude. The young horse stamps the ground, restless and excited. It has witnessed more in the past two days than it has in its entire life. Fanny rubs its forehead and goes to release the bandits' horses, which are still standing drowsily in the middle of the road. Then she sits next to Zizek, hoping that he will wake up before first light, before they are found.

When Zizek opens his eyes and takes stock of his surroundings, he decides that the blow to his head and the darkness have distorted his vision. His gaze rests on three rocks, a short way off, which look like the shapes of three people, lying with sprawled arms and legs. But when he turns his head towards Fanny and sees her widened eyes, he grasps the severity of their situation. He is indeed looking at three bodies, there can be no doubt about that.

He tries to get up, only to collapse again in agony. His back is bruised and his head is bloodied, and Fanny has to help him stand. He staggers towards the horses and checks that the harnesses are fastened, and then looks towards the road to see if the way is clear. It takes him some time to realise that Fanny has done all of this already.

Zizek straightens up and looks around him. He throws his army coat, uniform and jacket onto the cart and starts to climb up to his seat. Fanny helps by pushing him up from behind and hops on after him. She attempts to take the reins in her hands, but he snatches them away from her and urges the horses to start moving.

She tries her luck. "Zizek Breshov?" But as always there is no reply – only this time she senses that his silence is charged with an unspoken accusation.

Sitting next to him, Fanny feels the sheath against her thigh: why has she continued to carry the knife even after abandoning her career of slaughtering? She does not know. She intended many times to bury it in the back of a cupboard, but whenever she removed the blade from her body she felt as though something were amiss, as if it were another body part in addition to the 248 that the Sages of antiquity had enumerated in the human body. Since she could not conceal its existence from her family, she had begun to use it almost absentmindedly, as if it were a perfectly natural thing to do. She would pull out the knife to chop vegetables, trim branches and cut rope; a banal blade for everyday use. But every time Fanny chopped vegetables she knew that the knife was not fulfilling its purpose, and that this was not the reason she wore it on her thigh. And although she was horrified by the very notion of going back to the slaughtering business, she kept sharpening the knife every day, exactly as the *vilde chaya* used to do.

Whenever she wielded the knife, Natan-Berl would look at her helplessly, perhaps even offended. Don't you trust me, Fanny Keismann? She heard in her heart the whispers of his silent questions. Did it not become clear to you on the day of our wedding that you would no longer need that blade? No-one knows better than she that she could not ask for a better husband than

Natan-Berl. He will give away everything he has and more before letting a single hair on her head come to harm, and no-one should confuse slow thinking with slow action. If anyone so much as raised their hand to one of his children, they would have a taste of the mighty arm of a man who, though he only uses violence as the absolute last resort, is for that very reason overwhelmingly formidable. The thing is, Fanny never believed that her safety depended on Natan-Berl; she always knew that her world hung by a thread regardless. And what does that mean? Well, the boys are indeed attending the cheder, and the girls are growing up, and Gavriellah, dear God – she has raised an extraordinary daughter, so bright and brave. Natan-Berl is absorbed with his work, her mother-in-law continues to complain in her cabin as a matter of course, and they want for nothing. But what about her? She steers their ship to the safety of the harbour, each and every evening, making sure that they drop anchor in the safest cove. But after everyone has gone to sleep, she sits in the kitchen for a while and listens to the howling of the wolves outside blending with the snores of her family. And she knows that the wolves are yonder and home is here, but the barrier between the two is either ephemeral or preposterously thin. At any given moment, the wind might roar and the waves might wash over them, and everything could come crashing down. And what does "everything" mean? Well, everything is everything. They will be adrift, without walls or a roof over their heads, defenceless. And this is why she needs the knife and cannot trust anyone.

One day, Fanny realised that such thoughts could overwhelm her, so she went to consult with Reb Moishe-Lazer Halperin. She found him in his usual place, in the stuffy rabbi's quarters in the synagogue yard, in the same run-down cabin that his predecessors had also had to endure.

When he saw Fanny, he tugged at his beard and said, "Everyone is leaving."

94

"Who is leaving, Reb Halperin?" she asked.

"You might as well ask who is *not* leaving," he said. "The Weissmans are leaving, and the Rosensteins and the Grossmans and the Althermans."

"Where are they going, Reb Halperin?"

"You'd better ask where they are *not* going. Some go to Ellis Island and some to Berlin and some to St Petersburg and some to Palestine."

"And what is wrong with that?" she asked.

"And what is good about that?" he said. "They get mixed up in politics like people in any other nation. They take a stand as if they were politicians all of a sudden: some with the proletariat and some with the intellectuals and some with the Russians and some with the delusion of Palestine. A disaster, I'm telling you; simply a disaster. What has protected us in the *golus*, do you know?"

Fanny was silent.

"Do you know, madam?" he asked again.

"Our faith?" she suggested.

"Faith? Yes, certainly," he was quick, even dismissive, in his agreement, touching his forehead and chest with his fingertips. "But as we have dwelled here, in these lands of our exile, what has protected us? I'll tell you what: we have not mixed with politics. Do you understand, or do you not? The righteous do not take political positions, they strengthen their allegiance to the Blessed Holy One instead, and they could not care less whether the nobility is bickering with the peasants, and it is all the same to them if Polish nationalists are clashing with Russian oppressors. If there is something to sell to the gentiles or to buy from them in order to make a living, so much the better – but this is where the line between them and us is drawn. We share with them the same soil but not the same world; we breathe the same air as they do, but not the same Work of Creation. Dear lady, you know why we say 'Pohlin' instead of Poland, do you not?"

She was still silent.

"Do you or do you not? So, I will tell you: 'Pohlin' means 'poh lin', that is, here – 'poh' – where the Jew will lodge – 'lin' – and rest and pray and keep the Sabbath and celebrate the festivals and wait for the Messiah Son of David to lead the way to Jerusalem. It is *here* that we lodge, not in *di golden medina* or in Palestine or Berlin. And now, who will stay? Do you know, madam? So, I will tell you who: the ones who stay are those who do not have the money to leave. All of the meek, miserable, luckless, beggarly stricken lot. And all of them – who do they beseech for aid? Who else but Reb Moishe-Lazer Halperin? Who else will they turn to? And can Reb Moishe-Lazer Halperin help? Once there were Weissmans and Rosensteins and Grossmans and Althermans who made donations to the rabbi. But today?" He kissed his finger and raised it to his forehead.

At this point, Fanny understood that the rabbi was signalling his expectation of a donation from a wealthy lady such as herself as soon as their conversation ended. Unlike his predecessors, who either died of dysentery or froze to death in the ramshackle hut in the synagogue yard, Reb Halperin had managed to survive thanks to his adamant refusal to trust in the spontaneous generosity of his townsmen and his extraordinary gift for tacitly demanding his wage. Fanny took out two gold coins and placed them on his table, whereupon he placed one of his felt hats as a cover over them and said, "I have thought a lot about your sister in the past few days, is the dear lady aware of that?"

Fanny was not aware.

"Does the dear lady understand what I am referring to?" he asked, and she nodded without having the slightest idea what it might be.

"So, I will tell you," he said and proceeded to wax lyrical about the moment when a family's unity is put to the test and about the price that the community is required to pay when a man such as Zvi-Meir grants himself a liberty that was not his to have. "But your sister, Mende, unlike the other geese in the flock – and you will have to excuse the expression – she knows her place in the world. So gentle, so humble, all the Daughters of Israel should look up to her. As it is said, 'go out and look', Mende Speismann: she accepts her predicament with humility, she does not court controversy, she puts her trust in the all-merciful God who sees the reasons for her grief."

Fanny nodded in embarrassment and said that she had actually come to see the rabbi about another matter as well.

"Certainly." He rose from his seat and said he would like to walk her out. "As much as half the kingdom for Mrs Keismann."

They were already standing on the cabin doorstep and Fanny sensed that she should get to the point quickly. She told him about the knife she had been given as a child by her father and how she could not now part from the blade. The rabbi's eyes lit up and he proceeded to calm her, saying that the matter was crystal clear: the knife had no significance as a knife, only as a memento of her father Meir-Anschil Schechter, righteous man of blessed memory. It could be that she was having a hard time parting with a memory from her childhood, and also, if he might venture, that she was craving a strip of the beef her righteous father used to serve her on a silver platter, which again evoked the knife. Perhaps it was time, the rabbi suggested, for her to embrace once more the customs of the congregation, for it is said in Genesis 1:28, "And have dominion over the fish of the sea, and over the fowl of the air, and over every living thing that creepeth upon the earth", and the knife made a third appearance. And does she know what the difference was, between Cain's offering and Abel's offering? Does the dear lady know what it was? So, he will tell her: Cain brought an offering from the fruit of the earth, and Abel from the firstlings of his flock and their fat. Which offering did the Creator accept? There's nothing to add, and the knife makes its fourth appearance. And it has already been said that, because Cain was so merciful with animals, he raged with cruel violence against humans, and ended up taking the life of his innocent brother, since, as it is said in Hosea 13:3, "They offer human sacrifice and kiss the calves."

"And much more can be added," said the rabbi. "Reams of words can be said; the conclusion will remain the same: when it comes to the things that really matter, one should follow the community and its customs."

Fanny said nothing and waited patiently for him to finish his midrash and add congratulations and adulations to her and her household, to her sister and her household, and to all their relatives and their households. And when she left, she felt the knife and knew that it did not symbolise anything that called for a long and winding explanation. She missed her father, Meir-Anschil Schechter, righteous man of blessed memory, but the knife represented nothing more than the knife itself. More is known than unknown. It was an object that her father had given her as a child because he recognised that she had what it took to use it. And even though she had sworn an oath never to slaughter again, she could not let go of the confidence the knife exuded. Few people were as adept with the knife as she. Her father had known this when he sent her to Motal. Known, and said nothing.

"The world is on the brink of complete annihilation," he simply told her before they parted. "If my daughter wants to gird her thigh with a knife for slaughtering chickens, so be it."

Now the path is empty and she is riding next to Zizek in a daze, and she does indeed believe that the end of the world is here, like the Flood. She, of all people – a child-shochet-cum-murderer – is being sent to Noah's ark, to sail along with this shadow of a man, this lifeless dust.

V

It is the second watch, and Colonel Piotr Novak is sitting in the town of Baranavichy, tucked away in a dark room he has rented from one of the locals, comparing surveillance reports sent in by the secret agents he is operating, Lucian Ostrovsky and Mikel Simansky:

Top Secret

Lucian Ostrovsky	Mikel Simansky
0945 – Vladimir leaves his home carrying a leather satchel.	0945 – Vladimir leaves his home and hides a suspicious bag beneath his shirt.
1001 – Vladimir slips two envelopes into the постальном ящик.	1001 – Vladimir enters the post office and looks around. He slips into the box two letters to be sent abroad, one of them is addressed to a Levine family in Paris.
1013 – Vladimir buys cheese at the market.	1013 – Vladimir holds conversations with market-goers while buying cheese. Alleged cheese is wrapped in brown paper.
1026 – Vladimir goes to have a haircut.	1026 – Vladimir enters the barbershop. Four men are waiting in the queue appearing to read the newspaper. Every now and again they exchange glances, but no "cheese" is exchanged.

Any other officer in the Okhrana, Novak knows, would have immediately dismissed Lucian Ostrovsky for his dry and dreary report. Yet it is Simansky's document that Novak crumples and throws into the bin. How can one tell if a bag is suspicious or not? And why would men sitting in a barbershop read anything other than the newspaper? And what makes cheese "alleged"?

The next day, Piotr Novak meets his deputy, Albin Dodek, and the latter asks his commander if Simansky's report was not even slightly useful, since it revealed that one letter had been sent to Paris, and to a Levine family, of all addressees. But Novak rebukes him: "Is it not obvious? Simansky discovered nothing of the kind. All he did was slide in a Jewish surname to spice up the story he was concocting."

"But how do you know that it wasn't the address?" asks Albin Dodek.

"The man they were tailing told me," Novak mutters. "He is working for us."

"I see." Albin Dodek lets the matter drop. Ever since Piotr Novak saw that his deputy had misspelled his own name on an envelope, he could not help but hear him uttering misspelled words whenever he spoke. Dodek is a bureaucrat who started out as a cook and switched jobs throughout the army until the rank of major suddenly landed on his shoulders. At the Okhrana, the Department for Public Security and Order, most deputies try to demonstrate their intellectual inferiority in order to avoid being suspected by their superiors of conspiring to stage a coup. In Dodek's case, this behaviour is simply the result of his natural limitations. Many times, Dodek has suggested a new lead in an investigation only to discover that it had already been ruled out from the outset. Maybe Dodek is not solely to blame for these misjudgments, however; the unusual investigating protocol in the Grodno and Minsk districts under the command of Colonel Piotr Novak should also be taken into account.

In all other regions of the Russian Empire, the Okhrana busies itself chasing after small fry. Thanks to its highly motivated secret agents, low-ranking undercover police and informants with vivid imaginations, it picks up a steady stream of second-rate revolutionaries. They arrest a moth circulating pamphlets, or shoot down a mosquito staging a protest, only to wake up the next morning and learn that the Czar has been assassinated by the giants of the Narodnaya Volya. You can be sure that nothing of this sort would have happened on Piotr Novak's watch.

In Novak's secret police department, all is calm. He has no interest in proving to anyone that he is making new arrests every day. For the most part, he tries to become inconspicuously embedded in the social fabric of the large cities within his jurisdiction – Minsk, Grodno, Kaunas and Vitebsk – and can sometimes be found in the small villages whose residents would never guess that an Okhrana department could be bobbing about in their sewer. It was not a whimsical decision on the part of Field Marshal Osip Gurko to let his loyal reporting officer Piotr Novak take charge of these two districts. Gurko had summoned Novak to his chamber and said, "Piotr, I need you here, and you know why." And indeed, Novak did know why. In these densely populated districts, everyone is everyone else's acquaintance, including the men of the secret police, and the Okhrana's outdated methods have proved ineffective.

What, then, are Novak's special methods? So-and-so wants to stage an uprising? Let him, says Novak, and what's more, undercover secret police agents will be more than happy to help him organise the revolt. The same rebel wants to spread socialist ideas? Let him! And if he needs money, the Department will gladly provide the necessary funds. What will the secret police ever find out, if it does not become part of those groups? How will the agents gain the rebels' trust if they do not fan the flames of the revolution themselves? The best proof of efficiency for the secret police, Novak knows, is to quash the revolutions it foments itself.

And so His Excellency Governor Osip Gurko regularly sends his secret police officers to be trained by Novak. "Whatever can we learn from him?" the St Petersburg and Moscow top brass ask each other, only to discover that there is quite a bit to learn from him. To begin with, there are several ground rules. First, Colonel Piotr Novak is rarely seen in the big cities. In the buzzing metropolises, he has come to learn, the swords that people sharpen are, by and large, metaphorical ones; and ideas, as far as he can tell, do not lead to revolutions. True, these cities boast quite a few universities, and there is no shortage of young and zealous students. But as each of them wants to be the indisputable leader of the revolution, they distinguish themselves from one another only by developing minuscule variations on the same theme. A socialist is more likely to loathe his revolutionary comrade than the most Czar-loyal aristocrat, even if said comrade has merely omitted a comma from the movement's manifesto. Experience has taught Novak that the revolutions that matter are led by an angry mob. And an angry mob— well, an angry mob doesn't care for nuance. This is why Novak prowls around villages and towns, places like Baranavichy, for example: places where peace abounds until all hell breaks loose.

Second, as everyone knows everyone else in these smaller places, one might gauge the level of dissent by posing as a passer-by forced to spend the night at the local inn, with money that suffices for nothing more than a cave-like bedroom.

The taverns and inns are the front line in this battle, and all one needs to do is sit there and listen, nothing more, and let the vodka do the rest. No need to introduce a wedge between the locals. The wedge has been there since the dawn of time. The only capacity that good secret agents should develop, Novak knows, is their capacity to drink: they should grow the liver of a pig, the ear of a dog and the hide of an elephant. Mingling with tramps and drunks is not for the self-indulgent. Those who want to enjoy the perks reserved for the powerful should not work for the secret police; that's what the roles of governor and army general are for.

Third, as already mentioned, the revolution must be created in order for it to be crushed; but this is easier said than done. If a man were to travel across the Russian Empire asking people what they wanted, he would find some very similar answers wherever he went: health, a roof over their head, a decent wage, peace and prayer. Gentile or Jew, Russian or Polish, merchant or craftsman, rich or poor – this is what they would say: things that speak for themselves. But if our traveller were to confront them with questions about Socialism, democracy, education and nationality, these mortals would look at him as though he had lost his mind and would offer him a drink to calm him down. Why should you inquire about such lofty matters? Are you an aristocrat, or a general? Sit with us and tell us about your travels: who did you meet in Minsk and what did you see in Vitebsk? Stop talking about imperial decadence and stop throwing around ideas that jeopardise the little we have. This is how it has always been: the rich have mansions, pedlars have carts, and beggars have hands. Sit down with us, and stop being provocative before blood starts washing the streets. Revolutions always end the same way: one corrupt ruler is replaced by another, and the pauper remains a pauper.

It is therefore in the nature of things – and this is something Piotr Novak understood as soon as he stepped into office – that the sublime ideas of freedom and equality must take root in less lofty sentiments, such as bitterness and envy. If a provocateur finds it hard to persuade a peasant to join the "Just Revolution", and if a townsman has never heard about "equality for all", all the agitator has to do is turn their attention to their neighbour's affluence or point out that so-and-so is a burden on the taxpayer.

This insight has also led Piotr Novak to concede the importance of the Jews. It is said that they constitute no more than fifteen per cent of the population, and yet, if you go to relax in a tavern, it will be Jewish-owned; if you lease a plot of land to grow vegetables, the promissory note will bear the name of a Jew; if you need an interpreter, a Jew will show up; if you are looking for train tickets to Warsaw, the Jews will sell you the cheapest ones; if you want to buy an Arabian horse you go to the Jews at the market. Need a cart driver? They'll give you a Jewish driver along with the horses. Czech crockery? At the Jews' shop. For God's sake: if you want to find solace with a tanned prostitute, she will be Jewish. In the name of the Father, the Son and the Holy Spirit, the Jews seem to be the only ones who are doing anything in this country, and if you do not want to do business with them, you'd better go and live on the moon. In short, if, after saying all these things, your partners in conversation still have no interest in joining the revolution, the damned sloths, and they do not harbour any loathing for the Jews, and if you fail to incite them against the rich, and if even the gypsies, Armenians and Germans leave them unruffled, this is when the real suspicion arises. This is an indication that one is facing a particularly shrewd sort who does not disclose his true feelings to a passing traveller.

Fourthly, and briefly, the agents, undercover police and informants do not care a jot about any of the above. It makes no difference to them whether the Czar or a rat is on the throne. This is why one has to say the magic words "expense account" (which for some reason appeals to them much more than the word "salary") to prompt them to deliver consistent surveillance reports without any gaps or holes in them.

The Okhrana chiefs are mightily impressed by Novak's methods. Before they met him, they believed themselves to be standing firm against a tiny, divided minority that threatened the prevailing peace and order. Every now and then, socialists, liberals, intellectuals and democrats would form an alliance, and the secret police's job, so they had believed, was to prevent these germ cultures from proliferating. Novak has led them to the realisation that their goal is to divide the people, to turn them against one another and to undermine the prevailing order, to separate chaff from grain. Only when everyone is a culprit, to some degree, and every household across the Russian Empire tarnished, only then will suspicions be aroused sufficiently to uncover the truly dangerous rebels – at which point the real dimensions of the revolution will become apparent, and the commanders' courage will be properly tested.

VI

After the conversation with his deputy Albin Dodek, Colonel Piotr Novak summons Mikel Simansky in order to dismiss him from service. But before Novak can utter a single word, Dodek charges back in with a shocked expression, dishevelled clothes, a sweaty brow, and alarming news: three bodies have been found on the road near Telekhany. Their informant is out of his wits with fright. He has told them that the victims were the Borokovskys, known bandits; the mother and two boys were found on the path with knife wounds, and the whereabouts of the father, Radek Borokovsky, are unknown. Their horses have been stolen, but the wagon and its contents are untouched. Dodek ends his report by proudly informing the colonel that he has already sent out agents to find the father, who was probably involved in the murder.

Piotr Novak listens to all this attentively and then asks Mikel Simansky to summon Lucian Ostrovsky and wait outside. He decides to postpone the dismissal, assuming that he will need as many people as possible on this job. He feels the thigh of his crushed left leg, which has been paining him, and pours himself a cup of slivovitz, draining it with a single gulp. He belches, frowns and then sighs.

"A straightforward investigation ahead of us, eh, Dodek?" he says, turning to his deputy.

"Indeed," Dodek says, puffing out his chest and adding, "rather than an investigation, this will be a manhunt."

"A manhunt, Dodek? Which man are we hunting?"

"Radek Borokovsky, of course," says the deputy, who never learns from past mistakes.

"I see, I see . . . and there I was thinking we should hunt for the killer," Novak says, getting to his feet. At this point, Dodek realises that he may have performed what his commander calls an "incorrect deduction". But as his superior seems to be enjoying their conversation, Dodek pretends that he cannot quite follow him.

"Aren't Radek Borokovsky and the killer one and the same?"

"What do you think, Dodek?"

"I have no idea."

"Well, we're already making progress with the investigation, aren't we? A moment ago we knew who the killer was, and now we're not so sure."

Dodek makes a careful note of this tip on his notepad. "The fact that one of the people present at the scene of a crime has not been murdered does not necessarily lead to the conclusion that he is the murderer." In the evening, before going to bed, he will read through his notes and go over the day's lessons.

Now Novak is signalling to him to give twenty roubles to the informant, Mr Otto Kroll, who, surprisingly, does not close his hand over the notes, but keeps it outstretched. Novak limps over to Mr Kroll and gives him an additional ten roubles, on the condition that he leads them to the crime scene as quickly as he can. Dodek notes down: "Small change buys precious time."

Mr Kroll stinks, and in no uncertain terms. It could be his teeth, or perhaps the lack thereof. It took Novak a while to understand that his role would force him to associate with people of the lowest sort, but he has long since accepted that the secret police is a despicable and corrupt organisation, utterly devoid of all decency. When he served in the army, it was clear to all the soldiers who the enemy was and what a victory or a defeat would mean. But here all is lies and deceit, and he knows that to get to the bottom of this investigation, he will be forced to pull countless tricks and scams. Colonel Piotr Novak is under no illusion: anyone who serves their country with subterfuge is not a true patriot. Anyone who pulls an old **man out of** his bed in the dead of night in the name of national security, and tears children from their parents' arms in the name of an ideal, by necessity must follow an illusion of security and false ideals. But does he have the strength to change the world? Not with a crushed leg. And who can say if a different method of investigation would be better than the current one? Only a fool could countenance such a thing.

And during the five hours of strenuous riding to the scene of the crime, forty versts away, he recalls the time when he proudly rode under the command of the great General Osip Gurko, when he fought fearlessly against the Turkish cavalry. Colonel Piotr Novak never roused his troops with speeches before battle and never went to console the wounded in its aftermath, and yet they charged behind him towards the Turks with their eyes closed. He excelled as a tactician and led his soldiers only into clashes in which they outnumbered their enemy. And when shrapnel from an Ottoman shell tore through his knee and shattered his leg during the Battle of the Shipka Pass, Novak still led his cavalry into the conquest of their target. He lay wounded and bleeding on the ridge of the Shipka Pass for an entire day, until he was evacuated to a nearby village, where he was informed that his left leg had to be amputated above the knee. Novak vehemently refused, knocked the doctor out cold with a single punch and, just before losing consciousness himself, demanded that his leg be amputated only at a point just above the ankle, using the Pirogov Method. The surgeon obliged, probably thinking that Novak would not survive the operation in any case, but the colonel regained his strength to spite both the doctor and himself.

If he had lost his life along with his foot, perhaps he would not be drowning in the river of doubt that is presently washing through his mind. The ruined leg has not only affected his body but also disrupted his mind, so that – instead of cherishing the memory of the pure moments of war – his thoughts keep dwelling on other details: torn limbs and wails of pain and the heartrending cries of soldiers calling for their mothers. And every time he struggles to dismount from a horse, or leans on the cane that provides the support that his missing foot can no longer offer, he does not think of his military honours, or the St George's Cross for his courageous service on the Shipka Pass; instead, he recalls the bodies they found on the pavements of the besieged city of Plevna – as passers-by stepped over them or trod on them, indifferent – and the wounded, tens of thousands of them, who gathered in churches and mosques as several hundred carcasses were evacuated each day, and of the countless soldiers who'd had their ears cut off and their faces mutilated and their genitals severed by the Turks under the command of the infamous Othman Pasha, and the tens of thousands of Turkish prisoners of war whom the Russians had abandoned for days on end without shelter, starving and steeped in mud, a quarter of them dead by Christmastime. It was impossible to tell good from evil, liberator from oppressor; who was right and who was wrong.

Novak's wound also destroyed his life's dream. It became impossible for him to be promoted to general, and yet he could not bear the thought of becoming an administrator. His illustrious commander, Osip Gurko, had no wish to renounce his excellent service, however, and when he was appointed governor, he persuaded Novak to transfer to the secret police. Novak accepted the offer to become chief of the districts of Grodno and Minsk, having no wish to snub his commander. Colonel Piotr Novak remains loyal to Osip Gurko, and does not count the few letters the governor sends or worry about the infrequency of his visits. Gurko is the last shred of dignity left in his life.

And now Novak is following the informant Otto Kroll, a certified fool, who is leading them down shadowless trails beneath a burning sun and almost drowns them in one of the tributaries of the Shchara. With his help, they arrive at the crime scene exhausted and dehydrated.

They are wearing plain clothes, but the agents' fine steeds give them away and the gathered vagabonds and passers-by make themselves scarce as they approach. Kroll has left his wife watching over the evidence, and this new simpleton is waiting for them on the bandits' wagon, chewing on a sausage she has found in one of the sacks. Novak dismounts, pretending not to feel the excruciating pain shooting from his left thigh all the way up his side. Recently, the leg has started to come back to life, and the shockwaves of its blasts have spread to his upper body. Novak trudges over to the wagon and knocks on a wheel with his cane, but Kroll's wife, surprisingly, does not take the hint and carries on with her placid chewing. Kroll motions to his lady to climb down, but there are varying degrees of stupidity among the asinine, and she pulls a face, stuffs the sausage into her pocket and clambers down, widening one of the rips in her dress.

Emboldened by his wife's acquiescence, Otto Kroll turns to Novak to demonstrate further proof of his indispensability.

"The wagon is here," he explains. "And the bodies are over there, and the road is here." And here is the ground, Novak thinks, and the skies are up there, and that is the sun. Kroll lights his pipe, adjusts the brim of his hat and says, "Horse thieves, definitely." An unimpeachable deduction, thinks Novak, and he motions to Albin Dodek to rid him of this amateur detective. Time is short and there is much to be done, and the regular police investigators are expected at any moment.

Kroll wanders away, and Novak turns to examine the bodies. The two sons are lying on their bellies in pools of raspberry-coloured dried blood, their bodies bloated and their skin pale yellow. Their arms rest alongside their bodies and they each have a cheek pressed into the ground. Their mother, on the other hand, is curled up in a foetal position, her knees bent and her head tucked in. And Novak, who has seen thousands of soldiers' corpses in his lifetime, knows that the positions of the slain gives away how they died. The two sons, without a doubt, were dispatched quickly, while the mother suffered for some time before she expired.

The colonel takes out a handkerchief from his pocket and pulls a flask of slivovitz from his jacket. He soaks the cloth with the plum brandy, covers his nose, and rolls over each of the two male corpses.

Nature has no consideration for the needs of police investigators.

Clouds of bluebottles and an assortment of other evidence-obliterating vermin come to light, their frenzy undeterred even by the flapping hands of the detective in charge of the investigation. What is more, the trousers of one of the sons have been pulled down, and Novak is suddenly face to face with a lifeless pink hose that resembles a repulsive blind mole and is peeking out from the man's underwear. Novak notices the startling slits in the victims' throats, deep cuts in the trachea and oesophagus that would not have given them a chance. They must have twitched for a few moments in their own blood and excrement before parting from their lives. He notices contusions on the mother's head, which, he concludes, did not lead to her death. The deep slit in her own throat will have sufficed.

The singular slaying method notwithstanding, Novak decides that the secret police do not have a particular interest in the affair. This is indeed a horrifying murder, and Novak is curious to know who the killer might be, but he believes that the case is more relevant to the regular police than the Department for Public Security and Order.

"Let's get out of here," he says to Dodek, but then he realises that his deputy has gone over to sit with the Krolls and join them in wolfing down radishes from another of the sacks.

What kind of a deputy chief would whistle with admiration at the sight of Mrs Kroll demonstrating on her own neck the slaughter of the victims of his investigation?

"Dodek!" Novak calls.

"I'll be right there, sir, the lady is just finishing her story . . ."

"Now!"

Dodek returns, looking sheepish, duly upbraided.

"I hope I did not interrupt a fascinating conversation with the distinguished Mrs Kroll?" Novak says, mounting his horse, his leg throbbing.

"The lady had almost finished her story, surely we could have waited just a moment longer—"

"Be thankful I spared you from having to spend another moment with the village idiot."

"I don't know if she really is a village idiot," Dodek says. "She's actually seen quite a bit in her time."

"Alert the police, Dodek, we don't have time for tall tales. Tell them that three bodies have been found at the roadside between Telekhany and Baranavichy. Probable motive, robbery. Let them open their own investigation. We are closing the file."

"Yes, sir." Dodek instructs the other agents, still perturbed by the reprimand for his interaction with Mrs Kroll. "The lady is rather shaken," he says, turning back to Novak. "She won't calm down."

Novak looks over at Mrs Kroll, who is once again demonstrating the slaughtering motion on her own neck to the crowd of nosy onlookers who are now gathering around her.

"If she keeps raising an imaginary knife to her throat, I imagine that'll make it all the more difficult for her to calm herself."

"She says this is how the *żyds* slaughter animals."

Novak reins in his horse. During his time in the army, he had encountered young Jewish boys who had been forced to become soldiers. Some of these recruits had insisted on observing the primitive customs of their religion and had slaughtered animals in a pagan ritual that involved a unique way of slitting the beast's throat, even though they knew that they would be flogged for doing so. This was the first time that he had understood the popular belief that the Jews are born blind and have to drink blood in order to gain their eyesight, and why every mother warns her children that the '*żyd weźmie do torby*': the Jew will carry you off in his sack if you misbehave.

All this notwithstanding, Novak thinks, it would be a

complete surprise, perhaps even unprecedented, if the murderer turned out to be Jewish. If there is one thing that amazes him about the Jews, it is the ease with which they capitulate when threatened. Novak has taken advantage of this trait several times, and his technique has always worked: catch a Jew in a strategic setting, threaten him with disaster – family disasters are particularly expedient – and proceed to extract all the information you need. Nevertheless, Novak has learned, this is not due to their being spineless or faint-hearted, but rather by virtue of their reason and pragmatism. Their perilous situation as a numerical minority in the empire is clear to all; their segregation has indeed protected them but it has also isolated them, and before a violent mob they have little hope of help or escape. Jews therefore have to believe that, if they succumb without a struggle every now and again, they will buy themselves peace for the rest of the time. If ever they mounted any kind of militant defence, recriminations would immediately follow, and then it would not be long before vicious decrees were deemed justified, houses could be burned down, property pillaged and people exiled to Siberia. No, thinks Novak, it is hard to believe that a Jew would countenance the risk of murdering three people and jeopardising himself and his brethren.

And yet, there is some suspicious evidence to consider. If indeed the Borokovskys were well-known robbers, and if this was an act of self-defence, why would the killers not turn themselves in to the police? Might they also have something to hide? This question becomes all the more pertinent when the manner of defence is taken into account. Slashing the sons' throats was understandable. No-one would want to leave their fate in the hands of a pair of drunken thugs, especially when one of them is flaunting a pink and repulsive worm between his legs. But why did the killers feel the need to slay the mother as well? Should he presume that they had not wanted to leave an eyewitness behind? But if that is so, why didn't they chase down the father? And why didn't they take possession of a wagon loaded with goods? And what did they imagine they could do with the horses? After all, the county is small, and rumours about horses gallop faster than the horses themselves. Strange indeed. Very strange.

Precisely at that moment, another informant arrives on the scene. This time it is Otto Kroll's brother, Nikolai – genius number three – who has been sent on Otto's behalf to reveal more evidence and give the family's income another boost. It turns out that Radek Borokovsky has been found unconscious in one of the nearby villages. He has been drinking pálinka all night long and "singing like a canary". From what they can make out, Mr Borokovsky maintains that a number of Russian army soldiers attacked his innocent little family on the road to Baranavichy. There were at least three or four strapping cavalrymen, along with one large and terrifying woman. He himself escaped the merciless attack by the skin of his teeth.

"Should we arrest him?" asks Albin Dodek.

"Of course not," says Piotr Novak. "But don't let him out of your sight."

Dodek nods, regretting the question. He should have remembered that his commander does not believe in arrests, because they only relate to crimes that have already taken place. Novak reserves the right to apprehend anyone for crimes that will take place in the future, and if he avoids taking action now, it must mean that he expects that the charges will become more severe. I must write this down in my notepad and memorise it, Dodek thinks. "Give the suspect latitude, and prioritise surveillance over arrest."

Novak pays Nikolai Kroll twenty roubles, which join the thirty that the Kroll family has already earned that day. The information would have reached Novak for free, but time is of the essence here, and the bribes he has paid in order to be at the forefront of the investigation are money well spent.

It is now time for the regular police to take over, as he has already instructed, and for him to leave this case – officially, at least. Naturally, he has every intention of keeping up his indefatigable investigations behind the scenes. In the meantime, he sends his deputy off to alert all available agents. They must set out immediately on a search of the surrounding area. Informants in the markets of the nearby towns, Telekhany and Baranavichy, are asked to keep their eyes and ears open, horse dealers are told to watch out for any unusual transactions, and innkeepers are ordered to report on any suspicious guests. It is not every day that one comes across three dead bodies, Jewish slaughter techniques, accusations against a belligerent military convoy and one large and terrifying woman, all of which are supposed to come together to form a consistent story. I'll be damned, thinks Novak. This country is losing its mind.

VII

With first light, their predicament becomes clear. Both of them are beaten, battered and tattered, and Zizek urgently needs a doctor. They have nothing left apart from the rum barrel, neither food nor water.

Zizek stops the cart by a small lake where they can wash and fill their water flasks. Fanny climbs down and crouches among the reeds. Zizek assumes she is urinating, but when she does not return, he walks over to check that she is alright. He finds her sitting on a rock, her dress rolled up almost to her knees, sharpening her knife on a smooth stone.

He approaches hesitantly, careful not to make a noise, assuming that Fanny is in a state of shock. He wants to say something, but his words argue with each other inside his head and he can't get them out.

His failed attempt at speech is not lost on Fanny. For the first time, Zizek's enormous body is showing signs of life. They've been riding together for two days and he has not yet said a single word.

"Why did you come with me, Zizek Breshov?" she asks in Polish, standing up to face him.

Zizek scratches his head, the gaze of his bright-coloured eyes lowered. He retreats. She chases after him and grabs hold of his arm, and he recoils like a child receiving a scolding.

"I am sorry, Zizek Breshov, I . . ." She can feel a sob crawling up her throat.

Zizek looks at her hand gripping his arm as if it were a thorn that had penetrated his flesh. He keeps quite still, as if the slightest movement would make the thorn scratch into his arm until it bleeds. And yet he does not want to pull away. He feels ants creep beneath his skin and march in a column up his spine, all the way to the nape of his neck. A raw, addictive pain paralyses his limbs, and the sudden thought of death comes to his mind. He is ready to die at this very moment, as her fingers are biting into his skin. He feels as if he has been kicked up in the air, and a few first words are launched out of his throat to bridge the distance.

"We must return to Motal." He is suffocated by his own words. "I'm sorry, but if we stay here, they will find us."

Fanny lets go of his arm and walks away. If he has waited so long just to say this, it would have been better if he had remained silent. She slashes at the stalks of oats and then goes to feed the horses.

Zizek knows he has made a mistake. His first words after decades of silence, and they have not met with the desired reception.

Perhaps it would have been better if he had never opened his mouth, what an idiot he was even to try. He had only wanted to avoid more trouble, now that they are left without food and are wanted for murder throughout the region. If they do not hurry back to Motal, they risk imminent arrest, or even ending up in the clutches of an angry mob. Fanny could return to her village, she could resume her normal life without arousing any suspicion, and all would be well. And then he looks up and sees that Fanny has unharnessed the young horse and is leading it towards him.

"Here, Zizek Breshov." She hands him the reins. "Here you go; I will take the old one."

Zizek cannot utter a word in response before she turns towards the veteran steed, which nervously shifts back and forth, rocking the cart and advising them that he has no intention of pulling all that weight on his own. Fanny tries to quash the dissent with a brandishing of the whip, and the horse punishes her for this insolence by shoving her straight into a muddy puddle.

Zizek rushes to help her up, failing to hide the beginnings of a smile at the sight of Fanny wallowing in the muck. She sees his scarred lips starting to twitch, and bursts out laughing.

"This is quite a horse indeed!" she says, imitating the voice of the gang leader, and they both collapse with the contagious laughter of madness and despair.

Fanny seizes Zizek's hand and pulls herself out of the muddy embarrassment, and they sit together at the edge of the pond, which, at first light and from a distance, had struck them as a lake, and now, close up, reeks of swamp. They gaze out at the boggy plain, which resembles the surface of a burnt cake, and they peer at each other, their energy spent. When they had first set out on this journey, they could not have dreamt that by this point they would be in the middle of nowhere with three corpses to their credit. Zizek pulls out his snuff box and wipes his nose with his sleeve, and Fanny notices that the cut in his lip is deep and still oozing.

When they are under way again, he pours out two cups of rum and proposes a new plan, with the sudden excitement of one who has found a precious thing believed lost for ever.

"Baranavichy!"

"What?" Fanny says, taken aback.

"Baranavichy. I'm sorry, but I know the owner of a small inn there, perhaps you can stay there, just for a few nights, until they stop searching." Zizek fires out his words at great speed, without pausing for breath, as if compelled by a need to make up for lost time. "In the meantime, you must burn the bloodstained uniform, please – do it quickly – and get yourself new clothes, of course."

"Not 'myself', Zizek Breshov," she corrects him. "Ourselves."

"I'm sorry, but you must ride to the next village and rely on the villagers' charity for food and clothes, there isn't any other choice. Anyway, you won't be able to linger there for more than an hour, any rumour about two killers wandering between towns will spread quickly, and this is why you can't keep travelling at night. Your only option is to blend in, to pretend you have a family there, a father and daughter. If they ask questions, say nothing. And then go to the inn, you can stay there for a few nights, until they call off the search."

"*We* can stay there, you mean," she says. "I am not going anywhere without you."

"Hurry, please," he says, again ignoring her.

Fanny stares at him in amazement. The revival of Zizek's speech is dazzling, but why won't he include himself in the plans he is making for her? She doesn't know. But his instructions sound reasonable, and so she answers his pleading gaze with a nod. Apparently petrified by the outpouring of his own words,

118

Zizek lowers his eyes, reins in the horses, and gets to work. He gathers the uniform, coat and jacket and rolls them in thorny bracken he pulls up from the edge of the bog. He sets fire to this incriminating bundle and stokes the flames to ensure that his entire military past is incinerated. A whole life goes up in flames, and Zizek looks at Fanny, his face furrowed with anguish, like a man who has just lost everything he owns. He purses his lips with the intensity of a starved baby. Fanny takes his arm, still stunned by the verbal stream that just gushed from the man whom everyone considered the town fool, and together, caked in dried mud, they stand and watch the dying flames.

VIII

Emboldened by the success of the first stage of Zizek's plan, they climb back onto the cart and set off for the next village. But before they have gone very far, the remainder of the plan suddenly goes up in smoke: they come across a man lying face down by the side of the road. Zizek chakes the reins to urge the horses to speed up, but the old horse chooses to slow its pace instead, making it very difficult to ignore the body. They can see at once that the man is an unfortunate Jew, wearing a torn kaftan tied at the waist and a tattered hat covering half his head.

Two black ravens perch on the brim of the deceased's hat and peck at his neck, and Fanny mumbles, "We should at least . . ."

Zizek puts a stop to this at once. "I'm sorry, but it's out of the question."

But just when it seems that the danger is past and that the stranger at the roadside cannot trouble them unless they torment themselves by looking back, Zizek pulls the horses to a halt. He takes a shovel from one of the crates in the cart, alights with a groan and limps with his bruised body and wracked nerves back towards the corpse.

Fanny jumps down and hurries after him, and turns the man onto his back – only to discover that he is still breathing. Elated, she yells, "He's alive!", but the expression on Zizek's face tells her that they now have a new dilemma: how will they flee with a Jew suspended between this world and the next?

He gives Fanny an apologetic look. If the stranger were dead, they would be able to bury him properly, but in their present circumstances they will be risking their lives to save a stranger whose own life is hanging by a thread. Zizek shuffles back towards the cart, gesturing to Fanny to be reasonable and follow him, but then he sees, horrified, that Fanny is bending over the Jew and pulling out her knife. Has the woman gone mad? Will she now dispatch everyone they meet on this road as a matter of course? Then he realises that she is merely cutting the stranger's sidelocks and trimming his beard a little to try and disguise his Jewish appearance, and then she calls to Zizek and beckons to him to bring the cart back. Zizek refuses and implores her to leave the Jew where he is, but, with an unnerving stubbornness, she bends down to wrap the stranger's arm around her neck.

As they ride on to the village, with the unconscious fellow now reposing in the back of the wagon, Fanny explains to Zizek that the authorities are searching for a couple, a man and a woman, not a trio. In other words, they might have just arranged an alibi for themselves. If the human toothpick in the back there recovers, perhaps he will sacrifice the truthfulness of his testimony for them, in gratitude for having had his life saved? He won't even have to lie – not knowingly, at least. They will help him refresh his memory.

"Can't you see, Zizek Breshov, this Jew is a sign from Heaven?"

Zizek looks up at the skies, his wounds raked by the sun's scorching fingers, then glances back at the Jew who has been sent to save them, and whose sidelocks and beard have been trimmed to hide his incriminating Jewishness, with limited success. All Zizek can do is nod at Fanny in reluctant agreement.

As soon as they enter the village, their peril becomes clear. Usually, when strangers arrive in a village during the summer months, the locals greet them and offer them borscht and salted fish, or at least some sweetened tea. But not a single household is prepared to offer hospitality today. To the gentiles, the unconscious man in the cart, whose lips are cracked and whose beard was undoubtedly clipped in haste, is Jewish; even if a cross had been carved into his forehead, he would remain a Jew, and they are immediately wary of the Poles (supposedly a father and daughter) who are transporting him. The inhabitants of the three houses with mezuzahs on their doorposts – that is, the few Jews, *yishuvnikim*, who are still living among the peasants – are also suspicious, although they flag down the cart nonetheless and throw them an old blanket, a shirt with a hole in it, mouldy bread and half-rotten fruit, and even a broken stool.

Fanny knows that they are living on borrowed time. These one-street villages never fail to miss even the arrival of a new fly, and every insect buzz is taken for a sting. Nevertheless, they manage to amass enough alms-clothes to put together a change of peasant outfits: Fanny in a red dress, trimmed with pins instead of buttons, a babushka coat and a head scarf. Zizek puts on a ragged woollen tunic, a peasant's jacket and a worn red sash. They are given permission to draw water from a well to fill their flasks and let their horses drink. Someone sees Zizek's bruised face and tosses them bandages and a bottle of herbal medicine, and someone else adds a flask of smelling salts, perhaps to help revive the man lying in the back of the cart. Fanny knows how country life works, knows that their strange appearance will have already become the topic of the day. It is time to disappear, they must hasten on to Baranavichy before rumour of the three dead bodies reaches the village.

Thanks perhaps to the smelling salts, the old Jew finally wakes, his black eyes widening at the sight of Zizek's scarred face looming over him. He tries to get to his feet and flee from the wagon, but his legs tangle like a newborn lamb's, and he collapses again. However, once he has understood that the horses have been stopped for him and that he has been offered water and dry bread, he is no longer in such a rush to get up. His back aches and his muscles are feeble, but if he could only take a bite from one of those apples that his saviours have accumulated on their travels through the village, his body would surely regain its strength. On the other hand, he has bad teeth, so perhaps they would be so kind as to peel and slice the apple for him? It doesn't take long for Fanny and Zizek to discover that this Jew is quite demanding.

He tells them that his name is Shleiml and that he is a *hazan*, a cantor. Fanny is surprised by this revelation. *Hazanim* are usually devout men, greatly respected by Jewish communities. What has happened to him, and why was he lying at the side of the road in a filthy kaftan? What is more, how can he understand their Polish? *Hazanim* usually speak only Yiddish and Hebrew; they have no use for other languages. Shleiml the Cantor merely shrugs and offers no answer. They found him by the wayside? He is surprised. Perhaps he fell victim to sunstroke, or maybe he was robbed by bandits – yes, yes, it's all coming back to him now: there were two of them, maybe even three, ogres, sons of giants, who accosted him, demanding to know why he was roaming around the villages on foot like a government spy, and he explained to them that he is a *hazan*, delighting the Jews with

122

his beautiful melodies. And the bandits asked him what kind of profession is that, and he replied, certainly a most honourable occupation. Then they forced him to demonstrate his talents, and sing for them – and to illustrate this point in his story, Shleiml Cantor launches into song for Fanny and Zizek, as he did for the bandits: *"Adon olaaam osherrr molochhh . . ."*

"Enough!" Zizek claps his hands over his ears and looks at Fanny in horror, as if to say, I'm sorry, but if Shleiml is a *hazan* then Zizek is the Czar. It then dawns on them why this songbird has been forced to wander destitute about the villages: he was struck by neither sunstroke nor bandits. He is simply a cantor who sings like a bar-mitzvah boy whose audience prays for him to become mute.

All the same, Shleiml the Cantor is now stretching out his hand in expectation of payment for his toil. Fanny cannot help herself and bursts out laughing. Undeterred, the cantor goes on, *"Be-terremmm kolll yetzirrr nivraaa . . ."*, his hand still out-stretched, and it becomes clear that he will continue to sing until a few copecks have landed in his palm. When Fanny pulls out two coins from her sash, they realise that this *hazan* does not earn his living by singing, but rather by being paid to stop. He imme-diately feels "much better" and is ready to hop down from the cart and be on his way, knowing he will not squeeze any more money from these shegetz peasants. He must keep courting the custom of country Jews, who may be inclined to listen to his charming melodies, or else beg him to stop. But before he can take a step, Zizek seizes him by his collar. "If you please, Cantor, you are coming with us to Baranavichy."

As they ride on, the *hazan* starts singing again, *"Azzzai molochhh shemooo nikraaa . . ."*, but Fanny waves at him to stop pushing his luck, because Zizek is already at the end of his tether. She tries to ask him where he studied, where he comes from and where his home is, and his answers make his story even clearer. Shleiml the Cantor is a homeless, uneducated nobody who can sing "Adon Olam" and a handful of piyutim for the mussaf prayer for Rosh Hashanah. He travels the countryside, away from the big cities, where synagogues are scarce and Jewish *yishuvnikim* are willing to pay generously to listen to the tunes they grew up hearing, or for the abrupt truncation thereof. He picked up his Polish as he lurked in taverns, back when his business prospered and his lucky streak in cards and chequers was guided by interventions from On High. But, now that he is better known in the area, his income has dwindled. He is banned from entering taverns and no longer offered a place to sleep in the stables. His former gambling colleagues have ruined his reputation, denied him a livelihood, and ultimately caused his collapse at the roadside. And now, if they would be so kind as to explain, why is his presence required in Baranavichy? Not that he has anything against the town, it's actually quite pleasant, with many Jews and a nice synagogue and a mikveh and a market and tavern. But it is still a town just like any other, and houses there are not made of gold, so perhaps the lady could plead with the nice gentleman holding the reins to let Shleiml the Cantor get down from the cart?

Fanny looks at Zizek and they know that the time has come to refresh the *hazan*'s memory. So Fanny explains to Shleiml the Cantor that he has been riding with them for the past two days – can he not remember? They picked him up near Telekhany, he asked them to drop him off in one of the villages, but then he was sun-struck and lost the soundness of his mind. This is why they are taking him to Baranavichy, to the large Jewish community there. Perhaps he can find work there, or maybe receive charitable help, but in any event he will be out of harm's way.

Shleiml mulls this over as he scratches his clipped beard and feels about for his missing sidelocks, and only then does he realise that they have desecrated his Jewishness. He thanks Fanny for her well-intentioned act, even though her description of the past two days sounds rather odd to him. He could have sworn that he only lay in the ditch for an hour, two hours at most; could it be that this sorry state really lasted for whole two days? Let it be so. Anyway, if it was indeed two days, and he is not saying it wasn't, then he must be even more debilitated than he first thought. His body has clearly reached its limits, and if he does not have more food and water in double and quadruple amounts he surely won't make it. Fanny cuts him another slice of bread and sneaks him another apple, and Zizek grips the reins and stares straight ahead, trying to keep his ire in check. Since they mentioned Baranavichy, the cantor goes on, it is a lovely town indeed, and a large Jewish community is usually an advantage. But Shleiml the Cantor has reason to expect quite a few, well, *disagreements* there and also, it would seem he has some debts from various card games and chequers matches where the Guiding Hand had left him to his own devices. And then the chief cantor of the town, fearing competition, has declared war on Shleiml's livelihood and forbidden him to sing anymore. Shleiml the Cantor's vocal style, he was told, is no longer welcome in Baranavichy, and should he try singing there again, the authorities would be called in. In short, seeing as they are forcing him to visit a town where they know he will be in danger, Shleiml the Cantor would like to know if he isn't entitled to any form of compensation other than the bread?

Fanny and Zizek are doubly relieved when they reach Baranavichy at sunset, because another day of riding with such a schnorrer would have cost them the shirts off their backs.

IX

The town of Baranavichy has three inns. The one on Post Street is run by Tomashevsky, a man with a highly developed business sense and a hatred of paying taxes. Consequently, tax collectors and police officers frequently install themselves there, enjoying free drinks and "veal sausages" with the compliments of the house. Which really means that they must endure a menu that is entirely derived from cabbage: cabbage soup and cabbage salad and cabbage sausages and cabbage pie, all of which Tomashevsky passes off as "meat delicacies". But nobody goes there just for the food, and hungry drunks do not have refined tastes. It is unlikely, Piotr Novak thinks, that the killers will go to Tomashevsky's, and he is thankful to be spared the dubious pleasure of this cabbage den.

The second inn, on Alexander Street, is run by Vozhnyak. Even before entering the main hall, one finds oneself in a sumptuous foyer with a doorman and a place for coats. The inn's walls are made of stone, for a change; there is a fireplace in every room and imported alcohol is served – French, at that. Anyone wishing to see and be seen in Baranavichy will come to Vozhnyak's dressed in their finest, to smoke cigars and enjoy fine brandies. Is this a fitting locale for killers on the run? It seems unlikely, Novak decides, thinking regretfully of the fine caviar he enjoyed there on previous occasions.

All things considered, it seems likely that if the killers do indeed reach Baranavichy, and if they lack contacts in the town, they will put themselves up at Patrick Adamsky's tavern, down one of the alleyways off Marinska Street.

A wastrel in threadbare clothes is slumped in there at this very moment, one of his soot-stained cheeks resting on a table. He orders a second shot of the cheapest vodka, a sort of jaundiced, urine-coloured juice probably concocted in a soap factory, and, when no-one is looking, he empties the drink under his chair into one of the cracks in the wooden floor. Then, he carefully pours himself a shot from the slivovitz bottle hidden in one of the pockets of the rags he calls his clothes. While there is certainly a chance of making himself conspicuous among the crowd of tramps, it is worth the risk, if only to remind himself that, unlike all the other derelicts around him, he still has a shred of dignity left.

There is another reason why Novak chose Adamsky's tavern over all of the others. The first night after a murder is critical. The killers will not have gone far, and they might have to rely on local help. After all, for better or worse, we are all bound up together in a cycle of give and take. And if we recall that, of all the town's innkeepers, Patrick Adamsky is the only one who boasts a military past, and link this fact with Radek Borokovsky's testimony about the Russian army soldiers who allegedly attacked his innocent family, we might find a plausible connection.

To be frank, Radek Borokovsky's testimony has already lost much of its credibility. As he was found inebriated and unconscious, his concerned relatives and acquaintances took him to the region's best clinics, which happen to be its taverns, where he was administered the remedy of more liquor. Nikolai Kroll, the informant, who has already expressed a wish to make his service with the Okhrana more official, was among his treating physicians and reported the different versions of the story that emerged from Borokovsky's mouth. After each drink, Borokovsky blurted out another tale: initially he was attacked by six soldiers led by an officer and a woman; then the officer was a woman; and, later still, he recalled two giant soldiers with a rifle who were accompanying a woman, or were they horsemen riding a horse-shaped woman? In short, he is no longer very sure of anything.

Albin Dodek pleads with his commander to arrest Radek

Borokovsky and force the truth out of him through torture. "He is a born liar, a chronic drunk and a compulsive gambler."

But Novak gives his deputy a cunning smile. He knows that the truth is not torn out of people. It is nurtured and coaxed. What good will come of interrogating this incompetent? Just another story at most, and a dubious one at that, which he will stick to for fear of being thought a liar. If they follow Novak's methods, they will have several versions, which will allow them to compare the details, look for patterns, and deduce that the affair involves a certain number of soldiers, between one and six; one large and fearsome woman, who by force of necessity is neither an officer nor a horse; and, as Novak has already clearly identified, the throat-slitting style characteristic of *żyd* ritual slaughter is also evident. Moreover, if Novak insisted on interrogating Borokovsky and others of his ilk himself, then his face, the face of the authorities, would become familiar to the people of Baranavichy, and then he would not be able to blend in with the crowds at inns. For the people around him in Adamsky's tavern do not have the faintest idea that the good-for-nothing vagabond sitting among them with his cheek flat on the table is none other than the highest ranking secret police officer in the entire region, the man who used to be Colonel Piotr Novak.

BARANAVICHY

I

The Master of the World extends his arm and overwhelms the sun with a mighty hand and an outstretched arm, and now the heat is over and the wind is blowing on the three travel companions. Shleiml the Cantor offers another explanation: "The famished sun has wasted away. And if the sun is not immune to hunger, what will become of Shleiml the Cantor, the orphaned matchstick?"

A single glance from Zizek is enough to make the Cantor brace himself at the back of the wagon. The journey has been long and uncomfortable; it seems that their vital organs do not have fixed locations, and a lung can suddenly replace the throat, or vice versa. Finally, they cross the bridge over the Shchara and approach Baranavichy's main street. Now the silence is welcome. They must pretend to be strangers passing through the town and nothing more; just a father and daughter en route to Minsk, with a beggar they had picked up along the way. As they pass by the synagogue, Fanny takes Zizek's arm, as a daughter would, but the pretence makes Zizek uneasy, and he recoils. Suddenly, they both realise how foreign they really are to one another and how far away from home they have ventured: Fanny from Natan-Berl and her children, and Zizek from his boat on the Yaselda. Melancholy strikes them. In their most desperate moments, when they were on the verge of despair, they were able to find solace in each other, but now merely linking arms is irksome, even if it is necessary for their safety. The more they avoid looking at one another, the more each of them is present in the other's sight.

Twilight is the best time to enter a town where Jews comprise half the population. The year expects the High Holidays, the week anticipates the Sabbath and the day awaits prayer, so the Jews are quick to pack up their stalls and close their shops before gathering in the synagogue. Fortunately for the trio of travellers, they are not scrutinised, nobody turns to look at them. If they had arrived at midday, everybody in the town would have wondered who they were and where they were going. At the very least, they would have been invited to buy something. But at this time, not a single soul asks why they are passing through.

Even the peasants have left Baranavichy, returning to the nearby villages after selling their produce to their Jewish neighbours. Muzhiks do not have much of a nightlife. For them, nightfall does not mark the passage of time, but the occurrence of an event. Diurnal animals make way for nocturnal animals, colours fade and sounds multiply. The boughs of trees wave in unison, leaves hiss in the wind, frogs protest in chorus and packs of wolves begin to roam. The peasants prefer to sit out on their porches in the evening, their fingers wrapped around teacups and their bodies curled in comfortable chairs. Some of the muzhiks will gather to share some vodka, but come midnight bitterness will strike and they will return to their homes angry, and hopefully remember to take off their boots before falling asleep.

The three travellers pass through the town's main street until they reach Marinska Street, and stop outside Patrick Adamsky's tavern. Taverns and inns are always full at this time in the evening. It is the hour when idlers forget their laziness and make peace with their destinies or, in other words, bask in self-pity. Zizek asks Fanny and the *hazan* to wait for him in the cart while he goes to seek the owner's help.

"Do you really trust him this much, Zizek Breshov?" Fanny whispers.

"I am sorry, but I trust him even more than that," Zizek replies.

Zizek's first few steps are hesitant; he opens the front door a crack, and surveys the tavern. It is more cramped and mustier than he remembers it. The walls are made of rough, rotten wood, and the rafters are in such a state that they barely support the upstairs rooms. Every step on the upper floor winds around Zizek's nerves, and he thinks that the place seems busier than it used to be. The last time he was here, many years ago, the patrons of the inn lay idly on their beds and passed the time by counting the cockroach corpses and rat droppings that accumulated in the cracks in the wooden floor beneath them. But now, strange, unexpected sounds drift down from the top floor, the squeaks and muffled whimpers of adulterers or monks or God knows who else.

The dining hall downstairs is divided by garish Ottoman-style arches. A mural of Christ at Golgotha is so faded that the Saviour's body appears to have melted in the sun and Mary Magdalene seems to be rejoicing at his misery. Icons are everywhere, little booths with flowers and gold-coloured frames, beneath which the "pilgrims" are sitting, praying for a jug of kvass.

In a corner, Zizek spots a bunch of card players, mere small fry, gambling with roubles they don't have. One of them glances at his hand and laughs bitterly. At the other end of the room, three men are huddled in conversation, perhaps about politics, pointing their fingers at one another. Three other idlers are sitting alone at separate tables. One is leaning against the wall, owl-faced and empty-eyed. The second is so fat he cannot sit comfortably in his chair. And the third – well, five empty vodka glasses and a cheek flat against the table guarantee that he will not remain with them for much longer. In any event, there are no police officers here, and there are no women. Zizek walks in.

*

Patrick Adamsky descends the stairs from the upper floor, followed by a servant boy with a broom in his hand. "Over there," Adamsky gestures without looking at the boy, and the servant scurries away to sweep one of the corners. Adamsky has an overpowering, authoritarian bearing, to which all his underlings have grown accustomed over the years, but Zizek cannot erase from his memory the image of the orphaned boy who was abducted with him by Leib Stein the *khapper*, the child catcher.

II

Back then, Patrick Adamsky was called Pesach Abramson, and he lived with his older brother, Motl Abramson, in the house of his uncle. Pesach and Motl's parents had both contracted tuberculosis and received a summons from On High, and the two brothers had joined the seven children of their uncle and aunt, Scholom and Mirka Abramson. Theirs was the poorest family in Motal, and the townspeople would offer them charity from time to time, but not too often, lest they should stuff themselves until their bellies burst open.

When the accursed wave of army quotas reached Motal, the conscription of Pesach and Motl could have been easily justified as a way of lifting some of the burden from Scholom and Mirka's shoulders. And yet, with an unfathomable stubbornness, the uncle and aunt refused to turn in their orphaned nephews and defied the *sborchik*'s warrant. On the night when the foul child catcher Leib Stein knocked on their door, Scholom Abramson even dared to face him wielding a pitchfork. The pitchfork, needless to say, was quickly broken in two, with a single blow over Leib Stein's thigh, and Scholom Abramson felt closer to his Creator than he ever had before when a second blow hit him full in the face. Nor did the abductor spare Aunt Mirka: when she rushed to her husband's help, Stein slapped her across the face too. The blow was so surprising, and so violent, that everyone instantly stifled their sobs and screams and stared at Leib Stein, aghast, as though everything he had done up to that point had borne the hallmark of pure reason. The man's sadistic smile was unequivocal: he delighted in beating women, and if they resisted, he would move on to their daughters. In any case, Motl and Pesach were seized by the scruff of their necks by Stein's thugs and joined another petrified boy who was already waiting in the prison next to the synagogue.

Scholom and Mirka Abramson swelled the cries of Selig and Leah Berkovits. The people of Motal cried along with them, the heart of the town's rabbi broke in two, but that night many sighed in relief, thankful that at least their own children had been spared.

But then something happened that took even Leib Stein by surprise. His task had been to take the children to the ispravnik, the regional governor, and from there to the cantonist camp. But before dawn, as they were about to stop off in one of the gentile households where they had arranged accommodation and meals, fourteen-year-old Motl Abramson leaped from the wagon and hurled himself towards the black marshes. Leib Stein and his crew chased after him, but the boy vanished as though swallowed up by the swamp. Leib Stein searched for him until sunrise, but in the morning mists, earth and sky became one, and the boy was gone without a trace.

Where did Motl Abramson go? No-one knew. But a series of events that followed his escape led to the hypothesis that he had not gone far, that he had remained in the area to avenge the forced conscription of his brother, or perhaps to avenge the entire

Jewish population. First, a month after Motl's abduction, the houses of two low-ranking officials went up in flames. This was arson, without a doubt, and the usual suspects were members of the Polish underground. But then, two months later, there was a similar incident in Baranavichy, and this time a fire was started at the house of the assessor, the governor's local representative. The police declared a state of emergency, a reward was offered in exchange for information about the arsonist and heavy penalties were announced for anyone who dared to aid the criminal's escape. Threatening envoys were sent to the leaders of the Jewish community. After all, the Russian army provided a living bulwark against rioters and pogroms, and if it transpired that Jews were indeed sheltering the outlaw, the soldiers would no longer be able to protect them from an angry mob.

The next victim in line was one of Leib Stein's thugs. No-one knew how it happened, but while the child-catcher was on the road, an unknown perpetrator broke into his home and abducted his blameless son.

The last person to pay the price was Motal's very own *sborchik*, whose role required that he fill the conscription quotas imposed by the army. In this case, the fire was considered exceptionally violent, at least to the minds of the people of Motal, although it was not clear how one arson could be more violent than another, save for the fact that it had taken place in their town and had targeted a Jew, one of their own. At this point, though, it became clear to all that Motl Abramson was involved in this affair, and the community leaders had no doubt that these despicable acts of vengeance had to be stopped. If he continued, Motl might draw the entire Jewish community into a bloodbath. After all, the King of Kings had not consecrated the Jews above all other nations, only for them to drown in the slime of secular politics and deals. This is why they accepted any form of government that came their way and why they would sell their wares to the Russian army and also to the Russians' enemies, without thinking that this created any conflict of interest. They were not political because they had only come to lodge in Poland, "Pohlin", until the coming of the Messiah, the Son of David who would lead them to Jerusalem. The Abramson affair, however, pitted them against the authorities and threatened to drag all the Jews into a vortex of escalating violence. If a sheigetz turns out to be a murderer, he is nothing more than a madman, but if a Jew is an arsonist, then all *żyds* are traitors. They had no choice. Motl Abramson had to be turned in.

However it was done, and whoever gave him away, the information was accurate enough to prompt ten policemen to surprise the Abramson household in the middle of the night and arrange a roll-call of their children. Scholom Abramson asked them to count the children in their beds, but the officer in charge insisted on waking all of them, including a one-year-old infant. Indeed, the tally was seven children, an exact match with the records, three boys and four girls, the same number as the Patriarchs and the Matriarchs in the Torah. Scholom Abramson shrugged as if the matter were settled. But instead, the officer examined the papers of each child, until he reached the eldest of them, a boy of about fourteen, and yelled, "Name!"

"Yaki Abramson," the boy answered confidently, and the policeman carefully inspected the certificate, and muttered, "Well, then, um . . . How old are you, Yaki?"

"He doesn't speak Polish," Scholom Abramson said.

"Age!" the officer shouted, and then unexpectedly added in Yiddish, "*Elter?*"

"*Seben . . . acht . . .*" stammered the father, adding, "seven, eight, they grow up so fast."

The officer glowered and, in the blink of an eye, the boy posing as Yaki Abramson shoved past him and ran for the door, and the other police officers, who had been standing guard, chased after him and subdued him with punches and kicks.

The information that reached the police had been horribly accurate. Motl Abramson had indeed been hiding in his aunt and uncle's home, pretending to be one of their children, while one of his cousins, Yaki Abramson, had been sent away at the age of eight to apprentice as a blacksmith in another town. The policemen cuffed Motl and his uncle Scholom, while his aunt and cousins wailed. The court sentenced the accused to twenty years of hard labour in Siberia. A month later, the family was informed that they had both died before the sentence could be carried out. Official cause of death: typhoid.

Broken into a thousand pieces, Mirka Abramson completely rejected any comfort that Motal's community leaders and residents offered her. She agreed only to meet with Leah Berkovits, Yoshke's mother, and in secret at that. And if the Berkovitses and Abramsons recovered with the years, the mothers of the two families continued to keep to themselves, their one concession being to meet once a year with Rabbi Schneerson of the Chevra Techiyas Hameisim, who came to Motal to report on what was known to him about their sons.

The town's residents respected the mothers' wish to remain shut away in their houses, even though a decade later this seemed rather extreme and excessive – if only for the sake of their other sons and daughters, who all deserved a proper shidduch and a better future. After all, more children remained at home than had been snatched away. Nonetheless, whenever people tried to explain this unassailable fact to their faces, however gently, they were met with an impolite rejection bordering on ingratitude. They came to offer comfort and help, and left feeling reviled and humiliated. When Rabbi Schneerson passed away, no-one else tried to break down the walls of their solitude.

Pesach Abramson and Yoshke Berkovits arrived in the cantonist camp where they were to be re-educated. They refused to sit in the Christian prayer classes and would not participate in the marching drills. Their teachers explained that this was their only ticket into Russian society, and the pair's rebellion earned them serious floggings which tore open their backs but did not break their spirits. The continued obstinacy of the two friends resulted in the worst punishment of all: cleaning the latrines, which was as good as a death sentence, what with the exposure to the plague and dysentery.

Motl's escape gave Pesach hope that his brother would return and rescue him from that hell. He continued to secretly perform the commandments as he remembered them and to pray to the Father of Orphans, although he reflected that, in the light of his job in the latrines, it would have been better if God had not created man with so many pores and orifices, reversing the meaning of the blessing said upon relieving oneself. But once Pesach Abramson heard what had happened to his brother and uncle, Yoshke never again saw him cry or show any other kind of emotion. The nauseating work at the latrines appeared to compel Pesach Abramson to shed the customs of his people at the tender age of twelve. On completion of his education, he asked to train with the infantry corps, and in due course he was baptised into the bosom of the Son of God and christened Patrick Adamsky, a name that allowed him to become a field officer. He was honourably discharged with the rank of captain, and most people simply called him "Captain".

His bravery in the Crimean War made him famous among soldiers, as did his hatred for the Chosen People. Rumour had it that whenever he was told to ward off an excited mob on its way to lynch *żyds*, he wouldn't urge his soldiers to carry out their mission right away, but would let a few Jewish homes burn down first. In the war against the Ottoman Empire, he stood at the gates of the city of Stara Zagora and did not even blink at the sight of its synagogue going up in flames. There were only two exceptions to his hatred. The first was the fond memory of the boy who had been abducted with him on that night of damnation, Yoshke Berkovits. The second were the envelopes he sent once a month to his aunt, Mirka Abramson, containing half his military salary and no word of explanation. The other half of his salary he saved, and after being discharged he bought the tavern in Baranavichy. Needless to say, Jews were not welcome there, and he was not welcome among them. As they whispered behind his back: "His brother was a murderer, and he is even worse."

III

Zizek notices that Captain Adamsky's hair has turned grey. His sideburns have grown wider and his eyebrows bushier. But his movements are still vigorous and his eyes are still as wild as a hawk's. Immersed in paperwork at the counter, Adamsky addresses Zizek without raising his head.

"What will it be, sir?"

"I'm sorry, but I'd settle for pigeon droppings," Zizek mumbles.

Adamsky staggers back, as though he'd been slapped hard in the face. Craning his neck, he peers carefully about him, like an animal about to leave its den.

"Yoshke Berkovits?"

He has to be sure that the man standing before him is indeed the only person who could know the private joke from their latrine days, when any food they put in their mouths tasted of pigeon droppings.

"Captain," Zizek says, his eyes shining.

Adamsky drives away the half-smile that is attempting to stretch itself across his face and mutters, "It really is you . . . fucking hell."

Zizek knows that, were he not so obviously injured, Adamsky would likely throw him out of his tavern without fanfare. Instead, the captain pulls Zizek outside to the lean-to behind the inn, hurriedly pours him a glass of red wine and serves him bread, cheese and sausage. Zizek gulps down the wine and stuffs most of the food into his pockets, and, without explaining his urgency, asks the captain whether he and two companions could take refuge at the inn. Adamsky's tangled eyebrows meet above his prominent nose. He agrees: the tavern is fully occupied, but they can stay in his own room for tonight and wait until the following night for a room of their own. Noticing the pallor spreading across Zizek's face, the captain grasps the gravity of the situation. This visit is no mere courtesy. Zizek and his companions are in trouble.

"This isn't a good time," Adamsky says. "The place is swarming with police. There's a warrant out for . . . Wait a minute . . ." Adamsky's careful scrutiny of Zizek's face is met with silence. "It can't be. Fucking hell! They are searching for you everywhere. They have an agent on every corner. Anyone who shelters you will end up in Siberia."

Oh, how he has missed Adamsky's direct way of speaking. He implores the captain, "Please help us, as fast as you can without getting into trouble. Don't complicate things even more."

"'Without getting into trouble', he says. Ha!"

"I didn't mean it that way."

"Of course you did," the Captain says. "Fucking hell."

Adamsky orders Zizek to tell his two companions to come inside separately and sit in different corners of the main bar until he can put them up in a room. Who knows how many spies may lurk within the tavern's walls? The captain promises that someone will take care of their horses in the stables and warns Zizek that they must not to dare to come out of their room or speak a word to him until the place is completely empty. Zizek explains that his entourage includes a woman, and Adamsky's eyes widen with surprise.

"Yours?"

Zizek blushes and shakes his head.

"Pretty, at least?" Adamsky is curious, and Zizek almost chokes.

"In that case," the landlord growls, "the shit just keeps piling up by the minute. It won't take more than a second for all the drunks in the place to surround her and start offering her half the world. Men are pigs, Breshov, don't you understand that? She must sit with her companion at the same table and they must pretend that they are a couple. And you, Yoshke, you will set yourself up with me at the bar. Understood?"

Without waiting for a reply, the captain disappears upstairs. Zizek goes back outside to Fanny, who is waiting anxiously, and he sees that Shleiml the Cantor is lounging in the cart, munching on his third apple. Zizek relays Adamsky's strict instructions and tells them where they are to sit. He grasps Shleiml the Cantor by his ear and warns him against any idiotic behaviour and tells him that he must not utter a word of Yiddish. The cantor turns to Fanny.

"*Wus hat er gesugt*? What is he saying?"

Zizek grabs him by the throat, only to realise that the cantor is thoroughly enjoying himself; he is perfectly aware that they need him far more than he needs them – a most precarious state of affairs. So Zizek explains to the cantor how the landlord of this

142

tavern feels about Jews, describing the burning of the synagogue in the city of Stara Zagora, just one of many examples of Adamsky's cruelty. This only petrifies Fanny even more, and her grey eyes become alive with an animal-like vigilance. Zizek gives them both a lump of cheese as a sign of peace from their host.

Fanny and the cantor enter a place that might as well be a snake pit. No observant Jew, and certainly not one of the fairer sex, would ever set foot in a secluded establishment with the dual function of tavern and brothel, a place that plays host to the sort of people who give the night a bad name. They sit in a corner, as per Zizek's instructions, keeping their distance from the group of card players, who luckily do not even notice them, and from the company immersed in political debate, who size them up with a few quick glances – one of them seems to be making a point about strangers infiltrating their town and stealing the livelihoods of honest citizens – but soon after that, they return to their heated discussion of some issue or another. The few solitary drunks are cocooned by their inebriation and long past being able to register their presence. Fanny and Shleiml do not know where Adamsky might be, but they assume that the lame little boy serving them grog cannot be the fearsome captain who tortured their people.

A few moments later, Zizek enters and sits by the bar without looking at them. Suddenly, a squeaking of wooden floorboards echoes from the floor above like the cry of an eagle, followed by a raging female voice and a thunderous stamping on the staircase. The commotion ends with an old man tumbling down the stairs in his underwear and landing in the hall below. Roars of laughter from the card players and boos from the diplomats spark an already volatile drinking den.

"This is not a brothel!" Adamsky bellows at the client he has just kicked down the stairs, as he brandishes the arm of a woman whose otherwise naked body is draped in a flimsy nightgown. Adamsky drags her downstairs, shoulders bare, breasts dangling. The humiliated man raises a chair and brandishes it at the landlord.

"So now it's *not* a brothel?" he bawls back at Adamsky, but his feeble shaking of the chair, combined with his drunken gaze and flabby chest, invites an accurate right hook to his belly from the captain, who pushes him towards the door, the chair still in his hand.

The half-naked woman refuses to leave without her clothes and insists on receiving her full pay, even for a job half-done. Adamsky presses a few notes into her palm and orders the boy to bring her pile of clothes from upstairs. In the meantime, the Captain glares around his inn, the card players and the debating club go back to their own business, and the few other wretches who remain will doubtless have to be scraped off the tables before anything can disturb them. Yoshke is hunched at the bar, and only now does Adamsky notice the strange couple sitting in the corner.

In the middle of his tavern, Adamsky fixes his gaze on this petrified pair and quickly becomes enraged. The woman's dress is buttoned all the way up to her neck, her fair hair is tied rather loosely, her eyes are wolf-like and suspicious, her nose is sharp and her ugliness is oddly attractive. The man, however, is a walking toothpick. His beard is sloppily trimmed and there are traces of sidelocks. Adamsky could recognise them from five versts away: *żyds*. He is furious with Yoshke, who placidly looks back at him, as though their presence in Adamsky's tavern were the most natural thing in the world.

The captain takes a deep breath and looks over at Fanny, and she, feeling his eyes upon her, assumes a frozen expression. He motions to her and the toothpick to follow him upstairs. Fanny glances at Zizek, who nods reassuringly and turns away. As they pass Zizek on their way to the stairs, Adamsky whispers to him, "You're a pig, Yoshke! Two *żyds* you've brought here? Fucking hell."

IV

Even for someone posing as a drunk, Piotr Novak has an impressive array of shot glasses on his table. Four hours have passed since the three strangers entered the inn, and Novak has observed that Patrick Adamsky, the celebrated captain, did not have them sign the register, has not sent the boy to collect their mandatory identity papers, and did not exchange even a single word with two of them. Novak has had many chances to launch into action. He could have sent the boy off to sing to the police, or asked the card players if they knew the strange couple huddling in the corner; the question alone would have been enough. He could have, even hinted to the groom, with a wink and an extra tip, that their two tired horses should receive special treatment. But instead, Novak makes a mental note to dig into the captain's past.

In Adamsky's defence, at least two of his three guests look nothing like killers, so perhaps he was right to decide that there was no need to report every sorry soul that comes his way. The woman isn't large or terrifying; on the contrary, she seems gentle and fragile, while her husband looks like a cross between the village fool and a twig in his oversized clothes. His black eyes are so sunken they might have been gouged by an eagle. On the other hand, there are several details that would seem to connect these guests with the murder. First and foremost, they are obviously *żyds*. Their attempt to pose as Poles makes Novak chuckle. They have not touched the rum they've been served, they have not exchanged a single word between them – probably so as not to give away their accents – and the woman can wear a babushka's coat and an embroidered kerchief as much as she likes, but if there's one thing she is not, it is Polish. And then there is the older ruffian, the one who first came in to talk to Adamsky. Well, Novak knows this type of camaraderie. Men don't behave like that with each other unless they have seen the fear of death in each other's eyes. This older man – the one with the scarred mouth who went into the shed in the back with Adamsky, left the tavern and then returned to sit by himself at the bar – must therefore be an old army comrade of Adamsky's. And yet they had seemed restrained when they talked. No embrace or handshake. No visible excitement. Perhaps their days of fighting shoulder to shoulder at the front have caused a rift between them?

To sum up, we have several links to the multiple versions of Radek Borokovsky's story: an army connection, a woman (albeit not a large and terrifying one), and even a possible link to Jewish slaughter: there is no reason why that miserable, harmless-looking matchstick should not be some kind of apprentice butcher.

Could it be them? Of the three, the only one who seems capable of taking down the Borokovskys is the scar-mouthed thug. But if he was a soldier in the Russian army, why wouldn't he just turn himself in to the police and give his version of events? After all, Radek Borokovsky is hardly known for his credibility, and his testimony would be dismissed in a heartbeat when set against the report of a veteran of the Czar's army. Perhaps, then, the thug is the Jewish couple's hired knife, which is why he used the ostentatious slaughtering method that is uniquely theirs. There is no reason to prefer this style of slaying other than the fact that it is distinctive and therefore sends a clear message: the Jews are

146

responsible for the elimination of the Borokovsky family, who stood in their way. These murders might have been spurred by an ideological motive, after all.

In his head, Novak runs through the agents he has posted across the counties of Grodno and Minsk, and considers the variety of revolutionaries they are forced to confront in their daily work. He has planted fifty-two moles within the socialist underground, and fifteen more among the democratic agitators; two hundred and four agents are tailing intellectuals and thinkers, and he has one hundred and sixty informants keeping an eye on the students. Six others are looking into various charitable organisations, four are planted among the Hasidim, twenty-one among the followers of the mania for Palestine, and a dozen agents are tailing scientists. Could the three guests belong to any of these subversive movements? The socialists target Czarist officials, not humble peasants, and the democrats have such a naive hope of giving voting rights to backwards folk like the Borokovskys that killing them would be a grievous violation of their beliefs. The intellectuals, with their misguided faith in the sanctity of the human soul, usually condemn violence, even as the students are living proof that the human soul is all aloud reckless naivety and lustful passions. The philanthropists assuage their capitalist guilt by donating to revolutions that will ultimately lead to their beheading. The Hasidim devote most of their attention to fighting the Misnagdim, their opponents in the Jewish community. Those who dream of Palestine inevitably end up dying of malaria, and scientists usually take their own lives. It seems unlikely, then, that the killers of the Borokovsky family should belong to any one of these groups. But if they do not, what was their motive? Should Novak worry that he might have uncovered a new form of insurgency?

*

It has been a while since the three suspicious guests went upstairs, and Novak does not like the fact that they have lingered so long in their rooms, the very same rooms that Adamsky hastily made vacant for them. This tavern, which has always accommodated the men of Baranavichy and their prostitutes, is suddenly no longer a brothel? Do they now offer communion here instead? And what are those three doing upstairs? Sleeping? Plotting with Adamsky? Sharpening knives? How can a tramp as drunk as the one he is pretending to be weasel his way upstairs?

Novak takes up his stick and hobbles outside for a breath of fresh air. He looks up at the second floor of the tavern. The lamps are unlit, and the dark windows look like gaping mouths. He steals over to the stables. The stable boy is asleep on a haystack and a few horses are drowsing in their stalls. The night envelops Baranavichy with a soft, nebulous veil. A long way from here, in St Petersburg, Anna, his wife, and his two sons will be fast asleep. If he were to show up suddenly and surprise them, they would pretend to be happy to see him, but their smiles would only mask the intolerable embarrassment his presence imposes. Better to be standing here, dressed in rags, in the middle of the night, far away from them, because the rags are his uniform and this is his job, and because his absence from home at least has an honourable justification.

The pain in his leg grows sharper at night. Once he had recovered from his injury, he accepted Field Marshal Osip Gurko's offer to join the Okhrana without hesitation, mostly because he feared the purposeless life that awaited him otherwise.

"Our task now is to demonstrate the same courage and dignity on the home front that we showed in battle," Gurko told Novak, on summoning him to St Petersburg. And so Novak took up his new job filled with a sense of courage and dignity. And it was with courage and dignity that he deployed his network of agents, threatened civilians, made arrests and dragged terrified children from their beds. So far, so good. But over time, Novak has come to realise that his work requires the exact opposite of courage and dignity. The only justification for performing his despicable duties is to exercise the power vested in him by the Russian Empire.

Now he must return to the front line, which at that moment is none other than Patrick Adamsky's disreputable establishment. He knows that if the scar-mouthed roughneck is indeed a skilled knife-murderer, protocol dictates that he should call for reinforcements. With only one healthy leg, he must be particularly careful to avoid a fight. He therefore wakes the stable boy and tells him to take an urgent message to his agents, who have probably found their way to Tomashevsky's house of delights. The boy gets up and shakes the hay off his clothes, as if he thinks it quite normal to be roused in the middle of the night by a complete stranger and ordered to carry out a task. Specifically, this one: he must find a man named Albin Dodek, and alert agents Ostrovsky and Simansky too, at the double.

When Novak returns to his table in the tavern, he discovers with great satisfaction that he has lost a record of that the scrawny Jewish toothpick, who earlier sat with his prim and proper wife, is descending the stairs, eager to join the card game. The card players take one look at him and burst out laughing, but once he flashes a few coins they are happy to oblige. They offer him a drop of cheap vodka, anticipating a quick and easy profit. The human matchstick drinks up and manages to lose an entire rouble by the end of the first hand, after which he sits rubbing his unkempt beard as though trying to draw some lesson from his loss. During the second hand, he emits a series of thoughtful "hmmm, hmmm"s, and makes a show of playing his hand only after great consideration, though it is clear to all around him that his brain must be resistant to all manner of logic. During the third hand, he makes a mistake so blatant that they begin to suspect that, instead of a brain, he must have a head of straw, and he loses five roubles in one go.

By the seventh hand, the players tell him that he is out of the card game, because he has run out of money. The matchstick pleads with them to let him stay, declaring that he will soon sweep everyone's pockets and promising them a surprise if he does not. Happy to keep poking fun at this wretch, the card sharks let him stay in the game. After hands seven, eight and nine, he owes an additional five roubles that he does not have, and when they demand the promised surprise he takes off his hat and offers a free concert. "I am a famous singer," he announces, expelling a mist of vodka.

"*Adooooon olaaaaam . . .*" he goes on, now with an extravagant vibrato in his voice. Before he has quite finished the note, a fist lands in his face and he spits out a couple of teeth. Now he is not merely a man in debt but, more pertinently, a Jew in debt to a Pole – a situation that will inevitably end badly. But before a second fist can find its target, Novak gets to his feet, pulls up a chair and declares that he will pay the *żyd*'s debt. Instead of five roubles, he pulls out a twenty-five rouble note.

The card players look at one another in astonishment. A muscled member of the group is tempted to take the money, but his friend snatches the note from him and gives it back to Novak with a bow. "No need, Your Highness." In a flash, the party breaks up: one of them apologises and says that his wife is waiting for him at home, another volunteers to walk with him, a third is tired, and a fourth has to get up early the next morning. Novak knows that he has just blown his cover. A drunken vagabond like him is not supposed to carry this kind of money in his purse. He persists in trying to pay the *żyd*'s debt as they begin to leave, but the group persists in declining, and before they depart they even sit the matchstick in a chair and straighten his clothes, although it is not easy to spruce up a fool with a bloody mouth and missing teeth. The next to leave are the patrons from the adjacent table, dragging with them a stupefied drinker who had been sitting alone by the door. Finally, the only people left in the room are Novak and the *żyd*, who stares blankly in front of him and mumbles, *"be-terem koll, yetzirrr nivraaa . . ."*

Novak sits before him and empties a glass of water over his head. Dazed, the matchstick looks up at Novak like a man blinded by sunlight.

"Where is your wife?" Novak asks, calmly. "I'll take you to her."

"My wife?"

"Isn't she your wife?"

"How should I know who she is? How could she be my wife? We only met today, even though she claims it was the day before yesterday. They picked me up in Telekhany, so they say, although I do not recall having been in Telekhany. How could they have picked me up from a place I didn't go to? The Devil knows. Maybe the honourable gentleman could tell me, because all this is beyond me."

And now an excellent opportunity has presented itself to Novak. He could load this matchstick onto his shoulder and take the stairs to the next floor without ever being suspected of his true intentions. They will probably think it was chivalrous of him to rescue their friend from a pack of card-sharks, and will never guess that he is the secret police commander of the north-western districts. But Novak's one healthy leg can't manage even the matchstick's flimsy weight, and when he tries, he slips on the second step and the unconscious singer lands on his maimed thigh. Patrick Adamsky, who must have heard the thud, comes charging downstairs and grabs the two by their throats. "You miserable pigs, that's enough for today!" He throws the match-stick towards the door and kicks Novak in the belly. The colonel tries to stand despite this humiliation, but his cane is out of reach by the stairs, so he clutches at a table and drags himself along on one foot in the direction of his third foot. Adamsky beats him to it, looks at the etchings on the cane and realises that this is not the cane of a tramp. What is more, Adamsky has seen dozens of these men with their gaits warped by a shrapnel wound, and their legs amputated below the ankle, thanks to the innovation of the great surgeon Pirogov. Now he faces Novak apprehensively. It is clear to both of them that they can be either friends or foes now, nothing inbetween.

"So. Do you have a room for me?" Novak asks, brushing dust and dirt from his shirt.

"I'm sorry, sir," Adamsky says, assuming that this man is no more than a captain. "We are full tonight."

"I could share with them," Novak says. "We could all squeeze in together. Do you think they would mind?"

"They?"

"The nice couple for whom you went to such an effort to provide a room."

Adamsky is silent.

"Did they pay you at all? With money, I mean?"

"What else would I do it for?" Adamsky chuckles. "For nothing?"

"I couldn't say."

"If they don't pay, I'll kick them all the way to the police."

"Well," Novak sits down, "the police are exactly what I wanted to talk to you about."

Adamsky also sinks into a chair. "Are you . . .?"

"Not exactly," Novak says. He's been in the job for ten years and still finds it hard to admit that all he has become is a lousy mole in the police force, albeit a high-ranking one. "I won't ask you for your papers, Mr Adamsky – or, should I say, Captain Adamsky."

Novak notices that the landlord is trembling. The interrogator has gained the upper hand.

"Anyway, I am tired, it's late, and I need a bed. As you have seen – or maybe you haven't, busying yourself with tavern matters – I just rescued this fool from the clutches of those angry card players. I mean him no harm. And what do I ask in return? To share a room with the man whose life I just saved. His wife also seems nice – humble and shy. How did she end up in this sewer? The Devil must have had a hand in it, although I could not say for sure. Surely the two of them would like to tell me about their adventures out on the road? And in the meantime, you will have time to talk about the old days with that friend of yours. Or is he an adversary? It's hard to tell. Either way, if you wake up in the morning and find that the couple has indeed left without paying, I will gladly take care of their bill. We can even agree to keep this a secret between the two of us, can't we?"

At that moment, the man with the scarred mouth comes downstairs. He passes them and nods politely, then lunges at the wretch still lying near the entrance. For a moment, it seems as though he means to revive the wretch, but instead he kicks him in the face, yanks his ear and drags him away by the scruff of the neck. They disappear upstairs. Novak scratches at the filthy floor with his cane as though annoyed by a stain, then he plants the cane on the ground and stands up, looming over Adamsky, who remains seated.

"I can see you are concerned about that man, don't think that I haven't noticed," Novak says. "Is he really an old comrade, Adamsky? If he is indeed your friend, he'll be guaranteed immunity. I think we understand each other, do we not?"

Adamsky grows pale.

"I think that if we keep those we care about close, maybe locked up in a private room, it is a safe bet that no harm will come to them, at least not tonight. And as for the others, why don't we let fate take its course?"

Adamsky nods.

V

At about three in the morning, Fanny awakes with a start, with the feeling that a giant spider is crawling up her neck. There is a figure sitting in a chair by her bedside, holding her arm. She twists over onto her back and sends her hand to the scabbard on her thigh. But her movements are too abrupt, and the figure grabs her by the throat and pins her arm to the mattress.

"There's no need to be afraid," the man says softly. "It's just me here."

Fanny is breathless. The moonlight coming through the window has peeled back the darkness from a small patch on the floor, but left everything else almost pitch black.

"What do you want?" she says in a raised voice, hoping that Zizek might hear her from the other room, or at least that she will wake Shleiml Cantor, who is snoring in the other bed. She assumes that the man sitting beside her is Patrick Adamsky, the Jew-hater. A man who has burned down synagogues wouldn't hesitate to assault her.

"Well, my dear, we do not know each other, but I am not important right now, and I certainly do not intend to become the subject of this conversation. You, on the other hand . . . it's not every day that one meets a woman so quiet and fragile in a miserable tavern such as this, and especially not one with your foreign

154

accent. If I had to guess, I would say a Jewess, a Jewish mother even, but I wouldn't bet my life on it. For it is a well-known fact that Jewish mothers do not abandon their homes and children, is it not so?"

Every one of Fanny's senses is on fire. The landlord's clothes give off a reek of liquor that blends with the waft of stale breath, a smell of sweat and the faint scent of blood. The hand around her neck is rough and strong; it would be impossible to escape from its grasp.

"In any case, Adamsky, the landlord, has assured me that we can have our little chat without fear of interruption, and I've brought this fine plum brandy along with me to toast the occasion. As you people say, lechayim! If I loosen my grip a little, will you promise not to scream?"

Fanny nods. Evidently, the man pinning her down is not Adamsky. The bastard has betrayed them instead.

"Alright then. Sure you won't have a drink with me? No? Not to worry, the matter is settled in any case. Any moment now, a few close friends of mine will arrive and help me take in the thug you hired to do your dirty work. Forgive me for not including the vision of loveliness snoring at your side, but even after only a brief acquaintance I can safely say that if that fool is involved in any crime at all, it was without his knowledge. Wouldn't you agree? You took him along for insurance – an alibi, in legal parlance. But a reliance on the testimony of a wastrel like that is a double-edged sword that can easily turn against you. In any event, I would let you and your plot roll on, and maybe even assist you, if it would help me to understand what it is that you want. But there are three bodies to your credit already, and I'm afraid that the damage will only worsen if we do not get to the bottom of this right here and now. So, I have only one question, and if you are wise enough to answer it honestly, perhaps we can evaluate your position anew. My question is: why? That's all. Why?"

Fanny says nothing. The grip around her neck grows tighter.

"Zvi-Meir," she hisses.

"Zvi-Meir?" The grip slackens a little. "What the hell is a Zvi-Meir?"

From the road outside, they hear the sound of galloping hooves. The horses stop by the inn, and then the clatter of their riders' footsteps rises from the ground floor. The man at Fanny's bedside releases his hold on her throat and goes out to greet these new arrivals. He summons a brute called Simansky to guard Fanny, and then, with calm authority, Piotr Novak orders the two other men to follow him to the room of the tavern's landlord, Patrick Adamsky, with the warning that they should expect a certain resistance from the captain and his friend, two battle-hardened soldiers.

Simansky is not at all satisfied with his task. Keeping watch over a woman is a trifling business, the stuff of new recruits. Instead, he hovers out in the corridor, closer to the real action. Perhaps he will still get the chance to show his true worth.

The other two agents and Novak break into Patrick Adamsky's room and find the landlord and his burly friend fast asleep. Adamsky jolts awake, jumps out of his bed and yells at Novak, "You bastard! You promised you would leave us alone," only to be punched in the face by Albin Dodek. Ostrovsky and Dodek already have control of the scar-mouthed ruffian: they handcuff his arms behind his back and slam his forehead against the wall. Novak kicks Adamsky hard in the stomach, to return the blow the landlord had dealt him earlier, and jabs at his chest with his cane.

"Do you know the difference between a captain and a colonel?"

Adamsky squirms.

"Well, it will be my pleasure to explain it to you, my good sir.

A good captain must be an exemplary officer on the battlefield. He has to lead his men always from the front, he has to show great courage and conquer his foes. But a colonel must be more cunning, he has to design strategies, engineer diversions, even sacrifice one squadron for the sake of another. The long and short of it is that he has to be a sly bastard. The higher up you go in the chain of command, the more people you are required to deceive, not only among your enemies, but also among the ranks reporting to you. Is not that so? And now, let's return to us. During our last conversation, I sensed that you were not only sacrificing this strange couple in order to save your friend, but also that you would welcome their capture. But if this is the case, then according to the deal that we struck, I would be doing you a favour, and you would be sacrificing nothing for me in return. Therefore, if we evaluate our situation anew, our deal is void as of this moment. And now, let us all have a glass of plum brandy and a nice friendly chat, shall we? Simansky!" Novak yells into the corridor. "Bring the woman."

It has proved an impeccable plan, executed perfectly. Dodek and Ostrovsky gaze at their commander in admiration. Novak's instructions to his deputy and agents have been flawless from the start, and his assessment of the situation equally brilliant, especially when you consider the fact that he constructed the whole scheme after spending most of the night in this sewer, being kicked in the ribs and stomach. After the colonel's sharp, precise speech to Adamsky, his colleagues can only imagine what he might have in store for the interrogation.

There is one flaw in the plan however – albeit one that could not have occurred to any of them at the time. Simansky, despite his instructions to guard the woman, has been standing outside in the passageway for a while now, still stewing about having been denied any participation in the main action next door. In the room he was supposed to be guarding, he has left a poor, helpless woman and another miserable creature lying next to her, who, judging by his rancid smell, is slumbering in a pool of his own urine. And he, Simansky, instead of acting like a force for law and order, is expected to hang about here and play the nurse. His comrades might as well call him Florence Nightingale and replace his rifle with bandages and disinfectant.

And so, ever so slowly, he abandons his post and draws closer and closer to the main battlefield in the landlord's room. Finally, leaving his back exposed to anyone who should come along the corridor, he presses his ear against the door behind which the arrests are taking place.

Quite suddenly, Simansky feels a sting on his neck, followed by sharp pain. He freezes, expecting it to pass quickly, and then he slaps at the place where he has been stung to drive away the mosquito or fly. But when he turns back to continue his eavesdropping on the action in the landlord's room, he realises that his hand is wet with a strange fluid. He looks over his shoulder and sees the woman he was supposed to be guarding standing right behind him. She is watching him with equanimity, the crazy witch, and he thinks he should politely tell her to go back to the room. At that point, an unbearable pain cuts through his head, smashing down the gates of his consciousness, and his fists flail at the door, pushing it open.

At the sight of Simansky on the threshold, Novak regrets not dismissing him immediately after he submitted his fabricated report. It is a disgrace for the Okhrana to have an agent on its books who looks like this, eyes bulging and mouth drooling like a filthy drunk.

"Simansky!" Novak bellows. "Where is the woman?"

But before Simansky has a chance to reply, he falls to the floor with a muffled thud, quite dead. His collapse reveals his killer, still standing behind him, and, for a moment, all of the enemies in Adamsky's room are united in shock. Then Fanny erupts into the room and leaps at the neck of one of the two men holding Zizek. Unlike Simansky, Agent Ostrovsky has some idea of what to expect, but he is still unprepared for such swift and decisive blade-work. His throat is slashed and he sinks to his death, appearing almost to relish his last moments. He slumps onto the floor with his face between his knees, looking as though he is lost in thought about God knows what.

Albin Dodek grabs Fanny's arm and tugs the butcher knife out of her hand, and Novak breathes a sigh of relief. Prematurely, however – for Captain Patrick Adamsky, who had been pinned down by Novak's cane on his chest, takes advantage of the scuffle and springs up from the floor. Despite his two broken ribs, he manages to wrest the cane from Novak's grasp. He charges at Albin Dodek and thrashes his back with the stick, shouting at the colonel not to move. Dodek drops the knife, Fanny snatches it and raises it again, and Adamsky undoes Zizek's handcuffs. Before they flee, the captain stares at Novak, who looks back at him, sullenly. The colonel knows exactly what is going through Adamsky's mind. Captains are usually excellent fighters, and although their strategic thinking tends to be somewhat limited, they know what it takes to win in hand-to-hand combat. Adamsky raises the cane. Novak instinctively protects his head, but the captain opts for his leg, and the cane breaks asunder on Novak's already smashed leg. The pain shoots up it, just as it did in the battle on the Shipka Pass, when he took one look at his mangled limb and knew that his dream of becoming a general, like the great Osip Gurko, was over. He had crawled over the bloody earth like a broken lizard, hoping that the Ottoman swordsmen would impale the wreck he had just become. Instead, his regimental doctor scrambled to stop the bleeding and saved his life, which only went downhill from there. And now Novak is writhing in agony at Adamsky's feet, screaming loudly enough to be heard across all Baranavichy.

"Do you know the difference between a captain and a colonel?" Adamsky asks, and spits out of the side of his mouth. "A captain doesn't cry like a baby."

Just before dawn, a wagon leaves the tavern stables, pulled by two horses. Not too quickly, though, it mustn't look as though its passengers are on the run.

Patrick Adamsky and Fanny Keismann are sitting on either side of the driver's seat, which is occupied by Zizek. The three of them have not exchanged a word since their escape. Fanny was ambushed in her bed, but ended up victorious; Adamsky betrayed her, but then came to the rescue. And Zizek, who until very recently had been the main object of Novak's pursuit, was once more beaten, shackled and then rescued. In the back of the cart lies another man, Shleiml Cantor by name. He lived through the night's drama and horror either drunk or passed out or asleep, managing to squeeze in a performance of "Adon Olam" nonetheless. Now the monotonous trotting of the horses and the jolting of the wagon seem to perfectly complement his sound sleep, and his snores rival the clatter of the horses' hooves. The three of them turn to look back at the *hazan*, and even though they do not admit it, their hearts are joyful, if only for a fleeting moment.

MOTAL

I

The Jews know, and Mende Speismann is no exception, that the body can be chiselled with very little effort: all one has to do is pass up an extra portion here and avoid sweets there, and before long, one's clothes will loosen at the waist and ruffle in the wind. It is the never-ending work on one's soul, God help her, that is so daunting. How can one's faith in the King of Kings not wane in hard times? How can one resist the temptation of gossip and slander, *lashon hara*, or suppress heretical thoughts? It follows that, since we must choose our battles of the will with care, it is better to indulge the body with a sugar lump when it wants one, and to rigorously prod a soul that is too lazy to pray into action instead. For this reason, the Chosen People do not take it upon themselves to regularly scale mountains, they rarely stride through fields and pastures, and they stretch their limbs only once a day, in the evening. In their eyes, scholars can uproot mountains with the power of their minds, and the greatest warrior of all is he who conquers his own urges. They neglect corporeal concerns for the benefit of lifting up the soul, because it is clear to them that a healthy soul in a sick body is preferable to a sick soul in a healthy body. That is all there is to it.

And yet, from the moment that Mende Speismann learns of the disappearance of her younger sister Fanny, she can no longer bear to lie in bed. After reading the shocking advertisement in *Hamagid*, she looked down at her doughy thighs, her swollen ankles, her fleshy feet and bulbous toes. Mende Speismann has always urged herself to remember that the body comes second. If, God forbid, she should lose an arm, she would still be Mende Speismann. But if she stopped honouring the Sabbath, what would become of her? She would be as miserable as the goyim, a soulless animal without meaning or purpose.

Still, something about her body is disturbing her, to the point where she cannot escape her concerns in spiritual reflection. Her legs feel as if they have crossed a strange threshold, beyond which they are no longer her legs. Her swollen feet, and the thighs that ache beneath her flabby stomach – to whom do they belong? The rotting lump of flesh she is looking at right now cannot possibly be hers. The weakness of her limbs somehow doesn't seem to fit who she is. She must be looking at the body of a helpless child, certainly not her body. Who are you, Mende Speismann? With all due respect for the humiliation she felt after Zvi-Meir's disappearance, it should never have overridden other, more important concerns, like her children, for example, or helping her sister. The Keismann family clearly needs her right now. Natan-Berl and the children must be overwhelmed and stricken with grief, while she continues to lie in indolence. What a disgrace.

For the first time in months, Mende gets to her feet. A *mechaye*. Her head spins and her body is shaky, but she does not retreat to the safe haven of the bed and instead leans against the wall until the storm subsides. Feeling stable again, she examines her room with disgust. Like a king returning from a campaign to find his realm in shambles, she calls, in a ringing tone, "Yankele! Mirl!"

Squirrel-like feet patter in the next room. Yankele and Mirl were playing on the kitchen floor, and a sudden terror makes them hide beneath the table, as they have been instructed to do if they hear galloping horses. Rochaleh and Eliyahu place themselves in front of the children, she petrified and he uncertain. Authoritative as a field marshal, Mende sweeps into the kitchen, wearing a turquoise tasselled dress that she does not remember owning. The elderly couple exchange puzzled looks.

"Don't you ever read the newspapers?" Mende demands. "Can't you read? Don't you ever talk to the neighbours? Have you been hiding in your own home?"

"What dome?" Eliyahu shouts, tilting his ear towards her.

"Home!" Rochaleh shouts back.

"Why aren't you at Natan-Berl's in Upiravah right now?" Mende says. "Why didn't you tell me about my sister?"

"Why didn't we tell you what?" Rochaleh says, defensively. "You said yourself that she's in Kiev."

"I am aware that you have no interest in the House of Israel, that you couldn't care less about what happens in your own town. That's your decision. But now you want to alienate yourselves from your own family? My poor sister is gone, Heaven help us. Vanished. God knows where she is. She left behind five miserable children and a husband in shock."

"In stock?" Eliyahu is puzzled.

"In shock!" growls Rochaleh, and turns to stave off Mende's accusations. "A tragedy indeed, but we knew nothing of it, I promise you."

"But how can we stay here when we're needed elsewhere?" Mende says with consternation. "Come, let's gather provisions for the journey; we must take them good food and prepare to stay there as long as necessary. We'll help them run the household. Children!" She summons Yankele and Mirl who are still scrutinising her from their hiding place under the table. "Are you going to get dressed today or not?"

Rochaleh and Eliyahu look at one another. Their first instinct is to oblige. But then they recall their own poverty, and realise that they were about to indulge a preposterous madwoman, who is still yelling at them. What does she mean by "good food"?

When they have nothing but potatoes and carrots? What provisions will they take to the Keismanns – mouldy bread? As early as their negotiations over the terms of their son's marriage to Mende Schechter, the daughter of Meir-Anschil Schechter, the parents knew that they should expect trouble. They had heard the stories from Grodno. They knew about Mende's mother, sick with melancholy, and her sister – *die vilde chaya* – terrified them, but they succumbed all the same to the entreaties of the slippery matchmaker, Yehiel-Mikhl Gemeiner. He spoke highly of Mende and her singular qualities, and praised the education she had received from Sondel Gordon, the tailor. The only thing she shared with her sister, he said, was the generous dowry that came with her.

Well, that had come to nothing. Their son had squandered the dowry in his failed pedlar's business, the sister was and remained mad, and now it seems that their daughter-in-law is going the same way.

"Cook for them?" Rochaleh scoffs. "*You* cook for them. And you had better take care of your children yourself, instead of venting your anger at your elders and betters." Rochaleh points at the vegetable bowl with only a shrivelled potato on display. "There are your provisions, unless you can go back to the river and return with three roubles in your pocket again. What were you doing with such a sum, anyway? I've restrained myself from asking this question for an entire month. Where did you get it?"

According to their usual rules of engagement, Mende is now supposed to take a tongue-lashing from her mother-in-law. But Mende ignores Rochaleh. The old woman's fury chatters in the background like an orchestra of crickets. Mende focuses her attention on the wrinkly potato lying in splendid isolation. Two small leaves are emerging from its centre. Against all logic, this lifeless rock is sprouting new life, and Mende delicately runs

166

her fingers along the tiny leaves. She senses life throbbing everywhere. A great miracle has happened here, and she crawls under the table to embrace her children.

"My darlings," she says, now in tears. "Mamme is here."

The two children weep with their mother, and then laugh with her. Rochaleh and Eliyahu watch the trio's sobs and laughter, dumbstruck: they have not witnessed a scene like this in a very long time, especially not one prompted by a wrinkled old spud. They look at each other and wonder how best to distance their grandchildren from the corrupting influence of their deranged mother.

"To the market," Mende cries to her children, "quickly, before everything closes!" And she shoves the potato into her dress pocket.

"What will you buy without a rouble to your name?" her mother-in-law says. "Leave the children here, spare them the disgrace!" But Mende is already skipping to the door with her two children, and they make their way to the market like a trio of sprightly gazelles.

II

It is a sweltering summer day in Motal, one of those days when a Jew proves his faith even with the clothes he wears, as he is reminded that religious faith and comfort are often in conflict. After all, had the Blessed Holy One commanded His people to glutton on food, become inebriated in public and openly fornicate, the entire human race would have been devout followers of the Torah.

Even though the exertion shortens her breath, Mende skips

past the houses, a child grasping each hand. At first, she thinks it better to stay on the shaded footpath, but her feet lead her to the main road. She spots the church spire and heads towards it. Her son Yankele struts along, looking as proud as a peacock. On her other side, her daughter Mirl is ill at ease, she has a shadow on her face like someone trying to recall something important.

"Do not worry, daughter," Mende says, sensing that in spite of the hardships they've had to endure they are now walking as one. "Our family must be strong in order to help those who suffer."

My poor sister, Mende thinks. Is she a lunatic now? Maybe she got up in her sleep, walked off, moonstruck, and lost her way? Or perhaps she has always been miserable with Natan-Berl but too proud to share her secret?

The latter possibility seems the more likely. There has always been something about her sister's life that has never been completely compatible with what one might call "a family". Natan-Berl is – how should she put this – an ignorant *yishuvnik*, a graceless, cumbersome bear, whose dull eyes prove that silence is not necessarily golden. He protects his flocks from peril and disease well enough, and he is an accomplished cheesemaker, but the truth is that Mende has always believed that the general enthusiasm for his products has been exaggerated. Cheese is cheese, and it remains cheese even if you step on it. The nuances that connoisseurs marvel at are mere trifles blown out of proportion. After all, we are speaking of matured milk, Heaven help us. At least Zvi-Meir had a certain hidden sagacity about him, a certain keenness of mind. If anyone asked her sister why she liked Natan-Berl, her answers could amount to no more than "milking" or "seasoning". In her heart of hearts, Mende knows that she has played a part in her sister's disappearance. Instead of dissuading Fanny

168

and saving her from a senseless marriage, she kept quiet and enabled her sister's nightmarish choice.

But now she will help Fanny, and she will not be deterred by a lack of money. Mende resolutely comes to a halt before Simcha-Zissel Resnick's shop, as the church spire looms above them. The man is, as ever, leaning against the counter half-asleep, running his fingers along his *tzitzit* like a placid child. Most shopkeepers sit in their back sheds studying the Torah, while their wives, righteous women that they are, work at the counter to sanctify their husbands' ascent up the ladder of wisdom. At weddings, the women sing:

> Cobblers' wives must learn to hammer nails,
> Tailors' wives must work under lamps,
> Carters' wives must tar the boards,
> And butchers' wives must haul the meat.

But this Simcha-Zissel character, his wife came to learn, falls sound asleep as soon as he lays his eyes on the Holy Scripture. In the early days of their marriage, this infuriated her. "Shame on you, Simcha Zissel, sitting idly while your wife breaks her back." He pleaded his defence: "My darling, how can a man study all day long without closing an eyelid every now and then?" Over the years, his wife has realised that Simcha-Zissel Resnick will never join the learned elite, and has decided that he may as well spend the time half-awake at the counter instead. Alas, one cannot remain standing all day, and, as he leans on the counter, once in a while one eye will droop while the other stays alert, lest Mrs Resnick should ambush his moment of sweet slumber.

In walks Mende and clears her throat. Startled awake, the butcher sighs with relief when he realises that it is not his wife standing in front of him. He sweeps his beard aside and thunders,

"What can I get you, madam? Chicken?" And without waiting for an answer, he seizes the nearest knife and begins to cut slices from an unsolicited sausage.

Now that he has proved that he is awake, he glances at her, but fails to recognise her face. After another glance at her children, he sweeps the sausage scraps from the counter and charitably offers them on a sheet of newspaper. He wonders which cruel tailor might have donated such a tight dress to this poor, plump woman. Sights like these make Simcha-Zissel Resnick all the more convinced that the line between charity and abuse is often blurred. This is why he never gives the needy anything more than leftover sausage. If a beggar were to taste a decent cut but once, he could go mad thinking about all the flavours his life will never have.

But this relentless woman does not seem in the least satisfied. She is still in his shop and wasting his time. Typical of a beggar – they always confuse generosity with weakness. They will demand more and more from him, and if he refuses he instantly becomes a pinchpenny; if he acquiesces, he will instantly become a philanthropist whom they will never stop exploiting.

"Much obliged," he says to the lady and her two urchins. Their odour is intolerable, and the children's scrawny bodies are a depressing sight.

"Simcha-Zissel Resnick," the woman says, "it's me."

Me? What does this lady beggar mean by "it's me"?

"It's me, Mende Speismann."

Mende Speismann. Simcha-Zissel Resnick has not forgotten her. Since her last visit to his shop, she has often appeared in his dreams, sitting in the shack behind his house, biting into strips of red meat he has prepared for her. In his dreams, they are lying naked on mounds of raw meat, their teeth dripping blood and their appetites insatiable. Possessed, they devour each other, blood runs down Mende's frantic face as her canines sink into his skin. Once they have finished dining, they lie in each other's arms, fast asleep. Only this morning, Simcha-Zissel Resnick woke up in a state of excitement after dreaming of a frolic with Mende Speismann, and now this wretch says that Mende Speismann is her name. But the name alone is not enough to merge the Mende of his fantasies with the one standing here. It cannot be.

"Mende? It can't be Mende, only a month ago she was . . . and then in the river . . . they said that Zizek . . . I didn't know that—"

"Simcha-Zissel Resnick," Mende says, "you may be surprised to know that I am fine, but my sister is in trouble, God help her."

"Your sister?" The butcher is struggling to keep up with this overabundance of events. "Who? What happened?"

"No-one knows. But it's a serious business. Make haste! I must set out for the village before dark."

"Make haste?" says the butcher, still at sea.

"Pack up some of your juiciest cuts, please. Five hungry children are waiting."

The butcher hesitates. Subduing his wild fantasies, he has managed to identify something of Mende's features in the flabby face before him, but he cannot yet decide if she really has transformed from beggar to customer. He expects Mende to start searching in her pockets for roubles, but she stands there glaring at him, imperious.

"Simcha-Zissel Resnick!" she shouts. "I can see that the honourable gentleman is taking his time. Perhaps he expects payment? Perhaps he is forgetting his own debts. Does Reb Moishe-Lazer Halperin know how he took advantage of a woman in distress when she came to his shop on her birthday?"

"Took advantage? But you . . ."

"Does Mrs Resnick know how he lit the stove in the shack behind his shop, into which he lured said woman?"

"Lured? This is preposterous!"

"The cuts of meat, if you please, Mr Resnick, and do not imagine for one minute that they will pay off your debt."

At this very opportune moment, Mrs Resnick appears.

"Your debt?" She hastens to her husband's side and glances at Mende. "What debts are you discussing with this woman? Are we in debt now?"

Like any other Jewish man, Resnick knows that a wife has a way of taking the sting out of her husband's authority. All she has to do is let her face turn sour and cease talking – both things he cannot forbid her from doing – and the house will be awash with gloom. When the wife is happy, Resnick knows, the household is happy; whereas the husband could be either happy or sad and no-one would care. So he turns to his wife with a guilty air and tells her about the miracle that has just occurred. This "woman" he is talking to is none other than Mende Speismann, risen from the dead. It is his duty to give her the choicest cuts of meat, how could he do anything else?

Mrs Resnick is unconvinced, but Mende leaves her to bicker with her husband and resumes her stroll around the market with her children. The accomplices of her last shopping spree rush at her, their guilt at their part in her breakdown overcoming all business sense. Schneider is all over her, telling her that he has been thinking of visiting her for quite some time and now she has beaten him to it. After all, he needs to mend her turquoise dress, the one he sewed for her on her birthday. Now he can see that he miscalculated. It is too narrow at the waist, and he misjudged the breadth of the shoulders. He has no choice but to make the dress again from scratch. The tailor fusses over Mende as though she were a bride. Remembering her children, he takes Mirl's measurements for a brown dress with white muslin, and finds a new jacket and a smart white shirt for Yankele. And when Mende thanks him and promises to repay her debt, he dismisses

172

her courteous words. "Have we just met? There are no debts among friends."

Liedermann is not far behind. He gives Yankele and Mirl a pair of sandals each, and when the two of them look at him, amazed, he places in their hands two pairs of old galoshes for the coming winter months.

"For your mother," he announces loudly, "I intend to make a pair of leather boots. Now, I know what you are thinking, Mrs Speismann: he just made me a pair of boots, why do I need two pairs? Well, I shall tell you exactly why – today we are not settling for the necessary, but striving for the possible."

And before Liedermann finishes his job, Grossman the handkerchief salesman and Blumenkrantz the baker are standing at the entrances to their shops, arguing over whom she should visit next: will it be the finest handkerchief vendor in the district or the pâtissier whose reputation has travelled as far as Minsk?

But Mende comes out of Liedermann's store without heeding either of them. She has little time for them now, so perhaps they had better come to her house in the next few days instead.

"Your house?" Blumenkrantz says, unsure.

"I mean, this is unusual... But of course, your house!" Grossman agrees, stealing a march on his rival with his enthusiasm.

What a miracle. Only recently, on her twenty-sixth birthday, Mende Speismann had walked around the market with thirty-two roubles and seventy-one copecks in her pocket – quite a sum – and a few hours later she was unconscious and nearly broke. And now, without a single coin to her name, she is returning to her in-laws with an impressive catch: fine clothes and footwear, succulent cuts of meat and promises of calls from traders. How could she ever have doubted the All-Merciful's sagacity and faith in His people's generosity, knowing how eager they are to fulfil His commandments? "Bless His name for ever!" she cries as she skips with her children all the way back to her in-laws, feeling new life pulsating inside her. Could it be that a child is growing in her womb, even though her husband has been gone for so long? She believes in miracles, by God she does, for no-one predicted that she would ever get up from her bed again. And now she is preparing to go to the village and rescue her sister's household. As long as the Protector of Israel is up in Heaven, anything is possible, however outrageous it might seem.

III

People say: Rivkah Keismann, Natan-Berl Keismann's mother, is a difficult woman. The truth is that Rivkah Keismann is a good-natured woman.

People say: Rivkah Keismann complains all day long. Actually, most of the time, Rivkah Keismann says nothing at all, because her woes are beyond words.

True, every now and again, her old body will let slip the odd groan. She cannot help that she has gnarled hands from washing clothes in the river, or a crooked back from carrying buckets of water for years, or that her skin is not as soft as it used to be. One must remember that Rivkah Keismann is not a spring chicken anymore; she is fast approaching sixty. Still, she has never complained in her entire life. They told her to marry Shevach Keismann and she did. They told her she should be the valiant wife everyone sings about on Sabbath eve, and she was. They told her to follow her husband wherever he went, and she did, even though he chose to live alongside the goyim in the country. They told her that Natan-Berl would be all that the God-Who-Sits-On-High would ever give her, and he became the apple of her eye, her only son whom she loves dearly. They told her: your son has become a man and he has found a bride, so now you must step back and stay on the sidelines. Well, did she not step back? But they did not tell her that the couple would have forgotten the commandment to "honour your father and mother". And they did not tell her that "the sidelines" would mean a cabin in the yard rather than a room inside the house. Her son and daughter-in-law do not want to live under the same roof as her, so they send her to sleep in the outhouse, like a dog in a kennel. Instead of appreciating her help, they treat her as a burden. And what does she ask for in her old age? Money? God forbid. Love? In her dreams. Health? Not at her age. So what is it, in short, what does she ask for? A bit of attention and respect, that is all. Things that do not cost money and do not even take time: a word, a look, a mattress inside the house. If only God could see how she lives. She would be better off dead.

People say: Rivkah is making the life of her daughter-in-law, Fanny Keismann, a living hell. She criticises everything Fanny does. If Fanny has just cleaned the house, Rivkah will detect a speck of dust in a corner. If Fanny makes a lentil stew, Rivkah will recommend a different seasoning. When Fanny dresses the children, she will immediately hear a yell from the next room: "It's too warm for a coat!" Or: "It's too cold for just one layer!" No mistake goes unnoticed by Rivkah Keismann. And what is the source of each mistake? That the task was not placed in the hands of Rivkah Keismann from the start, of course.

The truth is that Rivkah Keismann is the only one to be subjected to such scrutiny. Why shouldn't she think that Fanny, her daughter-in-law, known in the Grodno congregation as a *vilde chaya*, a beast who slaughters sheep with a quick cut, why shouldn't she think that Fanny is not good enough for her son? Is it unacceptable to think that the rooms are not clean enough after

Fanny has swept them? Is it outrageous to say that Fanny's cooking is too salty? Did Rivkah Keismann not raise a child of her own to know the difference between playful and disobedient grandchildren? And what about her daughter-in-law's reckless spending? New clothes – is patching up old clothes not good enough? Sumptuous food – weren't they happy before they started eating trout? Hebrew and arithmetic lessons for her daughters – did Rivkah Keismann not marry and have a family without either?

Naturally, she keeps most of her opinions to herself; anything for a quiet life. She tries to stay on good terms with everyone, and perhaps this was her mistake. Because you cannot deny that this woman, Fanny Keismann by name, a righteous woman indeed, left her home in the middle of the night. She left a short, ludicrous message for her husband, Natan-Berl: "Take care of yourselves until I return." How will bewildered children abandoned by their mother take care of themselves? And the mother-bird has still not returned to her fledglings' nest.

At first, Rivkah Keismann told the children that their mother had gone away to care for their grandfather. But then she realised that these children were old enough to remember that Meir-Anschil Schechter died a while ago. So she told them that their mother had gone away, just for a week, to fill an important clerical position. Shmulke was surprised that his mother had been appointed a clerk, Mishka wanted to know why they needed to earn more money, and David counted seven days, one day at a time, and demanded an explanation when a week had elapsed. Not to mention little Elisheva, who every now and again sees her mother's apron hanging on the kitchen chair and screams, "Mamme!", and Gavriellah, the eldest, who picks up her baby sister and comforts her, an impenetrable expression on her face. Rivkah's heart is in pieces. What can she, their grandmother, tell them? She stares at the floor and says nothing.

And what about Natan-Berl? Well, this is simply heart-breaking. People say that nothing can penetrate her son's armour-like skin, because he accepts the world's wonders and afflictions with equanimity. People say that Natan-Berl ascribes any difference between what a man wants and the way the world is – a difference for which most people tend to blame the world – to his excessive wants and witless head. Would he not prefer people to care for their animals as well as he does? There's no question. Of course he would. But who is he? What is he? One of many. There is so much of everything, and so little of him, so why should everything align itself with his will?

But the truth is, as Rivkah Keismann permits herself to say, no-one knows a man's soul like his mother. Natan-Berl walks around the house as if lightning has struck him. He doesn't say a single word at supper, goes to bed early and leaves the house before first light.

People say: but this is how Natan-Berl has always been. He wakes up before sunrise to milk the goats, then he churns the milk and herds the flock, and before evening returns home to his family. The truth is, one can perform the same actions either with joy, searching for the sublime in one's daily life, or one can miserably go through the motions. No-one would detect a difference in Natan-Berl's gestures, of course. His face confronts each day without giving away any sign of crisis. His thick, hairy hands continue to milk the animals with their magical tenderness. But deep down, oh dear, deep down, only Mother knows how his soul is rent and his heart is paralysed.

The name "Zizek", which is yet to be uttered in Natan-Berl's home, is on everyone else's lips. In an uncanny coincidence that even the Devil couldn't outdo, both Fanny and Zizek disappeared on the same night. Of all the men in the world, her daughter-in-law has gone off with a good-for-nothing goy, a man who turned his back on his Jewish faith for a bowl of pork soup, a man who sits alone in his rowing boat like the village idiot.

Rivkah Keismann has been forced to swallow her pride and start sleeping inside a house where she is not welcome. She had to take the initiative, moving her belongings herself and laying down a mattress next to her grandchildren. Without asking for anyone's permission, she also sent an urgent missive to *Hamagid*. Let anyone say a word. Let anyone say that Rivkah is meddlesome, that Rivkah interferes. And what is the truth? That Rivkah is right! Rivkah knew all along. Rivkah suspected. Rivkah doubted. She is terribly sorry if you do not agree with her actions, but at times like these, she must choose between bad and worse for her family.

And if anyone still wants to bask in their scepticism, let them lie all night, wide awake, like her. Let them listen to her son wheezing in the next room and have their nights disturbed by the children's nightmares. People tell Rivkah Keismann that children have bad dreams, that this is how it has always been. And that Natan-Berl is famous for his stentorian snoring. Rivkah replies that a stranger listening in would certainly believe that this is a mere snoring sound. But deep down, my God, deep down, her son's battered heart is palpitating in agony.

IV

On Friday morning, as her son Natan-Berl is discussing the problem of wolves with his herdsmen, worried about the sounds of their howls being heard ever closer to his flock and wondering whether they should increase the height of their fencing, Rivkah wakes up in a panic. Her bones are on fire. The Sabbath is almost here. Her head spins with the number of tasks that await her. She doesn't know where to start. At her age, she should be the guest of honour at her family's Sabbath dinner. A moment before Queen Sabbath's arrival, she should enter a room filled with loving grandchildren surrounding a table laden with delicacies. But instead of this restful existence, she finds herself raising her son's family. And now, as she looks out of the window, she sees a disturbing sight. A large woman and two scrawny children are approaching the house, pushing a wooden cart loaded with sacks. They must be expecting some sort of alms from the Keismann household. If she had money to spare, would she not help? Of course she would, she is not a cruel woman. But these are hard times. When things get rough, there is no room for the smug generosity by which one seems to say: "I have, and you have not" – a meanness that only the rich can think charitable.

Judging by the beggarwoman's fancy dress, (despite its atrocious turquoise colour), this Jewess is no ordinary mendicant. It is obviously tailor-made, the collar is very elegant and the fabric is a linen of excellent quality, so this woman must be a lady only recently down on her luck. At this point fear creeps in, but also curiosity. Who can she be?

A knock on the door is followed by two quick, syncopated knocks. Is this how it is these days – strangers knocking on people's doors with such insouciance?

Three more knocks of the same rhythmic pattern follow, and Rivkah opens the door a crack and grumpily peers out.

"What do you want, madam?"

"Grandma!" exclaims the jovial beggarwoman with outstretched arms.

"Grandma?" Rivkah is taken aback and tries to close the door.

"Grandma!" The beggar pushes past her and strides into the house. "Don't you recognise me? I am Mende Speismann, Fanny's sister, and these are my children, Yankele and Mirl. We have heard of your great disaster, and have come to help Natan-Berl and the children."

Rivkah knows all about Mende Speismann. She has always been the better half of the pair of Schechter sisters. A well-mannered and humble woman, a model housewife and a fine mother. Her husband is useless, of course, a mere good-for-nothing, but Mende copes with the shame with dignity. She does not so much as hint that anything is wrong, never complains, keeps the pain to herself, as a daughter of Israel should. She's always had a certain inspiring grace to her, something pleasant and serene about her face. So who is this standing so boldly before Rivkah? A bloated vagabond. And judging by her outburst, a very rude one at that. She has a broad, flabby belly, and her face is cushioned with baby-like folds of fat; her cheeks almost swallow her eyes, her chin is sunken and her lips overstuffed. She just might be Mende Speismann, but even if she is, Rivkah Keismann does not need her help, and right now she is seriously considering driving her away from the house, even though the Sabbath is almost here and she is family.

"I have brought fine food," Mende Speismann declares and turns back to her cart to bring in the sacks. The grandmother stays the execution of her sentence as she sees the bags of vegetables and potatoes, and children's shoes, and fabric for new clothes.

"We need none of these things," Rivkah mutters, rummaging through the vegetables and plucking out the choicest radishes.

"So be it," Mende says blithely, as she spreads the fabrics on a chair. "As you wish."

"Not like that," says Rivkah, rearranging the cloths and smoothing out their creases. "Don't do it that way."

This strange new gang of four sits down to take a slice of bread with a little of the onion and cucumber Mende has brought.

Rivkah Keismann tells Mende about the disappearance of her sister, and the guest tut-tuts all through the story.

"It's simply horrendous," Mende slaps her own face. "What a tragedy. My poor, miserable sister."

She nods sympathetically when Rivkah says, "Do you really think she is poor and miserable? What about Natan-Berl? What about the children? What about me?"

Mende tut-tuts again. "God help the lot of you, you are all miserable."

The grandmother replies, "Not everyone is miserable, Mrs Speismann, not everyone! There are shades and grades in these matters!"

Amid this scene, however, the grandmother notices a strange smile stretching across Mende Speismann's face. What can possibly be amusing about such a calamity, Rivkah would like to know, and she begins to wonder if, just like her sister, Mende may not be of sound mind.

Mende gets up to slice some of the sausage from her sacks, and Rivkah's eyes dart towards the door in alarm. She has not seen meat in this household for years, and ever since she became a Keismann she has been eating mostly cheese. The Keismanns have abhorred meat since the dawn of time. She barely remembers the taste of sausage.

But now, as Mende puts a slice of sausage on her plate, Rivkah Keismann does not protest. She covers up the delightful spasm that the meat's sharp spiciness sends through her body with reprimands for Yankele and Mirl – their backs aren't straight and they mustn't eat with their mouths open or kick the table and they should ask for things politely – and they, in turn, eye her calmly and keep at it, completely unheeding her authority. To Rivkah's surprise, Mende joins her critical chorus, telling her children to obey Rivkah's instructions (all of which should have been obvious to them in the first place). Now that Rivkah Keismann has support, she continues; not only telling the children to be quiet but also forbidding them to communicate by their secret sign language. "Gestures are just like words," the grandmother says, and their mother agrees. In the end, Rivkah orders the children to leave the table and clear the dishes.

Mende obeys this command too, which is disconcerting for Rivkah. Evidently, Mende has none of her sister's spiteful temper. She has even taken up a twig broom and started sweeping the floor, with a smile even more foolish than the one she had before. What if she allowed them to stay? Rivkah could help this poor family after all, she could put them back on their feet and give meaning to their fatherless, husbandless life. They have been wandering hither and thither with a pedlar's cart, and now they are sitting in a decent household with an abundance of delicacies for the Sabbath. Much remains to be done before the Queen arrives, but Rivkah will fulfil an important mitzvah if she lets them enjoy a festive meal surrounded by family.

So without further ado, Rivkah takes Mende through everything that needs to be done before noon, and the guest takes responsibility for it all. Mende is perfectly aware that the grandmother treats her children cruelly and that she is taking advantage of her own helpfulness – Mende is not a complete fool, after all – but right now, integrating into the household of Natan-Berl's family is what matters to her most. And so she sets the Sabbath table according to Rivkah's instructions as if she, and not Fanny, were the old woman's daughter-in-law. Mende has done the right thing by coming over to help the poor Keismann orphans in their hour of need.

V

Preparations for dinner have stalled. Mende is doing the exact opposite of what she should. She lights the fire too late, risking a deviation from Queen Sabbath's schedule. She does not wrap the challah in its embroidered cover. The borscht is flavourless. The *kartoshkes* are undercooked. Fanny's five children cavort and caper about, and refuse to obey their aunt when she urges them to wash and get dressed properly.

Throughout the house, pandemonium reigns. David is wearing his Sabbath clothes inside out, and Gavriellah is polishing the candlesticks even though she has already scrubbed her fingernails. Mende scurries around the house as the children fight, and Rivkah Keismann sits at the table and directs proceedings with her last-minute instructions. If only they had listened to her from the start, all would have been fine. But everything that could have gone wrong has done just that. Rivkah should have assumed that Mende is incapable of rational thought. Next time she will rehearse every last detail with her.

The chaos is topped off by an argument, because Mende will not stop defending her sister.

"It's impossible to know what went through her head," Mende says.

This enrages Rivkah. "It is of no importance what went through her head."

"Don't judge someone else until you are in their shoes," Mende goes on.

Rivkah bangs her fist on the table. "If this was the case then no-one who committed a crime would ever face judgment."

"'Crime' is an exaggeration."

"Then what would you call it?"

"A mistake."

"A crime."

"A mistake."

"Let me ask you this," says Rivkah. "Would you leave? Never. Would you abandon your children? You know you wouldn't. Well, then: is it a crime or a mistake?"

"The word is of no importance; it could be that my sister has been miserable for years."

"And you, were you not miserable with Zvi-Meir?"

"I certainly was not," Mende says, appalled by the mere suggestion. "There were challenging times, but I was never miserable."

"And did you disappear from your home?"

"You go too far! I am not so wild."

"A-ha!" The grandmother clasps her hands together. "Why, then, are you so protective of your rebellious sister?"

"That is not what I meant. Every case is different. Something may have happened to her. Perhaps she was abducted."

"And the abductor wrote the note on her behalf?"

"That I do not know."

"Then what do you know?"

"That she is my sister, and that I should help her."

"No-one can argue with that."

"Then we agree."

"That your sister is wild? Absolutely!"

Nonetheless, in spite of these futile debates, and although the unruly children are rocking Rivkah Keismann's chair like a boat on the high seas, a calm pervades her limbs. This is how it should always have been. If only Natan-Berl had married another woman, a woman like Mende Speismann, then Rivkah could have entrusted her son to her capable hands and joined the Creator. Instead, the worries that she has endured in recent years have prolonged her life against her will, and she fears that if she leaves her son this way she will become eternally trapped between this world and the next. Who is she living for? She would have been better off dead.

As Mende pricks a *kartoshke* with her fork to test its tenderness, and David puts his yarmulke back on his head, and Gavriellah combs Elisheva's hair, and Mirl crawls underneath the table with a rag to help her mother clean the dining room, and Yankele and Mishka and Shmulke play with matches, the grandmother asks herself, why shouldn't it always be this way? Fanny will not return, and even if she does, Natan-Berl will not take her back. Perhaps eloquence and vivacity are not among her son's strengths. But there's nothing he cares about more than dignity and propriety. A mother knows her son's innermost thoughts, and Rivkah is confident that Natan-Berl has made up his mind to forget Fanny. Well, why should she not invert the practice of *yibum*, and replace the absent wife with her present sister? If Jewish men may marry their brothers' widows, why not marry Mende to her widowed brother-in-law? Certainly, this matter should be discussed with Reb Moishe-Lazer Halperin in the first instance. After all, she is not qualified to make halakhic rulings. Still, it is hard to imagine that the law would be opposed to a natural unification of the family.

With this in mind, when Mende absentmindedly pulls out the lamb shank she brought from Simcha-Zissel Resnick to place it in the oven for roasting, the grandmother stands up, lays her hands on Mende's waist and explains that it would be better if Natan-Berl never knew that meat had entered his kitchen. Mende trembles all over: how could she have been so stupid? But the grandmother soothes her; luckily for her, Rivkah is here, otherwise who knows what would have happened? Natan-Berl might have upended the table in his rage and never looked at Mende's pretty face ever again. But now that the disaster has been averted, Mende Speismann sighs with relief and starts to believe that her face has perhaps remained handsome despite its recently added poundage. Rivkah Keismann has said so herself. Upon hearing Natan-Berl's voice calling to his goats near the house, she feels a fluttering in her stomach.

Natan-Berl does not enter the house in his usual way. Perhaps Mende's cart parked outside raises his suspicion, or perhaps it's the commotion inside the house. It might be the unfamiliar smells coming from the kitchen – there's no knowing how Natan-Berl's mind works or how far his keen senses might stretch. In any event, as he stands on the threshold he peeks inside, counts the number of people and realises that it is higher than usual. Raising his eyes hopefully, he sees his sister-in-law, Mende. Embarrassed, Mende begins to explain why she is here, but the grandmother pinches her arm, as if to say: Natan-Berl's silence is a good sign. There's no need to ruin the moment with words.

The children immediately jump on the back of their bear-like father, and even Yankele and Mirl are happy to see him. David and Mishka are already arguing about who will go out with the shepherds on Sunday, and Gavriellah is angry with both of them, as they have broken a bowl of cabbage in their rush for their father. Young Elisheva slips in between everyone to hang around her father's neck, "Me! Me!", and the sudden relief in his face tells them all that he has made up his mind. Somehow, under their very noses, in a brief moment of inattention, the father and his youngest daughter have made a pact with a single glance. It is decided that Sunday will be Elisheva's day to go out with the flock.

But their envy does not turn to bitterness. Elisheva's siblings know that she needs their father more than they do. For the past three nights she has been calling for their mother without getting a reply, and although her grandmother has tried comforting her – "There there, Bubbe is here" – the little girl will not stop sobbing, falling back asleep only after yielding to her fatigue. The children do not talk about this among themselves, and yet they understand that this is not the time to act spoiled when they don't get their way. Their mother would have wanted them to be generous with their baby sister. After two weeks' absence, the memory of Fanny has blended with anger and resentment. Her soft voice still echoes in their minds, and their painful longing for her only grows stronger. Defying all logic, their inability to understand why she has disappeared doesn't shake their confidence that she will return. They will settle their accounts with her in due course.

And as for Natan-Berl, there is no knowing what goes on in his mind. He blesses the wine and then ritually washes his hands. Sitting down at the head of the table, he appears not to remember why they are gathered, or realise that he should pass around the challah after the *hamotzi* blessing over the bread. The grandmother clears her throat and Natan-Berl sits up, surprised. If someone had told him that today is Tuesday, he would have said, "so much the better", and started eating. Mende notes to herself that this household does not greet the Sabbath as extravagantly as Zvi-Meir and she once did in their home.

The adults do not exchange a single word during the meal, although they do turn to the children every now and again. The grandmother with reprimands, Mende with requests and Natan-Berl with the occasional nod. Mende thinks to herself that if Natan-Berl returned home and found the three Patriarchs and the four Matriarchs seated at his table, he would lower his head, sit down and gruffly chew his food. Can anyone blame her sister for running away from such boredom? If these were distant relatives, she would have thanked them at the end of Shabbat and gladly returned home. But these children, God help them, they are her nephews and nieces, her own flesh and blood. How can she leave them to their own devices, without a mother to teach them right from wrong? She is not free to choose. She has been commanded to help them. If she leaves when the Sabbath ends, she will never be able to look herself in the mirror again.

At the same time, she thinks that silence might have its advantages, too. She recalls a Friday night when she was very tired and Zvi-Meir had come home in a state of great agitation, wanting to discuss with her an issue that no Torah sage had ever contemplated before: how could Adam and Eve have grasped God's prohibition before they ate the fruit of the Tree of Knowledge that endowed them with reason?

"See how great this paradox is?" he had said.

"Sort of."

"What do you mean, 'sort of'?"

"Later," Mende had sighed.

"This cannot wait. Why can't you understand?"

The exhausted Mende had been forced to stretch the limits of her comprehension, and nod throughout Zvi-Meir's chaotic lecture that had lasted the entire meal. He saw that she was tired, and asked her to repeat the last thing he had said; she asked him to let the matter go, admitting to her fatigue. Zvi-Meir had risen from his chair and slapped the table. "Exhausted? You are simply stupid!" He'd sucked in his cheeks, which were reddened by alcohol, and hissed, "Why am I even discussing matters of Torah with a woman?"

Now, as she sits quietly, Mende thinks to herself that there is nothing wrong with flowing silences. And in any event, her experience has taught her that people can talk to one another endlessly without really communicating anything. Yet when Natan-Berl leaves the table without even gracing her with a sideways glance, she knows that her days here are numbered. Rivkah touches her foot and whispers in her ear, "Can you see how glad Natan-Berl is that you are here? I haven't seen him this happy for a long time."

VI

Mende's flaws are few. At her best, she is a comely, respectful and modest woman. Staunchly opposed to the frivolities of Hasidism, Mende does not ask questions about lofty matters and never doubts what she was taught to believe. Her faith rests on the fulfilment of the commandments. Even if someone presented her with irrefutable proof that the Creator does not require her to fast, she would still persist with this self-inflicted torture. Mende puts her trust in the millennia-old practices of Jews without ever concerning herself with why such practices should remain necessary. And being so accepting in matters of faith, she is not particular when it comes to family matters either. When her mother died during her childhood, she distanced herself from her father and her peculiar sister, harbouring a single wish: to have a family of her own. She did not dream of a husband who would be a brilliant scholar or a seasoned businessman. She could barely visualise a face. In fact, she had no notion of what he would be like at all. But whenever she thought about her five imaginary children sitting around the table as she served beef and potatoes, she knew that he would also be there. His figure was beyond her grasp, but his presence was beyond question.

Some would say that Mende Speismann had low expectations when it came to her future husband. Presence, being in a certain place at a certain time, is after all a clear necessity in a spouse. Yet, in all honesty, Mende never asked Zvi-Meir for anything more than that. Just as his sharp mind and studies at Volozhin's prestigious yeshiva were an unexpected gift from the God On High, so her husband's rudeness and tongue lashings were defects she had to endure. The good is always bound up with the bad, and life is never black-and-white. As long as they sat together for the Sabbath dinner then that was enough, and praise be to God.

And so the breakfast that Mende prepares on the seventh morning of the week for Fanny's family strikes her as the fulfilment of her vision. Five children are sitting around the table. Her Yankele and Mirl are helping her serve the krupnik she had prepared before Queen Sabbath stepped in. The bubbe is watching over everyone and Natan-Berl is eating to his heart's content. The household is bustling – clattering dishes and spoons, cries and laughter – and Mende does not have a second to spare. A humming heart free of cumbersome thoughts is exactly what she needed. The cooking and cleaning make lying idly in bed all the sweeter. One cannot rest if one does not work. An idle woman without a home to run or a family to care for sinks to the bottomless depths of the soul and drowns in an ocean of discontent.

But Mende is no fool. She knows that this commotion is not hers to have and that this place is not her home. With the sun's yawn and the first blinks of the stars as Sabbath the Queen departs, Mende wonders whether she can sacrifice so much for the sake of something that is not her own.

She quickly discovers that this choice is not hers to make, as the Blessed Holy One is leading her to her calling by giving out one sign at a time.

The previous night Mende and her children had slept on the dining room floor. But now the bubbe appears with clean sheets and blankets, and leads her and the children to the cabin in the yard. The grandmother explains that she herself used to sleep in this nice, cosy room. It offered her more peace and rest than she could ask for. But now she must sleep next to the poor children who need their grandmother. During most hours of the day, Mende and her children will stay at the house, there will be no difference between Keismann and Speismann. It is in their common interest to gradually merge the two afflicted families together. Two tragedies have occurred and their blood ties require them to take care of each other now.

"But is this really a tragedy?" Mende says, thinking of Zvi-Meir.

"Your sister's death is not a tragedy?" Rivkah asks, surprised.

"My sister's *death*? God forbid!"

Rivkah Keismann cannot understand why Mende should be so horrified. What did she think? Can a wife abandon her husband and not be considered dead by her mother-in-law? Then she sees that Mende has taken her words literally and is deeply shaken by the idea that Fanny might really be dead, and an idea flashes in Rivkah's mind.

"Haven't you worked it out by now, you poor creature?" she says, patting Mende on the back. "How could a woman fend for herself all alone in a world of violence and depravity, with a buffoon by her side who can't even talk? What did you think? That they were in Minsk, or in Pinsk, maybe? Living happily ever after? He in his rowing boat and she in a cabin? They must have left Motal only to be attacked by brigands or devoured by wild beasts."

"How do you know that?" Mende is in tears now. "You're provoking the Evil Eye."

"One cannot be more confident of the truth than when rumour and common sense are aligned."

"Rumour?"

"This is what people say in Motal."

"In Motal? Since when?"

"Since the first day of her disappearance. I'm sorry to be the bringer of bad news, but would you rather I'd hid this from you?"

"No, of course not," Mende whispers.

"Well, go and get some rest, my dear, we have a long day ahead of us tomorrow."

*

Mende tosses and turns throughout the night. She wishes that the world would be still, that the Blessed Holy One would open up the gates of Heaven for the angels to cry with her, or that the skies would show a sign that her sister is still alive. Could it be that at this very moment the angels of destruction are tormenting her poor little sister, just as Grandpa Yankel Kriegsmann of blessed memory used to describe? By midnight, she has yielded to her exhaustion. When she wakes up at the rooster's call, her eyes meet the sun, resplendent through the window. The world has continued to spin as if nothing has happened: the golden furrows, the harvested fields, and the black bogs guarding the horizon like drowsy monsters. Once again, Mende struggles to get out of bed, but, looking at her sweet children, she vows to never let them come to any more harm. Peeking through the window again, she sees courgettes nestled in the soil, boughs glistening with apples, daisies everywhere in between, and the tree in her sister's garden heavy with cherries. Fanny's favourite fruit. Is it a sign? Mende cannot tell. But for now she must concentrate on the things she knows with certainty. She is here. Her children are here. And what about her sister? Surely, Rivkah must care about her daughter-in-law's well-being; she wouldn't lie on that score. All the same, until Mende is given clear-cut proof that supports the claims made about Fanny, she will not believe them. In the meantime, she will wait for the day when her sister's family can finally come out of this living nightmare. Only then will Mende's work at the Keismann household have reached its end.

VII

All these family upheavals have sapped Rivkah Keismann's strength, compelling her to seek consolation and advice from Reb Moishe-Lazer Halperin. She first thought of sending a letter with one of the farmers travelling to Motal, but as she struggled to put her thoughts into words she decided that, in her old age, there was no need for her to make advance arrangements for a five-minute face-to-face conversation with the honourable rabbi.

She travelled into town on the wagon of one of their *goyische* neighbours, Tomasz Grabowski, who grows potatoes for a living. He made her sit above a rickety wheel, purposely she thought – but intentional or not, she arrived in Motal with a sore back all the same. The wagon inched its way along, because today of all days, he had decided to carry a double load of potatoes. Rivkah is not one to keep her thoughts to herself. "You young folk are in such a rush. Things that worked perfectly well yesterday are of no use to you today. So you're a businessman now, eh, Grabowski, and at my expense?"

Whenever she reaches the outskirts of the town, Rivkah Keismann is appalled by the filth and by the crudeness of its inhabitants. Rotting fruit lies strewn by the roadside like carcasses, and frenzied flies crash into her face like the sparks of a bonfire. The identical wooden houses are so quiet that one might think they were abandoned. The stench rising from the sewers is intolerable. This lot, these town-dwellers, who call themselves cultured, cannot even place their outhouses at a decent distance from their homes. And would you just look at their wells? They reek of mould and mildew. These enlightened men go out to taverns or discuss plays performed in Minsk, while dysentery spreads in their own back yards. Disgusting.

Rivkah marches towards the synagogue, a modest two-storey building. She knocks on the rabbi's office door and, without receiving an answer, walks in. The office is empty, and Rivkah is unsurprised to see that there are no holy books open on his desk. She has always suspected that Reb Moishe-Lazer Halperin prospers thanks to his pragmatism rather than his erudition. His predecessors overflowed with knowledge of the Torah, even as they let their bodies wither. Their dedication to the faith, to the immersion of their minds in study, was so great that they forgot to feed themselves. But this one? This one roves around Motal all day long. The pleasure he takes in his job is evident from his rotund figure. He assiduously collects his dues from the community; he never refuses even the donations of widows and orphans. It is rumoured that, on top of the state tax, Motal has the so-called Lazer Tax. Pay it late and you'll wish you'd died in a pogrom. Reb Moishe-Lazer Halperin will first haunt debtors with his piercing gaze, then he will corner them and start telling them everything about the assimilationists in Berlin and the young men who go to New York or Palestine in droves to chase futile dreams. And why do they do this, one might ask? Because the synagogue lacks funds and the community is losing its cohesion. After that, Reb Halperin ambushes his congregants at shul, in front of their relatives and neighbours, publicly demanding to know whether they've made their donation this month. The people of Motal know all too well that they had better pay in advance, lest they find themselves having to shell out the money after a public shaming.

But Rivkah Keismann wasn't born yesterday. She could see through Reb Moishe-Lazer Halperin even if she were blind. Over the years she has developed an arrangement with him: cheese in exchange for conversation. He can plump himself up with Keismann-made cheese, the best in Grodno County, and she can enjoy the attention of the head of the community. In the spirit of this arrangement, she now puts down the basket of cheese she has brought along and sits on one of the oakwood chairs.

Indeed, His Honour walks in two minutes later in the company of two men she has never seen before, neither of whom strikes her as a local. One is leaning on a peculiar cane and dragging a leg, maybe because of a crack in his spine. The other is wearing the elegant clothes of a foreign intellectual.

"Mrs Keismann!" The rabbi exclaims.

"Yes, as you can see." Rivkah Keismann says.

"I hope you are well, I know that these are hard times. Is there any news from the young Mrs Keismann?"

Every time, the rabbi's indiscretion surprises her anew. He has not even introduced her to the men by his side, and yet he is already talking about her problems in their presence.

"What a tragedy," he adds quietly, with a glance at the two strangers.

"God is watching over us," Rivkah says. She came to him to be consoled and now she finds herself consoling him. "I can't complain." At this point, she notices that the intellectual man is translating everything she says into Polish for the benefit of the limping man. Very odd. Since when did the rabbi start cavorting with gentiles?

"Of course he is," the rabbi mutters. "I mean, thanks be to God . . . Anyway, allow me to present these two distinguished gentlemen. They have wandered in the wilderness for forty years and now they have returned to the Promised Land. Do you know who they are?"

"Moses and Aaron?"

"Akim and Prokor."

"Akim and Prokor?" Rivkah is taken aback by these strange, frighteningly Polish names.

"Please don't jump to conclusions, Mrs Keismann, these two

righteous brothers were conscripted into the Czar's army when they were children and their original names were taken away from them. They served in the army for four decades. One has forgotten his mother tongue and the other turned his back on the commandments. But now, thanks to God, they stand firm by virtue of the faith that kept burning in their souls with its eternal flame."

Rivkah Keismann tries to recall the names of the boys abducted from Motal forty years ago. Apart from Zizek, the only children that come to her mind are the Avramson brothers, Pesach and Motl.

"They are not from here," the rabbi assures her. "They are from Vitebsk. Our Akim and Prokor are none other than Avremaleh and Pinchasaleh Rabinovits."

"Rabinovits?" Rivkah wonders at this suspiciously common name. "I don't know any Rabinovitses in Vitebsk." This is quite true: she does not know anyone from Vitebsk, Rabinovits or otherwise. And yet, she is making all of them uneasy, especially the polyglot maskil, the intellectual, who looks particularly hostile.

"Unfortunately their families have rejected them," the rabbi swiftly goes on. "They have imposed a senseless, unjust sentence. Do you know the secret to the survival of our small community? Do you, or do you not, Mrs Keismann? So, I will tell you. We in Motal are a community that is small and tightly knit. As it is written, 'all of Israel vouch for one another'. Pinchasaleh has pledged to found a yeshiva in three years' time that will rival those of Minsk and Vilna. This is the dawn of a new era for Motal, Mrs Keismann. A new era!"

The rabbi's last words clarify many things at once for Rivkah Keismann. Reb Moishe-Lazer Halperin can already see himself running a prestigious yeshiva, that much is obvious. But there is one thing that makes no sense to her: regardless of whether they

196

were or were not snatched from their beds as innocent boys, what business do they have coming here now? The names Pinchasaleh and Avremaleh Rabinovits could not be more incongruous. They made more sense as Akim and Prokor. Pinchasaleh's eyes are darting in all directions and he is clearly uncomfortable with the idea of his Jewish identity. He must have been a handsome and proud man in the past, but now he is bent and subdued. His physical disability has clearly spread from his leg to take over his entire demeanour. She thinks that she can detect a waft of alcohol coming from him too, *zisse bronfen*, a liqueur of some sort. If he was trained for life as a soldier, why not remain a soldier? Why dredge up murky childhood memories? Avremaleh seems like a lost cause too. It doesn't look as if he wants to be back in the Jewish fold at all. He cannot hide his contempt for his surroundings, and there's not a shred of excitement on his face of the kind you would expect from someone returning home after a long absence. So who can they be, these two? It is unclear, and, what is more, they do not seem to be the sort of men with enough money to finance a grand yeshiva. On the other hand, Rivkah Keismann has more pressing problems on her mind right now. She must speak with Reb Moishe-Lazer Halperin, after which the honourable rabbi can attend to his own matters, whatever they might be. She therefore turns her back on the strangers and politely clears her throat.

The rabbi, however, does not ask the gentlemen to wait outside. Instead, he explains to them that Mrs Keismann has travelled a long way to consult with him about a great catastrophe that has befallen her family.

"Her daughter-in-law, Fanny Keismann, has disappeared. What a tragedy!"

Rivkah is incensed. What do they think they're doing, making conversation at her expense?

"Fanny Keismann?" Akim asks in surprise, looking at his friend Prokor.

"Yes!" The rabbi's face lights up. "This is her mother-in-law, Mrs Rivkah Keismann, who has come over from the village. People flock here from all across the region, you know, for my counsel. Just look at this basket," he goes on excitedly. "You've never had such fine cheese in your life!"

"Cheese." Akim translates for Prokor.

"Cheese made by Natan-Berl!" the rabbi says, blissfully.

Now he has crossed the line. Not only is the rabbi wasting her time, he also intends to waste the fruit of her labour on these two nobodies. She did not take the trouble to come here to offer charity to all and sundry. If they want cheese, let them buy it.

"Well, I can see that the rabbi is busy," Rivkah Keismann announces, and gets up to leave.

Reb Moishe-Lazer Halperin knows better than to let Rivkah Keismann leave his office disappointed, so he hurries to block her way, grovelling in repentance. He asks the gentlemen to wait outside for a few moments, suddenly focused and alert, finally awakened from his daydream about the lavish yeshiva Avremaleh and Pinchasaleh have pledged.

"Your honour," Rivkah whispers, "I fear for my son's well-being."

"Of course, of course," the rabbi says, nodding. "This is a terrible mess. Is he not well?"

"I'm afraid not," Mrs Keismann pulls out a handkerchief. "And it is only getting worse."

"Why doesn't your son come to see me?" The rabbi peeks at his watch, his ears pricked to catch anything that might be happening outside the door. "He will find remedy in the warm embrace of the Motal congregation."

"In the meantime, he finds solace in the company of the ladies of Upiravah. They bring him cake and pie all day long."

198

The rabbi chokes. "Shiksas? Non-Jewish women?"

"They'd be willing to convert for Natan-Berl," Rivkah wipes away a tear. "I don't care anymore. I am exhausted. Look at me. I'd be better off dead."

The rabbi jumps up from his chair and starts to pace nervously around the room, his thoughts lost somewhere between Akim and Prokor, Natan-Berl and the shiksas. He passes his hand between his heart and forehead, letting it climb up and slide down his bushy beard.

"But this is inconceivable," he says at last. "Natan-Berl is still married!"

"A widower, you mean."

"A w-widower?" the rabbi stutters. "But what . . .? How . . .?"

"There's no need to be generous, Your Honour, you don't have to protect me from the truth. I am not a little girl. I have known many of Motal's rabbis in my day, but none of them were as immersed in the life of the congregation as you are. There is no point in hiding from me what everybody knows."

"Who knows what? Everybody knows? But—"

"—but there is always hope," she says, anticipating his words. "Even so, everybody understands that my daughter-in-law has been abducted and killed by a brute, and she will never ever return to be the mother of her children."

"But the Blessed Holy One is watching—"

"—the Blessed Holy One is watching over us," Rivkah finishes. "I do not doubt it. Of course, this righteous woman will rest in peace. But, in the meantime, the village women are taking advantage of my son's despair, and I am sure that one of them will end up living in my house. I am tired, your honour, and if it wasn't for Mende Speismann who has come to my aid to take care of my family, there's no knowing what would have become of us."

"Mende Speismann is a pious woman," the rabbi agrees.

"Only a widow can understand a widower. You should see these two together. A match made in Heaven."

"A widow? An *agunah*, an abandoned woman, you mean."

"Your honour, please, I am not a child. I hear what everybody is saying."

"What are they saying?" the rabbi asks with concern, still pacing around his office and glancing at the crack in the door to make sure that the gentlemen are still waiting.

"Mende is miserable, God help her, bearing the brunt of her husband's shame," Rivkah Keismann says, mournfully. "First he was seen in the company of anarchists, then people said he frequents sheigetz taverns, and most recently they heard that he had enrolled in the university. Unfortunately, the 'student' is studying the wrong religion, cleaving to misguided beliefs and embracing heretical ideas. 'Jesus and Moses are one,' he squeals on the streets of Minsk; he swims stark naked in the Svislach and hands out pamphlets filled with nonsense to strangers."

How on earth did she come up with that? The Devil knows. But, once uttered, these words become true as true can be.

Rivkah Keismann bursts into tears. "Reb Moishe-Lazer Halperin, please tell me: would you really want him to return to Motal? Is Mende Speismann still bound by her marriage, or is she a widow and are her children fatherless? Your Honour had better think about these matters seriously. As far as the people of Motal are concerned, Zvi-Meir, the devil, is dead and buried. And even if he stood right in front of them alive and well, they would say Kaddish in his memory to his face. Instead of worrying about the dead, Your Honour should leave your comfortable chamber and visit us country Jews. There is an unhappy widower, and a righteous widow, the sister of the late Fanny, may the Almighty avenge her death. The two of them, Natan-Berl and Mende, innocent lambs that they are, will face catastrophe without the rabbi's guidance: they can either succumb to the depravity of Sodom and Gomorrah or enjoy a consecrated marriage. We Jews are accustomed to the commandment of *yibum*, are we not?"

"Marriage? *Yibum*?" The rabbi is perplexed. "The Torah given to us at Sinai does not—"

"The Torah was given at Sinai to men and women alike. If a brother can marry his sister-in-law, then a sister can marry her brother-in-law."

"Mrs Keismann!" The rabbi gasps for air. "I'm begging you, please don't—"

"Of course, I will not say a thing, time is not pressing. Although I will consider it the rabbi's fault if one of the dearest sons of the congregation marries some Magdalena or Maria, Heaven forfend! I'd be better off dead."

"I shall visit the village as soon as possible," says the rabbi, panic-stricken. "I shall speak with both of them."

"The sooner, the better," Rivkah says, getting to her feet, her visit over. "And, naturally, you didn't hear a thing from me."

"Naturally," says the rabbi, accompanying her to the door. "In strictest confidence."

Rivkah Keismann knows that the next time Natan-Berl hears people talking about his wife, he will be informed that she was either abducted by Zizek or devoured by a bear. At first he might react with violence. Indeed, the rage her son hides behind his silence is without bounds. But in due course, he will come to realise that his children cannot remain orphans and that he should marry a woman who will become their mother, at which point she, Rivkah Keismann, will have peace and be able to leave this world at last.

VIII

People say: Rivkah Keismann always makes everything about her. The truth is, Rivkah Keismann is the last person on earth to be concerned about Rivkah Keismann. She is of no consequence. All she cares about is her family.

People say: there's no remedy for the tragedy that has befallen the Keismann and Speismann families. The truth is, Rivkah has discovered that trouble plus trouble does not always equal double trouble, but sometimes a solution. Trouble number one: a pretty, modest woman, whose only fault is wanting to be a mother and a wife, haplessly ends up in the arms of Zvi-Meir the rascal. Trouble number two: a mother of unsound mind who left behind a devoted husband and five children is said to have been devoured by a wild beast, if not worse. And the solution is: Keismann has what Speismann is lacking, and Speismann has what Keismann is lacking. Perhaps all's well that ends well.

People say that only in Rivkah Keismann's mind could this count as a "solution".

The truth is, nobody is saying that this solution is perfect. Natan-Berl has yet to demonstrate any feelings whatsoever for his sister-in-law, and Mende is far from feeling at home in his house.

The grandmother tells her: "Come over here, sit with us, rest a little." But Mende behaves as though she were their servant. She feels guilty if she does not keep busy.

The grandmother tells her: "We have let you into our house, you're always welcome to stay with us. How long will you keep on behaving as if you have to repay a debt?"

"Have you finished?" Mende Speismann asks, before clearing her plate.

*

This does not worry Rivkah Keismann in the least. People can say what they like. If she had listened to things that other people say, she would not have married Natan-Berl's father. Among the Jews, affection develops from cohabitation, and not the other way around. Man and wife learn to like one another out of a sense of duty and shared destiny. They will develop feelings for one another by facing the burden of everyday life and the pressures of their commitment together. Love should rest on solid foundations, not on a whim.

This is what Rivkah is thinking to herself, as she watches Mende clearing stones from the garden. Other people can say what they want. As far as Rivkah is concerned, this is a family in the making. Yankele has joined David and Mishka, and the three of them are studying with Schneor Mendelovits, the tutor who comes in every morning from Motal to bring them into the Tent of Torah. In the meantime, Rivkah Keismann's granddaughters are playing nearby as Mirl draws water from the well.

The father goes out to earn their bread, the mother takes care of the housework, and the children keep busy. Just like all good families. Her maligners will tell Rivkah Keismann that their own family members are also loving, that they talk to each other, the parents sleep in the same bed, and the children know who their father and mother are. True, there is not much loving or talking or liking going on in the Keismann home. But mind you, there's no cursing or fighting either. And can the same be said of other families? Exactly.

In the distance, Rivkah spies two horses approaching at a gallop. Before telling her darling grandchildren to come into the house, though, she takes a better look. She has never seen such a sight in her life: one of the horses is ridden by a strapping, handsome man, a skilful jockey, and perched just in front of him is none other than Reb Moishe-Lazer Halperin, riding side-saddle with both legs dangling from the same side of the horse. Rivkah Keismann cannot fathom the meaning of this, but she does know that any man who can be compelled to ride a horse like that has lost his presence of mind and could just as easily be persuaded to worship a false prophet.

Having recognised Reb Moishe-Lazer Halperin, she infers that the purpose of this visit is the conversation that the rabbi promised to have with her son, the necessity of which she is no longer certain. Her earlier idea of marrying Natan-Berl to Mende Speismann now strikes her as obsolete. Three weeks have gone by since Fanny's disappearance, and, in all honesty, Rivkah Keismann is quite satisfied with the course things have taken. Not only that, but the time that Reb Moishe-Lazer Halperin has chosen to invite himself to their house is highly suspect, as is the presence of his strange companions. Weren't they called Adim and Protor? (What kind of names are they, anyway? Perhaps she does not remember them correctly.) The rabbi knows full well that her son Natan-Berl leaves the house at the crack of dawn to herd his flock to the pastures, so in all likelihood the Keismann household would be one man short at such a late morning hour.

Frankly, Rivkah doesn't like the rabbi's continued enthusiasm for his two philanthropists for several reasons. First, if they are indeed from Vitebsk, and if indeed they went through what the rabbi claims, then she feels sorry for them; but now that they are no longer Avremaleh and Pinchasaleh but Adim and Protor, she is not so sure that she wants them to come anywhere near her grandchildren.

Second, it is not clear to her how two soldiers could have become so wealthy. People who earn their money through hard work are not usually inclined to be charitable. People who save up copeck after copeck, and put aside one rouble at a time to amass a fortune, usually leave their money to their children and family. Philanthropists are wretched, miserable people because they do not have to work for a living and they do not know anything about the hardship of daily toil that makes a nobody into somebody. Their generous donations are only meant to justify their existence and to clear their conscience as they watch most other people buckle under the pressure of earning a wage. The trouble is that the harder they try to be liked by the common man, the more he will try to distance himself from them.

Third, if they are Adim and Protor or Avremaleh and Pincha-saleh Rabinovits, people say that you cannot judge someone until you have walked in their shoes, and she makes no claim to know the secrets of their hearts as only the Almighty can. That said, she did hear of a few conscripted Jewish children who defied the Czarist army's education, preferring death to halakhic transgression, and starvation to impure food. For these reasons, and others that she'd rather not go into right now, Rivkah slips back into the house and asks Mende to tell their visitors that she is not feeling well, that the bubbe is going to lie down and cannot receive any guests.

Rivkah Keismann steals to the kitchen, pulls the curtain across the window and eavesdrops attentively on the conversation taking place on the other side of the wall. She hears a weak buzz of chatter, the grunt of an irritated horse, and then silence. Then three quick knocks on the door catch her off guard. The best thing to do would be to withdraw into one of the rooms at the back of the house, but before she can move, the door opens, unbidden. Reb Moishe-Lazer Halperin stands on the threshold with the two gentlemen, Adim and Protor, just behind him and letting in the blinding sunlight.

"Mrs Keismann!" the rabbi cries, raising his arms jubilantly. "We heard that you are not well and yet we thought we should come in, because we feel confident that the news we bring will heal whatever ailment you may have."

We? *We* feel confident? The news *we* bring? Have the three men suddenly become one?

"Why have you left your bed if you are not well?" asks the rabbi.

"Why did you leave Motal?"

"You asked me to," says the rabbi, stung by her scorn. "We said that I would come over—"

"That was a week ago."

"Not that long ago, I'm sure."

"A week to the day."

"Things came up," the rabbi says, apologetically. "You know how hard I work. But I bring you good news."

"Natan-Berl is not present to hear it," Mrs Keismann says, "and even if he was here, he wouldn't have liked to hear it in front of such a large audience."

The rabbi takes his time before replying, and Rivkah thinks that at last he has understood the cause of her irritation. In his rush for the philanthropists' money, he has neglected his obligations to his congregation.

"If I might be so bold, could the guests have a glass of water?" the rabbi says, drawing up a chair.

A glass of water for the guests, indeed? It always starts with a glass of water and ends with an open invitation for everything else.

"I am still weak," she says, feebly. "Perhaps Your Honour could pour some water from the jug yourself?"

Reb Moishe-Lazer Halperin walks over to the water jug and pours out three cups. With the air of a meek servant, he offers the water to his bountiful guests, who are still standing in the doorway. Now they enter the house, and the grandmother notices that

206

the limp of the one calling himself Protor is heavier than she remembered, and that without his cane he probably would have had to crawl. His shifting eyes spy out every corner, as if he is looking for something. Adim, for his part, looks around contemptuously, and whenever their gaze meets he immediately looks away, as if to say, I cannot believe how backwards you people are. You might as well be living in the Stone Age, whereas I have travelled all over the big, wide world. I am educated. I know Russian and French. Me me me. A man like this, who thinks that everything revolves around him alone, cannot be Jewish. The manners of the Jew bespeak self-deprecation and futility.

And yet there is something about Protor. Perhaps his disability makes her feel compassion for him, or perhaps she has gone soft over the years. Fortunately, the Blessed Holy One endowed her with particularly keen senses, and while most people favour sight, she is acutely sensitive to smell. She has no doubt that Protor is a slave to alcohol, and he has clearly tried to mask the smell of hard spirits by drinking some sort of fruit liqueur – peach, is it? Or perhaps plum? But there's a reason beside his limp or his intoxication for his unsteady gait. He is looking around like someone who has never set foot in a Jewish home before, with the all the wide-eyed gawping of a child. She pities a Jew who does not even recognise a Sabbath candlestick. It might have been possible to bring him back to the fold, were he not drowning in a torrent of drink and pain.

Reb Moishe-Lazer Halperin motions to his guests to sit at the table. Only once they are comfortable does he allow himself to sink into a chair and take a sip of his water. How did the faithful city become a harlot? Only greed can explain it.

"What we have to say," the rabbi declares on behalf of the three of them, "we will say in person and in private, and we vouch that none of it will leave this room."

Then that's another secret gone down the drain, the grandmother thinks to herself.

"These generous gentlemen," the rabbi goes on, "have been troubled since they met you. In fact, your visit made Akim and Prokor, excuse me, Avremaleh and Pinchasaleh, quite agitated."

So Protor is Prokor, and Adim is Akim. The names are of no consequence; her memory is not what it used to be.

The rabbi continues. "They suddenly recalled that, when they last visited Baranavichy, they happened to meet Mrs Fanny Keismann, in a tavern!"

"A tavern?" Rivkah scoffs. "*Kvatsh, kvatsh mit zozze*, nonsense with gravy on top."

"This is not nonsense," the rabbi says, defensively. "What is more, when I told them about the disaster that has befallen your family, I could not help but mention the sister, Mende Speismann, and her wastrel of a husband, Zvi-Meir. And do you know what they told me? That they ran into a man called Zvi-Meir in Minsk, and the more I described him, the more they were convinced that he is our Zvi-Meir. They saw him at the synagogue, Mrs Keismann – the synagogue!"

"Baranavichy?" The grandmother is dumbfounded. "Minsk?"

"Akim and Prokor can send someone to Baranavichy right away. They tell me she was staying at—"

"Adamsky's," Akim mutters. "Patrick Adamsky." And Protor – that is, Prokor – nods in confirmation.

"Adamsky," the rabbi echoes. "Patrick Adamsky. That's where they saw her, sitting in the tavern, not lying in the forest, torn apart by wild beasts. She must have simply stopped there for rest and refreshment. This is wonderful news – and there is more."

Please, no more, thinks Mrs Keismann, no more.

"I have already told you about Avremaleh and Pinchasaleh's generosity, and I have spoken at length about their compassion.

Well, the two of them are prepared to fund the search for Fanny Keismann and help restore peace to the Keismann and Speismann families. Therefore, the purpose of our visit is actually not to prevent further disaster, but rather to advise that no disaster has taken place at all, as the Blessed Holy One, father of orphans and resurrecter of the dead, has been protecting the missing family members from harm all along. In no time at all, husbands will return to their homes and mothers to their children, and happiness will prevail. Feeling any better now, Mrs Keismann?"

Actually, the grandmother's head has begun to ache and her limbs feel weak.

"In any event," the rabbi presses on, "we need all the details you can give us about your daughter-in-law and Zvi-Meir. The gentlemen ask that you keep nothing back, as even the most trivial details could turn out to be the most important. After that, the gentlemen will send out messengers, and they will bring our lost sheep back to the fold. Come on, Mrs Keismann, time is short and there is much to do. You will describe, Akim will translate, and I will take a little rest because my stomach is rumbling. If you have any leftover dry bread from breakfast, that would be most welcome. And if any cheese rind remains, it would be a pity to throw it away. Where should we start, Mrs Keismann? Let us begin! Time is of the essence! Spare no detail."

NESVIZH

I

When God created the Heaven and the Earth, darkness hovered over the void. There was no need to create darkness, only light. The Almighty illuminated even the miserable souls of men, lest they stagnate in their primordial form, that is, in terrible loneliness. This is why He created them male and female, in His shape and form, as though to say: "You humans are incapable of civility. You will only really be human beings once you have learned to live together in harmony."

But now, as the four of them are travelling on in a ramshackle wagon in the dead of night, the total darkness outside and the desolation within are flooding the abyss in their souls. Each of them wants to be alone, as far away as possible from any other living being, and forget everything that has happened. What do they fear? Each other, more than anything. Captain Adamsky buries his face between his knees. What, in the name of the Father, Son and Holy Spirit, has he just done? Fucking hell! The authorities will confiscate his tavern now, that's for sure. He had poured his life's savings into his business. The result of thirty-five years of combat service in the infantry corps – gone up in smoke. His friendship with Yoshke Berkovits is a thing of the past, it belongs to a time when Adamsky was just a helpless Jewish boy, a pathetic coward called Pesach Avramson. As soon as he learned how his community had given his brother away to the authorities, how their faith had driven its leaders to fabricate a story that would justify this monstrous injustice, he knew that he wanted nothing more to do with these pigs and their religion, whose immutable laws can always be bent to suit shifting needs and interests. True, Yoshke has saved Adamsky's life on more than one occasion, but this is not why the captain came to his aid. He did it in spite of that. He never asked Yoshke to save his god-damned life, after all. Why, then, did he risk everything and bury himself up to his neck in this affair? What is more, his formerly rational friend has clearly become a naive little lamb who has been duped by this mysterious fiend of a woman. She isn't Yoshke's wife, and they have obviously never been intimate. Is it some kind of business relationship? If so, what's in it for him? Is it too late to change sides?

Fanny is also preoccupied by her own thoughts. With one hand she feels her neck, which just a short while earlier was in the steely grip of an officer's fist, and with her other hand she touches the knife, which she intends to throw away at the first opportunity. This disaster could not be further from her original plan to help her sister. All she wanted to do was cross the Yaselda and ride to Minsk, confront Zvi-Meir and make him sign a writ of divorce, there and then. She never imagined that she would find herself slaying a family of bandits, and then fleeing the scene of a second crime with a synagogue arsonist in tow and the slit throats of two police officers in her wake. Natan-Berl must be sick with worry. When it came down to it, he might have been able to understand what his wife had intended to do. He knows her. And after all, what a man wants and what the world is can rarely be reconciled. Can anyone force the world into submission? Everybody knows that only the Blessed Holy One can. But in any case, even if Natan-Berl had approved of her initial plan, he would never accept its consequences: there are five dead bodies to her name, and her own life is in grave danger.

Natan-Berl couldn't possibly understand anything from the

ridiculous note she left him. "Take care of yourselves until I return." Is this what a wife and mother writes to her loved ones knowing she will be gone for a long time? What were you thinking, Fanny Keismann? Her children must be tiptoeing around their father, stricken with guilt and sorrow. Gavriellah will be the only one in the house who can somehow soothe them, Fanny knows this much. And her mother-in-law, Rivkah Keismann, will be relishing every moment. Rivkah, who always warned her son against the shochet's daughter, the *vilde chaya*. Is it too late for Fanny to change her mind and go home? Would she ever be able to salvage her former life? Or could it be that, really – and the thought makes her shiver – she knew all along that she would be leaving it forever?

These two runaways fear one another. Adamsky has seen with his own eyes just how dangerous the fragile woman can be with her knife, and she has seen the captain betray her without blinking. True, he subsequently risked his life to save hers, and he cannot ignore how she courageously rescued Yoshke Berkovits, contradicting everything he had ever thought about those cowardly Jews, but neither of these events was planned, and there's no knowing what will come next or how it will turn out. Fanny wonders: would the captain betray her again? Adamsky wonders: would she slit his throat, too? Only time will tell. Perhaps in days, maybe hours, maybe moments, they will have their answers. For now, they can only sit side by side, tense and vigilant.

And what about the forces of law and order? They have much to fear on that score. This affair is likely to end at the scaffold. Whether undercover or uniformed, every officer in the region will take this manhunt personally. It is no longer a matter of killing roadside bandits; now they are wanted for slaughtering secret agents.

The agents' commander, it turned out, was the limping drunkard from the tavern. It shocked them to discover that such a man could be a seasoned Okhrana agent, and that he could just as easily show up tomorrow disguised as a tzaddik. They should not underestimate his shrewdness, nor his thirst for vengeance, and they should not forget that the captain has smashed the officer's already wounded leg, adding agonising insult to injury.

The first scratches of sunrise do nothing to ease the tension between the passengers. They need to decide where they are going. What is keeping this band together, aside from the fact that they are all fleeing both Poles and Russians? And that they have managed to raise the ire of both criminals and law enforcement? During the night, the dark made it easy to avoid looking at each other. But now, as the sky is clearing and the horizon opens up before them, this intimacy seems to evaporate as the tangible presence of all four travellers becomes impossible to ignore.

Fanny peeks over at Adamsky. His eyes are a deep amber – how can such wise, owl-like eyes serve the forces of evil? He seems ill at ease, his bushy eyebrows give him a shabby appearance, and his upper lip is unnaturally thin. Perhaps once, before he started burning synagogues, Zizek thought of him as his true friend. But after last night, it is clear that his hatred of Jews is far stronger than any lingering sense of loyalty he may have had for his people.

Adamsky chances a glance in Fanny's direction. He hasn't seen such attractive ugliness in a long time. Her nose is sharp, her gaze cold and detached, her fair hair is hidden beneath a headscarf that makes her impassive expression seem only icier. A deep scar on her left arm leaves no doubt: she is a lioness, a fighter. But if she is devoid of emotion like any other Jew, why did she risk her life to save Yoshke Berkovits? It is a mystery.

He cannot stop himself from exclaiming, "Fucking hell! Now what?"

Fanny hisses to Zizek in Polish, "Don't tell him our plans, Zizek Breshov, he will only betray us to the police again."

216

Adamsky is furious. "If I still have my throat intact, of course. Unless you intend to slaughter me too."

"It's actually easier to burn down synagogues."

"What?!"

"You heard me."

"How dare you . . ."

"No, how dare you?"

Zizek tightens the reins and draws the wagon to a halt. Neither Fanny nor Adamsky seem to have given him much thought. He abandoned his seat in the rowing boat on the Yaselda to help Fanny Keismann find Zvi-Meir, after seeing her sister throw herself out of his boat. He brought with him his two horses, an elderly steed from his army days, and a headstrong colt, and since then Zizek has suffered in the sweltering heat, starved and collapsed with exhaustion. Then, in the middle of the night, he fell victim to an attempted highway robbery, was pummelled senseless by bandits and made a fugitive. In Patrick Adamsky's tavern, he was handcuffed by secret agents who smashed his forehead against the wall, and if it hadn't been for Fanny and Adamsky he would have found himself at the gallows soon thereafter.

"Oy!" Zizek suddenly exclaims, and then stops speaking just as abruptly. His own voice still sounds new to him, like a stranger's.

Adamsky is irritated.

"Oy what, you fool?"

Zizek is silent.

"Fucking hell," Adamsky growls, but Zizek notices that Fanny is watching him with anticipation.

"Oy," he says again, "stop your bickering. I'm sorry, but if anyone wants to get off the wagon, they should do it right now, and quickly. These horses will keep going until they reach Minsk, if you don't mind. Sorry, but if you two want to keep arguing, you will have to do it by the roadside, because neither of you comes out of this story a saint. We all have something to regret, and maybe, if we all get out of this alive, you will have your chance to argue over who is more at fault then. Understood?"

Fanny and Adamsky listen intently to his outburst, and his earnestness is heartening. At the end of the speech, however, they look at each other: they still have their doubts. Why would an observant Jew stay in the same wagon as a cantonist traitor? And what does a captain in the Czar's army have in common with a crazy Jewess? And what do any of them have in common with a useless pseudo-cantor, who might have been a music professor if melodious snoring could earn you a degree? To top it off, it is not at all clear who is sitting in the driver's seat: is it Zizek Breshov or Yoshke Berkovits? A hermit or a demagogue; a mute or an orator? To be sure, he did not include himself in his little remonstrance, he spoke as if they were the only ones sitting here and he was still back there, back in his boat on the Yaselda. And while it is true that they were all born Jews, a closer look reveals that the only thing they have in common right now is that they are all on the run.

All the same, none of them leave the wagon and their fears begin to subside after Zizek's speech, despite its hesitations and foolish apologies. So, what are they not afraid of right now? First of all, themselves. Fanny knows that the knife has returned to its true purpose again, after many dormant years on her thigh. Adamsky remembers how his tavern had drained him of his pride – instead of leading troops to battle, he brought prostitutes to his guests on the top floor. Zizek has regained his voice for the first time in a very long while. And the cantor – well, there is not much to say about him, but he is better off on the wagon with a barrel of rum than being left to his own devices in the road.

The question of which road to take remains. How will they

218

travel all the way to Minsk without going through towns and villages, along exposed roads or through open fields, all while avoiding the black bogs? There is no such road in the Pale of Settlement, let alone in the big, wide Russian Empire. Adamsky, however, knows the area well and whispers a few words in Yoshke's ear, who suddenly blanches. Without further ado, Adamsky grabs the reins. Fanny looks at him curiously, thinking that he may have finally lost his mind.

"*Ah! Che la morte!*" Adamsky shouts and stands up on the platform, looking like the general of a one-man army. "To the barracks, Yoshke!" He points north-east. "*Ah! Che la morte!*" To the death!

II

The brutal blow to Novak's crushed leg has left him humiliated. His deputy, Albin Dodek, has now seen him screaming and writhing like a frightened boy. And when the town doctor was called in, the illustrious colonel demanded a chloroform injection, no less: a powerful anaesthetic used to knock out horses.

How long has he lain in bed in this state? A week, judging by the sores on his back. Coming to his senses, he feels that his eyes are swollen, and from the smiles on the faces around him, his lips must have been mumbling nonsense. The leg hurts less, thank God, and Novak quickly breaks up the loud crowd in his room – mostly officers, agents and informants – and asks even the doctor to leave. He gets up from his bed, his head spinning, and leans against the wall for a moment to regain his bearings. Then he goes downstairs into the main hall of Adamsky's tavern, summoning Albin Dodek to join him at a table, along with two other agents whose names escape him. They are replacements for Ostrovsky and Simansky, may their souls rest in peace.

If only he could, Novak would ask to be left alone so he can think. But at times like these, he knows, the Okhrana expects a swift response. If he were to take his time, it would be seen as a sign of weakness. Instead, he asks his deputy to brief him on what has happened while he has been lying unconscious in the room upstairs, and he is surprised to learn that Dodek has been dedicating himself mostly to the victims' funeral arrangements. To be sure, he has updated informants, briefed shopkeepers and tavern owners in the region, and alerted all the relevant agents, but he seems more interested in describing the last respects they paid the two heroes, Ostrovsky and Simansky, taking special pride in the wreaths he sent to their families.

Novak's cheeks are burning. "A respectful funeral is important, is not that so, Dodek?" The two nameless agents, who rival Dodek in stupidity, nod in agreement. "You did call in the portrait artist to prepare facial composites of the fugitives, I presume?"

"Certainly," Dodek replies. "That is, I was going to call him in as a matter of urgency, but I thought I should send out a search party first."

Novak breathes heavily. "And did you?"

"Yes, yes," Dodek says. "Not yet."

Novak looks at the two agents, who are nodding along with Dodek.

"So, I presume you wrote to Lieutenant General Mishenkov, at the barracks near Nesvizh, asking him to send over regiments for back-up, did you not?"

"Yes, yes." Dodek's flabby fists pound the table in agreement. "We must write to him."

"But did you?"

"Of course, of course. I'll definitely write to him." And,

scrambling to his feet, Dodek urges the other agents to follow him and sets off to carry out the orders he has just received.

At last, Piotr Novak is on his own. An excellent opportunity to pour himself a glass of slivovitz and reflect on recent developments. His first conclusion from the events of the other night is that, sometimes, idiots are worth listening to. Radek Borokovsky, the only surviving member of a family of thieves, a drunkard and a fool, has given countless versions of the chain of events that finished off his family: at first he described six soldiers, then two giants armed with rifles, then a cavalry squad and then who knows what else. In none of his versions, however, did he omit the presence of a large, frightful woman. Novak had not thought much of this detail, because the Jewess he had seen in the tavern had been anything but large, and certainly not frightful. Her face was round, her hips carried the experience of childbirth, and she had twitched her cheeks every now and again in discomfiture, but not in agitation. A complete fool had been sitting next to her, but he was just some clown asking for trouble: not exactly a skilled accomplice to a throat-slitting spree. In the absence of any sign of danger from their corner, Novak had focused on the burly scar-face instead. What a mistake that had been. Out of the four people involved in the crimes at the tavern, the thug had been the most innocuous. Even the flabby-armed Albin Dodek had subdued and handcuffed him without resistance.

Novak's second conclusion from that night's events is that presuppositions obstruct one's judgment. He had presumed that, being a woman, she would be incapable of murder, whereas the thug, being a man, had to be the source of any violence. When he had entered her room and sat at her bedside, he had caressed her arm a little as she slept, and for a moment he had felt comforted; an almost inevitable feeling really – a force majeure, if only because he was sitting beside a woman.

But there was more to it than that. The knowledge that he was about to touch a Jewess – a follower of alien customs – did not repel him, but rather excited him all the more. Strange, isn't it? But then, the demands of his life as an army officer has driven a wedge between him and Anna, his wife, and their two sons. He was never any good at writing letters, addressing the envelopes in which he sent them money with the words "To my wife and two sons, from Piotr", as if this relieved him of any additional obligations to them.

When he had returned home injured after the battle on the Shipka Pass, he'd had to lie in his room for weeks. He had felt like a foreign object lodged in the household's throat, because with every impatient look she gave him, Anna seemed to be trying to eject him from their home. When he told her about the direct invitation he had received from Osip Gurko to join the Department for Public Security and Order, she did not even ask what his position would be. If someone had asked her today what her husband did, she would not have been able to give an accurate answer, other than that he was somewhere near Grodno or Minsk, doing something for the security services, she has no idea what.

Novak will never forget the way she cared for him while he was bedridden. When she brought him his meals, he could never decipher her evasive eyes, which seemed not to see him, even when they looked in his direction. When she returned to collect the dishes, he would compliment her cooking, and she would pucker her lips in an artificial smile. She looked at him with the contempt she reserved for cowards. No-one had ever looked him like that before. When he tried telling her about what he had endured on the Shipka Pass, she had pressed her lips together to stop herself from laughing. It took him a while to realise that he had missed the opportunity to make her think of him as a hero a long time ago. He had not been around when his sons were born and he had almost never sat down to dinner with them; she had raised his sons as fatherless children. To her, he was not a courageous officer but a mundane coward, and a saboteur of routine, which in her eyes made him the worst criminal of all.

But as he was touching the Jewess's arm, his emotions got the better of him. How he would have liked to abandon the investigation and slip beneath her blanket. He wouldn't have undressed her under any circumstances – for heaven's sake, he is no barbarian. All he would have done would be to cling to her warm body and sink into deep sleep. That was how he imagined her to be, soft and tender, and he had failed to register her surprising composure when he began interrogating her. Oh no, to him she was a woman, and like all other women she carried within herself the promise of consolation, or at least that was what Novak believed, until he witnessed her slaughtering of two of his agents.

Novak's third conclusion is that the more he discovers about the killers' identity, the harder it becomes to discern their motive. First, the name "Zvi-Meir" has been mooted as the cause of everything. A Jewish name, of course, but one that is unfamiliar to him. Novak does not recall any "Zvi-Meir" in any group of socialist insurgents or Palestine dreamers. He must find out quickly who he is and what he is involved in. Second, Novak is convinced that Adamsky would not risk his livelihood for the sake of such a bizarre assortment of patrons, even if one of them was an old friend. But if a man with something to lose acts so irrationally, it means that he is fighting for an ideal. And yet, the ideal usually dictates the course of action, which, in turn, alludes to its underlying principle. Ideals and struggles must be reciprocal. Whereas in this case the actions are unfathomable and illogical: why get into hot water with both outlaws and the law? And why butcher people as though they were cattle?

Novak decides that there is only one key to the investigation: he is willing to bet that there are not that many female slaughterers among the *żyds*, and that all it will take to find her home is a spot of snooping around the nearby towns. Novak knows that he only needs to start knocking on a few doors for women to start fleeing, screaming, "Gevalt! Gevalt!" What is it with these people, that they are startled by the merest gust of wind? If you so much as light a cigarette in their presence, they believe you have come to burn down their house. And therefore, once they realise that all you want is a bit of information, they sigh in relief and tell you everything they know.

III

What does a soldier want in peacetime? War. Adamsky knows that if the Czar's enemies could have seen the courage of the Russian army in times of calm, they would not have dared to declare war on this disciplined bear. Just take a look around the army base near the town of Nesvizh. Spartan canvas tents propped up alongside makeshift wooden buildings, which transform the area into a city of officers and soldiers. Each unit is a family, and every regiment has its own bakers, tailors, cobblers and blacksmiths. And naturally, the most important thing for the morale of the troops: bands of musicians and portraitists for immortalising the war heroes.

Soldiers are sitting around in large groups, stout, tall men, wide of chest and narrow of waist. They each wear a fancy kepi, which tops a loose dark-green tunic and wide trousers tucked into knee-high boots. Morale is low because they are stationed at Nesvizh, which is a long way from the few areas where their army is still fighting the Turks. There is nothing more depressing for soldiers than feeling left out.

As a rule, Czar Alexander III, "the peacemaker", tends to avoid conflicts with other countries. Much to his soldiers' dismay, he spends most of his days building alliances, creating coalitions, and conquering tracts of land in Asia simply by signing agreements. At this rate, these men will end up retiring from military service without ever seeing any action. In the meantime, they dutifully clean their weapons, change guard posts and train during the day. At other times, they play cards, examine the reflection of their eyes at the bottom of empty glasses, and scorch their throats with cigarette smoke. Their favourite pastime is to spread rumours. Right now, new plans to mobilise forces towards the Danube are raising their hopes.

They earn thirty-two roubles a month, which is twice the salary of Turkish soldiers, but only a third of that of the French and a quarter of that of the British. This will not prevent them, however, from marching at a pace of five versts an hour when ordered to do so. Their equipment is always at the ready: a haversack containing a tent, a sleeping bag, a copper jug for brewing coffee, bandages, and a grey, thick coat rolled and tied up with rope.

The cavalrymen are different altogether. Armed from head to toe, they each shoulder a new musket with bayonet, and the hilts of pistol and sword protrude from their belts. They are compact, their faces wise, eyes small and mouths large, resembling one another to the point of indistinguishability. Their hair is thick and no longer than their shoulders, its hue tending to be lighter than the colour of their moustaches. They can be told apart by the pedigree of their horses and the quality of their tack. They are all, however, terribly narrow-minded. For them war is not a political issue; it is the place from which a man can emerge either proud or humiliated. The battlefield is where one can give the loftiest expression to one's humanity, they believe. And if the Czar, God's emissary, has decided that they must attack Constantinople, they will never ask why, only when.

The officers sleep in separate tents. The degree of veneration they enjoy is usually in inverse proportion to their seniority. The junior officers are the most admired, but serving in such close promimity with their troops leaves them exhausted. They do not necessarily come from aristocratic families, and so their honour depends on deeds rather than titles. They are battle-ready, brave and intelligent, resent dogmatism and admire impromptu solutions. A good platoon commander is a good listener, to both his own soldiers and the enemy.

Going up a level, one will find the colonels and major generals, regiment and division commanders. These usually come from prominent families, and grow up thinking that life in St Petersburg is too bourgeois. Their reasons for joining the army are almost existential, and they think of the battlefield as the only place where one may find self-fulfilment and lead a meaningful life. Their leadership style is philosophical and aloof; how else would they be able to send hundreds of men to their death? They tend to observe their subordinates from a distance, and reflect on human nature: what makes them follow my lead? Why don't they run away, or defect? How can I be confident that they will listen to me tomorrow? And so on.

The army general stands at the top of the pyramid, a prince or a count who can recite French chansons and Italian arias. By the light of the night lamp he pores over Machiavelli's *The Prince*, and takes morning walks through the camp to survey his domain. The average general can command twenty thousand subordinates or more without having fired a single round in a real battle. He will have acquired his professional qualifications at the military academy in St Petersburg, studying mostly obsolete tactical manuals written by inflexible conservative strategists like Professor Levitzky. The main flaws in the leadership skills of such a general are usually: foot-dragging over decisions, failing to exploit an advantage, failing to engage the enemy, striving too hard to engage the enemy, strategic miscalculation, insufficient familiarity with the terrain, ill-judged division of his soldiers, and, in short, a general lack of any understanding of the battle-field whatsoever. A typical general will conceal his incompetence by claiming to be hiding his "true" intentions and his "secret" manoeuvres. After all, his subordinates cannot fathom the wider picture as he can, and lack the totality of detailed information that he alone has at his disposal. Nonetheless, despite the resent-ment they harbour towards him, the general's subordinates still idolise him and address him as "Your Magnificence", no less. The very fact that he is the one in possession of this rank, rather than anyone else, makes everyone think there must be something special about him, even if it is not so immediately apparent. After all, in the absence of substantive reasons for such admiration, they can still talk endlessly with him about the fine Sobranie cigarettes he keeps in the golden box in his coat pocket.

At the military camp near the town of Nesvizh, just by the village of Uzanka, everything is running more or less as it should, under the command of Lieutenant General Mishenkov. The General himself is not in camp right now. Two days earlier, he was invited to a feast at the assessor's house and he has not yet returned. At the military academy, Mishenkov learned that a good commander is judged by how well his unit functions in his absence, and he often tests the strength of his leadership skills by disappearing from the camp for days on end – sometimes weeks – and leaving his deputy, Major General David Pazhari, in charge. Every time Mishenkov returns, he is pleased to note the fruits of his superb leadership: the camp is shipshape, training is progressing according to schedule and all the reports are waiting for him on his desk, scrupulously filled in by his second-in-command.

IV

Another day in the camp is drawing to a close. Weapons have been polished to a mirror-like sheen, all equipment has been stored, and a changing of the guard is about to take place. And then the sergeant in charge spots a wagon carrying three beggars approaching in the distance, and sends out two soldiers to see them off.

The fugitives have been travelling along back roads all day. As they have gradually begun to trust each other, they have taken turns to keep watch, giving the others a chance to sleep. First Fanny joined the cantor in the back of the wagon, then Zizek replaced her, and even Adamsky allowed himself to doze next to the urine-drenched drunkard. People are pigs. It's a rotten world.

They re-emerge onto the open road and a great field stretches before them, the site of the army camp well known to Adamsky. Two infantrymen are approaching, their rifles shouldered and cigarettes hanging from their lips. One of them picks up a stone and throws it in their direction, and Adamsky stands up on the wagon's platform and waves his arms about like a man lost at sea.

"Get lost, you fools," the other soldier calls, indifferently, and continues his relaxed stroll towards them, as his comrade picks up another stone.

Zizek tightens the reins and halts the wagon. The two soldiers also stop, keeping their distance, and the second soldier, who is now rolling another cigarette, calls to them again, "Get out of here, scum," without even looking in their direction. The soldiers exchange a few words and laugh, clearly enjoying their respite from camp.

"I am Captain Adamsky," shouts the man who until recently had been the owner of a disreputable tavern. "Third Regiment, Fifth Division, Eleventh Army."

"And I am Peter the Great," the first soldier shouts back, and hits the wagon with his next stone. Enraged, Adamsky, jumps down from the wagon.

"Soldier," he roars, "I demand to speak to your superior!"

"He's right here," says the first soldier, pointing at the second, who is now choking with laughter, expelling cigarette smoke through his nostrils.

"And who is your superior?" Adamsky asks the second soldier.

"He is," the second soldier says, pointing at the first, who picks up yet another stone and bounces it towards Adamsky's boots.

"And who do the two of you report to?" Adamsky says, now walking towards them.

"To Him." they both point at the sky, and the stone-loving soldier says, "Seriously, Grandpa, not another step closer, we don't want to hurt you."

Adamsky looks back at Zizek and Fanny in a fury, his face purple, his jaw clenched. He climbs back on the wagon and snatches the reins from Zizek.

The horses notice that a different hand is now grasping the reins, a hand that pulls at them aggressively and urgently, but they heed Adamsky even as he directs them straight at the guards. Suddenly alarmed, the cigarette-smoking soldier grabs his rifle and fires a shot in the air. The horses baulk at the explosion, but keep going, and the stone-throwing soldier brandishes his rifle with a bayonet at the end of its barrel. Fanny's hand twitches towards her knife, but Adamsky anticipates her actions, and warns her with a sharp look to not even think of such a thing.

"I am Captain Adamsky," he bawls again. "Third Regiment, Fifth Division, Eleventh Army."

"Stop, or I'll shoot!" shouts the formerly amused soldier, now terrified.

The rifle shots are heard in the barracks, and in times of peace and boredom such a sound can easily fire up the imagination. Soon two more hussars approach, the first to respond, quickly followed by dozens of other soldiers eager to engage in battle. Before long the wagon is surrounded by an entire infantry platoon, and the first two soldiers, the unexpected heroes of the hour, give an account of the incident thus far. They gave the trespassers a warning, and then pelted them with stones to ensure they got the message. But then one of the wagon's passengers, either a fool or a madman, yelled at them: "I am Captain Something, of Such-and-Such Regiment, and Such-and Such Division," and started racing the wagon in their direction, intending to run them over. With no other choice, they fired their rifles in the air to end the assault.

Silence falls on the rocky field cut through with rivulets that the sun has carved with its blades, stagnant waters welling up in the crepuscular light like shed blood. A sword is drawn, with the squeaking sound of a bird's chirp, by a stocky, broad-shouldered hussar whose face is sweet as a child's. He stops his horse behind the wagon and peers inside, looking for the source of the strange noises coming from within. To his surprise, he discovers a drowsy fellow lying there, soaked in urine, with a sloppily trimmed beard and grog-reddened cheeks. The passenger rubs his eyes, twists a lock of his hair around a finger, and then sucks on his thumb – why not? These are the last indulgent moments of his slumber. When he opens his eyes again, he sees more or less what he was expecting, and, being accustomed to waking up to bedlam, he raises his hand to his forehead, still lying on his back, and salutes the sword-wielding soldier.

The hussar lets out a roar of laughter and the soldiers guffaw too, even without being able to apprehend the ridiculous sight in full. But Adamsky knows every nuance of this laughter, and he knows that there is a sinister side to the soldiers' relief. They have all realised that the wagon poses not a threat of danger, but an opportunity to loot. Sure enough, the hussar is already rummaging through the empty sacks on the wagon and eyeing the barrel of rum. Adamsky draws himself up to his full height and turns on him.

"I am Captain Adamsky!" he bellows. "Third Regiment, Fifth Division, Eleventh Army!"

"You are nothing more than a filthy *żyd*" the hussar scoffs. "Stay where you are."

Many things can be said about Patrick Adamsky. Filthy? Sure. A depraved inn keeper? Definitely. A pimp and a scoundrel? Why not. But a *żyd*? Anyone suggesting this does so at his own peril. Adamsky has devoted too much of his life to the single goal of erasing his past and denying his identity. No fat non-commissioned hussar will return him to the night when he was abducted by Leib Stein. For this reason, Adamsky doesn't pause to consider whether this is the best time or the right course of action – surrounded as they are by an entire infantry unit – before leaping at the soldier, throwing him off his horse and wrestling with him in the muddy road. Surprisingly, no-one rushes to disentangle the brawl and slice Adamsky in half, and Adamsky realises that if he can ignore the disadvantages of his own age, he can withstand the counter-attack of a hussar who is thirty years younger than him.

Captain Adamsky did not make a name for himself because of

his size or strength, but because of his wild temper, which was like that of a ravenous predator. While his comrades stormed enemy positions, throwing fists and blows and rolling on the ground until they could grab an enemy by his throat, Adamsky bared his teeth and tore off noses and ears, rammed his fingers into eye sockets, and tore the skin off necks and mouths. Overpowering his foes without much effort, he would leave them bleeding on the ground, ripped and gouged, feeling after a missing earlobe or piece of nostril. This included not only his own melees but also the entire course of the battles he fought in. Turkish soldiers watched the Czar's wolf in disbelief as he flashed blood-dripping teeth and amber eyes thirsty for yet another fight. Nobody else fought that way, shedding every shred of their humanity, or worse, mercilessly striving to crush the very possibility of being humane.

Now, though, Adamsky feels his bones shattering under the hammering fists of the hussar, his legs buckling like pillars on the brink of collapse and his ribs cracking beneath the strain. And yet, mustering his strength, he leans forwards and sinks his teeth into his rival's chin. The hussar is taken aback by this novel type of assault and tries to shake off the wild brute, but Adamsky's jaws are ripping into his flesh. The watching soldiers can only watch in astonishment as their comrade screams in pain, fending off the attack on what is left of his chin with one hand and punching thin air with the other. Facing him with his newly gained upper hand, Adamsky tries his luck again. "I am Captain Adamsky," he says, spitting out bits of leftover chin. "Third Regiment, Fifth Division, Eleventh Army."

The bleeding hussar draws his pistol from its holster and aims it at Adamsky. But his grip is weak and he fires too low, and the bullet swishes past the captain's knee and shatters a spoke on one of the wagon wheels. Adamsky is on the point of his next charge, but another bullet whistles past his ear, this time fired from behind him. He turns to find the other hussar, a lieutenant, shouldering a smoking rifle and drawing a pistol.

"What do you want, Captain?" the lieutenant asks, quite politely. His bright eyes have a slight squint, and his full head of blonde hair has not yet had a taste of the trenches.

"Who wants to know?" Adamsky pants, wiping his mouth. "You or the gun?"

"The gun is to be sure that you will not kiss me on the chin," the lieutenant replies, pleased with the rumble of laughing soldiers around him. "I, on the other hand, would like to know why you aren't getting the hell out of here."

"Shoot him!" yells the bleeding torn-faced hussar, his eyes still searching for the rest of his chin on the ground.

"I want to talk in private," Adamsky says.

"You are in no position to bargain," the officer says, raising his voice.

"I am a captain in the Czar's army," Adamsky says. "I have served Russia for thirty-five years."

"Shoot him!" the maimed hussar shrieks, as the magnitude of the damage done to his face begins to dawn on him.

"Served Russia?" the lieutenant laughs, ignoring his comrade's torment. "You served yourself, your family."

"And risked my life!" Adamsky is dumbfounded. No-one would have dared to speak like this in his day, certainly not hussars, and certainly not before the ears of infantrymen.

"And you were paid handsomely for it, were you not?"

"You evidently haven't been in battle, boy," Adamsky hisses, taking a step towards him. "I demand to speak privately with your commanding officer."

"As you wish," the lieutenant says and cocks his pistol. "I will make sure your last words are relayed to him."

A deathly silence falls. The gun and Adamsky's obstinacy confront each other. Both are made of steel. The troops wait for a signal to storm the wagon. Fanny and Zizek huddle together, and even the cantor is watching, wondering whether this might be a good time to try a burst of "Adon Olam" to break the tension.

"Shoot him!" the hussar implores.

The night before, when Adamsky still had something to lose, he had acted like a complete fool and risked everything he owned for Yoshke's sake. Now, when he has nothing to lose, he still acts like a complete fool and ignores the barrel of a gun pointed between his eyes. One can only conclude that Adamsky is an imbecile, putting his life in the hands of a junior lieutenant whose sharp tongue has already demonstrated cruelty and malice, not uncommon traits in the younger generation. He must have been educated in one of those bourgeois schools that, rather than teaching their students to show respect and seek justice, expose them to the web of interests and hypocrisy behind those "principles". They hide their corrupted souls behind quotation marks, which, like laundry pegs, fasten words to the washing lines of cynicism to desiccate their beautiful meaning – to the point where conscience and dignity become empty words invoked in intellectual jousting sessions with their friends.

Who knows if the blonde lieutenant will really pull the trigger? Adamsky takes another step in his direction all the same.

Stupidity, perhaps even superciliousness, must be admirable qualities in the army, because still the lieutenant hesitates to pull the trigger, and a murmur of admiration begins to rise from the soldiers standing around Captain Adamsky. Without a doubt this man is an officer, a fearless warrior, and the thought of splitting his skull with a bullet seems inappropriate under the circumstances. Adamsky considers taking another step, but of all the stupid things he has done so far, he decides that continuing to edge forwards in the twilight, surrounded by twenty soldiers who are watching his every move, would be pushing his luck. So he breaks off his ceremony of careful approach and confidently strides towards the young officer, who realises that, now that the old man has taken such a risk, he cannot respond with a cowardly blast of the gun. If he has to wrestle in the dirt and risk the integrity of his pretty face, so be it. Even the bleeding hussar is holding his peace, hoping that he will not be the only one to come out of this incident humiliated.

The young lieutenant, however, dismounts from his horse and leads Adamsky out of the circle of watching soldiers. They talk quietly for a few moments. The lieutenant points towards the camp, Adamsky draws something on the ground, and then they continue to exchange quiet remarks for a long while. Finally, they return to the group, arm in arm like old friends. Adamsky points at Zizek, and Fanny is convinced that the sheigetz has made yet another deal behind her back. The captain will extract himself and Zizek from the situation, and she, along with the cantor, will be left as easy prey for the mob. But then the lieutenant asks Fanny for permission to climb onto the wagon, and gives Zizek a warm handshake.

"It is a great honour, sir," the officer whispers. "Had we only known, all of this could have been avoided." He smiles apologetically at Fanny, too. "I beg you, madam, forgive us for our lack of manners." Without further ado, he turns to the watching soldiers. "These people are our guests of honour for the coming days. If I hear that any of you have dared to approach them without permission, I will personally remove his tongue."

Adamsky climbs back onto the wagon and sits beside Zizek. Fanny, still eyeing him with contempt, cannot help herself and demands, "What did you say to him?"

"Two words, that's all," Adamsky says.

"Zvi-Meir?" Fanny asks, in disbelief.

"Zvi-Meir?" Adamsky says. "What the hell is a Zvi-Meir?"

"Never mind," Fanny growls.

"I said to him, 'Yoshke Berkovits,'" Adamsky says, mysteriously, and Fanny notices an almost imperceptible change in Zizek's expression.

"Yoshke Berkovits?"

"That was all that had to be said," the captain replies. "Fucking hell."

V

Some people can never be satisfied. They have an image in their heads of how things should be, and if reality does not fit the image in their head they never suspect that there might be something wrong with the image, but blame reality instead. Well, Shleiml Cantor does not have any images in his head. Like most beggars, his life is a succession of humble wants, momentary aspiration and immediate gratification.

An orphan since childhood, as the Almighty had wished, he was first sent to his uncle in Krakow, then to his great-uncle in Pinsk, and from the moment he could think for himself, he made a living polishing shoes for a pittance. If only there were a tale to tell about how, soon thereafter, he had caught the attention of a wealthy philanthropist who had extracted him from poverty and given him his first opportunity in life! How nice would it have been to imagine Shleiml Cantor as an apprentice metal-worker who ended up as the owner of a railway construction company. Alas, his expectations of the Creator were far more modest. If all He had done was produce bread from the earth and not bring it to Shleiml's mouth, this would have been enough. If all He had done was to bring it to Shleiml's mouth, where the bread would prove unpleasant, this would have been enough. If the bread had tasted fine and He hadn't send a potato his way every now and again, this would have been enough. If He had sent a spud his way every now and again, but did not let him have chicken thighs on the High Holidays, this would have been enough. If He had let him have chicken thighs on the High Holidays, but not gladdened his heart with brandy, this would have been enough. If He had gladdened his heart with brandy and not blessed him with the talent of singing "Adon Olam", this would have been enough. Yet the Merciful Father doubled and trebled Shleiml's good fortune, and often treated him to a stable or a barn for laying his head to rest. Can anyone appreciate Shleiml Cantor's joy as he walks through the snowy nights of Uzda, stray dogs barking from all directions, when suddenly a Jew comes out to open the stable gate for him? Can anyone picture the moment when he is generously invited to join a festive dinner, take off his water-soaked boots and huddle with his hosts around the stove? Can anyone fathom how lucky he is?

But the Almighty's charity is boundless and He does not turn His back on Shleiml Cantor. Look at him now, as the itinerant cantor is ceremoniously led into an army base. And he is shown the way to a tent! They give him a folding bed, with a mattress! And they give him a uniform, a clean set! True, it is too big, but why should a man complain when his own rags are soaked in . . . well, fortunately no-one has noticed. Now the emaciated cantor is wearing the uniform of the Czarist army, ready to entertain the soldiers by singing "Adon Olam", especially when they are asking him such welcome questions. Have you eaten? No! Have you had anything to drink? Would you like to, maybe? Yes!

Frankly, the sour-faced trio that came along with him are

ruining the atmosphere. He recognises one of them by his menacing eyes, but cannot remember from where. The lady who dragged him into this adventure seems out of sorts and won't stop rubbing her cheek. He must remember to have a little heart-to-heart with her. A few words from Shleiml Cantor might improve her mood, and if not, a song will surely do it. And the burly character with the scarred mouth they call Zizek is so sombre that one might think he had just witnessed the third destruction of the Temple. They all sit dejected, as if disaster were about to strike, while bread, potatoes and preserved meats are brought into their tent. One piece of advice from Shleiml Cantor: disaster may or may not strike, but in the meantime, they should straighten their backs and enjoy a feast the likes of which he hasn't seen in a very long time. But while the itinerant cantor is asking for more bread, without caring whether it was baked today or the week before, the three of them are sitting sullen-faced, picking at crumbs, drinking little and exchanging morose glances.

Any fool, and Shleiml Cantor is no exception, knows that the human soul separates itself from the body at the point of death with great agony. Most people imagine that the soul extracts itself from its corporeal bonds on one's deathbed and ascends On High. But Shleiml Cantor is convinced that most people do not understand that it is the body that separates itself from the soul and withers away, because people yield to their mental torments from their most tender age to the point where, like his travelling companions, their anxieties deny them the pleasure of bread and potatoes. This is what happened to Adam and Eve, who were given the Garden of Eden to satisfy all of their desires, and instead of indulging in the bounty of God's creation agonised over the prohibition to eat of just one particular fruit. So from the time of First Man until today, people learn to ignore their child-like bodies, which scream whenever they do not eat or

238

sleep, imagining that the needs of the soul are more important. Unlike them, the cantor's soul cleaves to his body, and when the latter asks for more bread, the spirit obeys. And when the body asks for more potatoes, the spirit says: no reason to delay. And when the body asks, is there any brandy, the spirit joyously replies, why not? By all means, have as much as you like.

Therefore, the cantor does not adopt the indifferent diet of his three companions. Their stomachs must be thinking that their mouths have lost their mind. And if they leave something on their plate, be it a crust of bread or a potato, he immediately inquires after it. Is it not to your liking? Why aren't you eating? And what about this? Such a pity to leave all this food on the plate. What a shame. And when a soldier walks into the tent to inquire after them, the cantor does not clam up like his friends for fear that they will be thrown out into the black bogs, but shamelessly asks the soldier if he might wet his throat with anything other than tepid water. Any "variety" would do. The strange humour of the wretched rake makes the soldier grow serious, and for a moment it seems that the itinerant cantor will be punched in the face. But then the soldier walks out of the tent without a word, returning with two bottles of mead a moment later. And the cantor is beaming.

His melancholy troupe, however, obstinately refuses the drink, as if they were in the middle of serious negotiations. Is what is on offer so bad? A bit of joy for the heart and repose for the body? What is it exactly, that they are refusing? To feel better than they are feeling right now? There's no reason for him to complain, though. Sometimes people's souls isolate them from reality, forcing their minds to become obsessed with tomorrow and yesterday, chances and risks. This way, they leave freedom to those whose eyes are intent on the present and whose souls follow their bodies. Indulging in a tin of preserved meat and two bottles of mead never hurt anyone.

VI

Adamsky cannot stand his present company. Were it not for his old friend, Yoshke Berkovits, he would have liked to burn down this tent along with all its occupants. The cantor is a gluttonous pig. In an hour's time they'll find him snoring and pissing himself again. The woman is so bitter she has not even deigned to thank him for saving her life. She thinks she can depend on her knife as if that blade could help her inside an army camp teeming with ruthless soldiers. What is it with these Jews? Why are they always waiting for the next catastrophe? Why are they always bracing themselves for disaster?

Adamsky remembers the day Stara Zagora went up in flames. The Turkish forces and the Bashi-Bazouk unit had raided and ransacked the city. Adamsky's regiment was called in for support a few hours too late, and when he reached the city outskirts he watched a long trail of Bulgarian refugees, including Jews, with wagons loaded with all they could salvage from their burnt homes. They seemed to have thrown onto the wagons a stool here, a shelf there, a few blankets, without rationale or order, probably leaving jewels and valuables behind.

The Bashi-Bazouk, a barbaric pack of mercenaries wearing broad sashes and red turbans, armed with pistols, *shibriya* daggers and cries of *"Allahu Akbar"*, terrorised the town, massacred the residents who failed to escape – more than ten thousand of them – gang-raped women and plucked ears and genitals from dead bodies.

Adamsky will never forget the appalling sight. A valley of death with scorched, defiled corpses, a cloud of stench and decay, and swarms of blue and green flies. A herd of dumbstruck survivors crawled out from this mayhem: screaming babies, shushing mothers, petrified children and stunned fathers pulling stubborn mules. Their hesitant steps proved that they were not fleeing the havoc. They lingered amid the carnage, coalescing with it. Subhuman faces passed by Adamsky without saying a word, piercing him with their gaze: now what? Where do we go? How could you let this happen? They even burned down the church, the savages!

Suddenly he heard animated voices and saw a mule approaching, pulling a wagon with a large Jewish family: elderly people, women and children. Leading the mule, the men of the family were engrossed in a heated debate. Half-suffocated by the smoke they had inhaled, the elderly in the wagon seemed barely alive. The women were dehydrated. Remembering the sound of Yiddish from childhood, Adamsky became interested in the men's conversation.

"They are fighting each other, the Muslims and the Christians, and we pay the price," said one.

"This is how it has always been," added another.

"But what do the Turks have against us?" a third one asked. "We sold them three tons of wheat this year alone."

"The Turks have always hated us," a fourth said.

A fifth man did not say a word.

"And when the Bulgarians return with the Russian army," the first one said, "will it be any better?"

"Worse," the second said.

"One is as bad as the other," the third observed.

"The Bulgarians have always hated us," the fourth asserted.

The fifth man remained silent, gritting his teeth.

"They burned down the yeshiva," the first declared.

"And burned the Torah scroll," the second hissed.

"Itzhak Galet, Aryeh's father, was killed."

"Itzhak Galet always had it in for me," the fourth said wistfully.

The fifth remained mute and glum.

Adamsky continued eavesdropping because he could not

believe how isolated and indifferent these people were, living in their own little world. Why did they not even mention the terrible disaster that was befalling the city and its residents? As far as they were concerned, the catastrophe affected only them, their family and their synagogue. They were innocent and everyone else was to blame. In their eyes, anyone who did not speak their language was useful only for trade. Their obliviousness had led them to think that they could sell wheat to the Russian army one day, then to the Turkish army the next, and continue to be seen as neutral.

Most of all, though, Adamsky noticed the men's relief, detecting beneath their fatigue and the soot on their faces a hint of elation, as if the disaster they had expected, once it had finally struck, had released them from the claws of anxiety. And then Adamsky realised that these people did not anticipate catastrophe but lived it, letting it shape their way of looking at the world. Disaster was not a possibility but a necessity. The seeds of destruction did not lie idly in the hands of barbarians but were sown everywhere. And so, if a goy refused their offer in business negotiations, he couldn't possibly be a businessman making a business decision but had to be a murderous Jew-hater, who would show up at their doorstep one day with a mob wielding torches and pitchforks.

And now, just as expected, Fanny is sitting next to him absorbed in bitter contemplation, even though he has just found an ideal hiding place for her. Without him, she would have been hanging from a noose by now, and he still can't understand why on earth he has risked his life and defied fate for her sake. It is time to understand what he has really got himself into, and he demands that she tell him who the hell is this Zvi-Meir, and how is he connected to Yoshke Berkovits. So Fanny reluctantly tells him about her sister Mende Speismann (how interesting) who

242

was abandoned by her husband Zvi-Meir (oh, really? Adamsky is on the verge of tears), and that she, Mende's sister, simply wanted to go to Minsk and confront the missing husband (so . . . when does the real story begin?).

This *is* the real story.

What?!

That is to say, more or less – the rest wasn't planned. They were attacked on the road, things happened, they escaped and found themselves in trouble with the law, and he knows the rest.

"That's it?"

Fanny nods.

"I'll be damned. Fucking hell."

Adamsky takes a deep breath, shuts his eyes and sinks back onto his bed. Shleiml Cantor, who has also just heard the story for the first time, raises his glass of mead. "Lechayim! May we find the scoundrel Zvi-Meir as soon as possible!" Adamsky opens his eyes and looks at the imbecile, and then at the woman who has just explained to him, drily and coldly, the ridiculous reason why he has just lost everything. He shifts his gaze to his friend, hoping for an explanation, if only a partial one. But his friend is still suffering and withdrawn, refusing food with a shrug. Yoshke's face offers no shadow of an explanation for why he has pulled Adamsky into this pathetic entanglement.

Adamsky remembers how he heard about the betrayal of his brother as he was cleaning the latrines in the camp. Another boy, who had been abducted from Pinsk, told him about the rumours from Motal. In return for generous rewards, a neighbour of his uncle and aunt, Itche-Schepsl Gurevits, an expert on cleaning pendulum clocks, would tell the assessor about the tax evaders and name-forgers among his Jewish brethren. A staunch Misnagid, he began by betraying his arch-enemies, the Hasidic Jews. But in due course he also started singing about his fellow

Misnagdim, and some say that he even grassed up his own brother-in-law. Everyone knew, and turned a blind eye because his actions rarely affected them directly, and because they did not want to get into trouble with the authorities themselves. The police searching for Adamsky's brother, Motl Avramson, ended up contacting Itche-Schepsl Gurevits, who said that he hadn't noticed any suspicious activity in the Avramson house, but that perhaps their papers should be checked more carefully. That was all.

Everyone knew what the outcome of his betrayal would be and nobody did a damned thing. Behind his back, they said that Itche-Schepsl polished the clocks as though he were cleaning his conscience. But as long as the skies did not fall on his head, Itche-Schepsl Gurevits continued to walk around Motal as if nothing had happened, attending the evening prayer at shul like clockwork.

Then one day he disappeared from his home and never returned. Who had abducted him? Well, it's not hard to guess. What hellish torments did he suffer? One can quite easily imagine. All that can be said is that when Adamsky pierced him with a dagger and threw his corpse into the Polesian marshlands, he felt that he had irreparably severed his bond with his people and that, from now on, he would only face them at the other end of a blade. And now, the humiliated captain stands up and furiously leaves the tent, although not before noticing that Fanny, that brazen woman, is staring at him with her frozen, wolf-like gaze, almost threatening him. He has been a fool until now. From this point onwards, everything will change.

Fanny never dreamed that she would don the uniform of the Czarist army. But here she is, in an army camp, wearing a green tunic and baggy trousers, a lone woman surrounded by thousands of men. On one side of her sits a dim-witted beggar and on her other side sits Zizek from the Yaselda. It turns out that Zizek is a famous war hero. How else can one explain the hospitality they started enjoying as soon as the name of Yoshke Berkovits was mentioned? In the past few days, she had actually begun to like him, thinking that she could detect in his bright eyes a heart-wrenching fragility. Instead of the clumsy man who sat in his boat with a bovine mien reeking of gefilte fish, she had started to notice his softer side, his hair always carefully combed over to one side, forehead taut and nostrils alert. And now it emerges that Zizek is a ruthless killer who has butchered enemy soldiers by the dozen, maybe even by the hundreds.

She wonders if it is just happenstance that she has ended up in the company of killers. How could it not have occurred to her as she left her home at two hours past midnight, travelling by back roads, that it would be impossible for her to reach Zvi-Meir without passing through places where a Jewish prayer shawl has never been seen, where no Jewish woman has set foot before?

Her longing for her children is like a rock rolling down a mountainside, subject to the force of gravity and the momentum of necessity. She rolls towards them in dreams that shatter when she wakes. In her imagination she runs her fingers through the hairs on Natan-Berl's back the same way he touches the ends of his prayer shawl, the *tzitzit*, one tassel at a time, and then she kneads the fat on his shoulders. She tortures herself for not being there to put her children to bed and watch over them as they sleep, for listening instead to Shleiml Cantor ostentatiously releasing belches that stink of tinned meat. She misses and yearns and she is exhausted, but there is one thing she does not feel: regret. No, she has no regrets. How could she?

As they were led into the army base and made their way through the fanfare, army officers bowing and waving at them, Fanny hoped that her mother was watching from above. Malka Schechter used to sit in her room, overwrought with anxiety, muttering, "With God's help everything will be alright." This phrase was her mother's favourite, always accompanied by a heavy sigh, which perturbed the other family members all the more. Nothing terrified her mother more than the unknown. In her eyes, an uncertain future was a greater threat than a concrete disaster. Malka Schechter never stopped complaining that if only she could be told where and when catastrophe would strike, she would be able to deal with it. It was the element of surprise she could not tolerate. And while she knew that her daughters' odds of being run over by a cart were close to nothing, the possibility existed nonetheless! If two children out of a hundred died of diphtheria, those two were clearly destined to be her own daughters! What is the difference between the odds of two to one hundred and two to two? For this reason, she wove a dense web of mental constructions of "if . . . then . . .", thinking that she could at least keep the "if" side of the question under her control. If she does this and that, such and such will happen. And so, with God's help, everything will be alright.

From a young age, Fanny had watched her mother hiding in her bed as the layers of her humanity peeled away from her, one by one. "Not now, Fannychka, not now, Mamme is tired." Hearing her daughters moving about the house, she would emit that same heavy sigh that thundered in the girls' ears like storm clouds, pelting down the words, "With God's help everything will be alright." The night her mother died and her body was placed in the kitchen until morning, Fanny could not close her eyes. As disasters raged in her imagination she began weaving her own "if . . . then . . ." constructions. Praying that with God's help everything would be alright, she had wet her bed.

Driven by an instinctive impulse, she had thrown away her blankets and crept to her mother's resting place. In the light of the lantern, Malka Schechter's face had been pale and serene. Fanny had never seen her so calm before. The daughter had squeezed her mother's lifeless hands, which sent back a strange warmth. The bags underneath Malka's eyes had softened and her lips were parted as though she was about to say something. To Fanny, her mother's death was a show of splendour compared to the crushed life that had inhabited her body. With her pretty, peaceful face, her mother's lips carried the promise of a tender word. Fanny knew that no game of hypothesis and consequences could overturn the fact of her mother's death. So she did not beseech the Almighty to bring her back from the dead, nor did she pray that He would protect her from the angels of destruction. She clung to her mother and lovingly stroked her hair. It was by not praying that she felt the closest she had ever felt to the God On High, and it was through her lack of faith that He would bring her mother back that she found her consolation. In the sheer meaninglessness of death, she found God for the first time in her life.

Fanny slept next to her mother until the break of dawn, promising herself that she would never yield to fear. With the same passion with which she dipped her fingers in her mother's meat stew, Fanny vowed to get her hands dirty in the cauldron of this world and immerse herself completely in earthly life. Alas, her access to that life was blocked when she was forced to become a seamstress. Fanny drifted away from her calling with every day she spent with Sondel Gordon the tailor, as the eye of the needle lay her eyesight to waste. To her, everyone in Grodno was like her mother: isolated from the world in the safety of their homes. A Jew cannot call himself a Jew unless he hides behind the walls of Yiddish and dwells in the citadel of the shtetl. Men cannot fulfil the commandments unless they ward off temptation and enforce the modest conduct of women. Women cannot be whole without their husbands, even if their husband's virtue is nothing to put on a pedestal. Every minute detail must be regulated and ordained, everything must be in its proper place. Trying to flee the rule of halakha is courting danger.

To Fanny this way of thinking was not just a life of self-deception but actual sacrilege: these people had turned their backs on the work of Creation. So she grew closer to her father and learned his trade, and then went all the way to Motal to marry Natan-Berl and embraced country life, enchanted by the villagers' customs. Compared to Mende and the women of Grodno, Motal, Pinsk and Minsk, Fanny was a renegade. To them, she was a little crazy, a *meshugene*. Behind her back the gossipy *klaftes* whispered that if you lie down with dogs you should not be surprised if you wake up with fleas, meaning that it was only a matter of time until tragedy would befall the Keismanns who dwelled among the gentiles. For her part, Fanny was emboldened by her need to prove to the women of Motal that Jews should not turn their backs on the world, and that their seclusion was actually a recipe for disaster. So she learned to speak Polish and befriended her neighbours and ran a successful cheese-making business, all the while continuing to observe the commandments and running a traditional home. And while we are speaking of dogs, and especially ones with fleas, Fanny had never forgotten Tzileyger, the stray who had endured a lifetime of misery, until the night he had fought for his freedom with every scrap of courage he possessed.

Like the dog, she wished she could tear down the boundaries of her fate and mutilate the face of anyone who stood in her path to freedom.

When she was paraded through the barracks, she had believed herself to be in grave danger, and that she had every reason to be on edge. The past has taught her that the gentile soldiers of the Czarist army do not tend to spare any pity for women, and definitely not for Jewish ones. But now she knows that she will not come to harm. She feels safe with these soldiers who bow their heads to her and offer her their food. And she is bursting with curiosity about how Yoshke Berkovits earned his reputation among them.

"Zizek Breshov?" She turns to him.

He does not answer.

"Yoshke Berkovits?" she tries again, sensing that she is crossing a line.

No response.

Like a man hiding in a bunker with his ears covered during a bombardment, Zizek is lying on his bunk with his arms covering his head. Despite the honours he has been showered with, Fanny sees that entering the barracks under this old name has clearly unsettled him. He reluctantly pecked at the bread when they sat down to eat, and then lay down on the bunk and stared at the canvas above him. In the past few days, grey whiskers have sprouted on his usually smooth face, contributing to his scruffy appearance. The beatings he took from the bandits and the agents make it hard for him to find a comfortable position. He looks like a man lying in a barren field trying to clear invisible stones from under his back.

Strange lights filter through the tent flaps, and, for a moment, Fanny fears that they are surrounded by a mob with torches. Peeking outside she sees soldiers approaching the opening of their tent, carrying offerings of candles and flowers, as though Zizek Breshov were a Christian saint.

Delighted by the sight, Fanny raises the flap slightly, thinking it will please Zizek. But he only turns away and covers his head with a blanket. She takes the hint.

Fanny goes out to greet the gawping soldiers. One of them approaches, carrying a canvas stretched on a frame and a brush, and asks her in Polish if it would be possible to paint the Father today.

"The Father?" She is confused.

"Yes, Yoshke Berkovits," the painter says.

"I'm sorry, he's not well, we have travelled a long way."

The painter immediately translates what she says into Russian for the other soldiers, who are buzzing around them like bees. "Of course," the painter says, beaming. "I understand. Could you ask him if he could manage tomorrow? In the entire Russian army, there's not a single portrait of the Father."

"Why do you call him that?" Fanny asks.

The painter draws closer and says, mysteriously, "He is the Father who saved us."

"Saved you? One soldier saved an entire division?"

"A division? How about a corps? Or an army? Don't you know? I thought you were his wife."

"Oh no," Fanny bursts out laughing, but then she sees that the painter looks offended, apparently on the Father's behalf. "We are travelling together," she begins, and the painter looks disappointed. "I am his niece," she lies, and the painter's face lights up again. "But we have not seen each other for many years."

"And you will ask him?"

"Of course," she promises. Then, unable to stop herself, she asks, "Was he an officer?"

The painter whispers, "A corporal, maybe a sergeant."

"A mighty warrior?"

"A coward."

"What? How, then . . .?"

"With the power of words. How else?"

"Tell me more."

"On one condition."

BYALA

I

A man and a woman are sitting on a wagon. He is holding a brush, she is all ears. Earlier, they agreed that she would learn the truth about Yoshke Berkovits, the Czarist army's most timorous hero, on condition that the artist would have the honour of painting the Father's niece.

The moonlight is like a tie around the night, its beams sliding down a suit of darkness. Starry lanterns flicker in the sky. A cool wind caresses the earth's curved back, which has grown limp beneath the weight of the day's heat, pleading for relief. Toads are sounding their amorous calls, and the air is imbued with the scent of grass and dung. With the first brushstroke the painter begins.

Outline of the Face

Forgive me, madam, I am a man of many faults, but no-one has ever accused me of being a man of words. No-one! I have been granted a heavenly gift that I call a sense for beauty. Forgive me, madam, but most people have eyes. And what do they see with those eyes? God help us. Can you believe that people invented the word "ugly"? Truly, this word is used for describing people with a certain flaw in their face. But I, the painter, have never seen a thing that is "ugly". For years I lived with the feeling that my mind was weak and I was slow to understand, because I was fascinated by people whom others found unappealing. Everyone mocked me: if everything is so beautiful, they teased, then nothing in this world is repulsive, not even the giant mole on so-and-so's buttocks, they said. Well, I was embarrassed. I did not mean to say that everything was perfect, symmetrical and attractive. I meant that even the things we find repugnant are beautiful in their own way, and even giant moles can stir one's soul.

Forgive me, madam, for the long preamble, but the story you are about to hear is told by a painter. Is this what happened down to the last detail? I do not know. Is this how I was told it? I cannot remember. But this is the way I tell it to myself: a story told by a man who senses beauty, even in latrines or a mass grave. If you would like to hear another version you can ask someone else, a blacksmith or a baker, who will surely relate the course of events from the viewpoint of metal or bread. Perhaps they would think you a strange or even terrifying woman. Your fair hair and wolf-like eyes and sharp nose and small ears seem to have been brought together from different parts of the world. But I think, and please forgive me if I am blunt, that you are beautiful. I detect a big secret behind your serene, Madonna-like eyes.

Forgive me, madam, but the word I am forced to open Yoshke Berkovits' story with is "shit". To be sure, I am not using either "faeces", "dung" or "excrement", for good reason. I am using "shit", that brownish, sausage-like lump that comes out of people's behinds once a day, and twice on a good day. Well, the story of shit is in fact the story of the human race, or at least the story of the departure of the spirit from the body, which to a large degree is bound up with the ridiculous distinction between beauty and ugliness. If you are indeed a relative of Yoshke Berkovits' (a fact I find hard to believe as I sketch your round face, which is nothing like the angular face of the Father), then you are Jewish. Either way, if you know your Old Testament, you must be familiar with the story of Adam and Eve, who ate from the tree of knowledge. Perhaps you remember, dear madam, what was the first thing they did after they began to see the world differently? They got dressed! Suddenly the body became a source of shame, and for no reason, do you understand? The moment it became possible to distinguish between good and evil, the culprit was found: the body is evil, and the mind is good. At that very moment, my dear lady, the history of shit began. For, if we are ashamed of our body, we are disgusted by its waste.

Forgive me, madam, perhaps these words sound too harsh to your ears? What is more, a cultured artist and sublime painter is not supposed to take an interest in shit. Bollocks to that! The artist in question actually does preoccupy himself with shit, and he has no intention of letting the matter drop. Do you know why? Because Yoshke Berkovits took his first independent steps right into a pile of shit.

Yes, indeed, my dear madam, the day he was taken by an accursed child-snatcher, Yoshke Berkovits was sent with other poor Jewish boys and delinquent Polish lads and Russian orphans to the cantonist school near Kiev, on the banks of the Dnieper. And what did they learn at that school? Well, useful professions for army life: some of them learned to bake bread, others to bandage wounds, some of them learned to beat drums, and a few of them were even sufficiently athletic to be trained for battle.

Please, madam, I would ask you not to move. I am about to complete the contour of your face and every movement changes the angle, and consequently the whole sketch, so if you wouldn't mind . . . exactly. That's it.

In any event, Yoshke arrived at that school at the age of twelve with his friend Pesach Avramson, and the two of them became the most stubborn cadets in the camp. When students were summoned for Sunday mass – they did not attend. When they were offered twenty-five roubles to be baptised in the river – they disappeared. The kitchen was not kosher – they refused to eat meat. It was strictly forbidden to wear a yarmulke – they both covered their heads with a hand. Pay attention, madam, because you must understand: their backs took close to one hundred lashes every week. In the end, they were sentenced to the worst punishment a cantonist could be given: latrine-cleaning duty, a job that cut short, not to say obliterated, the life expectancy of those sentenced to do it. In the first month the body would contract a disease, in the second month it would run a high fever and in the third month it would be interred in the furthest plot in the cemetery. Mind you, the two managed to persevere thanks to their sense of humour. They called one another Colonel Shit and General Piss. They pretended that each day at school they studied the doctrine of the body's structure and orifices, and they argued at length like two scholars whether so-and-so had had corn or wheat for lunch. They consumed their food indifferently, since it consisted mostly of turgid mashed potato. Before long, they could no longer distinguish between their insipid meals and the pigeon droppings they were ordered to clean from the windows. "What's to eat today?" one would ask. "Pigeon muck," the other would reply. The usual joke.

Forgive me, dear madam, but I do not know if you can understand what I'm trying to tell you. Two boys aged twelve who grew up in a remote Jewish town were snatched one night from their beds and hauled along in a wagon for hundreds of versts, to be offered far-reaching privileges in exchange for obedience. And yet something in the depth of their souls told them to resist. And we, in the Russian army, appreciate stubborn resistance, and nothing makes us happier than trying to break a stubborn mule. This is why their instructors exiled them to that mound of shit, in effect giving them two choices: repentance or death. The two of them would wake up early each morning and march to the outhouses. Initially, they tried to keep their clothes clean, vomiting profusely when the stains of dung spread well beyond their uniforms. They started to breath only through their mouths and ignored the swarms of maggots and worms they encountered. In time they realised that this was to be their world, stinking as it might be, and that their protection must consist of shut eyes and blocked nostrils.

They continued to pray every morning, afternoon and evening, not even knowing why, reciting the bits and pieces they could remember. As the days went by, they changed. People say that God started laughing when he heard them praising His name while they were smeared with shit. This doesn't happen very often, you know, your God laughing His head off. He makes constant demands and metes out punishment, and sometimes He even shows some mercy. But laughter? Our own God is also as dry as stale bread. I wouldn't want to attend family dinners with the Holy Father and Son.

Well, God's laughter emboldened the pair the more they prayed, and at their young age they discovered something that most people do not understand until they draw their final breath: there is nothing wrong with the body, not even with its excretions. Every day they waited in the long cabin for the thousands of well-fed soldiers who visited the latrines. Like attentive bartenders at a tavern who always remember what their regulars order, the two learned to recognise soldiers by the smell, shape and colour of their turds.

They would joke: here comes the captain's pink sausage, followed by the blacksmith's puffy nugget, and then the splatter of the artillery sergeant (who can never seem to find the hole), and the baker's sheep dung. Oh look, today the cooks have changed the menu from mashed potato to rice and beans, as may be inferred from this stringy crap. We are dust and to dust we shall return, isn't that a phrase from your Scriptures too?

Eyes

Could you relax your face a little? Let us start with the eyes. They are dominant as it is, so please don't frown. Thank you.

Forgive me, dear madam, but Yoshke and Pesach worked at the latrines for two months without once falling ill. If I had to guess, two full years would not have broken their spirits. Other things crushed them, of course. Some would call it "emotions" or "mental torment", but these are flowery ways to describe the wounds and contusions the soul sustains when it is ripped apart.

Forgive me, madam, but as you may have already realised, I am not much of a patriot. I like Russia, but I will not die for its sake. In the army I am given food in exchange for my art, even if it only amounts to painting flattering portraits of generals. I pray to God, like everyone else, so as not to attract the wrong sort of attention, and to avoid being seen as a snide intellectual, Heaven forfend. Even if you tried, you would not find an idea for which I'd be willing to sacrifice my body. This is why I've always admired you Jews (that is, if you really are Jewish), for your resolute avoidance of patriotism and your strict loyalty to your family and community.

One ordinary day, as Pesach Avramson was leaning against an outhouse after emptying a latrine tank, one of the cantonists approached him to report the rumour that his brother had been arrested. I don't know all the details, but apparently Pesach's brother was also conscripted, managed to escape and decided to have his vengeance. His considerable acts of retribution ultimately led the Jewish community to turn him in to the authorities.

Forgive me, dear madam, but when I heard this story for the

first time I found it hard to believe. Can one's hand punch one's own face? Can one's knee jab one's own stomach? It turns out that once fear is sown among you people, hatred erupts and you become your own worst enemies. One resents the other, the other loathes him, this one betrays, the other squeals, and the whole community is fractured. Finally, someone gives up the culprit on everyone else's behalf. That night Pesach Avramson lay on his bed with his eyes wide open, as heretical thoughts assailed his defenceless heart. He started recalling incidents he hadn't paid much attention to until then, which now struck him as highly significant.

He recalled, for example, that several days after his abduction and his brother's escape, their abductor, Leib Stein, had dragged him and Yoshke to the house of some goy farmer in a village along the way, with whom he had arranged accommodation and food in return for a generous sum. There were Sabbath candles on the dinner table, and Pesach looked at Yoshke in disbelief: they had ventured so far away from home that they hadn't even noticed the arrival of Queen Sabbath. In a sudden display of devoutness, the abductors prayed like cantors before the embarrassed farmer. Then they made kiddush, washed their hands and passed the challah around the table, and Pesach watched them with equanimity, for what Jew does not greet the Sabbath with joy? A stranger like the farmer could never understand that.

But when he learned how his brother had been handed over to the authorities, Pesach recalled that evening with consternation. Interpreting the farmer's expression in an entirely different way, he realised that he had shown not embarrassment, but shame and resentment, thinking, how can these serpentine villains sing praises to the Guard of Israel after ruthlessly abducting the children of that very same guard? The bastards see no contradiction between their cruel deeds and their pleas for protection and safety and health and a decent living; that is, they aspire to have the very things they are denying others. Pesach trembled at the idea that for some people religion is only there to serve their egotistical needs and the commandments are paid mere lip-service. He then began to wonder what use the prayers of their venerated community leaders could have, if these leaders had let their fellow townsmen surrender his brother to the police? In what name did they sacrifice him? Faith? Torah? Oh no. It was to merely serve the selfish interests of men who fear the authorities. And what lie did they tell themselves to suppress their guilt? What verse did they cite to rationalise this transgression? Sharp pain pierced Pesach's body, but he neither screamed nor cried, knowing it was the pain of detachment. He was to purge himself of their presence in his life without leaving a single trace. He was to eye them with the same resentment that the farmer had shown. And what about the scum who betrayed his brother? Well, his day would come.

Yoshke Berkovits was lying in the next bed, and could sense his friend's fury. He had also stayed wide awake and reached out his hand to hold Pesach's. An important gesture because, after that night, it became clear that Pesach could no longer remain Pesach. The next morning, he reported to his instructors and asked to be baptised in the river. He was relieved of latrine duty and joined infantry training. Yoshke Berkovits was sent a new apprentice, Imre Schechtman was his name, and he hardly ever saw Pesach Avramson, now Patrick Adamsky, during the day. But at night, without uttering a word, Yoshke and Pesach lay in their beds holding hands, knowing that their bond owed nothing to religion or nation.

Your expression tells me that this story about Pesach Avramson surprises you, or perhaps even makes you uneasy. It is strange

262

that, as the Father's relative, you know nothing about how Patrick Adamsky came into being. Your astonishment will find its way into the painting. I'm afraid it cannot be helped.

Forgive me, dear madam, but we had better say a few words about Imre Schechtman too, for I find him especially endearing. You might understand why later on. Imre's family came from the faraway kingdom of Hungary in search of a better life. His father was a salt merchant who moved with his family to Odessa to sweeten his profits by being closer to the trade routes on the Black Sea. The southern weather, he was told, might ameliorate his wife's shingles. Indeed, after one summer she felt better than she had in a decade. But whoever gave his father this advice failed to mention the cruel winds that blow across the Gulf of Odessa in wintertime, and these gales duly carried off Mrs Schechtman and left Imre Schechtman, the youngest of seven children, motherless. The father's business faced merciless storms too. His powerful competitors also knew that the Black Sea was the key to their success. Unlike the father, though, they had several advantages: fluency in the local language, high-profile contacts and solvency. Before long, Mr Schechtman was stuck with sacks of salt ruined by damp due to a lack of storage and buyers, and it's not hard to understand how he came to convince himself that his youngest son would face a glorious cantonist future in the Czar's army.

Young Imre was not yet eight when he was signed up for military service as a twelve-year-old. Before long he was widely considered a fool: he struggled to read and could not write, and would bite his tongue and stay mute whenever he was scolded. The only task he could be assigned was latrine duty, as it did not require any rhetorical or cognitive skills whatsoever. This is where he met the highly experienced Yoshke Berkovits, who taught him everything that an eight year old needs to know about shit.

But Imre Schechtman was no Pesach Avramson. Oh no! His spirit was crushed and his body was weakened. Unlike his predecessor, he did not find any consolation in his job. He spent each day in silence with an increasingly listless expression on his face. Yoshke Berkovits gave up his own pigeon-droppings meals and offered them to the boy instead, but Imre Schechtman was vomiting whatever he ate and quickly becoming as brittle as a twig, and before his first week was up, he collapsed with exhaustion. His innocent, fragile face seemed ready for death. Yoshke took him to the infirmary, certain that the boy's days were numbered.

Forgive me, Madam, we will return to Imre. Indeed, this story may seem long and disjointed to you, but we are still only at the beginning, far from the heart of the matter. In the meantime, if you please, I shall dedicate more time to your eyes, which tell me a lot about you, far more than I wanted to know.

Every morning, Yoshke Berkovits reported for duty alone and did not speak to a living soul all day. He forgot all the prayers save the one pertaining to orifices, because of its connection to his work. The memory of his father and mother, Selig and Leah Berkovits, grew dim. The principles for which he had fought so hard faded away. The body, it turned out, needed solid ground, but Yoshke Berkovits felt that he was hovering in space. He dreamed of the day when he would be able to leave the cantonist school and find his way home by following the stars. In his imagination, he did not proceed along rocky paths and dirt roads, but lightly flew over Polesia's mountains, forests and bogs, quickly crossing the Yaselda and landing at Motal. But once he arrived back in his home, he forgot why exactly he had set out to reach it, and could not remember what he was doing there. He then returned to the here and now, and to the knee-high shit he was standing in.

Unable to sleep at night, he continued to hold the hand of his converted friend. Patrick Adamsky's body grew broader in training, bristles appeared above his thin lip, and his posture became enviably august. The other boys raved about Adamsky's athletic feats, and, more than once, Yoshke wondered if his friend was no longer extending him his warm hand out of need. Yoshke's obstinacy became ridiculous. No-one would come near him because of his job. He had no choice but to face reality and embark on a new road in the bosom of Christ. And yet, dear madam, for some reason, Yoshke Berkovits felt he could never consent to be baptised in the river. The cause for this reluctance was no longer his Jewish descent, for which, just like his friend, he felt nothing. His defiance derived from nothing more than defiance itself. Pragmatic considerations did little to change his mind, as he continued to reject the offers that Patrick Adamsky passed on to him. Yoshke Berkovits wanted to rebel, and his Jewishness was primarily a rebellion against convenience.

Forgive me, dear madam, for now we reach the worst part of our story. On a night like any other, Yoshke was lying in bed, waiting for his friend Pesach Avramson to return. He could hear him chatting and laughing with the other boys. When Pesach entered the dormitory, he approached Yoshke's bed and undressed as usual. Yoshke waited patiently for his friend to lie down and stretch out and sigh deeply as he relaxed. But when Yoshke extended his hand, expecting the familiar touch, his fingers were left grasping thin air. Patrick Adamsky was lying next to him, breathing peacefully, but did not stretch out his hand and, after a moment or two, Adamsky got up from his bed, folded his things and moved to another bed, closer to his comrades.

Yoshke remained lying there, with a weight upon his heart. For him, this was his first night away from home, even though it was now many months since he had been snatched from his bed in Motal. He felt as forsaken as a dismembered body part: useless and without hope. He had loved Pesach Avramson like a brother, and he could even live with Patrick Adamsky. But now he felt overcome by a vertiginous fear, and he struggled for breath.

Every person knows, and Yoshke Berkovits knew this better than anyone, that incontinence means the loss of one's dignity. This is why you Jews bless your God with this strange prayer, one that we would never dare to utter in church, praising him for having made man with orifices and cavities. I admire you for that. But that night, a new chasm opened in Yoshke Berkovits' heart, from which no tears or secretions flowed. It was filled only with a dull pain that extinguished his wish to live. The next morning, the inspector kicked him to work without breakfast, and after he had emptied the first few buckets of the morning, Yoshke let himself sink into a pit of shit, and lost consciousness.

Nose

Dear madam, now that we have finished with the eyes, we are moving along to the nose. Considering that shit has been our main topic of discussion up to this point, we could also have worked our way through your portrait from the bottom up, if you know what I mean. But a painting can follow a story in an uncanny way: let the eyes smell, the nose see, the mouth hear, and the ears talk. On to the snout, then, the centre of the face.

Yoshke Berkovits is still in deep shit, and not figuratively. His rebellion ended in a foul pit, and if not for one of the sergeants, Sergey Sergeyev by name, our story would have ended there too.

Sergeant Sergey Sergeyev hated meat. He ate inordinate amounts of bread and potatoes instead, which is why his bowel movements were particularly slow and painful. That morning, Sergeant Sergeyev was crouching for yet another agonising defecation when he spotted a hand poking out of the hole below him. He immediately called for help to pull the body out. "He's still breathing! To the infirmary, quick! Maybe there's still a chance!"

Forgive me, dear madam, but it is often better to turn one's back and shut one's eyes on such occasions. A sergeant is crouching and groaning, his body stiff and tense, strained to the limit. Not a glorious moment, by all accounts. He sees a hand jutting out of a hole. He can just as easily keep on at his business, knowing for a fact that the Czarist army will not notice the absence of such a soldier. No-one will come looking for him, and some day he will be added to the list of those missing in action. But Sergeant Sergey Sergeyev did not turn his back, nor did he turn a blind eye. Instead, he took the unconscious Yoshke Berkovits to the camp doctor, Dmitry Yakunin.

Dr Yakunin used to say that he could cure any curable illness. He had other tautologies that seemed just as pregnant with meaning: he could only do what he could do, and in such situations all one could hope for was what one could hope for, always ending with the quip that one should expect the best and prepare for the worst. The patients, irrespective of whether they got better or worse, were perfectly happy with his treatment methods, because he made sure they received the two things they cared about the most: a chaplain and drugs.

The doctor allowed Father Alyosha Kuzmin to enter his infirmary, but would not let other priests anywhere near his patients. He thought that all other clergymen were hypocrites. They wandered around the tent, dangling their annoying bells and flashing their icons about, and they always told everyone exactly what they wanted to hear. Father Kuzmin on the other hand would slam the truth in the patients' faces. Between his gorging on either vodka or olives (why did he like olives so much? Only the

267

Devil knows), he would pass along the beds, spitting out olive stones and cursing every patient he met. "Why should you be cured? You stinking bastard! You've been sinful and reckless your entire life . . . And you? You lowlife! Why should Christ remember you, you pathetic gambler!" For some reason, the patients loved him. Perhaps because he told the truth, or because he was just as depraved as they were.

Dr Yakunin administered medicines strictly in inverse proportion to their necessity. He kept chloroform from the dying and let them writhe in agony, whereas patients overcoming mild infections were given sedatives in high doses. Surprisingly, this absurd system worked because all his patients tried to show signs of recovery, to obtain prescriptions if nothing else. This spared Dr Yakunin from having to deal with the usual charades of screams and groaning, and his clinic was consequently an oasis of tranquillity.

Therefore, dear madam, you can imagine the reaction of Dr Yakunin when he first laid eyes on the filthy, unconscious form of Private Yoshke Berkovits. He immediately instructed the nurses to put him in the worst bed in the infirmary. Two of the bed's legs were stacks of bricks, and it was located under a large hole in the tent's canvas, which let in the rain. The doctor gave orders to clean the body of this human wreck, in preparation for his imminent interment, and they left him lying naked on the bed covered by nothing but a thin blanket. The doctor invited Father Alyosha Kuzmin, who spat two olive pits at the boy and observed, "He's a *żyd*, can't you see? He's going straight to hell!" As Private Yoshke was delirious with a raging fever, Dr Yakunin had no intention of wasting any medicines on him.

Yet Yoshke Berkovits had one advantage, madam, a remedy that few patients are lucky enough to have. Every morning, noon and evening, Sergeant Sergey Sergeyev came to see him. This long-serving soldier had seen it all in his day. As the adjutant to many a general he had roamed half the world. He had met dark-haired, almond-eyed women on the steppes of Mongolia and stocky men in Yerevan. He had watched thousands of Russians making pilgrimage to Jerusalem and sleeping under the open sky near the Holy Sepulchre. He had been witness to the sadistic troops who had pillaged and raped, and the soldiers who had shown mercy in the most dire of situations. There was nothing he did not know about human nature, and he had been led to conclude that virtue is overrated. For the most part, he maintained, people who are taught to hate will hate, and people with their backs against the wall will do whatever they are told. Reality is not shaped by the choice between right or wrong, but by opting for the necessary and the expedient. And yes, there are always exceptions to this rule, but what of it?

There was one thing Sergeant Sergey Sergeyev never had a taste of, dear madam: the love of a family. He joined the army before he had an opportunity to marry, and the career he chose did not leave him much time for such trifles. He never had children, at least none that he knew about, and his parents died before he was twenty-two. You, on the other hand, are clearly a family person. You exude the confidence that only a mother can have, even if right now your husband and children are far away. This raises an intriguing question: did you part from your family willingly or under duress, out of choice or necessity? We will let that one go for now.

Dear madam, Sergeant Sergey Sergeyev had always wished he had a son. And when the opportunity arose, he didn't get his perfect choice. At almost thirteen, Yoshke was not a young boy anymore. His body was broken, his spirit was crushed, and his Polish and Russian non-existent. But you can't choose your family, and so Sergeant Sergey Sergeyev duly paid his visits and fought for his "son's" rights. Dr Yakunin disliked having visitors walking around his infirmary. He told Sergey Sergeyev that he might as well grind water, because the boy was a lost cause. Father Kuzmin hinted to the sergeant that he would be better off adopting a sap-head of his own ilk rather than taking a killer of Christ under his wing. But Sergey Sergeyev was not impressed by their insinuations and warnings, and demanded that Yoshke be given a proper bed.

The sergeant spent hours and hours at Berkovits' side, dear madam. Perhaps you are thinking that his tender words and other such nonsense helped Yoshke recover? You are quite wrong. It was what Sergeyev did for Yoshke, rather than what he said to him, that saved his life. Before I go on, though, allow me to pour you a cup of rum from the barrel here at the back, which I've been eyeing for a while. If I had to guess, I'd say this is dark rum, the Father's favourite, the brown liqueur that saved the life of your so-called uncle.

Yes, indeed, Yoshke Berkovits is often considered to be nothing more than a worthless drunk by those who fail to understand why he always has a barrel of rum within reach. But he is not a drunk, and he is certainly not worthless. He learned from his adoptive father, Sergeant Sergey Sergeyev, a secret that has kept him healthy to this very day: that the special qualities of rum lie in that which it is not. When Yoshke Berkovits first heard the sergeant's explanation, he thought that his delirium had returned. His adoptive father, however, forced the drink down his throat, refusing to relent even when his son spilled the contents of his stomach on his pillow. The sergeant told him, "You will learn to drink rum whether you like it or not, because the qualities of the rum lie in that which it is not." If you can believe it, the boy was better within a week.

Rum is a rotten, extremely strong spirit. Its sweet taste soon turns bitter, and it paralyses the stomach for hours at a time. Drink it on a hot summer day and you will burn; comfort yourself with it in the snow and you will freeze. Its qualities lie in that which it is not: in other words, in the fact that it is not water.

Why shouldn't it be water, you ask? Or rather, what is so bad about water? Well, my dear madam, we draw our water from contaminated wells, and at that time terrible plagues were raging across our poor continent. Even Florence Nightingale, if you've ever heard of her – the celebrated nurse who served enemy armies in the Crimean War – even she lost half her patients. Therefore, dear lady, anyone who drank rum could abstain from water, and this is why the spirit's remedial qualities stem from that which it is not.

Yoshke Berkovits had survived the latrines for months, but the Yoshke Berkovits of that period had been as rebellious as they come, and as long as he had Pesach Avramson by his side, he could have endured torture by the Bashi-Bazouk if he had to. The separation from Pesach, however, had left him dejected and apathetic, and even a small dose of contaminated water would have easily wiped him out. So it is a good thing that he didn't drink any water – under Sergeant Sergey Sergeyev's close supervision, which I can only describe as an act of kindness, even if I do not fully understand what that word means. You see, madam, from the moment Yoshke Berkovits came to his senses, it became clear that the distance between him and the sergeant could not be bridged. The sergeant was almost sixty, a sombre recluse, who quickly realised that he would not get a loving son out of this affair. Berkovits' Jewish descent, that is, his foreignness, was obvious to him from the very start, and they could barely communicate in a language they both knew. Sergeyev was never even properly thanked for his care, because the boy was completely devastated at being saved. During each visit, Berkovits would rise from his bed, mostly as a sign of respect. He would sip a cup of rum with Sergeyev and then lie down again with a steely face. The sergeant kept coming to the infirmary nonetheless, because the body, dear madam, is prepared to make great concessions for the sake of intimacy. Sergeyev not only kept Yoshke company. He refused to let him slide back into melancholy and started teaching him Polish. When Yakunin and Kuzmin asked him to leave the pitiful boy alone, he mocked them by saying that people of merit would never use the word "pitiful", the most awful word in the dictionary, an infuriating combination of ignorance and arrogance.

"What nonsense," Father Kuzmin said and rang his bell to catch the other patients' attention. "Where would we be today without Christ, the Son of God, whose entire gospel is based on love and pity?"

"Love and pity?" the sergeant said with a chuckle. "They are two opposites. How can you pity someone you love? You cannot feel close to someone you call pitiful." Noticing that the patients were not inclined to favour Father Kuzmin's position, Dr Yakunin put an end to the exchange.

Know, dear madam, that Sergeant Sergey Sergeyev was true to his word. He did not pity Yoshke Berkovits and he did not go easy on him. When the boy grew stronger, the sergeant accompanied him on walks around the courtyard every morning and evening, and, before long, he had Yoshke transferred from the infirmary to his private tent, against Dr Yakunin's advice, and despite the warnings of Father Kuzmin, who was sure that another month in the infirmary would be enough to convince the heretic to join the Orthodox Church. Sergeyev changed the boy's name to Zizek Breshov, a name with the closest ring to Yoshke Berkovits he could come up with, and made sure this change was registered on all his official documents. For his part, Zizek did not show any sign of concession or objection. He was utterly crushed and no longer had any reason to live. He couldn't care less if his name was Zizek or Yoshke.

Did I not already speak of kindness, dear madam? Indeed I did. I have tried to explain it in different ways. I have described Sergeant Sergey Sergeyev's need for family. I have told you about his loneliness. I have noted his tenacious and resilient opposition to Yakunin and Kuzmin. I have shown that he did not gain much from this affair, because his adopted son was not ready to have a father. But can any of this explain the sergeant's decision to bequeath Zizek Breshov all of his assets?

I can tell you are surprised, dear madam, and luckily, I have finished drawing your nose, which now has a slight twitch. We will begin drawing your lips at once, but we had better take a moment to collect ourselves first. To put your mind at ease, I will only say that the sergeant's "assets" amounted to a few dozen roubles, not exactly a fortune. The sergeant had squandered almost his entire pay on women and rum. To the acquaintances who pleaded with him to put aside money for rainy days, he explained that he always kept a few coins in his pocket for an overcoat and an umbrella.

Dear madam, I was not referring to money when I mentioned assets, but rather to words, that is, to languages – Polish, Russian, French and English – the four languages that any skilled adjutant would do well to master. Every morning, Zizek Breshov woke up to the "inheritance" that was bequeathed to him by way of a strict training regime. There was not enough time to teach each language separately, so instead he learned common phrases and essential words in all four languages simultaneously. What he did with this knowledge was up to Zizek, but, for his part, the sergeant made sure that by breakfast-time the boy had learned twenty new sentences in Russian, Polish, French and English.

Zizek studied without enthusiasm, memorising each day sentences such as "What would you like me to bring you?" and "Where would you like to go?" in four different tongues. He had only one condition, or a request, rather: there was another boy in the infirmary called Imre Schechtman, who was lying in a corner burning with fever and coughing out his lungs. If Sergeyev could spare some rum and rescue him from Dr Kuzmin's death-trap, Zizek could use the company of a fellow student. The sergeant agreed to his request, because he saw it as a positive sign of life. And so Sergeyev found himself tutoring two young boys.

Unfortunately, the rum had a powerful effect on the eight-year-old Ignat Shepkin, the boy formerly known as Imre Schechtman. His head lolling, dozing off throughout the day, he was only able to stay awake for two hours at a stretch. The sergeant's fury over the feeble boy was met with a foolish smile and rosy cheeks.

Sergey Sergeyev had no choice but to punish him. He pulled a pendant out of his pocket, which housed a miniature of Nikolai the First, the Iron Czar, and told Ignat Shepkin to copy the portrait with utmost precision. The slightest deviation from the Iron Czar's features led to the drawing paper being snatched away and thrown into the waste-basket, and meant that the boy would have to start all over again. A week later, Ignat could draw the Czar's moustache, high forehead, curly locks and noble gaze with admirable precision, thereby earning himself some sleep after a sip of yet another bittersweet cup of rum. Within a year, Zizek Breshov could hold conversations in four languages, at which point Sergeyev decided that it was time for his protégé to learn about eloquence and refinement. He pulled Pushkin's *Eugene Onegin* out of his "library", which was no more than a charred munitions crate, and instructed Zizek to memorise Tatyana's letter to Onegin.

Dear madam, no true Russian will be able to suppress his tears on reading this letter. Our friend Zizek did not remain unaffected either. Who was he thinking about, when he read those lines of verse? His mother? Possibly. An old flame from his hometown? Perhaps.

Unlike Zizek, who memorised his Pushkin from dawn to dusk, Ignat Shepkin barely opened his mouth. Instead, he learned to draw the Iron Czar so accurately that at night he suffered terrible nightmares for fear that he had deviated from the stately features of Nikolai the First, which meant that he had to start drawing them all over again.

Such was the legacy of Sergeant Sergey Sergeyev, and it is impossible to overstate the value of his bequests to his two adopted sons. The rest of the story will make this clear.

Mouth

Forgive me, dear madam, but my watch tells me that it is already gone midnight, and yet your travelling companions have not come looking for you. Most strange. What kind of companionship is this? I beg your pardon, the rum makes me inquisitive.

The eyes, as they say, are the windows to the soul. And if, as I have said before, our main concern here is not with the soul but with the flesh, one might say that the mouth is the window to the body. Granted, the mouth crushes our food and enables us to yawn, satisfying two distinctly corporeal needs. One might add, though, that it is also used to kiss and to speak: two distinct needs of the soul. What should we make of that, then?

You should know, dear madam, that there is no greater danger than the separation of a body from its soul. For, if you are indeed Yoshke Berkovits' niece, as a Jew you have surely encountered goyim – or whatever you call us – from time to time, who looked at you with contempt. The goyim claim that you are foul and spread diseases. Some are convinced that you are soulless ghouls. A loving mother will touch her children's foreheads and warn them of the diabolical Jew, scheming to snatch them away. What should we make of that, then?

But do you know why they hate you so much? Do you have any idea why I hate you? They will talk about your betrayal of the Son of God until the cows come home. They will say that it is a war between the two faiths, citing their envy of your financial success, or fretting about your estrangement and alienation. But let me tell you my opinion as a painter: it could not be clearer to me that they see in you their worst traits, their innermost characteristics. The Polish peasant believes that he is far more just and generous than he really is, while the Russian aristocrat thinks of himself as brave and stately, no doubt to an excess. Neither of them would ever admit that they too suffer from fear and loneliness and alienation and greed and lust, and above all, that they also have bodies made of flesh and blood: wrinkled, flaccid, ugly and vile. They are not as sublime as they like to think, which is why they place on your backs the load they try so hard to be rid of themselves. The paradox of it all is that they hate in you the very same things that keep haunting them.

I made this preamble because the story of Yoshke Berkovits is the story of the body. I am not talking here about the body as a mass of organs and bones. I am talking here about a creature that understands that its humanity is intractably an expression of its body, because without a body its humanity could not be expressed. I am talking here about a boy who began life in the deepest shit. Not in faeces, defecation or excretions, dear madam (and forgive me for repeating this foul language over and over again), but in shit. Yes, shit! One doesn't need to be a scholar to follow with one's eyes that brownish lump that emerges between one's legs every day. One doesn't have to be a genius to know that it is thanks to this lump that you – your loves, feelings, words, notions and reflections – exist. No point in going to university to learn about human nature if you cannot grant this much, or if such issues strike you as obscene and embarrassing. You must be crazy if you believe that wanting a hand to hold as you fall asleep is a matter for the mind. If you do not understand that it is the flesh that pines for warmth and intimacy at nightfall, you are a fool. If you have not realised that extending your hand one night and only grasping thin air will break your heart, then you have never lived. If you do not know that words can be as sharp as a knife, and not just figuratively, a real knife, then you do not know what words are. And if you no longer want to reach out to touch someone's hand heedless of the outcome, and you do not realise that your trembling body and broken heart prefer death to loneliness, then you may be dead already.

Now that we have got that straight, it will be easier to understand Zizek's progress through the ranks of the Czar's army.

The bequest he inherited from Sergeant Sergey Sergeyev turned out to be priceless. Most soldiers could not even write or read, and the few literates among them usually knew only Russian. Therefore, a prospective adjutant fluent in four languages after two years' training, even if he was a lowly private, was a sought-after commodity among the higher ranks. Naturally, Sergeant Sergey Sergeyev was well aware of this, which is why he trained up his adopted son to become the perfect aide-de-camp. And when the sergeant heard that a new regiment was being recruited for the region near the Danube, not far from Bucharest, he said the right words to the right people and Zizek Breshov, at the age of not-quite-fifteen, was promoted to corporal and rode north-west in the company of Ignat Shepkin. The sergeant registered Shepkin as a military artist, despite the fact that he could only draw the Iron Czar, thereby enabling him to join Zizek

Breshov on his way to the newly established unit under the command of Colonel Gregory Radzetsky.

Interlude

Since the mere mention of the name "Radzetsky the Terrible" is enough to make me shudder, perhaps we should pause the painting at this point to avoid spoiling the line of your lips. Contrary to popular opinion, dear madam, the painter's soul need not suffer unduly in order to capture the immortal, and neither madness nor muse are necessary for him to sketch the lips with utmost precision. A painter can be happy, or even elated, and still produce a worthy work of art. Therefore, in view of the emotional turmoil we are about to encounter in our story, allow me to set my brush aside for a little while, if you please. You may take the opportunity to relax, too.

Where did Gregory Radzetsky come from? No-one knows. Some say that he was the tenth son of a Yakut man from Siberia, a reindeer herder who forced his children to take the suicidal journey to join the army, even though their district was not required to send any cantonist recruits. Travelling thousands of miles, they crossed the Ural Mountains, enduring temperatures close to minus twenty, and then marched all the way to St Petersburg. Only two of the brothers made it, including Gregory, and rumour has it that they survived by feeding on their fallen brothers' flesh. Others dismiss this story altogether, arguing that both the distance and the climate would be impossible to overcome. Yet even those sceptics, having made the acquaintance of Radzetsky the Terrible, are prepared to grant that he may have partaken of a spot of fraternal cannibalism, even without the long walk.

And now for a riddle: over the hills and across the vale a black, double-headed eagle is laying eggs – the gift of God. What are those eggs? Well said, madam: potatoes. Catherine the Great and Pavel the First had tried to persuade their subjects to grow this nutritious bulb. But the Russians are a stubborn people, and they were convinced that potatoes were dangerous, toxic and malignant, implicated in a highly suspect conspiracy of the crown. Only the Iron Czar dared to impose his will on the empire's peasants. Overcoming stubborn resistance and even rebellion, he persuaded the muzhiks that the motherland's soil would be ideal for growing spuds. Later on they realised that no family can live on the *kartofl* alone.

Another story is probably as close as one can get to the truth about Gregory Radzetsky: it is said that he was the son of a penniless but patriotic farmer living near Kazan, who started growing potatoes like others in the region. The landlord from whom Radzetsky's father leased the land collected such high taxes that he was left without any profits. But like every true patriot, the father embraced his fate and thanked Mother Russia for letting him work, even without pay. He saw the cantonist conscription as a blessing more than a curse, a rare opportunity to make the ultimate sacrifice to show his dutifulness. To be sure, he did not want his sons to die. But if they were to die, it might as well be in battle, defending country and Czar.

In those days, the battles waged in the name of Russia's defence were really triggered by the empire's expansion into new markets, or by the need to quash local rebellions. Wars in Greece, the Caucasus, Persia and Turkey certainly did not serve to defend St Petersburg. Yet patriots, being patriots, tend to think that justice and their country's interests are one and the same. Being of such a mind, the young and enthusiastic Gregory Radzetsky joined the Imperial Infantry Corps.

Now a second riddle: an infantry platoon is ordered to take a hill. The hill is occupied by Ottoman soldiers with superior equipment and artillery. One officer says: "This is a suicidal mission

– we had better wait for support or create a diversion." Another officer says: "These are our orders, and we must follow them without question." Who do you think the Czarist army will promote? Will it be the wise, resourceful officer anticipating the outcome of the battle? Or will it be the obedient officer who would charge into the mouth of a volcano if so ordered? Well, you've guessed it, and do you know why? Because the Czar's army, dear madam, is built on discipline. Obedience means promotion. Following orders means honour. An officer is not measured by his victories or defeats; what matters the most is whether his soldiers march in straight lines, whether they report for duty well dressed and groomed, whether his marching band plays constantly, and whether his troops would ever dare to defect. The riddle about the hill, dear madam, is not hypothetical. Gregory Radzetsky, then a sergeant, took command over a platoon whose lieutenant reached the conclusion that their orders to storm the hill from the south meant suicide and that they should therefore outflank it from the north. Sergeant Gregory Radzetsky turned the other soldiers against the recalcitrant officer and led them uphill to their death, roaring, *"Ah! Che la morte!"* Only three survived – Radzetsky among them – from the thirty-man unit, and when they returned to camp, he was immediately made an officer.

In many ways, this was the right thing to do. Ever since the Napoleonic wars, the Russian high command had realised that they could only win a campaign if they persevered long enough and kept sending a steady flow of soldiers to the front line. Even if they lost troops in droves, more than any other army, and even if the vast majority of them died because of the miserable decisions of their superiors, because they abandoned the wounded and advanced without waiting for their lines of supply to catch up, the Czarist army would still have illiterate patriots in sufficient numbers to keep up their attacks. The war would be won by wearing down the other side, and the generals' blunders would be covered up when victory was declared. Do you know, dear madam, what was the most dangerous enemy of the Czar's soldiers back in those days? Do you think it was the courage of the Turks? Or the shrewdness of the Persian generals? Nothing of the sort. For every soldier killed in action, dozens of others would die of the plague, disease and injuries sustained away from the battle. Do you know why the soldiers did not dissent, dear madam? Well, just you try disobeying Gregory Radzetsky.

Radzetsky was in his element in the army. It permitted him to pass on to his troops the obedience and overwhelming sense of loyalty to the Czar that his upbringing had instilled in him. Back then, it was the officers' prerogative to flog soldiers, but Radzetsky considered it an obligation. Soldiers had to be flogged each and every week as long as they could not prove their innocence, and they not only had to prove their own innocence but also that of their comrades. Radzetsky's standard procedure was collective punishment. A defecting soldier knew that his entire squad would be taken to jail and that, because of him, each comrade would be flogged fifty times every day. A marksman knew that if he did not charge to certain death in battle, he would be hung by his ankles in the scorching heat until he begged the Angel of Death to carry him away. One's sense of duty to the Czar was absolute.

Gregory Radzetsky's rapid rise up the ranks can be attributed to his contribution to the suppression of the Hungarian revolution. A regiment from the Czar's army was called in to assist the Austrian Empire in crushing the uprising, and more than eight thousand of the infantrymen who crossed the Carpathian Mountains were defeated by the superior Hungarian forces. A mere two thousand Russian troops survived, having escaped either death or captivity. Radzetsky's platoon did not fare much better than the rest of the regiment, but his tactics caught the attention of the army's top brass. At first, the generals found the stories about him hard to believe, but as the rumours persisted they left little room for doubt. For one thing, the young lieutenant did not allow his soldiers to evacuate their wounded comrades after battle. In his eyes, being wounded meant one had failed to perform one's duty; it was a mark of mediocrity whose bearers were left suspended between the only desirable outcomes: victory or death. A wounded soldier also strained the unit's logistics. A casualty might put healthy soldiers at risk, and, what is more, the country would be required to spend a fortune on the recovery of a man who might never return to the battlefield, which was tantamount to ransacking the Czar's coffers. Instead, if wounded, a brave carabineer was expected not to indulge in self-pity but to rejoin the ranks and carry on fighting, thereby making his death worthwhile. Indeed, dear madam, Radzetsky forbade his troops from evacuating the wounded, and in principle, however ridiculous it may sound, he forbade them to be wounded at all. Brothers in arms were forced to watch their comrades sprawled on the ground bleeding (the traitors), moaning in pain or taken captive (the cowards), either suffering a slow death or being murdered and robbed by the enemy. Radzetsky maintained that the wounded could have died promptly and spared themselves the ordeal, and few dared to disagree.

Then there was a sensitive religious point: Lieutenant Radzetsky refused to evacuate dead bodies. He declared that removing the corpses would crush morale, because such palpable encounters with death make it extremely difficult to deny its imminence. And this denial is essential for a soldier's ability to function on the battlefield.

Furthermore, as you may have deduced from what has been said thus far, Radzetsky believed that an officer should not strive to be liked by his soldiers. Soldiers do not charge to their deaths out of love, and they do not keep their formation out of affection. A soldier should know that obeying orders is his only chance of survival.

And finally, Radzetsky did not care for his platoon's camaraderie. Soldiers should not be friends with one another. Discipline in battle, as we already know, should be based on obedience and duty alone. In short, dear madam, Radzetsky did not demand from his soldiers anything that he did not demand from himself. And all that he demanded from himself amounted to steely discipline, boundless fervour and a heroic death brought about by obedience.

The young lieutenant spared nothing in his attempt to subdue the Hungarian rebels. He demolished his unit completely in pointless ambushes near Hermannstadt. Then he attacked mountain passes in the Carpathians from weak positions, drawing an entire Russian company into the debacle. The force commander was killed and it seemed only natural that Radzetsky should take his place. But instead of retreating to Walachia and letting his unit lick its wounds, Radzetsky sent his soldiers on a desperate outflanking manoeuvre and, thanks to an orienteering blunder, led his troops directly into the enemy's main line of fire. The army commanders watched the new major in admiration: had he attained any notable achievements? No. Had he caused unnecessary losses? Without a doubt. Had he proved to be an impressive tactician? Not really. Well, let's keep an eye on this promising officer. And why? Very simple: there had been no defections, the soldiers marched in impeccable formations, the military band blew their trumpets until their last breath, the soldiers charged to their deaths without question, and in a remarkable display of logistical frugality, the division had been spared the need to take care of either wounded or dead soldiers. Give us a thousand more Radzetskys and we will set out to conquer the British Isles – even if twenty Russians will die for every British soldier.

As you can imagine, dear madam, if Sergeant Sergey Sergeyev had known that he was sending his adopted sons to this madman, he would have done everything within his power to prevent such a mistake from happening. But when he heard that a "new" regiment was being set up not far from Bucharest, he did not know that this regiment's history went as far back as Catherine the Great. Nor did he know that most of its soldiers, the adjutant included, had perished in one or other of Gregory Radzetsky's misadventures. So it was that our protagonist, who is today called "the Father" and back then was a fifteen-year-old apprentice, reported to Radzetsky's unit. At his side rode Ignat Shepkin, who was not yet eleven, and possessed no useful skills save his talent for serial productions of the Iron Czar's portrait. Now I can finally continue drawing your mouth; just the name of this duo, Zizek and Ignat, is enough to calm me.

Mouth – continued

Radzetsky was very excited at their arrival. His regiment had not yet been allocated a new adjutant, let alone a military artist. He immediately ordered Private Shepkin to paint a portrait of him poring over maps of the Danube. What did Shepkin do? Just as he always did. He painted the Iron Czar, covering Nikolai the First's receding hairline with tufts of hair, and adding the brown bandana that Radzetsky kept knotted around his own neck.

Dear madam, let me tell you something: people like nothing more than to look at a flattering portrait of themselves. Sergeant Sergey Sergeyev knew what he was doing when he punished Ignat Shepkin by forcing him to copy the Czar's portrait. Suddenly, Gregory Radzetsky saw himself – the son of muzhiks from a village near Kazan who had risen to the rank of colonel with neither title nor ties – as he had never seen himself before. He looked at the painting of his dull face – elongated skull, rough skin, brown eyes, dishevelled hair, nose twitching in contempt and lips glistening with foam – and saw the face of an aristocrat. The green eyes, groomed moustache, trimmed sideburns, slightly high forehead, perhaps, and somewhat bulky chin, all formed the image of a model officer, a man of honour and duty.

Radzetsky examined his portrait for a long time, and Zizek noticed that his eyes seemed to soften. Later, Zizek would realise that this was the first time that Radzetsky had not seen himself as the illiterate son of a worthless potato grower. Now he was a learned officer, a true-blue member of the nobility! A bona fide artist has painted my portrait, he was thinking to himself . . . Gregory Radzetsky, this is you, this is you without a shadow of a doubt.

"Can you march?" Radzetsky asked Private Shepkin.

"Yes, sir."

"Can you continue to paint even if shells fall around you and bullets whistle past you?"

"Yes?" Shepkin hesitated. He pulled himself together. "Yes."

"Do you know any goddamned words other than 'yes'?"

"No, sir." Shepkin wasn't sure what he was supposed to say, but the tone indicated that this question had right and wrong answers.

"Private, you do realise that you have just contradicted your-self?"

"Yes, sir."

"Does it not bother you?"

"No, sir."

"Excellent. The job is yours! Next time make the hairline lower. Understood?"

Shepkin nodded, even though he was not sure if he did.

"And try not to give me a double chin, goddammit. And you,"

Radzetsky turned to Zizek and spat through the gap between his front teeth, "what the hell are you doing here?"

Zizek began listing his impressive adjutant skills: he could manage the rostering of men on duty and on leave, survey the wounded and optimise deployment. The colonel was unimpressed. In his regiment, there was no need for a roster. Soldiers were counted three times a day, and if each tally was the same as the one before, their names did not matter one bit. Radzetsky's troops were never granted leave, and wounded soldiers, as we know, were to be avoided at all costs. "In other words," he said to Zizek, "your skills are useless. Go to the armoury and have someone teach you how to operate a musket. Then report to one of the goddamned platoons."

Zizek was not surprised by the outcome of his interview, even though it had not gone according to plan. He made no mention of his fluency in four languages, which could have spared him from becoming a rifleman in Gregory Radzetsky's regiment. Two days later he reported to his new platoon, and, like every other junior soldier, he was ordered to polish the soldiers' boots and serve them their meals. It is hard to blame Radzetsky's troops, dear madam, for forcing young Zizek to serve their bread and tinned meat wearing a prostitute's ribbon on his head. These soldiers faced almost certain death, despair was a constant feature of their lives, their separation from earthly temptations was near, and they were prepared to believe in the afterworld more than ever before. The only way they could feel better about themselves was to debase and humiliate their inferiors, relishing the fact that the fate of these boys was even worse than their own. Mind you, Zizek was not the only one who was left without a modicum of dignity. Every other new recruit entered the tents either as a butler, a shoeshine, or to carry out tasks that it is best not to mention in the presence of a lady.

Your lips are pursed with horror, dear madam. Pray relax, this will not help me portray your hardy, tenacious face. I wouldn't want you to think that the story I am telling you is one of only despair and submission. Not at all. The body is never defeated, and even the Father managed to find a way to extract himself from his predicament. Although it didn't happen overnight. In the camp by the Danube, Zizek suffered humiliation for months at the hands of Gregory Radzetsky's regiment.

Do you know, dear madam, what is the soldier's worst enemy? No, not hunger, thirst or fatigue. Neither nostalgia nor death. Soldiers are prepared for these well in advance. Even if such hindrances are unpleasant, a solution can always be found, except for death, of course, which is the ultimate solution for everything else. The answer is "the cold", dear madam. Yes, yes, the cold. Anyone who has ever worn an army uniform will tell you this. While the heat can be obnoxious, the cold is sheer agony. You try to protect yourself from it, you curl up and summon your defences, you wear every layer of clothing you've got, even your helmet when the cannons are silent. You cover your ears and block your nose. You'd give anything for a sheepskin coat and a mongoose fur. But if the cold is determined enough, if it finds a loophole and reaches your skin, it will penetrate your flesh and nest in your bones no matter what you do. As long as you lack the means to buy a fur coat, you will find yourself, as Zizek did, huddled with a few other boys for a pointless ambush on the Danube in peacetime, your body shivering, your bones angry, your bowels groaning, shaking and hurting all over. These are the moments when the body is drained of its last drop of strength, dear madam, when the mind can think of nothing but the freezing cold. You would sell your own mother for a mug of tea, your children for a steaming bowl of soup, and you would set fire to your own home for a hot bath. At moments like these the heart comes undone.

This is when young soldiers, who are usually indifferent and reticent and don't have fur coats, allow themselves to become poets.

A private shares a memory of a day like any other: sitting at the dining table in his home in Yaroslav, his father serving chicken soup, his brothers exchanging kicks under the table. The story flows without much happening, and then suddenly his comrades are muffling their sobs, releasing dams of tearless sorrow and boundless longing. Another soldier says, "I wish I could write to them," and the storyteller says, surprised, "Why would you want to write to my family?" The soldiers exchange smiles and thank the Lord for this moment of grace that makes them feel human again. Emotion breaks through the icy crust of obedience and duty, making them recognise their love for each other, their brotherhood, and the consolation they share. Then Zizek says, "I can write that letter for you."

Everyone is silent. The older soldiers do not take the opportunity to punish this clever-clogs daring to condescend to the illiterates in the group. Normally, there is nothing that riflemen detest more than learned people, who think that sitting in libraries makes them wise, and yet Zizek's offer is not ridiculed. Instead, the older soldiers reverently turn to him to make appointments for letter-writing, bickering over who will go first, and for how long, suddenly fighting between themselves instead of against the enemy.

And so Zizek became the most indispensable soldier of his platoon. His comrades took his rifle away and replaced it with quill and paper. In utmost secrecy, he began writing one letter after another for the older soldiers. After midnight, barely able to keep his eyes open, he tried his best to do some letter-writing for the new recruits as well. Before long, Zizek even started offering editorial advice. "Instead of 'say hello to the children', how about 'please tell the children that a day doesn't go by without my thinking of them'?"

The soldier dictating the letter would hesitate. "Does that sound better to you?"

"The meaning is the same," Zizek would reply, "but the wording is more idiomatic."

"Idiomatic?"

"Yes, idiomatic."

"Well, if it means the same thing then let's be idio-whatever."

Zizek would tell another soldier, "'I miss sitting in my chair by the fireplace' isn't bad, but perhaps you could say, 'I miss watching you as I sit in my chair by the fireplace'."

The soldier would grow defensive. "Don't you think it's embarrassing for a man to write like that?"

"Why should it be embarrassing? You'd be saying the same thing – don't you miss your chair by the fireplace?"

"Of course I do."

"And what do you see when you sit in that chair?"

"My wife standing in the kitchen."

"Well, then it's one and the same."

"So it's not embarrassing?"

"Of course not."

Some soldiers did not seek out Zizek and did not wait in the queue for his help. Perhaps their letters were too personal. Perhaps they feared that others would overhear their innermost secrets. Who knows. In any event, Zizek had met one of them before, and the two of them avoided each other's gaze whenever their paths crossed in the camp. The soldier in question was a young sergeant who had joined Radzetsky's regiment only recently, but had already built up a reputation for courage and intrepidness. His name was Patrick Adamsky, and Zizek's heart seemed to stop every time he walked past him. Of broad torso and burning amber eyes, Adamsky subjected his subordinates to a rigorous discipline that made them admire him all the more.

Zizek hoped that at some point Sergeant Adamsky would want to dictate a short letter to his aunt, Mirka Avramson. But Adamsky never approached Zizek or addressed him. Instead, he chose to send money in wordless envelopes from the Bucharest post office.

Adamsky, however, was an anomaly. Everyone else flocked to Zizek as though he was the Messiah. Dear madam, the winter months of the year eighteen hundred and fifty-two were the happiest that Russian soldiers' wives had known since the birth of the Russian empire. Not only were they fortunate enough to have dutiful husbands and reliable breadwinners for their families, but their men also turned out to be sensitive poets attuned to the nuances of the feminine mind. However, this proved to be a mixed blessing. Before, the soldiers' wives had believed that their loneliness was a form of sacrifice on a par with that of their husbands, and told their neighbours that it was an honour and a duty to bear this burden, even as they secretly resented having to raise children on their own and had affaires with men of lesser courage but closer proximity than their husbands. And now, suddenly, these women wanted their husbands back, and for all they cared the whole Russian army could fall apart.

You might ask yourself, dear madam, how could a fifteen-year-old write such affecting letters? What could he have known about love and women, how could he have had the nerve to correct a father's expression of longing for his children? True, he knew little about women and he certainly had no children of his own. But he did know a fair bit about longing, about pain and about missing your home. Add this to his Pushkin-inspired prose, and behold! Any one of these elements alone would have sufficed. But Zizek had it all. Dear lady, those letters were masterpieces.

At his age, had he not been in the army, Zizek would have married a damsel from his own town. Thus, as he drafted the soldiers' letters, he revelled in the life that should have been his, which is to say, the life of Yoshke Berkovits. He did not write to a sergeant's wife in Kiev or to a hussar's children in Yaroslav; he wrote to Mina Gorfinkel from Motal, whose eyes he had sometimes caught when they met at the market, although Zizek had never been sure whether they really had exchanged glances, or if he had imagined it. You see, dear madam, after Patrick Adamsky left, and Pesach Avramson and the town of Motal dissolved altogether, the letters Zizek Breshov wrote were the only thing that kept Yoshke Berkovits alive. As he wrote, Zizek Breshov conjured up Yoshke Berkovits the way he had never been and never would be. He described him at his betrothal and on his wedding day, imagined him on his wedding night. He wrote about his frolics with his children, he conjured an image of himself as an authoritative and confident man, soft and sensitive, dependable and brave. Inspired by Tatyana's letters to Onegin, he wrote imagining himself sitting in the one place he would never reach: his home.

Once a year, Zizek Breshov saw Rabbi Schneerson of the Society for the Resurrection of the Dead, who would bring him a letter from his mother, Leah Berkovits. Zizek would scrutinise every inch of the envelope. The paper was unfamiliar, the stamp strange, and the Hebrew script denoting his name, Yoshke Berkovits, might as well have been a cryptogram. Zizek had not forgotten his Yiddish, but he failed to understand what he was reading. There were words such as "my boy", or "my *zissale*", or "Mamaleh is here", which Zizek read over and over again, trying to grasp their meaning. He could not bring himself to write letters to his real home. He was only capable of using his quill to create his imaginary life.

And what was it about that home? What was the thing that Zizek managed to convey in all the letters he wrote for others that touched the regiment's wives so deeply? What was the distilled essence of these letters, common to any manner of love and all relationships between husband and wife, that stirred so many hearts? Well, it had nothing to do with essence or relationships, distillation or purification. The opposite was true. Zizek Breshov wrote about such boring and stale minutiae that the soldiers had every reason to punch him in the face when he suggested, for example, that their letters should mention a kettle.

"A kettle?" a soldier would ask, puzzled.

"A kettle," Zizek would insist. The urge to resurrect Yoshke Berkovits with words inspired Zizek to visualise life together with Mina Gorfinkel down to the smallest detail. The kettle, which he imagined to be cast iron with a spout shaped like an elephant's trunk, portended idyllic moments: a couple sipping tea and enjoying delectable *lekach* sponge cake. Or, as he wrote letters for a young father, he would imagine an infant waking up crying in the middle of the night, and one of its parents putting on the kettle to make porridge. In yet another letter, busy parents would exchange smiles at not having a moment to spare for afternoon tea. Zizek could even feel the tea's warmth, his mouth watering at the imagined taste of the cake melting on his tongue.

The riflemen knew not to interrupt Zizek as he wrote, even if he described a heathen comrade walking to mass, arm in arm with his wife, or expressed a father's regret at not being able to look in on his sleeping children, when the father in question would never have done such a thing. For Zizek, it was paramount that they wrote these things in their letters. The soldiers liked his way of describing them, not minding that he merged them, momentarily, with the lives of Yoshke and Mina Berkovits.

Would it surprise you, dear madam, if I told you that Radzetsky's headquarters was suddenly flooded with requests for leave? Can you imagine a battle-thirsty major being ordered one morning to look up his troops' entitlements, because the high command has received complaints about soldiers who have not been home in more than two years, and now this major has to take into consideration the servicemen's needs, goddammit?

"Needs?" Radzetsky spat. "Entitlements?" he yelled as he entered the tent that served as his office. "I'll show them entitlements!"

Needless to say, Radzetsky did not consider the orders he received worth following. Every so often, Radzetsky believed, the high command's corruption and narrow-mindedness would yield orders that were either illegal or unmilitary. This is where the plain soldier, in this case a young major, must exercise his judgment and stand his ground. What was more, this problem of entitlements had to be eradicated once and for all, for which purpose Radzetsky needed to know what his soldiers were writing home. As Zizek Breshov's name came up whenever letter-writing was mentioned, Radzetsky summoned him to his office.

"They tell me you can read," Radzetsky growled.

"Yes, sir," Zizek replied, looking at Ignat Shepkin who was sitting next to the major, brush in hand. "In four languages."

"In four languages?" the officer chuckled. "Are you a goddamned intellectual?"

"No, sir."

"Are you a fucking clever-clogs?"

"No, sir."

"What are you, then?

"An adjutant, sir."

"A fucking adjutant?"

"Yes, sir."

"See this pile of letters?"

"Yes, sir."

"Take one of them and start reading, goddammit."

"Yes, sir."

The urgency of the request clouded Zizek's judgment. He took a letter and started reading it out loud: "My beloved Lyudmila, the harsh winter is about to end. Despite the chilblains on my foot I managed to survive. I can't wait for the day when I will return home and embrace you . . ."

"Stop!" Radzetsky cried. "Who sent this letter?"

Zizek did not answer, even though he knew very well it was Private Yevgeny Stravinsky writing to his wife Lyudmila and his children who were living near Kiev.

"Yevgeny Stravinsky?" Radzetsky seemed shocked by the name on the envelope, as if he knew who Stravinsky was and felt betrayed by his words. "Just wait 'til I embrace *him*," he hissed.

Forgive me, dear madam, but you must realise that this turn of events was most significant, historic, I would say. For at that moment, letter censorship in the Russian Imperial Army began. Zizek was transferred from his infantry squad and appointed as Radzetsky's chief adjutant. His main job was to read to the major the very letters he had written a few days earlier. Naturally, after Yevgeny Stravinsky's unfortunate case – the poor man was flogged to a pulp and never served in a battle unit again – Zizek would carefully adapt the letters as he read, to keep Radzetsky happy. And so, instead of "Winter is wearing me down", the line was read to the major as: "There's nothing like the cold to forge a man's soul." Instead of "I miss home", he read: "My dutiful submission to the command of the Czar and my officers has earned me the right to miss home." And instead of "I miss you all so much", or "I think about you all the time", he read: "The platoon is my family. I feel safe in its embrace, and think of you too." Before long it became clear, however, that the five hundred lashes the major ordered as punishments were not on account of the content of the letters so much as the sending of the letters in the first place, which he took to be a sign of weakness and cowardice.

Soon Zizek realised that the soldiers had better refrain from sending letters altogether. He advised the regiment's troops that until further notice they should send their families nothing but money, without even an accompanying note. He stopped writing their letters, and the regiment's correspondence shrank to almost nothing.

To tell the truth, Radzetsky, for his part, had become addicted to the hours of listening to the miserable letters of his soldiers, and he decided that it was unbecoming and cowardly of his soldiers to have given up letter-writing for fear of punishment. He issued a new order that henceforth every soldier must write to his family once a month, no fewer than four hundred words, on pain of a punishment even more severe than five hundred lashes.

Dear madam, in a few months the soldiers became walking corpses. Their backs were scarred from the whip, their spirits were crushed, and there was no escape. Regardless of what they dictated or Zizek wrote on their behalf, the outcome remained the same. Since Zizek had introduced them to letter-writing in the first place, their once-beloved comrade became an unbearable liability.

At this point, dear madam, it appears that several miracles happened. Before we get to the most important miracle, let me tell you about some small but noteworthy ones that preceded it.

Throughout history, humans have been convinced that their race, like all of nature, is compelled to fight for domination over others. Doesn't the lion hunt the gazelle? Doesn't the shark devour the seal? Are humans really any different? Just try refuting this argument – try saying, for example, that when the lion hunts he does not kill an entire herd, but rather a single gazelle. What of it, your interlocutor will reply. It makes no difference; lions are beasts but we are humans. Imagine that!

Still, gullible fools continue to join the army to serve God knows what purpose. Ask these soldiers why they are enlisting and they will lecture you about duty, love of country, defending their home, following courageous leaders and fighting against the enemy's evil despots. Clearly, however, they are not doing it for the sake of ideology alone. Most soldiers, unless they are complete idiots, are rewarded sizeably with respect or money, which makes their lives easier compared to most people. Even if their benefits were cut in half, they'd still get credit for fighting for an important cause.

But once every few centuries there is an awakening, or a disillusionment, if you will, and then all those principles are reconsidered. This is exactly what happened in Gregory Radzetsky's regiment. Over time, the soldiers began to think that their enlistment in the Czarist army was a sorry mistake, and that they would have been better off working on farms for greedy landlords, which would have spared them the floggings if nothing else. They started obsessing over weighty questions: were we really born just to hide in trenches and fight against other men, be they Turks, British or French? Is it truly in our nature to kill each other? What is it about the Turkish peasant that means we must hate him? Wouldn't it be better to reach out to him, become friends, perhaps trade with him, rather than pop a bullet in his forehead? Are we brought into this world only to end up on a battlefield which will soon be strewn with rivers of blood and mutilated corpses, some of them our own? Do the Czar's interests necessarily coincide with our own?

Dear madam, you can call me naive or think me mad, but I tell you that the soldiers in Radzetsky's regiment lost any desire to fight. However much he urged them on, his troops could no longer think of the men they faced in battle as enemies. What was more, they came to realise that the principles drilled into them during their training had been mere indoctrination, designed to instil fear and erect barriers between them and their enemies – indeed, between them and their humanity. Naturally, this new awareness could not be translated into concrete actions. Obedience was still essential for avoiding the gallows and for salvaging what was left of their mutilated backs. Therefore, they continued to trudge along, losing comrades by the dozens, by the hundreds, remaining bitter to the core, and free, if we can call it that, only in spirit.

It did not take long for the second miracle to occur. Or was it the same miracle as the first? It's hard to tell. Anyway, it was only to be expected that the soldiers would direct their anger at the famed letter-writer, Zizek Breshov, whose every ten words granted them one lash of the whip. As time went by, however, the soldiers asked Zizek not to modify their letters to suit Radzetsky's whims anymore, and instead to write what was really on their minds. Once they were free to think of things other than acts of bravery and had stopped imagining their breasts adorned with the St George's Cross, they were left only with life itself, or at least what remained of it. Since they were thrashed no matter what they did, Radzetsky no longer terrified them and they felt comfortable enough to follow Zizek's initial advice and return to the poetry of the first letters.

I have to fight back my tears, dear madam, thinking about the lines they wrote. I wish you could have read them. They contained memories of the future and plans for the past, laments of wasted lives and the last wishes of the not-yet-departed. The soldiers reminisced about the lost childhood that a boy abducted from his family could never have, and suddenly the realisation flashed through Zizek's mind that they were writing the lost life of Yoshke Berkovits. Indeed, as he wrote each letter, Zizek had to imagine himself in their homes, crossing the threshold, hearing the door creak, admiring the dinner table by the fireplace, wrapping his arm around his wife and hugging his five children.

At that point, Zizek decided that he could not remain an idle onlooker anymore: he, Zizek Breshov, adjutant, would save his comrades' lives. Mind you, this idea was nothing new. The desire to rescue the regiment from the scourge of its cruel commander was ingrained into each and every one of its troops. And if you can keep a secret, I can tell you that the idea of assassinating Radzetsky had come up more than once. There was no shortage of opportunities: they could have popped a bullet in his back during battle, or even poisoned his food. Zizek's plan, however, was entirely different, and, if I may add, it was entirely becoming of his profession in the army. Zizek wanted to save them by writing letters.

The idea came to him as he sat with Radzetsky, reading a letter he had randomly pulled out of a pile. It had come from St Petersburg and had been written by the wife of Sergeant Surikov, a tall, baby-faced grenadier known for his courage. Surikov's wife, Agata, had unknowingly inflicted great suffering on her beloved's back. In each letter, she wished for his imminent return and wondered when those "stupid battles", as she called them, would finally end. In previous letters she had told him that their only daughter, Yelena, wanted to marry her sweetheart, and the only thing the couple were waiting for was the consent of the "long-lost soldier", as Agata called her husband. Skimming through the letter, Zizek reported to Radzetsky that it was of no particular interest: other than their soon-to-be-married daughter, the wife wrote about her grandmother's good health, a play she had seen at the theatre and gossip from Kazan. Noticing that the officer's ears pricked up at the mention of "gossip from Kazan", Zizek decided to make his move.

"There is another letter here," he said, before Radzetsky could blurt out an order to punish Surikov, "from the wife of a Captain Venediktov, or something. Must be new to the regiment." Zizek's knees trembled as he uttered the invented name.

"Mmmm . . ." the major mumbled. "Venediktov? Of course . . . of course, I know him. A rotten sort. Well, what does she say?"

"It's quite interesting," said Zizek. "The family is from St Petersburg."

"Damned aristocrats?"

"Something like that," said Zizek. "Should I skip this one?"

"Did I say skip it, Breshov? Read the goddamned letter!"

My Darling,

The children and I send you our greetings and love, but I am very worried. The winds of change are upon Russia, and it is rumoured that the Czar fears confrontation with the other powers on the continent. Here in St Petersburg, they praise General Paskevich for foot-dragging all spring over the planned assault on the Ottomans, the lame duck of Europe. If you were here you wouldn't have believed your eyes: Paskevich received an explicit order to besiege Silistra, and responded by saying that he must have more troops and artillery. And how are his demands met here in the capital? With praise for his genius and foresight! Gorchakov hides with his forces on the banks of the Danube and hesitates to go into battle, and the princes want to promote him!

What a sad age we are living in, if we are no longer prepared to pay the price for Russia's honour; if we refuse to redeem the motherland with our blood! Will we become one of those pathetic countries that drown out their cavalry's cowardice with the roar of cannons? Will we hide away in our forts like effendis while the empire crumbles?

I tell you, my darling, at least in this household, this woman and these children know you are of a different stock.

Yours always,

Yelena Venediktova

For the first time in a long while, the major listened to the letter in silence. His expression was calm but his hands twitched.

"Quite a woman," he said, finally. "What did you say was her name?"

"Yelena Venediktova," replied Breshov, still trembling.

"St Petersburg?" Radzetsky inquired, curling the tips of his moustache.

"Yes," Breshov replied, now expecting to hear the punishment that would be meted out to the non-existent Captain Venediktov.

"Call in this Venediktov."

"Certainly. Once he returns from Bucharest, of course," Breshov said, his heart pounding.

"At the first opportunity," Radzetsky concurred, and sent his deputy out to call off the ambush he had ordered to be set up near the Danube.

Zizek experienced the rush of elation that washes over explorers or scientists when they discover one of God's secrets. Was it Mrs Venediktova's fictional letter that prompted Radzetsky's order to retract the ambush? Perhaps. It should not be ruled out, in any case. It was clear that Zizek had disoriented the major, and had done so intentionally. He had conflated a relentless patriot, a symbol of national pride, with St Petersburg's spineless aristocracy and, lo and behold, something about this item of gossip from the capital had penetrated Radzetsky's tough hide. The stronghold the major had worked so hard to build around his sense of duty had cracked, and something like "personal interest" now knocked at its gate. And finally, Zizek had found his own voice.

He no longer used Pushkin's words, or let Tatyana speak from his quill. There he was, writing in a new language of his own invention: the language of Mrs Venediktova. It had worked. Zizek had no choice but to try again.

The following week, another envelope arrived.

"A new letter from Mrs Venediktova! We already know she is loyal, let's move on," Radzetsky said, beaming. Then, trying and failing to stifle his curiosity, "What is she saying? Anything interesting?"

"Not really," Zizek said. "Petersburg and more Petersburg, and more noblemen afraid of fighting, and more gossip, and young generals quoting Sun Tzu's *The Art of War*, and what people are saying about Paskevich's injury, and . . ."

"Breshov!" Radzetsky cried. "We had better read this letter at once."

My Darling,
The children and I send you our greetings and love, but I am very worried. Russia is in danger. You soldiers are probably unaware of what goes on behind the scenes. You take orders: go there! Come here! But you do not know what people are saying in St Petersburg. They say that Paskevich faked his injury. Can you believe it? They say that he used a scratch he sustained from a shrapnel shell as an excuse to retire as a national hero and abandon Russia at her darkest hour, leaving her in the hands of cowards even worse than he.

I was at the theatre with my father and my aunt. We were sitting next to a few generals and some dissolute princes. They praised Paskevich's restraint and argued that Russia should discard its outdated doctrines. They said that officers who continue to storm enemy positions head-on and shed the blood of their troops should be reassigned to the Siberian border. Then they praised Sun Tzu – can you believe it? Now we are learning from the barbarians! – and admired advanced tactics that use the units' potential. Everyone here is obsessed with military pragmatism and sophistication, optimised firepower and leveraged opportunities. They talk about the high command in terms of cost and benefit, and I can already see the next war being led by bankers and accountants. You wouldn't believe this latest idea: that soldiers should be happier! Let them drink rum instead of water, is what they say. Can you imagine your troops charging into battle in a state of drunkenness? As God is my witness, this is what they are saying.

Floggings are also a constant subject for debate, and many claim they are "inhumane". By God, I don't even understand what this word means. They make up new terms that shine a revealing light on the truth, you see. Discipline has lost all meaning. What happened to honour? What happened to "charge ahead"? Is there a loftier aspiration than to die for our motherland?

And who are those new officers who constantly get promoted, anyway? Our ideals are in shambles, our faith is weak, the fashions from Paris and London are roiling our women's sound judgment, luxury mansions are offered for sale in the newspapers, gentlemen admire fine food with words such as "succulent". What does "succulent" mean, anyway? Our beloved country has become one great, lecherous, decadent bordello.

Wherever it is you are stationed, my darling, I'm sure no-one talks about succulence, because you soldiers are the true heart of this nation. My darling, at least in this household, this woman and these children know you are of a different stock.

Yours ever,

Yelena Venediktova

The expression on the major's face was unreadable, but Zizek noticed that he was tapping his foot on the ground and that the veins in his neck were bulging. For the first time in his life, Radzetsky was facing a dilemma. On the one hand, he had a clear image in his head of his own heroic death: being unhorsed, but still charging straight into the enemy's jaws, his final words leaving an indelible impression on his admiring, if somewhat resentful, troops. Of this he was certain. On the other hand, he now felt a bit reluctant to die the old-fashioned way. Should he give those spoiled Petersburgians the pleasure of remembering him as a foolish hussar who galloped to his death? Is it really beyond his powers to prove to them that he can be a "modern" officer – one of far higher quality than any of them?

Radzetsky got up from his chair, cleared a nostril with his finger and faced Breshov. The adjutant braced himself for a blow from the major. He was sure that the letter was too dense, that the inclusion of the Sun Tzu quotations was too artificial and had given away his ruse. Should he have left out the comments about floggings and rum? Now Radzetsky will surely ask for Captain Venediktov and what will he, the adjutant, say then? Has Breshov really resolved to rescue his comrades, or to have himself killed? The major tweaked Breshov's nose as though trying to clear his adjutant's nostrils too, and then said, in a hoarse voice, "Yelena Venediktova, eh? Quite a woman."

Dear madam, that week the floggings stopped in Radzetsky's regiment. As God is my witness. Of course, there was no official notice to this effect, but no contravening orders were issued either and in the absence of clear instructions either way, the commanders chose to abandon the practice. Two weeks later, under the influence of the next letter from Mrs Venediktova, Radzetsky requested his superiors' permission to ambush retreating enemy forces.

"Meeting them head-on," he explained to the division commander, "would not make the most of my unit's potential."

"Potential?" repeated the division commander in astonishment. "If you want to organise an ambush in the east, be my guest, Radzetsky, but stop spouting nonsense."

As the Russian forces besieged Silistra, Radzetsky mobilised his unit to the north-east, deploying his cavalry and infantry in an area overlooking one of the Danube's narrow valleys. Since he had begun to read the works of Sun Tzu with the help of his adjutant – and with great interest – he knew that "a wise general makes a point of relying on the enemy for supplies", and he would send his troops to recuperate in nearby villages, drink mead, whore to their hearts' content and return with their morale high. "In order that there may be advantage from defeating the enemy, our men must have their reward." Thus spoke Sun Tzu!

Dear madam, we are about to complete the line of your lip. Even though the lines themselves are not uninteresting, the mouth's true enigma is its colour. Your lips are not red but a light pink that verges on white. Their pallor seems to reflect your natural composure. I find great interest in this incandescent, impenetrable face of yours, which radiates both longing and resolve. I cannot decide whether your heart is full of freedom or restraint, passion or pain, deceit or truthfulness, beginning or ending. In any event, we have reached the ears, the organ most amenable to sniffing, tasting and seeing.

Ears

The ear, dear madam, is the only part of the face that painters can hide, fully or partially, by using either hair or angle. Sometimes we will only outline the earlobe, sometimes we draw the inner canals. For painters, the ear is a real challenge. It tests not only our precision, but also our ability to depict the sort of listener we have before us.

Dear madam, we may confidently say that Zizek Breshov was a good listener. By this I do not mean he had the patience to sit and listen to other people's problems. Of course not. I mean that Zizek Breshov listened to the pulse of space and time; he listened to the heartbeat of his era.

What kind of an era was it? Well, it was an era when, as Sun Tzu says, to kill the enemy one's men must be roused to anger. Imagine this: two people in two different parts of the world: one in Russia, the other in either England, France or Turkey. They know nothing about one another. They do not know their counterpart's wife, children, not even his mother-in-law, God help them. Nonetheless, because they were raised in a certain time and place, they learn to harbour bottomless hatred, and are eager to destroy each other, one aspiring to slash the ears of his enemy and the other planning to sever the head of his – and why? Because the former grew up in Kazan and the latter in Constantinople. Bloody rot!

You might ask, what was the great discovery yielded by the Father's listening skills? Well, he noticed that, contrary to popular assumption, men do not join the army because of ideals: men enlist, and ideals justify their enlistment after the fact. In other words: the loftier the values professed the likelier it is that they were concocted by some goddamned prince (this is how Radzetsky put it) to legitimise his decrees and injunctions. The more one invokes the name of God, the more one is likely to do it in the name of licentious ends.

Zizek noticed a gradual shift in Major Radzetsky's thinking, in light of the fabricated gossip from St Petersburg. Overturning all his earlier plans, he ordered his regiment to remain stationed where they were, and while the imperial forces suffered a miserable defeat in the battle of Silistra, Radzetsky's cavalry waited patiently for reinforcements that never turned up. The division to which Radzetsky's regiment belonged was ground into the earth – thousands died in battle and tens of thousands more succumbed to cholera – but Radzetsky's troops were left unscathed, except for the odd liver broken by excessive rum-drinking, and a few victims of syphilis. When Radzetsky was summoned to report on his soldiers' performance, everyone was astonished to learn that his unit had emerged without a scratch, and that they had even escaped the cholera. In response to his colleagues' inquiries, he feigned surprise at their old-fashioned approach: did they not know that Sun Tzu had said that "there is no strategy worse than the siege of a walled city"? Was it not common knowledge that "he who knows when to fight and when not to fight will win"? The other regiments' commanders stared at Radzetsky, unsure whether they were looking at a genius or a fool. Still, it was a miracle that his troops were so unaffected by disease. In other regiments, for every Russian martyr killed in battle, ten men had been lost to plagues: shivering, vomiting and incontinent, their souls separated from their dehydrated bodies only after unbearable torments, unable to relieve their parched bodies with water, which they had no access to anyway. "Water?" said Radzetsky, dumbfounded. "My soldiers drink rum and a little coffee, on the recommendation of the Czar's representatives in St Petersburg. Didn't you know?" But indeed, how could they have known about the letters of Mrs Yelena Venediktova from St Petersburg?

In any case, even though they could not decide if Radzetsky was an exceptional tactician or a complete fool, two things seemed certain: one, Radzetsky was surely connected to St Petersburg's aristocracy, and two, God had to be on his side. And therefore, he merited immediate promotion.

Becoming a *polkovnik*, a colonel, and entering the senior army ranks, shocked Radzetsky. He suddenly realised that he had been too quick to judge those spoiled St Petersburg grandees, and that his attitude towards the high command had been too harsh, perhaps. After all, they had recognised his abilities in the end. According to Mrs Venediktova, it was rumoured that secret units were preying on the Bashi-Bazouk by laying sophisticated ambushes, and the names of their commanders were known only to the highest echelons of the Russian army.

Naturally, Radzetsky continued to be guided by his sense of duty, and suppressed his excitement at the admiration he now received from his troops. As he walked through the camp, officers stepped aside to let him pass, hussars stood to attention, tailors bowed before him and cooks invited him to try some freshly baked bread. Yet he would still scrutinise them from head to heel, checking that their arms were well oiled and that their belts were straight and tight. Admiration is all well and good, but he had a regiment to run.

Radzetsky kept his adjutant by his side at all times, but he never imagined that the admiration he enjoyed was actually addressed to the Father, the man who had extended the soldiers' lives far beyond all expectations, the man without whom they would have been wiped out in their thousands and tens of thousands. Zizek continued to send soldiers' letters to their wives and children, and in his spare time he even taught many infantry-men how to read and write. They were like his children. Sitting around him in two circles, as they would around a bonfire, they absorbed his teachings, working out the words they might use in their next letter. For his part, he listened to their stories and learned about the life that could have been his: he imagined all their wives to be Mina Gorfinkel, all their hometowns Motal, and all their houses resembled the home he had been snatched from as a young boy. They needed his words to kindle their hearts, and he needed their lives to kindle the soul of Yoshke Berkovits: husband, father, family man.

All this time, Imre Schechtman continued to paint Radzetsky's portrait. As a colonel, Radzetsky viewed his portrait, which was in fact still that of the Iron Czar, in a completely different way. He was a member of the aristocracy now. Strange as it may sound, his features had become more noble, perfectly adapting to his rank. A common man looking at Radzetsky's portrait would never have guessed that the dignitary pictured there was descended from peasants. He would not have imagined that the son of potato farmers could acquire the unassailable, aloof appearance of a Spartan leader, an aspiring army commander. And why not commander in chief? Yelena Venediktova kept saying that Russia had lost its sanity, and that there was talk of ousting the old guard, which had spent so much of the empire's military force in vain. And who would step in once they were gone? Who else would be made commander-in-chief, if not a modern officer of the sort Mrs Venediktova finds so loathsome? Yelena Venediktova, eh? Quite a woman, despite her old-fashioned ideas.

Therefore, when Radzetsky was made major general and assigned the task of reinforcing the besieged corps in Sevastopol that was facing defeat, he requested permission to deploy his troops north of the Crimean Peninsula, to block any surprise attack from the combined British and French forces on that flank. The generals of the high command listened to him carefully, reluctant to deny his request even though the likelihood of such an attack seemed minimal. And so, as the battles of Balaclava and Inkerman raged in Crimea, in a bloody attempt to break the

308

allied forces' siege, Major General Radzetsky's division settled in the Ukrainian lowlands without firing a single round.

"Another letter from the lady?" the major general asked, languidly, as his peers sustained heavy shelling in Sevastopol. "What's the matter, Breshov, have you swallowed your tongue? Read the goddamned letter!"

My Darling,

The children and I send you our greetings and love, but things have become unbearable. Russia is falling apart, and I am not talking about the odd defeat in Crimea. No, my darling, for we have known greater losses. Mother Russia is facing a spiritual collapse, and this is why I am so anxious for its future. You soldiers, may the saints protect you, are bearing the brunt in the trenches, unaware that a revolution is forming at home. Noblemen and princes from St Petersburg are speaking of peace, in effect shooting you in the back, and people say that the Czar is under their sway. Rumour has it that his health has deteriorated, and some are even saying . . . my hand is shaking, forgive me, darling . . . some are saying that he has only a few weeks left to live, and we know all too well who will succeed him to the throne. Alexander Nikolayevich certainly cannot be called a military man, and they are saying that all the officers responsible for the defeats in Crimea will be stripped of their rank and sent to Siberia.

Yesterday we went to the opera and heard a new production of Glinka's "A Life for the Czar". This is without a doubt his best opera. We were surrounded by the great and the good of the capital, and as they were watching the wonderful drama of Ivan Susanin, the Russian hero who sacrifices his life for the Czar, they were saying that the army should retreat to the border and bring the pointless carnage to an end. You see, darling? If tomorrow, God forbid, you should lose your life in a cruel battle, they will think your death unnecessary. For them, courage for its own sake is not reason enough to give one's life away. To them honour is currency, loyalty an object, and love for the motherland just one idea among many. They want to foster a new breed of officer, who thinks independently, preserves the forces under his command and above all else protects his soldiers from cholera. The next commander-in-chief will have to be a nurse and his officers will serve their own soldiers bread and beef.

They say Sevastopol is about to fall. Yet this does not stop them from dressing up for the opera and looking for the culprits. They say that the entire high command will be exiled to Siberia. To our great shame, half the Russian army is holed up in a tiny peninsula. I know that in your eyes it is a good thing to attempt to break the siege at the cost of tens of thousands of lives. Yet we know that officers like you are called "old-fashioned", and that thanks to your courage and loyalty you will end up being hanged like a despicable traitor. Worry not, my darling, at least in this household, this woman and these children know you are of a different stock.

Yours ever,

Yelena Venediktova

If all warfare is based on deception, as our friend Sun Tzu taught, Breshov concluded that non-warfare can also be based on deception. But if there was anything that could be stated quite truthfully, it was that the Crimean War ended terribly for Russia and taught Radzetsky's troops the following: that one had better

avoid mixing rum with coffee, root vegetables can soothe indiges-
tion, and that Odessan whores get very angry if you don't pay them.

At this point, the Father's first "sons" were discharged from
the army, veterans between the ages of forty and fifty who had
lived to see retirement age. They told their children and grandchildren about their second Father, Zizek Breshov the adjutant,
or rather Yoshke Berkovits from Motal, who before the age of
eighteen had saved their father's life with the power of words.
Zizek was the first father in history who could boast at such a
young age of having tens of thousands of descendants, all of
whom were older than he was by at least twenty years.

Patrick Adamsky also became one of Breshov's children.
Adamsky, a junior second lieutenant back then, was spared time
and again from carrying out suicidal missions on Radzetsky's
orders. On several occasions Adamsky's squad was deployed to
vulnerable locations, surrounded by the superior forces of the
Bashi-Bazouk, a perfect recipe for disaster devised by Radzetsky
whenever he did not want to feel completely left out of the war.
In the nick of time, however, the adjutant would read to the
major general a letter that had just happened to arrive from
Mrs Venediktova, and would prompt Radzetsky to wonder if it
was really such a good idea to attack. It transpired, according to
the letter, that St Petersburg's counts and princes had become
so impressed with Radzetsky's cunning that they had started
referring to him as "the Hussar". The Hussar, people were saying,
defeats the enemy while keeping his forces unharmed, and his
name, princes were whispering, had even reached the ears of the
Czar. Did he really want to ruin his reputation with a fiasco on the
battlefield? Perhaps not. Instead, Radzetsky would send orders
to secure the flanks and retreat, telling his reporting officers that
their mission had been accomplished. And what was their mission? No more than keeping the unit intact, as it transpired.

Mind you, dear madam, this does not mean that the friendship between Avramson and Berkovits was rekindled. Quite the opposite is true. Adamsky was not much of a patriot, but he was driven by an uncontrollable death wish. And so, when the Crimean War was over, he was transferred – at his request, actually – to another unit. At his new unit, reporting to an old-fashioned general, Adamsky got his wish. He fought countless battles in the Caucasus War, managing to die at least a dozen times in the eyes of the riflemen who watched him take apart enemy lines with his bare hands. Adamsky, for his part, was simply indifferent to the idea of getting himself killed. Even the Angel of Death preferred to leave him be rather than risk losing an earlobe or an eye. Adamsky was decorated with every class of the Order of St Gregory and never once requested leave. His greatest pleasure was in ransacking Jews' homes as they watched. He stomped on loaves of bread and vegetables, emptied casseroles on doorsteps, smashed all the porcelain he could find, ripped up clothing, and pissed on firewood. When one of his reporting officers asked him why he didn't just enjoy the loot, Adamsky replied, as he crushed a cabbage beneath his heel, "Who says we're not enjoying ourselves?"

But that was after he had left Radzetsky's unit. As long as he was with the regiment on the Danube, Adamsky ignored Zizek's many attempts to catch his eye, assuming a hollow expression whenever the shadow of his childhood friend was near. Zizek was beside himself whenever he saw Adamsky in the distance. The tension peaked when they chanced to run into each other and Zizek twitched a hesitant half-smile.

"Soldier," Officer Adamsky barked. "Who do you think you're smiling at?"

"But if this was so," Fanny says, "why did Adamsky risk everything and shelter us in his tavern?"

"His tavern?" the painter asks, surprised, and lifts his head from the canvas. "This I do not know, dear madam, such matters belong to the present. But if I had to make a guess, well then . . . Never mind. Let us finish painting your ear."

Intervals

We have the contour of the face, and the nose, mouth, hair and ears. The portrait is still incomplete, however, because the proportions are not set. People tend to think that proportions are naturally determined by the intervals between the features. Place the nose here and the lips there, and there's already a space between them. But make it too wide and the expression dissipates. If it is too narrow, the face becomes grotesque. The correct proportions are not created by the face's features, but rather the intervals between its parts determine its shape. Intervals, dear madam, form the heart of our story. May I continue? Then sit up straight, please.

A little over twenty years is the interval of time that brings our story to its conclusion. At that point, perhaps you could tell me about the Father's life since, as you say, you are his niece, although I remain sceptical. However, I doubt that whatever you can tell me would surpass the next part of my story, in which the Father met the Czar, no less. To top that you would have to tell me how the Father met the only one who outranks the Czar, which is to say God Himself. But this, I presume – with all due respect – is something you cannot do.

When the battles on the Danube resumed, Radzetsky was made lieutenant general. He had no need of Mrs Yelena Venediktova anymore. A corps commander does not follow the advice of a St Petersburg lady, high-born though she might be. In other words, by then Radzetsky had completely assimilated Venediktova's way of thinking. On the one hand, be shrewd, Radzetsky: give those damned aristocrats what they want. Beat them at their own game. On the other hand: never forget that you are of the same stock as the men admired by Mrs Venediktova.

Indeed, his efforts were fruitful. Who would have thought that when Alexander the Second assembled the high command at the height of the Russo-Turkish war, a messenger would be sent post-haste from the Bulgarian city of Byala to Radzetsky's forces stationed near Bucharest, asking him to urgently report to the Czar in the white city on the banks of the Yantra?

Everyone was there. Living legends, walking myths, the titans of glory and splendour. The hard-headed Osip Gurko and the fearless Mikhail Skobelev, and many other famous generals, including Radzetsky, the potato farmer's son who had paved his way to the top without selling his soul to the Devil.

Zizek had passed through Byala several times during his military service, and had fond memories of the city. It was small and clean, surrounded by white hills, and home to friendly residents and merry taverns. But now the Russian army that had swept through the city and driven out the Turks marched down streets that reeked of rotting cadavers. The air was viscous and thick, and the waters of the Yantra were putrid. It was impossible to find a meal for less than a rouble, and Radzetsky was incensed by the damned locals taking advantage of honest Russians and babbling on about inflation, when they should have been grateful for their civilised conquerors. They would have done well to ask themselves if they preferred waking up every morning to muezzin calls from mosques.

The locals, for their part, were generally indifferent to whichever uniform festooned their streets. Their crops were plundered, their wine consumed and the virtue of their women assaulted, and it didn't matter to them one bit whether this was done in

Russian or Turkish. These colossal historical developments took shape far above their heads but hit them right in the gut, and they preferred to sit on their doorsteps and watch events unfold.

The Czar occupied an abandoned Turkish mansion in the heart of the city surrounded by fences and weeping willows. He was staying in a temporary residence set up in the courtyard, while the meetings were held in the main pavilion, where meals were also taken. Radzetsky and his adjutant were invited to wash and change into their dress uniform (it would be improper to meet the Czar wearing dusty, well-worn fatigues one has ridden in for almost a week). Ignat Shepkin had already portrayed General Radzetsky in a white uniform, exuding might and pride, and the radiant general instructed his talented painter to depict the meeting with his usual skill, in order to surprise the Czar with a gracious tribute.

We've somewhat neglected Ignat Shepkin in our story, dear madam. This is probably due to my disinclination to upset both you and myself. In any event, with your permission, I'll say a few words about him now.

Shepkin's job was indeed dreary, but over the years he became completely absorbed by it. Adamsky burned the bridges to his childhood and focused on his future, that is, his death; Breshov hoped to resurrect his past; whereas Shepkin immersed himself in the present, that is, in the art of painting. You might think, dear madam, that in his spare time Shepkin painted horses, landscapes, battlefields and culinary delights. This is a common mistake. Shepkin never tried to paint anything other than that same accursed portrait he had been taught to draw almost thirty years earlier by Sergeant Sergey Sergeyevich. Most of the time Shepkin lay dozing in his tent, waiting to be called in by his commander. Radzetsky's satisfaction with his work had yielded Shepkin status and perks, but he drew his inspiration from elsewhere: he aspired to produce the perfect portrait, the most vivid artwork ever made in the history of painting.

Shepkin taught us artists an important lesson in humility. Is inspiration essential? Absolutely. A muse? Most welcome. Outbursts of creativity? Never hurt anyone. But without accuracy and mathematical precision, one has no right to call oneself a painter. Today, even the advent of what is called a "camera" has not made our services superfluous. And why? Because, as Shepkin taught us, a painting can be more accurate than a photograph.

If this observation strikes you as strange, dear madam, think of a man looking at his own photograph and failing to recognise the ageing face before him. Radzetsky, on the other hand, thought that Shepkin depicted him impeccably in his portraits, give or take a wrinkle or two. Ultimately, a painting better reflects the image we have of ourselves.

Shepkin often left camp to holiday in the mountains, where he would occupy himself with his private affairs, which consisted chiefly of bordellos. Waiters fought over him and prostitutes jockeyed for his attention. As Shepkin lacked almost any conceivable desire, his holidays really meant time off for them too. He ate whatever they served on his plate, gave exorbitant tips, and caressed the prostitutes without ever forcing himself upon them. The sons that many of those women produced were all christened Ignat Shepkin, but no-one knows if they were indeed the fruit of his loins. Nonetheless, Shepkin sent all of them money and visited his putative offspring whenever he could. The youngsters were initially afraid and cried at the mere sight of him, but he treated them like no other man they had met; that is to say, he enveloped them with warmth and love. They, for their part, needed time to grow accustomed to the gaunt man who showered them with kisses, lifted them up in his arms and even rocked them to sleep. Once they became used to his presence, he dedicated himself to teaching them the craft that had saved his life. By the time they turned ten, all of his children could draw the portrait of a proud man wearing a sumptuous army uniform.

Now I may tell you that my name is also Ignat Shepkin, and therefore I am somewhat invested in this story. If you can believe it, I even remember him, the milksop: however meekly he arrived at the brothel, his presence brightened up the faces of everyone in the room. My mother marvelled and rejoiced, and whatever she wanted, he would give her.

Why, then, did I warn madam that this story would make her sad? Well, our story is not over yet. I wish, dear madam, that it had ended here. But we were discussing intervals, and at this point, one interval became impossibly narrow.

When the Czar graciously received his army chiefs and warmly shook Radzetsky's hand, the newly appointed general felt as though his life had reached its zenith. His Highness recognised him! There could be no doubt now that the Hussar had made a name for himself. Radzetsky could not take his eyes off the Czar and motioned to Shepkin to start painting. At his side, Adjutant Breshov waited, tense and worried, wondering what turn these events would take.

The Czar was exhausted, his head drooped and his throat was sore and congested. But he was thrilled to hear about the loyal troops who had given up their lives in the battles on the Danube, the units that had charged at the superior enemy forces of the Bashi-Bazouk, and about the small victories on the Danube and the Shipka Pass. Then the conversation shifted to the besieged city of Plevna. Skobelev was furious that the army had not attacked it sooner, while other generals defended their decision to hold back.

Radzetsky's moment had arrived. He gargled, coughed and then mumbled, "Why lay siege to it at all?" Skobelev and the other officers fell silent and looked around for the source of the buzzing sound that had interrupted their conversation. When their eyes rested on Radzetsky, he turned red with pride and launched into a Sun Tzu quotation: "A siege will consume your strength. The general, unable to control his irritation, will send his men to attack like swarming ants, with the result that a third of his men will be slain and the town will remain untaken. Such are the disastrous effects of a siege."

The Czar raised his head and looked straight at Radzetsky.

"Who is that?" Skobelev asked the Czar's adjutant, rather than addressing Radzetsky directly.

"This is General Radishevo," said the chief adjutant, checking his lists.

"Radzetsky," Adjutant Breshov corrected him. "General Radzetsky."

"Yes, of course," the chief adjutant mumbled, with another look at his lists. "Radzetsky of the Ninth Army."

"The Eleventh Army," said Breshov.

"Of course, of course, the Eleventh Army."

"The Eleventh Army?" said Skobelev, chuckling and turning to the Czar. "This is the force we are keeping in reserve near Bucharest." The officers sitting around the table roared with laughter, and Skobelev rounded on Radzetsky. "You haven't fired a single bullet in years, so why don't you keep your mouth shut."

Radzetsky's face was on fire. He had never been humiliated this way before. He remained sitting at the table but his hands were shaking and he was burning with rage. What is more, as another senior general entered the pavilion, he noticed Shepkin's portrait of the Czar. He removed the canvas from its easel, turned it towards the assembly and remarked, "Your Highness, it seems that this painter misses your father, Nikolai the First." More laughter thundered from the generals and they demanded to know how the artist had produced such a strange picture.

"Sir," the general shook Shepkin by the shoulder, "a new Czar ascended the throne more than twenty years ago. Who is your commander?" And so Radishevo's name, that is, Radzetsky's, was mentioned in yet another humiliating context. He was now the laughing stock of the high command.

"Such are the disastrous effects of a painting," Skobelev said, paraphrasing Sun Tzu and instantly improving the mood around the table. Radzetsky shot Breshov a look that promised nothing good.

The humiliated general remained huddled in his chair until the meeting ended. In an instant, he had gone back to being the lowly peasant's son from Kazan, an object of scorn for St Petersburg's nobility.

When the meeting was adjourned, the Czar continued his consultation with Skobelev and Gurko. Breshov and Shepkin felt the same sharp stab that had punctured Radzetsky's heart. The Czar briefly raised his eyes from the maps and looked straight at Radzetsky. The general stood up straight: was the Czar about to ask him for advice or share the confidential matter at hand? But the Czar merely stared vaguely at a button of his coat, as though he could see right through him. Radzetsky took a deep breath. He'll teach them to call him "Radishevo". He will prove them wrong about "not firing a single bullet".

Dear madam, you can probably guess what happened next. No letter can stop a man from trying to prove a point with his own death, not even the surprising letter that one of Radzetsky's officers received shortly thereafter from his mother. A fervent patriot and an eighth-generation Petersburgian, the concerned lady warned her son that there was talk in the capital of the aristocracy's intentions to dismiss the entire cohort of generals who, she said, were leading Russia to its demise. Two names that kept coming up, she went on, were Skobelev and Gurko, who insisted on sending their troops on suicidal missions that failed miserably. They would be guillotined and replaced with more prudent officers, the letter concluded. Radzetsky listened attentively as Breshov read and then exclaimed, "Bullshit! No-one remembers the prudent."

And so Breshov, who had rescued tens of thousands of lives thanks to the power of words, was helpless two days later as Radzetsky ordered his unit to move south-west towards Plevna. The troops marched for weeks in the heavy heat, and close to four hundred of them died of dehydration on the way. Half of those who remained alive marched with stress fractures and sprained backs. And who joined the march? Shepkin and Breshov, the painter and the adjutant, who had been cast out of headquarters because portraits of a former emperor and fabricated letters were no longer in demand. Radzetsky was determined to throw his unit into the fray.

Near the village of Pordim, Radzetsky came across Skobelev's units. Instead of joining forces with the larger army of a more senior general, Radzetsky did not even stop to encamp but pressed on to flank the next village, Lyubcha, exposing his troops to Ottoman fire as they crossed an open field in territory completely under Turkish control. Ignorant of Skobelev's plan to attack Lyubcha, which had been conceived months earlier, Radzetsky ordered his soldiers to charge directly at the enemy's cannons. It was late at night when the first shell fell among his soldiers. The Ottoman gunman had fired it almost reluctantly on hearing rustling noises rising from the cornfields, not even sure whether it came from the battlefront or from his dream. But once he heard the commotion stirred by the shell, he alerted his comrades to take up their positions as they realised they were facing an entire

Russian corps, about to attack. Radzetsky, who had been eagerly waiting for this moment, rode to the first line of attack and ordered his cavalry to charge.

What were they supposed to charge at? Dear madam, I'm sure you can imagine. Shells, bullets and spears in fortified positions. One by one, Radzetsky's horsemen fell into the jaws of fire as their commander-in-chief urged them to their death: *"Ah! Che la morte!"* Straggling behind, the infantry regiment gradually disintegrated, veiled by shrapnel and smoke. A few dozen came within firing range of the Turkish positions, but every shot they fired was met with lethal return salvos. Before half an hour had elapsed, Radzetsky's troops were scattered in all directions. Some of them retreated towards Pordim while others fled straight into the hands of Ottoman reinforcements. A lucky few hid in the fields and waited to be rescued. Only when day broke did the true scale of the catastrophe emerge. Not only had an entire Russian army corps been decimated, dear madam, there was not a corpse left without a sliced-off ear or severed genitals. Heads rolled about like rocks, uniforms had been stripped away, and dead bodies became the fodder of carrion-birds and wild animals. Radzetsky's head lay at a fair distance from his body, his eyes staring towards his torso with neither pride nor peace.

Shepkin sank to the ground as soon as the first shot was fired. Zizek tried to pull him away, but my father sat down on a rock, took out pencil and paper from his backpack and started to sketch a portrait of Nikolai the First, the Iron Czar, as the cannons thundered from all directions. He was still breathing when the Turks found him. They laid down their swords for a moment and peered at the drawing. It was my father's best work, without a shadow of a doubt. He departed from this world, dear madam, leaving a thread of light in the heart of darkness. Women and children across Russia silently wept. They were not necessarily lamenting the loss of a husband or father, since they weren't used to having him around. But when I heard about his death I felt that I'd lost something I never knew I had, and my grief was unbearable.

We should not be talking about the sorrows of an obscure painter, though, dear madam. We should be talking about the Father and how the saints protected him in Radzetsky's death-trap. No-one knows how he survived, and I was hoping that you, his so-called niece, would know something about his mysterious disappearance from the battlefield. Did he lie on the ground and pretend to be dead? If so, how did he keep his ears intact? Did he dive into the river? If so, how did he not drown? Did he manage to hide in a nearby village? If so, someone must have known about it. He disappeared into the bloody soil without a trace. Such circumstances, dear madam, are the stuff of legends. Soldiers who survived this massacre couldn't agree about whether he ascended to the high heavens on a storm cloud, was swallowed whole by the earth, or was snatched by a seraph mounted on a grey dragon. A carabineer swore he saw this miracle happen with his very eyes: "The Father charged together with the rest of us, but suddenly an angel of God landed on the battlefield riding a fearsome dragon, put Zizek on its back and flew up to the heavens."

If the extravagance of the legends about the Father tells us anything about the admiration soldiers have for him, then this tale is a fine example. There may not have been a grey dragon, and it is doubtful whether anything descended from the heavens. But many imagined that Zizek the Divine was extracted from that valley of death by the Holy Spirit Himself.

One might expect this escape to have enraged his comrades, as he ultimately failed to rescue their unit from destruction. But from the moment Radzetsky appointed Zizek as his adjutant, generations of soldiers had been rescued, and those soldiers had children, wives, parents and friends. It can be said without fear of exaggeration that countless Russians are indebted to the Father, and if he had not been born a Jew, he would surely have been declared a saint.

We are almost finished, dear madam. I believe that your curiosity has had its fill, while my own curiosity is still ravenous. Before I present you with the outcome of our session I have one request for you: I want to hear that the Father has a child of his own. Even if you have to lie, and I can already see your eyes twitching, tell me that he managed to live a full life, where words became words again instead of tools. Tell me he found consolation in the arms of Mina Gorfinkel, and that the baby she gave birth to healed his soul, and that he found repose in a modest Motal house. Describe to me how Zizek Breshov went back to being Yoshke Berkovits and I will ask for nothing more, not caring whether you are a niece or a foe. No-one believed we would have the honour of meeting the Father before we die, which is why we find his solitude intolerable. We want to know that he lacks nothing. Our only dream is to know that when Yoshke Berkovits goes to bed he can tell himself that his home is his castle, and that those distant days of Yoshke and Pesach at the latrines are gone for ever. Did Mina Gorfinkel wait for him? Was he happily received in his hometown upon his return? Did he have any children? Did any of this come to be, dear madam, or are these all empty, wishful thoughts?

I can assure you that the reason why you are here is none of our concern, though it certainly piques our curiosity. What is more, as long as blood is running through the veins of the soldiers and hussars serving here, you will come to no harm. Even if the Czar himself ordered your arrest, we would escort you to safety and foil any plot against you. There is one thing we would like to know, though: is the Father happy? Yes, as simple as that. Is there any joy in his heart? Has his odyssey come to an end? Did he manage to retrieve the words that had been expropriated for the common good, and make them his own again? Did he manage to put longings into words, not for others' sweethearts, but for his own beloved? Was he able to use words as they were uttered by the First Man?

Your face is not reassuring, dear madam. Your wordlessness speaks volumes. I do not want to hear you mumbling half-truths. Let us part ways, then. Please forget the fable that I have just told you, for it is nothing more than a fable. Any soldier here in the camp will tell you a completely different version of this story, depending on his imagination and how much time he has. Nevertheless, I delivered my part of the deal, and cannot complain about yours. You sat here for a long time listening to an emotional, grieving artist, who now has a memory of someone who purports to be the Father's niece. Your portrait is the only memento I have of my family. For I was born Ignat Shepkin, with the name of a man who surely was not my father but treated me with nothing but kindness. Would you like to take a look now?

II

Ignat Shepkin bows to Fanny and turns the painting around for her to look at. She is not accustomed to seeing herself in the mirror, and certainly not on a canvas, not to mention in the presence of someone else. Indeed, she recognises her moon-shaped face, light-coloured hair, and bright eyes that the artist has left blurred. She thinks her nose is out of proportion, however, and the wrinkle between the eyebrows is only hinted at. Fanny cannot say that this is a faithful portrait, she rather thinks that Ignat Shepkin has failed to follow his father's advice to limit himself to drawing a single theme. The face on the canvas is sad, the puffy bags under the eyes suppress any sign of vitality they might have had. Wait a minute . . .

Fanny touches her cheeks, feeling the skin and fat they have acquired of late. Impossible! She notices that her eyes in the painting have dark circles around them, and her chin even has a small, sharp dimple.

"What is this?" Fanny says. "Who did you paint?"

Shepkin smiles and folds his canvas.

"Give it to me!" She tries to snatch the painting from him.

"Absolutely not." He pushes her arm away.

Her thoughts turn fleetingly to her knife.

"A deal is a deal," the painter says, now upset, and jumps off the wagon. "What is wrong with you? Clearly, you're not his niece," he says as he disappears into the dark.

What is happening to her? She cannot stop thinking about the portrait. The painting showed submissive eyes, which are everything her eyes are not. They were the eyes of Malka Schechter. How could Shepkin have known about her mother who died more than ten years ago, in Grodno? Could he have discerned in Fanny the resignation that consumed her mother? Impossible. Unlike her mother, even as a child Fanny forbade herself to play if-then games and took her fate into her own hands. She decided to hunt down Zvi-Meir herself, instead of praying like the rabbis for the release of husbandless wives from wedlock. How can a stupid artist confuse frivolity with vigour, or weakness with resolve?

Pent-up rage ignites Fanny's face, and her fingers slide towards the knife on her thigh. Touching the blade calms her, but this quickly turns to fear and in her distress she struggles to breath.

She claws at her own neck as if trying to free it from someone else's grip. Fanny is impelled to draw her knife: who's there? Who dares try to strangle her?

Placid and indifferent, the night gives nothing away. The moon is shrivelled like a dried pear, the landscape dissolves, and Fanny listens to the snores teeming in the tents. Now that she is finally her own master, the prospect of losing control of her life terrifies her. Her mother's old if-then thoughts creep back in. If she falls asleep here in the field, she'll be captured by dawn. If she stares into the eyes of Zizek's old horse she'll be sent to Siberia. But if she gets off the wagon with her right foot first, the four of them will certainly be saved. And if she lets go of the knife, this whole mess will be forgotten. What is she to do?

She descends from the wagon and hurries back to the tent. In the lantern's dim light, she can tell that Adamsky and the Cantor are not there. Only Zizek is in the tent, lying across the bed with his back to her. She steps over some boxes to see if he is awake. His eyes, the eyes of a dead carp, are heedless of her presence. She gently taps his shoulder.

"Zizek," she whispers, "I'm sorry about everything. I didn't mean to . . . But what made you help me in the first place?"

Zizek does not turn but his eyelids flutter. His refusal to look at her, like a stubborn child, stabs her directly in the heart. His spurned body, which has never been touched, is rigid to the point of prickliness. His anguished look projects a lucidity she recognises from her children: the look of a scolded boy pleading for forgiveness. If a woman touched him he would beg for a mother; if a mother touched him he would withdraw into himself. His body has never been necessary; the only affirmations of its existence have been the imaginings he dictated to his comrades. The act of love with Mina Gorfinkel is as implausible now as it was when he was a young boy.

326

And yet Fanny touches him: first she touches his scarred mouth, then she runs her fingers across his lips, strokes his cheek and brushes aside the hair on his forehead. This touch, even if forbidden, does not feel like an act of infidelity, because it is not in the least arousing.

A sigh of pain escapes from Zizek's lips. How far did her touch reach? She cannot tell, but as she strokes his forehead, she notices that his shoulders grow stiff and he arches his back as if shrinking away from her. She lies down next to him, presses her body against his, and wraps her arm around his belly. Zizek lies without uttering a syllable, but his breathing grows softer. Now she cannot move away from him, and she cannot say whether it's for his sake or her own.

TABULKI

I

No man in the camp has a bad word to say about the deputy commander, Colonel David Pazhari. As Lieutenant General Mishenkov's absences grow longer and more frequent, Pazhari is seen as the regiment's acting commander. While Mishenkov is away, Pazhari could choose to do whatever he liked. He could drink fine wines from dawn to dusk, smoke excellent cigars, or fornicate with the local women. But sometimes, when one meets a St Petersburg aristocrat, one realises that certain things tolerated in the capital are not tolerated elsewhere.

The deputy commander is tall, broad-shouldered and has a chiselled face. His yellow hair, which flops across his forehead like an egg yolk, is carefully trimmed at the back in a straight line that would make a draughtsman proud. He shaves daily, even in wintertime, and you will never see him wearing ragged boots held together with cheap glue, as his peers do. Even when he gets up at night to piss, the colonel puts on his belt before leaving his tent. Pazhari, people say, will never be caught with his trousers down.

In addition to his impressive stature, distinctive features and a small scar above his top lip, Pazhari is distinguished by a rare quality of holding sway over both men and women. A trivial comment of his at a staff meeting can make officers unsure whether it has annoyed them or filled them with love, if not to say passion, for him. And since passion between men is tenfold more inspiring than its trivial alternative, men can interact with Pazhari only if they love him unconditionally or are made nauseous by his presence.

The nauseated among them face a dilemma. If only they could point their finger at a fault in Pazhari's conduct they would at least feel that their attitude was justified. But the colonel's behaviour is impeccable. He could easily follow Mishenkov's example, leave his own deputy in charge and go off to dine with government officials in the city. Such a handover of authority could go on for ever, ending with a humble private as commander-in-chief. But Pazhari prefers the routine of life at the barracks to sensual delights and political intrigues. He likes chatting with new recruits, crawling onto an empty cot in a tent for a quick nap, running a kitchen inspection once a week and smoking with his officers. If something escapes Pazhari's attention it means that Pazhari let it escape on purpose, because it gives him peace of mind to know that there are some things he does not need to know. The colonel has come to learn that every soldier breaks at least one rule a day. To his mind, it is preferable that such transgressions should pertain to opium, morphine and mead rather than weapon smuggling or – God forbid – espionage.

One morning, a few days after the quartet's arrival in camp, Colonel Pazhari receives an urgent telegram from "the Department for Public Security and Order". A nice name for the Okhrana's rats, Pazhari thinks to himself. The letter is addressed to Lieutenant General Mishenkov, and the colonel wonders what it could be about. Looking for the signatory's name at the bottom of the page, he is surprised to find it was sent on behalf of none other than the commander of the Okhrana's north-western districts, Colonel Piotr Novak.

Although Pazhari served under Novak for no more than a fortnight, he knows his former commander better than the officers who served under the colonel for twenty years, by virtue of a random accident: Pazhari, a cavalry captain at the time, was there when a shell hit Novak's horse during the battle on the Shipka Pass. Determined hussar that he was, Pazhari found himself among the first line of attack and witnessed the senior officer writhing in agony on the ground, dragging his leg along like a snake with a severed tail, with no sense of where he was going. Leaving a trail of blood in his wake, Novak leaned on a rifle in a desperate attempt to stand up and, contravening all orders, Pazhari jumped off his horse with the idea of dragging his commanding officer away from the line of fire, but took a punch to the face as soon as he tried it. "What do you think you're doing, you fool?" Novak yelled. "Mount your horse and get back to the attack!" Pazhari obeyed the order, but he could not help staring at the gory, sooty, horrific pulp that had once been a leg. Blood was gushing from the shrapnel-torn knee, drenching the scorched flesh. As he grimaced, Pazhari realised that Novak had seen the terror in his face. Raising his eyes, the colonel seemed to plead with him: is it that bad? Is there really no hope? Pazhari did not have the gumption to lie to his commanding officer. He ignored Novak's plea and returned to the mayhem.

Contrary to what people tend to think, our moral compass does not necessarily give us the ability to do the right thing in critical moments. If anything, the opposite is true. The inherently just are not virtuous, since they have never had a weakness or flaw they had to overcome. Alas, most people become a pale version of themselves and lose their wits altogether when evil makes an appearance. It is therefore a mistake to judge one's morality in times of crisis. Most people, and Pazhari is no exception, become aware of their morals only in hindsight, once they have recognised their blunders and the irrevocable injustice they have unleashed. In the same way that a novice tailor makes inferior clothes before learning to produce flawless garments, people develop a moral sense through failure, flaw and sin.

For many years, Pazhari had replayed that scene at the battle on the Shipka Pass in his mind, and had come to realise that his role as a commander in the Czar's army was to teach his men to accept reality as it was. Nothing more. If he could go back to that moment – and how often he imagined that he could, not a day passed without him wishing that he could – he would have turned to Novak's pleading face and said sternly: "The leg is gone, deal with it." And even if Novak would have expected him to offer consolation, Pazhari would have fulfilled a basic moral obligation: to see people as they are – in this case, with a mangled leg – and not as they ought to be.

Either way, even if Pazhari had had no idea who Piotr Novak was, a request from a district commander at the Department for Public Security and Order is no trivial matter. What is more, the telegram unequivocally demands to know whether four fugitive outlaws have been sighted in the camp, three men and a woman, members of an underground organisation of some sort, probably Jewish, who have murdered an innocent family and two agents in a cruel attack, and managed to escape on an old freight wagon headed for Minsk. Further below, a line written by a different hand reads: "Anywon hiding informashen abowt there identity or wherabowts wil be considerd ful akomplices and wil be I for conspirasy and eiding and abeting merder."

Whoever wrote this line had to be a complete idiot. It couldn't possibly be Novak's doing, thinks Colonel Pazhari. But the smile that these spelling mistakes bring to the lips must not mask the seriousness of the words they express. Scaffolds can still be set up by fools who cannot spell their own name. Pazhari knows that it is customarily believed that the secret police follows laws of its own, but anyone who can think for himself knows that the secret police do not follow any laws whatsoever. If they decide tomorrow that David Pazhari has to go, then David Pazhari will be gone; and if they decide the next day that David Pazhari never existed, then he never existed.

Therefore, after reading the telegram, the colonel immediately orders his officers to find out if anyone knows anything about four fugitives in their midst. He tells the unit commanders to check their furthest outposts, and instructs the cavalry to send out horsemen to the nearby villages. Not even thirty minutes elapse before his question is answered in the negative, which makes him suspicious. First, such rumours usually stimulate the imaginations of bored people and prompt them to invent things they know nothing about. Give a muzhik a reason to report and he will come up with impossible tales that implicate four innocent people without an alibi, but in this case no-one saw anything. And second, how could they have already reached the furthest outposts and come back, if these outposts are half an hour's ride in each direction?

Mind you, under normal circumstances Pazhari couldn't care less if his soldiers have their secrets. If any other matter were at stake he would have left it at that. But the combination of the telegram's exigency with the celerity of the responses makes him uneasy.

"Glazkov!" Pazhari says to one of his battalion commanders. "I want you in Nesvizh today. Starting tonight you will set up roadblocks near all the town's gateways. Demidov! Mobilise towards Minsk, starting tomorrow. Zarobin! Mobilise south towards Baranavichy. Your soldiers don't sleep a wink until we catch them. Is that clear?"

Pazhari has never seen his officers in such a state.

"To Nesvizh?" Glazkov mumbles.

"Where did you say we should set up roadblocks?" Demidov asks.

"Where should I go again?" Zarobin is confused.

"Are you still here?" Pazhari demands, now scrutinising maps of the area. "Go! Every minute counts!"

The colonel finds his officers' hesitation amusing. Once they have left the tent, he peeks outside and sees them huddling together. They never question his orders normally, but now they are uneasy and dithering. Pazhari knows it will not take long for their secret to come to light.

Indeed, once the orders reach the ranks and the futility of pursuing their guests of more than a week makes itself evident, Zarobin returns to his commander with news: one of the sentries in his regiment reported that two of the four fugitives were spotted near the camp last night. Search parties have been dispatched to bring them to Pazhari.

"And what about the other two?" the colonel asks.

"Like I said, sir, the sentry only reported two people."

We may surmise that the soldiers feel obliged only towards the Father and his niece. No-one cares about Adamsky, even though he was a decorated captain in his day, and clearly no-one has grown fond of the gluttonous, tone-deaf cantor.

If truth be told, some of the soldiers said that it was a cast-iron rule never to mess with the Department for Public Security and Order. If the Department demanded that four people should be handed over, they should hand over four people, even at the cost of giving up Breshov. However, others believed that giving up even one member of the Father's entourage would be tantamount to sacrilege. Out of respect for the Czarist army and its troops it would be best not to dwell on the arguments that raged in the soldiers' tents, which quickly turned into fist fights, bitter altercations, the settling of accounts and a few broken noses. Eventually, it was decided that they would give up two of the guests and save the other two, although it was unclear where the two now destined for arrest had gone. They were not in Zizek Breshov's tent, and no-one knew where they had spent the week following their arrival.

II

After realising that Yoshke and his companions, led by that vile woman, have tricked him (how could he have lost his entire fortune because of a stupid spousal quarrel?), Captain Adamsky leaves the tent and descends into the night with the saunter of a local. He can tell just by looking at the ropes tied to tent pegs which of them will survive the autumn winds and which will be torn away and fly off to the Black Sea. The tents are abuzz with snores, muffled sobs, broken-up words and cracking bones, sounds so familiar that he could use them to compose a symphony: an opening fart, followed by a curse and a stone thrown at the farting man that will accidentally hit a snoring man, who in turn will shout, enraged, "Let me sleep, you bastards!" Others will hush him: "Kiss my arse!" Silence will be reinstated briefly until a sentry enters and calls: "Get up, Igor!" Igor will bark back at him, "I'm not getting up!", and so on. This exchange will be accompanied by the open eyes and vigilant ears of a soldier praying for redemption, unable to sleep; the first to end up killed on the battlefield.

If he wanted to, Adamsky could easily seize an empty bed in one of those tents. Waking up the next morning and preparing for roll call would be the most natural thing in the world for him, he could even conduct a roll call himself. He knows all the procedures, and he could adapt them for this pampered younger generation. They are much more talkative, more understanding and empathetic; in other words, much softer than his generation. Oh well. This sort of shit he can live with.

The thing about army life is that one is rarely confronted by more existential concerns. A roll call is coming up? Get ready for it. No roll call? Sleep. A battle is on? Fight. No battle? Sleep. In between one can eat and, if possible, drink, and play chequers or cards in the evening. Adamsky knows all too well that a whole lifetime can be passed this way, a life where anything goes: the dismembered ear of a friend, severed genitals, chilblains and bodies sour with sweat. Dammit, you can even get used to army jokes. And as you sign your discharge papers, you curse your god-damned freedom because it makes you realise that your military service was arbitrary and pointless, and that you have nothing in common with most servicemen, even those you count among your closest friends.

No, he would be out of place in one of these tents. Instead, he picks up a light jacket and some trousers from a clothes line to make it easier to pass through the night without having to come up with endless explanations. Uncharacteristically, tonight he'd prefer to avoid clashes or brawls and relive his former, carefree life. Even for just a few hours.

Drifting away from the centre of the camp, he notices a distant halo in the dark, a bonfire probably. He turns in its direction, hoping to find liquor and company, and above all an opportunity to forget that heinous Fanny who has razed everything he had with a single stroke of her knife. Who will compensate him for his tavern? Who will give him his property back? She even has the audacity to stare at him with her cruel, wild eyes, without a modicum of . . . No! He certainly doesn't need her pity. What can you expect from a bloody Jewess? Still, she's not like others

338

of her ilk, she has something that they lack, or rather, lacks something they have. If she had been ordered to give away a boy under the Cantonist Decree, she would never have relented; she would have hunted down every single child snatcher and personally seen to their beheading.

By God, just the thought of her wolf-like eyes makes his blood boil. Such rage hasn't possessed him since his brother died. He had better keep walking towards that light, lest he return to the tent, take her knife and tie her up. It's best if he doesn't. Once he starts there's no stopping him.

Every seasoned soldier knows there's nothing more misleading than lights in the night. As long as no sound comes from the direction of such incandescence, it's nigh-on impossible to estimate how far away it is. Thinking you're almost there, you could fall into a brook or be forced to climb yet another hilltop, which you are convinced is the last one, but then there's a crest preceded by a crevice you have to cross, and then the light is gone and you're no longer sure if it ever existed outside your imagination. Sure enough, Adamsky trips and falls as he ventures into the mounting darkness, roundly cursing the Creator: if He wanted to have darkness, why did He bother with a moon? And if He wanted to have a nocturnal light, why does the moon set so early? Any fool could have planned this better. Fucking hell.

You have no-one but yourself to blame, echoes a voice inside his head. You're just a fool repeating the same mistake over and over again. What do you have in common with Yoshke Berkovits? What do you owe him, anyway? He chose to carry on working at the latrines until he got the plague. He decided to remain faithful to the community that made him an outcast and destroyed his family. He believed he could fool the entire world with his letters until it blew up in his face. Their entire corps was annihilated in one, miserable battle.

And you were actually on leave for once, in Bucharest, when it happened. Why did you ride back to rescue him? Why were you so distressed when you heard about Radzetsky's scheme? You rode for five days without a break, eating nothing but bread and onion and sleeping in the saddle. What were you chasing after? What did you set out to save? What did you want to prove? You spotted him, the coward, charging with the fourth or fifth wave of the assault. He didn't use his rifle once. He ran alongside everyone else like a perfect idiot, not caring if he lived or died.

And when he saw you, the great baby, he started crying. You slapped him twice. Stop crying, there's no time for that, you idiot. Put your head down and let's get the hell out of here. "Pesach," he called you, his voice trembling. And you let him. Like a fool you let him.

You should have thrown him off your horse and left him to the mercy of the Bashi-Bazouk. Enraged, you threatened him with your dagger – if he ever called you Pesach again you'd cut his tongue off. And the idiot snatched your dagger and slashed his own mouth, and kept mumbling with a bleeding tongue and torn gums, "Pesach, Pesach."

You couldn't believe your eyes. You threw him off the horse and dragged him along the ground.

"You fool!" you screamed. "What are you doing?"

The idiot kept wailing, "Pesach, Pesach."

"You're a lost cause!"

"Pesach, Pesach!"

"What do you have to live for, anyway?"

"Pesach, Pesach."

"Answer me, Yoshke!"

"Pesach, Pesach."

You dragged him to the nearby village to get medical aid. There wasn't any other choice. His mouth was gushing blood. You left him

340

in the care of a family in return for a few roubles, and left as fast as you could. And now? The same story all over again? Without thinking twice? He shows up in your tavern and you immediately come to the rescue. You deserve it, Adamsky, it's all on you.

Adamsky assumes that the people sitting around the fire are officers. They probably wanted to unburden themselves of the effort of having to feign uprightness, a duty they carry around like a hump on their backs. His assumption is confirmed by the sound of feminine giggles. Smuggling prostitutes into camp requires a measure of power and means, and if officers have any advantage over plain soldiers it is their higher salary and the range of opportunities that comes with it.

It's impossible to see the forest for the trees, though. Well, actually there is a forest, a dense one with the thin fingers of speckle-trunked birch trees protruding from the ground and scratching the sky with their sharp fingernails. Adamsky squeezes through the thicket in his bid to reach the light, wondering how he managed to glimpse the fire at all if he has to cross this damned thick brush to get to it. Once he is out of the woods, he meets neither officers nor whores, just plain soldiers and local women who had happened to be passing by. To his surprise, not one of them cocks their gun and orders the stranger to identify himself. They couldn't care less whether he is an underground Polish assassin or an old-timer who just wants to have a relaxing smoke in their company.

Three soldiers and five women stare at him blankly. One of them, sporting an unkempt moustache and an unshaven face, invites him to join them. "Come over here, Grandpa," he calls, and before Adamsky can reply, another soldier, slender and cricket-like, hands him a pipe filled with a strange tobacco. Adamsky suspects they may have packed it with opium, an assumption confirmed by the mellowness of the company. The men are not making much of the women, and the women are not pushing them away. They are all moored in a bottomless bay of complacency. If Adamsky were still an officer, he'd have thrown them all into a dungeon without further ado. But such thoughts are not even crossing their tranquil minds right now.

One of the women gets up and sits next to Adamsky. "You are really old," she giggles, but for some reason he is not offended. "You have wrinkles in the corners of your eyes." She touches his face, and Adamsky shuts his eyes and focuses on his pipe.

"Tell us, Grandpa," says the third soldier – who, judging by a corpulence beyond his years, is probably a cook – "did you fight in the Russo-Turkish war?"

"The Russo-Turkish war?" Adamsky snorts. "How about the blunder in Crimea?"

"Crimea!" The moustached man is suddenly alert. "The Battle of Inkerman?"

"Inkerman, Balaclava, Sevastopol." Adamsky puffs out his chest. "The Russo-Turkish war was child's play compared to Crimea."

"They say that things are heating up again in the east," the cricket-like soldier says, in a nasal voice. "We're going to the front too, maybe even next month. Who knows what's cooking there. We'll finally get to fight."

"What makes you think you'll be sent to the front?" his moustached friend scoffs. "What's cooking? Cold cucumber soup, if you're lucky. Our generation is doomed. Look at this old man. One soldier, two wars. And what about us? We oil weapons all day long. Tell us, Grandpa," he goes on, "tell us about the British. Are their snipers really that good? Is it true that they don't cry at funerals? Did you fight them face to face?"

"Yes," Adamsky says, "you could say that. That is, you couldn't actually see their faces, but . . ." Suddenly, the young woman sitting next to Adamsky lays her head on his shoulder and stretches out her legs. He had been about to tell them about lacerating enemies' entrails but now he thinks the better of it, looking sideways at his admirer, thirty years his junior, as she clings to him. It seems no coincidence that she has curled herself against him, although her gesture is not seductive, more a request for protection.

"Well?" the rotund man prompts him.

"What's your rank, anyway?" the moustached soldier asks. "Sergeant?"

"Yes," Adamsky lies, "retired."

"Retired," the cricket says. "Aren't *you* a grandpa."

Adamsky says nothing.

Once his companion has closed her eyes, Adamsky notices the unusual quirks in her face. Her teeth are far apart and her lips are bloated. Her eyes are strangely narrow and her nose is flat as a bulldog's. He wonders if she might have some kind of disability, or condition. The thought makes him feel neither pity nor revulsion. He strokes her smooth hair and closes his eyes too. His face is warmed by the fire's heat, and fatigue eases his tense body. Before long, he is visualising Ada – he has decided that this is her name – cooking him dinner and waiting for him in their home, as he returns from the fields with a goddamned pitchfork. He suddenly bursts out laughing, but he is unsure whether it is an expression of momentary happiness, or self-ridicule, for choosing to be a peasant and not a prince, even in his fantasies.

How much time did he spend with this gang? Who knows. The nights blended with the days, and Ada's breasts were soft and welcoming. One thing is clear: the pipe he smoked was not packed with tobacco; otherwise it would be impossible to explain his wild reveries, and the fact that he wakes up one morning on a straw bed in a tent at the far end of the camp. His new friends must have ended their week's holiday, dragged him back from the forest and left him here, not knowing who he was. Or could it be that this week, from beginning to end, has been no more than a sweet dream, and that Ada, like the distant halo in the dark, was only a figment of his imagination? Whatever happened, right now he feels as though he has rolled down from a mountaintop into a turbid bog. The memory of Ada sends unfamiliar pangs of longing through his body, vivid and intense, although he cannot decide for the life of him if she was imaginary or real.

He has never felt this way about a woman. In fact, he has never given much thought to women at all. In his army years, and even more recently as a tavern owner, women have always been a means of satisfying an impulse for him – passing whores, an outlet for carnal desires. In all honesty, he never felt that he needed anything else from them. Hard as he may try, the sight of a woman only elicits from him one of two reactions: attraction or repulsion. But of all of them, this innocent, unattractive woman who laid her head on his shoulder and asked for his protection without even knowing his name, has made him open up to a possibility he cannot even define.

And there's another thing. Adamsky senses that, before he can go out looking for her, he must return to Yoshke's tent and end that story; that is, if the others are still there and haven't left him to face the music all by himself.

He remembers the way back to the tent well enough. His senses, even if a little clouded, are still sharp enough to lead him in the right direction. He blends in perfectly with the crowd of soldiers, thanks to his borrowed uniform. No-one would guess that he is a retired captain. He finds the tent and cautiously enters through the flaps at the back. Although he recognises the belligerent expression in Fanny's eyes immediately, he does not feel the ire her presence usually sparks in him. He doesn't care whether she suspects him or intends to use the dormant steel dragon on her thigh. He is finished with her.

He crosses the tent, but stops short at the sight of Yoshke, who is lying prostrate on a bed, like a corpse. What has he done all week? Basked in self-pity? A man his size lying flat on his stomach like a bag of potatoes, weighed down by his childhood defeats, the victim of his own miserable choices. Adamsky surprises everyone by sitting at Yoshke's bedside. Yoshke doesn't budge. Adamsky shakes his defeated shoulder, and whispers, "Yoshke, it's me."

Magically revived, Yoshke rolls over, his glistening eyes directed at his old friend. "Pesach?"

Adamsky coolly scrutinises his face: tousled beard, dazed eyes. Yoshke's scarred mouth trembles.

"This is it, Yoshke," Adamsky whispers. "It's over, I'm going." The perfect serenity that slowly permeates Berkovits' face tells Adamsky that Zizek understands exactly what he means: no matter what happens, this will be the last time they'll see each another. Adamsky will not come to his rescue ever again. Their story has reached its ending. There will be no reconciliation.

"This is it," Adamsky repeats and extends his hand to Yoshke, who has turned over again, his eyes bright and beady.

"As you wish," says Yoshke and looks away.

"Patrick Adamsky, you are not going anywhere," Fanny says, her voice laden with contempt. "If they catch you, we will all be held accountable."

"Accountable?" he explodes, shattering his pledge to ignore her, unable to tolerate her insolence. "What do you know about accountability? You spoiled brat! Roaming the empire because of a stupid love story, destroying other people's lives on the way – is this what you call justice? Don't lecture me about accountability!" He turns to leave.

"I said, you are not going anywhere," Fanny says again. Unable to restrain himself any longer, Adamsky lunges and grabs her left arm before she can reach her thigh. Pinning her against the canvas sheet he growls in her face, "Not such a hero without your knife, eh? I could squash you like a mosquito, understand? Don't you tell me what I can and can't do. I'm finished with the lot of you."

He reaches under her skirts and rips the knife off her thigh. The fleeting touch of his hand on her leg excites him. He expects to see fear in her eyes, but he is met with a smile that seems almost inviting. She simply does not believe he is capable of going that far. Adamsky would like to prove her wrong, but he cannot harm her. He knows full well that he's making a mistake, that he will pay for his weakness later, but he cannot bring himself to tighten his grip on her arm.

"Pesach!" Zizek cries.

"Don't you dare call me Pesach, you bastard!" Adamsky points the knife at Zizek, who is now standing there, facing him. Despite Zizek's towering height, Adamsky knows that the woman is still the real danger here. He clamps her neck with his hand and keeps his eyes on her. Those who have left a crack in their defences around Fanny have ended up with a slit throat.

Then, suddenly, without warning, Zizek's iron fist lands right in Adamsky's face. Adamsky, who knows all about fights, realises that no defence is possible against this kind of fist, and that if he tries to stay on his feet and punch back, his flailing arm will hit nothing but thin air and he will end up on the ground. Drawing on all his experience, he turns to his opponent and dives at Zizek, ready to tear him apart with teeth and finger-nails.

They roll on the ground, struggling. Adamsky's skin is torn, Zizek bashes his ribs, and they try to strangle each other senseless.

Then Fanny seizes the knife Adamsky has dropped, and holds it against the back of the captain's neck.

"No!" Zizek gasps. "You stay out of this." He releases his grip on Adamsky's throat.

The captain also relents, and they lie on the ground, in a tangle of limbs, sweating and seething with rage.

"So you've finally decided to wake up, have you?" Adamsky wheezes. "You've been asleep for forty years. It's a bit late to start fighting now, don't you think?"

Zizek does not reply. His body is battered and bruised. His short breaths barely push the oxygen through his body.

"Did you understand what I just said?" Adamsky says.

Zizek looks at him, wordlessly.

"This is it," Adamsky says. "It's over. I'm going. If I ever see your face again, you will be no more than a stranger to me."

Zizek closes his eyes, as if an agreeable spasm has passed through him, and Adamsky, expecting more resistance, finds that he has no-one to argue with.

"I should have left you to die," Adamsky says, exasperated, as he rises to his feet. For the first time in years, since they were children in fact, Adamsky sees a broad smile spreading over his opponent's face.

"Is that what you want? To die?" Adamsky says. "It can be easily arranged."

Adamsky picks up a blanket and uses it to wrap up a few tins of food scattered around the tent. He takes one of the discarded bottles next to Shleiml Cantor's empty bed and fills it with water. He looks about him, ignoring Fanny and Zizek, and makes his way to the exit, but just as he is about step out of the tent, he finds his path blocked by five sentries, bearing orders to urgently bring Adamsky and Cantor to headquarters.

"I have nothing to do with them!" Adamsky protests, pointing at Fanny and Zizek, when he is told to drop whatever he is holding.

"Excellent," the officer says. "I didn't come for them."

"You're arresting me?" Adamsky is livid. "It was them . . . I arrived with them."

"I don't care who arrived with whom. I received a clear order and I intend to follow it. By the way, where is the fourth man, the one they call Cantor? Have any of you seen him recently?"

III

The guard commander's question perfectly encapsulates Shleiml Cantor's current situation. Indeed, another week will go by before they find the cantor. Put your mind at rest, he will still be alive. But the very fact that someone is looking for him, that someone should take an interest in him, can be explained by Shleiml Cantor's arrival in the army camp, since when he has been enjoying a life he had never tasted before. To wit, it actually matters to someone else whether he is around or not.

It all began, of course, with the sumptuous banquet he enjoyed the day of their arrival. Having ingested more than two pounds of tinned meat (kosher of course, or so the soldiers who brought the food claimed), a loaf of bread and three bottles of wine (also kosher, he was assured), the cantor unwillingly sank into deep sleep. And then, having gorged himself beyond capacity, he was compelled to get up in the middle of the night and rush off to answer his accursed body's shortcomings.

Even then, something troubled Shleiml Cantor, preventing him from going back to sleep. At first, he suspected that it was one of those sinister thoughts that possesses him without warning once in a while; a dark, rainless cloud that envelops him with melancholy and blocks his tears. A slight murmur in his stomach, however, announced that his hunger had simply returned, and that the heavy feeling in his stomach was merely a kick from an embryonic appetite.

In Cantor's eyes, his appetite was a small creature writhing in his belly, capable of assuming monstrous dimensions without warning, and sapping his strength. Accustomed to these pregnancies, he listens to his foetus's pulsations with a mixture of pain and pleasure. Given half a chance, he can give the details of each and every meal that has ever calmed his stomach, all the more so if they consisted of several courses. In the latter case, the mere memory of the dishes would make him feel full again days after the meal had taken place.

As it happens, the meal of the previous night – rich, abundant, his reward for escorting the Father (who is the Father anyway? He doesn't know) – has left him famished and thirsty, and just now he does not feel like facing yet another long gestation. In the army, he thinks, there seem to be immediate rewards to be earned, and if he plays his cards right such meals could become routine.

Before long, he runs into a group of card players gathered in one of the tents and offers to join them. They welcome him cordially, and he gathers from the low bets – twenty copecks a round – that this is a friendly game. Even so, this does not stop him from racking up some dizzying losses and he soon tops the losers' chart with a five-rouble debt. For some reason, his new friends are amused by his losses and do not demand immediate payment. On the contrary. They offer him kvass and veal sausages (kosher, to be sure) and laugh uproariously at everything he either says or does. "I win!" Shleiml Cantor declares, flashing the weakest hand of the table, and the pack gasps for air. "I raise!" he proudly announces, in his funny little hat, and a soldier merrily smashes a bottle against a tent pole to stop his laughter. "Is there anything left to eat?" the matchstick asks, having guzzled down twelve sausages, and his hosts are reduced to hysterics. When the time comes to say goodbye, they leave ten rifles next to him in a pile and tell him to have them oiled by sunrise. Cantor gladly accepts, surprised that this chore will settle his debt. Most of his luckless nights end with a bruising, but now his nose is in place, his ribs intact, and his spirits are high.

What does Shleiml Cantor know about rifles? Not much. He seems to recall that if the trigger is pulled at one end, someone dies at the other. Regardless, if he can pay his debt by cleaning instead of having his face smashed, then army life has turned out to be more appealing than he could have imagined. He has travelled constantly since childhood, escaping life in an orphanage by the skin of his teeth. Who would have thought that rationing a child's food could be allowed? All they served there was one slice of bread a day, a bit of cheese and vegetable soup without the vegetables. Alternating between famine and gluttony in the outside world is better than starving all the time in a so-called children's asylum.

Shleiml's chosen way of life is bound up with luck. It is hard to predict people's behaviour. Once, as a young man, he encountered a grumpy woman who started hectoring him before he could even open his mouth: "A boy your age, why aren't you working? Scrounger! You'll be a cantor only in your dreams. Just look at my children, hauling buckets from dawn to dusk." The lecture was followed by her producing a shoe out of nowhere and missing him by a hair. As he walked away, disappointed, she went back into her house, only to return with a trayful of delights: cabbage soup and warm borscht and meat casserole with *kartoshkes*, and *lekach* sponge cakes. Imagine that. Another time, he met a merciful mother who had come out of her house, dripping honeyed words: "I understand, how could I not? No-one is an orphan, my dear, we all have one father in Heaven. Nothing of what has happened to you is your fault. Come in, our home is your home too, sit down to dine with us, this is a mitzvah." But while she served her children goulash she scraped from a pot, she served him a sickly-pale, shrivelled carrot that looked like the finger of a cadaver. After all, one mustn't stuff a beggar's stomach with more than it can hold. She could not take responsibility for the death of a tzaddik.

As salvation has always come to Shleiml Cantor from unexpected sources, he has learned that there is never any reason to despair. His greatest triumphs came just as he was convinced that he was facing defeat and humiliation. This is why he agrees to clean the rifles, hoping it will yield him additional reward. This time, however, he thinks that his fortune is not down to lucky chance, but the conclusion of a perfectly logical process. On the one hand, he gambled and feasted at his hosts' expense. On the other hand, he didn't pay a damn thing. It is only natural to be asked to carry out a task in return, and it only makes sense for soldiers' tasks to somehow involve guns rather than something like flowers. As he oils a rifle barrel, Cantor wonders if this is the kind of order and discipline his life so desperately needs. If all he has to do is to clean a few metal rods in exchange for tinned meat – kosher, of course – then he would like to enlist in the Czarist army. The sooner the better!

The next morning, he announces his plan to the half-asleep and decidedly less welcoming group from the night before, who tell him to make some coffee. Intent on proving his dedication, he obliges, mentioning again his wish to enlist as he serves their brew.

"I'm all for it," a soldier yells. "He can replace Oleg."

"Great idea!" the others chorus. "Let him replace Oleg!"

Cantor inquires if replacing Oleg will involve food and drink, and everyone assures him that, from now on, food and drink will be the least of his worries.

It is hard to describe what happens to a man whose greatest worries suddenly become the least of his concerns. On the one hand, he is surely overjoyed. On the other hand, the core of his being disappears, his life has taken an entirely new course. If he is no longer supposed to scavenge for food, what else is he supposed to do?

"Come on!" another soldier orders. "Let's go and replace Oleg!"

"Should I take anything with me?" the cantor wonders.

"What have you got?" the soldier asks.

"Nothing."

"What would you take with you, then?"

Indeed, this soldier's military logic makes a good deal of sense. It'll take Shleiml some time before he masters it too.

The walk is long and the sun is blinding. Who knew that Oleg's post is not actually in the camp at all but lodged between two steep hills? Naturally, the cantor lags behind the sure-footed soldier. When they reach their destination at the pass, Oleg turns out to be Dmitry, a carabineer sent to guard the camp's eastern flank, and the real Oleg, Shleiml learns, was eaten alive by wolves in this very spot.

"I'm joking," his companion laughs, "it's just a joke."

"It happened a long time ago," Dmitry says, reassuringly. "They check up on me every two days."

"Every two days?" The cantor is concerned. "And what about . . ."

"See that crate?" the soldier says, pointing. "You could feed half the army with the food in there. Eat all you want."

The cantor opens the crate, shoos away a few flies and starts plundering its riches. If God had produced bread from the earth and not have brought it to Shleiml's mouth, it would have been

352

enough. If He had brought it to his mouth but not thrown in tinned meat and sardines and crackers and reasonably fresh vegetables and four bottles of liquor, it would have been enough. If He had thrown in tinned meat and sardines and crackers and reasonably fresh vegetables and four bottles of liquor, and not left him a small tent to stretch his limbs in, it would have been enough. If He had left him a small tent to stretch his limbs in, but no straw bed to lie on, it would have been enough. If there had been a straw bed without an old feather pillow, it would have been enough.

Can anyone appreciate Shleiml Cantor's elation? He will gladly replace Oleg. "You can trust me," he exclaims, and brings a hand to his ridiculous hat. "Sir!" he adds for good measure, and the two soldiers laugh their heads off.

After the change of guard, Dmitry kneels and crosses himself several times. Even Cantor understands that this gesture means this outpost is dangerous, and that one's chances of survival here decrease in inverse proportion to the length of one's stay. If they remember your existence after two days, you might come out of it relatively unscathed. But if they forget about you, a two-week shift that includes almost daily raids by bandits or wolves will see your chances of survival plummet. Dmitry, it emerges, spent four days here. The fact that he was not butchered by gypsies, Poles, Turks or wolves is very heartening indeed.

Dmitry and the other soldier begin their walk back from Oleg's outpost. "Don't forget, you've got Olga too," Dmitry yells over his shoulder, pointing at a scarecrow with straw hair. Cantor is impressed by its tarpaulin torso and arms made of planks, one of which is half the length of its counterpart. "Pleased to meet you, Olga!" He is happy to learn he has company. Shaking her good hand, he suggests, "Shall we dine?"

IV

As Adamsky is dragged out of the tent by the soldiers, the Father rushes after them with Fanny right behind him. "No!" he yells. An entire platoon bows its head at the sound of the voice they have been wanting to hear for so long. They know full well that the only way of rescuing the Father from the Department for Public Security and Order requires keeping him bound and gagged in his tent, and yet no-one dares to try it, even though they are painfully aware that their reluctance exposes their saint to grave danger.

Three of the four fugitives are brought to Colonel Pazhari. The fourth and easiest prey is the only one they cannot find. From what Pazhari can gather, this character is rather conspicuous: a gaunt, strange man, with tousled beard and sidelocks, as *żyd* as they come.

"Search for him," Pazhari orders. "He must be somewhere in the camp."

Pazhari could not be more right, although there is one particular fact that has escaped him, and the soldiers who sent Cantor to replace Oleg have kept this fact to themselves. When the order came to arrest the four suspects, without reflection or coordination they pretended not to know anything about Cantor. When the messenger arrived at their tent with the order, they sized him up and shrugged, surprised at the very injunction, let alone the possibility of finding a *żyd* in their tent.

Once he had left, they were struck by the gravity of their actions. Why had they risked everything for the sake of a wretched matchstick? If the truth came out, one of them, or all of them, would pay dearly. Good Lord, they might face a military court. And yet, for some strange reason, they resolved not to give him up, as if Cantor – that orphaned *żyd* and insatiable nomad – was one of them. Imagine that.

In any event, as the colonel turns to the retrieved suspects, he wonders about their missing friend, because none of these three strikes him as a killer. The woman is indeed unconventional, staring into his eyes without fear. What is she looking for? He does not know, but even if she is plotting something, her pale, exhausted and worn-out face assures him she won't get very far. Road dust and burnt gunpowder have painted her light hair grey underneath her headscarf, and her complexion resembles a blackened cabbage leaf. Her frailty and distress, as well as the fact that she is unarmed, make it hard to imagine that her fists could be dangerous.

The hulk standing next to her, however, is a colossus. Despite his age – fifty-five, maybe sixty? – Pazhari would prefer to see him handcuffed, mainly because of his scarred mouth, which suggests battle experience. His imposing figure is tamed, however, by a frightened demeanour, making the colonel seriously doubt that this massive body could take part in a lethal assault. The man is taciturn, introverted, with his eyes fixed on the ground. This cocoon will never grow a butterfly with iron wings.

The third suspect calls himself Captain Adamsky and won't stop babbling about the Third Regiment, Fifth Division, Eleventh Army, in which he supposedly served. What Pazhari sees, however, is a midget wearing a private's uniform, a gnome boasting a pimp's sideburns, a character one often sees coming out of taverns at sunrise to stagger about the streets like a headless chicken, making one ask oneself: "Am I really sacrificing my life for this?" If he was indeed a captain, there's no way of proving it. He doesn't have any documents to show, and right now his word is not worth a fart.

"Why aren't they shackled?" Pazhari asks the garrison commander.

"Sir . . ." the soldier hesitates. "We cannot shackle the Father. He is our guest."

"The father?" Pazhari asks. "Whose father?"

The head of the guard says nothing, embarrassed.

"He really is the Father," Zarobin says.

Pazhari is irritated by Zarobin's reverence for this man, but then, all of a sudden, he understands what they are trying to say.

"Which one?" he demands, astounded, guessing before Glazkov points him out.

"And this is his niece," Demidov adds.

"But as for him," Zarobin says, pointing at Adamsky, "no-one knows what he's doing here."

"I am Captain Adamsky, Third Regiment, Fifth Division, Eleventh Army."

"You are under arrest," Pazhari says, coldly.

Even though the unexpected arrest has undoubtedly disrupted Adamsky's ability to think clearly, he is still able to estimate the distance between his fist and the colonel's face and lands a lightning-fast punch on Pazhari's chin.

Adamsky has come to learn that punching faces can have varying degrees of effectiveness. You can crush a cheekbone, break a nose, smash eye sockets, break a man's teeth one by one . . . But a single strike to the chin will go much further. And indeed, Colonel Pazhari collapses on the spot, and Adamsky flees the tent like a demon.

If one were to assess his odds of escaping the camp, well, one would focus on these facts: a veteran long past his prime, who has celebrated fifty-six springs, breaks out of the camp commander's heavily guarded pavilion. Beyond a circle of officers' tents, tens of thousands of troops are performing their morning drills with their weapons at the ready. In the outer circle, thousands of fearless horsemen are waiting with their fit and well-fed mounts. And yet our man still thought it would be a sound idea to try and break through this line of defence.

There's one advantage Adamsky has always had, though. Most of the soldiers surrounding him do not know what combat is really about. Sure, they wrestle one another during training, shoot at fixed targets and jump over obstacles on horseback like English gentlemen. But all one has to do is chew off one of their ears, and you'll have them crawling on the ground licking the dirt in search of it.

Adamsky exceeds his own expectations. He pushes past the sentries, runs through the circle of officers' tents, pierces fifteen eyes (two of which belong to the same officer), crushes seven noses (leaving one man completely snoutless), tears off twenty-one earlobes (three of which are quickly found, though their rightful owners cannot identify which one is theirs), and one hundred and twelve bullets, two bullets for every year of Adamsky's life (the captain counted them all), miss the man Pazhari thought a gnome and a pimp.

Why does the getaway fail? As always with Adamsky, his hot temper is to blame. Had he used the turmoil he unleashed to get past the furthest guard and flee on the back of a young colt, he might have reached Ada, the young woman with whom he wants to build a future. But Adamsky can't help but attack every ear that comes his way, and finally a furious mass of men-at-arms are pinning him down.

Now he is surrounded by dozens of sentries, all of whom know exactly what his mouth is capable of, and the mere sight of him compels them to touch their noses and ears to make sure they are still there. Exhilarated, Adamsky gets down on his knees, crosses himself four times and stretches out his arms for the chains.

Bound and bruised, the captain is dragged back to the camp's deputy commander. After all, there's no better proof of courage and cunning in combat than attacking a chained soldier. Pazhari has since recovered from the blow to his chin, despite his rattled head and aching tongue, while Adamsky lies on his side, groaning and spitting blood. Zizek and Fanny are paralysed at the sight of his mangled body. Pazhari bends down to take a look at his face.

"Why?" the colonel asks Adamsky.

"Why not?" the captain says.

Pazhari respects the honest answer, but he cannot let it pass. "Take him away," he orders the sentries. "I want three guards on him even when he pisses. And you!" Pazhari turns to Fanny and Zizek. "You are coming with me."

V

Inside Mishenkov's tent there is a sequestered section that the general calls "the office", and his subordinates prefer to call "the bordello". Mishenkov has planned his office in a way that allows him to repay his high-ranking friends by entertaining them with the finest delights modern life has to offer. Despite the military backdrop, he has managed to put many a lavish salon to shame.

Behind the entrance flap a new world awaits the guests, a space painted in bright colours, scented with rare perfumes and adorned with silky fabrics. A green velvet sofa faces an oak rocking chair with satin cushions, an Asian coffee table in the middle offers a chessboard with pieces carved from seal teeth, an ice bucket nestles a fine bottle of Wyborowa vodka, complemented by the barrel of English rum next to a box of French cigars. There's a shelf stacked with the plays of Racine and Molière, and a pantry stocked with caviar, fish, ostrich eggs, beef and tropical fruit – how does Mishenkov manage to find tropical fruit? – compels one to sink into the cushions on the sofa and stuff oneself senseless.

*

Normally, Pazhari would never dare to set foot in Mishenkov's office in his commander's absence, but now he ushers in the distinguished guests and invites them to sit on the sofa. If the governor, or even the Czar, had been there, Pazhari would not have dreamed of receiving them in a dusty tent, and would never have served them tepid tea with stale biscuits. In the same way, he wants to entertain the Father to the best of his abilities. So now, the deputy camp commander turns and offers Zizek and Fanny a glass of the Wyborowa, even though he has never tasted it himself. They both refuse, but Zizek is ogling the rum and the colonel takes the hint. Zizek drains his cup and hands it back for a refill. Pazhari smiles to himself and gladly serves him a second.

Like everyone else, Pazhari also knows one version or other of the Father's legend, although he is certainly not as immersed in the details as Ignat Shepkin. Pazhari's generosity towards Fanny and Zizek does not surprise his troops nor his guests. Fanny wonders if perhaps Pazhari's own life hadn't been saved thanks to one of Yelena Venediktova's letters, and if not his, then perhaps the life of his father, or a brother or uncle. Only the Devil knows which of them was suspended between life and death until Adjutant Zizek Breshov intervened. But the truth is that Pazhari served in a unit deployed much further north, never met Radzetsky, and none of his family members, as far as he knows, ever served in the army – for the simple reason that he has no family. So it can be said with confidence that his emotional attachment to the Father is not based on gratitude for his life.

Be that as it may, all the soldiers in the camp, from private to captain, are pleased with the way their commander is treating the Father, glad that Zizek Breshov has been given a gracious reception by a scion of Petersburgian nobility. If truth be told, they are wrong about that too. That is, they are wrong not about the gracious reception, but they are wrong about the noble origins of their deputy commander. In order to explain their mistake, we have no choice but to inquire into the past of Colonel David Pazhari, who might appear to be a marginal figure in Fanny's and Zizek's journey yet, by virtue of being deputy camp commander and the officer in charge, will play a decisive role in shaping their destiny.

VI

The colonel's first mistake was to be born in a tavern, for reasons that remain unclear to this day. The publican – that is, the whoremaster – may have been the real father, and his mother probably tried too late to correct her mistake. One thing is beyond question: a tavern is no place to raise a child.

Although the records indicate that Pazhari was sent to an orphanage at five months old, he could swear he has a memory of his mother: a fleshy, vivacious woman of curly hair and low brow, who he remembers singing a lullaby in a French accent: "*Mon chéri*, my sweet, my jewel, *mon petit.*"

This lullaby, or, rather, the memory thereof, may provide all the information necessary for telling David Pazhari's story. He never resented his mother and never dreamed of the day when he would take her to task for the wrongs he suffered. Not even when he was flogged by the orphanage headmaster, a pious priest, when he tried to escape at every opportunity. He accepted the floggings, knowing that they were a necessary deterrent for other children who might follow his example, and with every lash he calculated his next escape.

On his ninth attempt, on Christmas Eve, the holy matrimony between the birth of Christ and the resulting general inebriation permitted the boy to successfully flee the city and take refuge in the forest. The only drawbacks to his plan were the snow that slowed his escape and the cold, which took his breath away and forced him to find warmth in stables along the way. Huddled under old harnesses and sheltering in haystacks, he somehow managed to survive for three weeks, suffering only three chilblains: two on his legs and one between his mouth and nose, which left a scar that is still visible today, disrupting the otherwise irritating symmetry of his features.

As far as food went, he didn't have much. He occasionally sneaked into empty houses and ransacked pantries. In the village of Tabulki, not far from Motal, he finally found work as a servant in the Komarov household, a peasant family who let him sleep in a small shed in their courtyard. As far as David was concerned, they had granted him a palace. It was bedecked with tools and nails, shelves and tins of paint, buckets of various sizes and even a barrel long enough to lay on its side and use as a bed, if he padded it with hay.

The Komarovs were a devout Christian family, and the boy learned to love Jesus as he never had done before. His favourite story was the family's own version of the Holy Trinity – Jesus, his mother Mary, and Mary Magdalene – which the head of the family, Lev Komarov, who was evidently endowed with a fervent imagination, described to his children with grandiloquence. Nothing moved the young David more than the love of Jesus for Mary Magdalene. In his dreams she was fleshy, of curly hair and low brow, singing to Christ in a French accent: "*Mon chéri*, my sweet, my jewel, *mon petit*." Lev Komarov noticed that the servant boy was listening in on his stories and allowed him to stop dusting the mantelpiece and learn about the crucifixion. The boy was charmed by this act of generosity.

One day, his idyllic new life was disrupted. A group of

peasants from neighbouring farms arrived at the Komarovs', demanding to know if they had noticed any suspicious activity on their land. They said that thieves had plundered Teplov's cabin in what was Tabulki's second break-in that week.

"No," Komarov shrugged. "What were they looking for in the cabin? Children, did you see anything?"

Komarov's children were silent, as was David.

"We haven't seen anything," said Komarov.

"The bastard threatened Teplov with an axe. Teplov swears it was a *żyd*, he saw him with his own eyes."

"A *żyd*?" spat Komarov, as though the word was a curse. "Wait a minute, I'll come with you. We'll take a few horses from the stable. David, go and saddle them."

What was it about that word, *żyd*, that had infuriated his master so much? David was curious and begged with Komarov to be allowed to join them. Komarov was in a good mood. He clapped the boy on the shoulder and let David sit behind him on his horse. The boy couldn't have been happier as he set off into the birch forest with the search party, hunting for the fugitive, and on their way they set fire to a *żyd*'s wheat field and burned down a log store belonging to another. Exciting stuff. "Death to the *żyds*!" Teplov's brother shrieked and David followed suit, "Let them die!" The search party was jubilant. David was consumed with a desire to catch the thief, all his senses sharpened. The bastard! Breaks into a cabin, threatens people with axes, who does he think he is, the filthy *żyd*? Death to them all.

They returned home a few hours later without the culprit but quite pleased with themselves nonetheless, feeling they had restored their defences by brandishing their might and courage for all to see and hear. The pack sat down together at Komarov's table. The men drank themselves into a stupor and the boy served them the leftovers from dinner: borscht, pork and potato cakes with soured cream. When David had finished cleaning the kitchen, Komarov sent him back to the shed, where a surprise awaited him.

Inside his barrel, in the darkness, there crouched a snarling figure. David didn't think for one second of running away. That shed was his home, and he was prepared to die protecting it. He reached for the saw, but the beast jumped on him and hit him over the head with a bucket. David raised the saw, but then he heard the terrified whispers, "No! No!" This was the only word the beast knew in Polish, and David dropped the saw and stared at the boy before him. He had found the cause of the peasants' riot.

All they could see of each other was their murky silhouettes, and they were unable to communicate. The fugitive spoke Yiddish and a bit of Hebrew, and David Pazhari spoke Polish and a little Russian. But they heard each other's breathing, and suddenly David realised that even if it cost him everything he had, he would help this boy as best he could.

The fugitive was wet to the bone. David immediately produced his Sunday shirt, an old scarf, a lynx fur hat he had found near the river, which protected his ears from freezing at night – who would have believed that a boy like him would ever feel the softness of lynx fur? – and a pair of old boots with rather loose soles. He even considered handing over the trousers he was wearing, the only pair he had. He lifted a floor plank and showed the fugitive his secret food stash: fresh bread (just one week old), half a cabbage, cow's milk cheese and blueberry jam. The terrified boy tore at the bread and stuffed his mouth with a chunk so big that it looked like a hand reaching out of his throat, stretching his teeth with its fingers.

David was pleased. He was overcome by satisfaction as he watched the *żyd* voraciously eating the bread he had saved for himself. Loyalty is a strange thing. One man can betray his most generous benefactor while another can blindly follow his adversary. David did not stop to weigh up the pros and cons of the matter, but turned to stack the pails, seal the holes in the shed walls, move his barrel-bed and create a hiding place for the boy. Had he found him in the woods an hour earlier, he would have beheaded him. Yet now, even though he knew that turning the fugitive in would make him a hero, David was prepared to give up his life to save his guest.

The rooster started scolding the sun as dawn sneaked in through the cracks that David had tried to seal. Judging by his deep and even breathing, the fugitive was still asleep. David sat in a corner like a sentry, unable to sleep a wink. For how many nights did the runaway stay? David could not remember. How many words did they exchange? If one said none, this would be correct, and yet if another said an infinite number, this would be equally true.

David still remembers his guest's last night. After midnight, the boy dared to leave his hiding place and sit next to David. He stank of urine but David didn't care. He had never imagined that a human body could emit heat like a hearth. The two ended up embracing one another tightly, and the guest raised his glistening eyes to the heavens, reassuring David that he had done the right thing.

David woke up the next morning to find that his friend had gone. Without the fugitive, the shed had become a strange, empty place that no longer felt like home. David packed the clothes he had lent to his guest, who had left them in a neatly folded pile, and started planning his escape from the Komarovs. His destination was St Petersburg. Why the capital? Because St Petersburg was the place that had been most maligned in David's ears. In the Komarov household, it was said that the metropolis was one big tavern, a sewer teeming with pompous cliques who aimlessly roam around Nevsky Prospect. They wear the latest fashions and talk favourably about social reform in the Stroganov Palace grounds. Who will benefit from this reform? Not them, of course. Not the rabble: villagers, muzhiks, serfs and all other slaves making a living by doing actual work and by growing things that can be actually tasted or smelled, all of whom have nothing to do with the aristocracy. In between their debates about reform, Petersburgians frequent the theatre, mainly in order to gossip, and even as the opera they have come to see reaches its climax, they simply gawk at so-and-so's latest beau. Officials and officials' sons, none of whom know anything about real work, that's who inhabits the capital, that's who devises the reforms. David gathered little from these critiques, but his heart was drawn to the place that the Komarovs despised.

How did Pazhari turn from a vagabond to a scion of Petersburgian nobility? Well, he didn't. As he disembarked at Moscow railway station at half past eight in the morning, the boy stood at the terminal, dazzled by the onrush of grim faces. What was he thinking? They were dressed differently, smelled different, spoke a Russian dialect he had never heard before. He wanted to ask how to get to . . . but did not even know where he was going. Worse still, he felt embarrassed when he finally did speak. He walked to Vosstaniya Square and kept on going until he reached the Nevsky Monastery and the banks of the Neva, sensing policemen eyeing him suspiciously as if he were about to snatch a purse. Seeing some soldiers who had gathered in a side street, he approached them and for some reason felt more at ease.

The next day the boy presented himself at the city headquarters and enlisted in an imperial military school in the east, beyond the Ural Mountains. When asked for his name and from whence he came he replied, "David Pazhari, St Petersburg," and noticed that his interviewers' faces had grown suddenly intent. "Are you related to Count Pazhari of St Petersburg?"

"Of course, I am related to Pazhari," David replied, as if this were obvious.

"You are one of His Highness's sons?" they inquired, intrigued.

At this point, David realised that there had been some misunderstanding, but decided to stick with his story. "I'm his nephew," he muttered. "His sons' cousin."

Count Alexander Pazhari of St Petersburg was one of the best-known and most venerated men in the empire. He was among the Czar's closest and most influential advisers, and an almost certain bet for the job of chancellor, the highest position in political office. He lived on Nevsky Prospect – where else? – and he was an intimate friend of the Stroganov family. David Pazhari, the boy now considered the relative of this senior statesman, was received in the army camp with a respect reserved for kings. His comrades treated him with great politeness, officers demanded weekly reports about his well-being, and every commander who took Pazhari on a mission of any sort deemed it necessary to state for the record that he had been scarred between his lip and nose prior to his stationing with their unit.

It soon emerged, however, that the pampered boy was quite a military talent. He did well in his studies, took on the strongest opponents, proved an excellent shot and quickly adapted to the climate. In winter, he walked around without any furs and at mealtimes he was satisfied with only a scrap of bread with some cheese and jam.

Pazhari's rapid rise up the ranks was absolutely justified. If his last name gave him any advantage, it was only that every commander wished to have him stationed in his unit. Over time, rumours began to spread in the capital about Count Pazhari's nephew warrior, who was by then a junior officer, and, surprisingly, the count did not deny the connection. None of Count Pazhari's sons – a bunch of indolent brats to a man – had chosen to serve their country in the army. The only requests they made were "Papa, make me an adviser here", "Papa, let me open a law firm there". Papa, Papa, Papa. They didn't have a shred of decency between them. It would do the family no harm if it became known that one of its descendants was a true-blue military officer.

If anyone discussed David Pazhari with him, the count would evade the matter of his descent. "Your Excellency, we hear that David Pazhari is doing well," they would tell him. "Not even thirty years old, and he's already been promoted to captain."

"A jolly good fellow," the count would reply, enthusiastically. "I always knew that he was destined for great things."

When David Pazhari was promoted to colonel at the age of thirty-five, he started receiving offers to join the civil service. Pazhari turned them all down, determined to remain with his soldiers.

"Your Excellency," Alexander Pazhari was asked in St Petersburg, "what is wrong with your nephew? Does he mean to grow old at the barracks?"

"David Pazhari is no ordinary man," the count said. "The blood of princes runs through his veins."

VII

As Pazhari sits down before Zizek and Fanny, he feels as if his whole life has been leading up to this moment, the peak of his existence, no less. When he had first heard the Father's story, he had known at once that he had met him before, that their paths had crossed at the Komarovs'. The fugitive that he had concealed in the shed had been Yoshke Berkovits. Pazhari felt it in his bones. People who knew more about the Father's legend would have probably made a more reasonable assumption: it could not have been Yoshke Berkovits whom Pazhari had met in the shed, but it might have been Motl Avramson, Pesach's renegade brother. It had been roughly at that time and in that area that Motl had fled; many details matched, more or less. Naturally, only a kind-hearted orphan like Pazhari, even once he had become a colonel and deputy camp commander, could believe that in the vast Russian expanses that stretch between the empire's preposterously long borders, such a coincidence could be possible. Once he heard about the Father, this conviction settled in his mind and would not relent, as if there had been no other thieving boys in the empire, including *żyds*, that he could have met. In fact, his belief was quite unfounded, but nonetheless, Pazhari's fancy might still benefit the arrested pair, which is a serendipitous coincidence in and of itself.

"So, what brings you here?" Pazhari says to the stunned duo, sitting across from him on the velvet sofa.

They say nothing.

"You are Zizek Breshov, correct?" Pazhari asks this obvious question with the idea of drawing the man into the conversation.

No comment.

"And you?" He turns to Fanny. "Do you know that half the empire is chasing you?"

Pazhari notices a strange change in her face. Her eyes have turned predatory and her face is tense. Her left hand is sliding down towards her leg. Something's up.

"Fanny," Breshov snaps, and Pazhari is taken aback. Could he have underestimated this lady?

"I'm sorry, but . . ." his guest says.

"It's fine," Pazhari mutters, "no harm done."

The deputy camp commander thinks of his pistol. One false move and he will draw. He has no intention of becoming the next victim of this strange pair, whatever their mysterious motives. Pazhari knows that now is not the time for rash acts. If the woman realises that he noticed her sliding hand, she might be spurred to execute her plan. In his many years as an officer he has learned that if a soldier lies to your face, it's best to avoid a direct confrontation and give him a chance to repent. Confront a conman with his lies and he will always feel guilty in your presence and loathe you for ever.

"Are you going to give us up?" the woman asks, almost making him feel that an answer in the affirmative would seal his fate. The gall!

"No," Pazhari says.

"How can we believe you?" Fanny demands.

"Madam, I can tell that my language does not come naturally to you," Pazhari says, trying to politely put her in her place. He points at Breshov. "You had better let him speak."

"I'm sorry, but . . ." Breshov bows his head.

"There's no need to apologise. Why are you here?"

"We are . . . Please, you must hurry . . ." Zizek stutters, "Patrick . . . Adamsky . . . is . . . hot-headed . . . he—"

"—he is an imbecile," Fanny says. "Lucky they caught him before he took us all down with him."

"I cannot help him," the colonel says, looking directly at Zizek. "He'll be hanged soon, and trust me, they'll be doing him a favour. You, on the other hand . . ."

Pazhari is completely unprepared for what follows. Zizek buries his face in his hands and dissolves into tears. The colonel watches him in bewilderment. The man whimpers, then howls, gasps and shudders. The hulk is a broken man, sobbing, "Pesach . . . Pesach . . .", and smothers his scarred mouth with the crook of his arm.

"Zizek." The woman strokes the back of his head. "Pesach

Avramson has been Patrick Adamsky for a long time. Do you understand that?"

"Look," the colonel leans towards them. "I'll see what I can do about Pesach . . . I mean, Adamsky."

Zizek raises his bright eyes to Pazhari like a man who has just seen a miracle.

"I don't care if the suspicions about you are true or unfounded," Pazhari goes on. "In fact, it's better if you don't tell me whether you are responsible for this killing spree or not. I have just one very simple question: what are you doing here, and where would you like to go?"

"To Zvi-Meir Speismann," Fanny says, at once.

"Zvi-Meir who?"

"Zvi-Meir Speismann," she says. "My sister's husband. He is in Minsk."

"I'm sorry, but . . ." Zizek mumbles. "You said, about Pesach . . . he is—"

"Don't worry." Pazhari touches Zizek's arm. "I'll see to it that your friend does not come to any harm." He has no idea how he will keep this reckless promise.

"Please," Zizek whispers, looking anxiously at Pazhari's hand as if it were a snake twisting around his forearm.

"I'll personally take care of Adamsky," the colonel says, embarrassed. "Just tell me what happened to Zvi-Meir?"

"Nothing happened to Zvi-Meir," says Fanny. "That's the problem."

Pazhari says nothing and looks at Zizek, who is looking at the ground.

Fanny launches into her story. "He abandoned my sister and his children, and now he must be held to account."

The colonel crosses his arms and shifts uneasily in his chair. "And what does Breshov have to do with it?"

"Breshov is helping me. I'm his niece."

"You mean to say he's helping your sister, whose husband is in Minsk. If you are Breshov's niece, then so is she."

"Exactly. Yes."

"And Pesach? I mean, Patrick?"

"He is connected to Breshov," Fanny says.

"And the fourth man?"

"He's not connected to anything."

"I'm sorry," Breshov says again.

"No need to apologise," Pazhari soothes him. "It's quite alright."

I've got myself into one hell of a mess, Pazhari thinks as he asks them politely, "Would you mind waiting?"

Pazhari hurries along to the garrison to make sure that they do not maul Adamsky any further, but his deputy's expression tells him that it's too late. The prisoner is lying unconscious, and every member of his guard detail has soundly pummelled him. One of them even went as far as to tear off his earlobe with a wild bite, which he then chewed and lustily swallowed. Adamsky smiled briefly at him before fainting. Only a true savage can appreciate the savagery of another.

Pazhari knows that if Zizek sees him in this state their entire quest will come to an end. On the other hand, how will it benefit Pazhari, if it continues? How should he know? What good comes out of hiding a fugitive in his shed? Less food and fewer blankets. Some will say that the colonel is soft and overly kind, but anyone who has seen him in the trenches will vouch that he is tough. Then why is he scheming like an outlaw? Well, these are too many questions to answer all at once. He has no idea.

As he returns to Mishenkov's office, where the duo awaits him, Pazhari concludes that it would make most sense to split the group in two. Zizek and Fanny will be escorted to Minsk, where they will sort things out with Zvi-Meir. The other two, including the fatally wounded Adamsky, will wait for them here in the camp, if, that is, their fourth companion can be found. In the meantime, Pazhari will delay Novak with some excuse or other, throw him a bone, fabricate red herrings, and when that story runs out, he will have to give one of them up, presumably the fourth miscreant. But before he can reach the office, he hears a garrison officer yelling in the distance: "Attention! General Mishenkov, sir! At your command!"

VIII

Lieutenant General Mishenkov usually sends prior notice of his return to camp. Two days before he arrives, he sends a messenger to obtain reports about the units' status and training progress. In his meeting with his deputy two days later, Mishenkov and Pazhari go through the updates that have been submitted for the general's review.

Mishenkov: "So, old man, I understand that you know all about the successful artillery manoeuvre."

Pazhari: "Certainly, sir! It went very well."

Mishenkov: "Did you know that only two soldiers defected this month, old man? This is excellent news."

Pazhari: "Yes, sir! Bazarov and Gossin. We will find them."

Mishenkov: "Well, when you do, hang them by their ankles, spare them no mercy."

Pazhari: "Naturally, sir."

Mishenkov: "And I understand that only twelve men have died of typhoid, I think this is quite an achievement."

Pazhari: "Yes, sir, I mean no, I mean, relatively speaking . . ."

The second thing Mishenkov likes to do when he returns is

to change some aspect of the camp's routine. There is much that is not to his liking, but he does not want to rock the boat too much. On one occasion, the flags annoyed him: "Old man, we cannot display the symbols of the empire on these rags. Replace them immediately!" Another time, it was the horses: "Why don't they report to roll call together with the cavalrymen? Prepare them to join the ranks!" To stave off Mishenkov's preposterous orders, Pazhari stays their execution, approaching the general an hour later to suggest attenuating amendments: there are no new flags in storage to replace the ones they already have and new ones would have to be ordered from Minsk; it's an excellent idea to include the horses in the roll call, but, overworked as they are, the grooms would collapse if this were added to their tasks. Wouldn't it be just as effective to have the hussars inspect their steeds in the stables? "Certainly, old man," Mishenkov readily agrees, glad to see his orders' contribution to the spirit of the unit. "That is exactly what I meant. Let's do it that way."

Mishenkov started calling Pazhari "old man" from the day he, Mishenkov, was made a general. Pazhari is older by several years, and this nickname is Mishenkov's way of reminding Pazhari that age, experience, and certainly pedigree are not necessary for promotion in the army. Just look at him, Lieutenant General Mishenkov, the son of a lesser nobleman than Count Alexander Pazhari, who grew up in Kazan, not St Petersburg, and nonetheless made it to lieutenant general first. What does Pazhari have to say about that?

Pazhari, of course, was offered Mishenkov's rank four years earlier, but turned it down after telling his superiors that he preferred to spend his time with the troops rather than with a desk. And the colonel does not want to stand out from the crowd too much. If the lie that had catapulted him to such a senior position was ever exposed, he would instantly lose everything he had.

In any event, Mishenkov is now returning from his latest jaunt on horseback. He is followed by a barouche driven by his personal coachman, who is trying to keep up with the general, mercilessly rattling his passengers, uniformed men who seem to be adjutants from another unit.

"Old man!" Mishenkov exclaims, waving and reining in his horse. "I hope you have good news for me."

"Always, sir," Pazhari replies. "Of course."

"So, you captured them?"

"Who?" Pazhari says, pretending not to understand.

"To my office, now," Mishenkov orders as he dismounts. "*Now.*"

When, minutes earlier, Pazhari had heard a garrison officer shouting, "Attention! General Mishenkov, sir! At your command!", he had bolted back into the office, pushed Zizek and Fanny out of the tent's rear exit, and ordered the garrison commander to place them immediately under arrest and hide them in a remote cell with Adamsky.

"It is my duty to inform you that the troops will refuse to follow this order, sir. No-one will agree to lock up the Father."

"This is the only way to save him," Pazhari had urged. "You must tell them that."

By the time Mishenkov enters his quarters, Fanny and Zizek are already in the safety of a fetid cell. As the hole they were thrown into is right next to a sewer, the stench of their prison cell prompts Fanny to vomit. For his part, Mishenkov empties his bowels more conventionally after his long ride, and then proceeds to slice himself some sausage and dip it in caviar.

Spotting a cup on his desk, the general raises it to his nostrils and exclaims, "My rum!" He turns to Pazhari, who shrugs helplessly, clears his throat and says, "I helped myself, sir."

"Oh, no need to explain," Mishenkov beams, "go ahead." He shoves the expensive bottle into his deputy's hands and looks

374

expectantly at Pazhari, like a chef waiting for his diner's approval. "Is my rum not the best you have ever tasted?"

Pazhari nods in embarrassment. Mishenkov grows serious. "Well, we have two urgent matters. Firstly, as I arrived, I noticed the tents of the Second Regiment. Why aren't they closer to the First Regiment's encampment? The regiments look as though they are facing off like enemies. Tell them to bring the encampments closer and remove the fences."

"Yes, sir," Pazhari replies, knowing that he will have to approach Mishenkov later to suggest they relocate just the one tent that had actually struck the general as being too far away from the others. It would take more than a month to shift an entire regimental camp.

"And on to the other matter, old man. As I was sitting with the adviser Bobkov – you know Bobkov, don't you? He's a good man, very close to Anton and Maria." Pazhari smiles to himself at Mishenkov's penchant for name-dropping. Anton and Maria Radziwill are the aristocracy's golden couple. It is highly doubtful that Mishenkov has ever met them.

"Well, we were discussing army business and state affairs, and Bobkov told me that Anton and Maria are organising a ball in Berlin, and that they are insisting I do everything I can to attend. They are just an adorable couple, Anton and Maria. Anyway, at that moment, two secret agents stormed in without bothering to knock, frightening the ladies. 'What's happened?' I demanded. 'What do you want?' And they told me they had a message from Novak. I calmed the others down and retired with the agents to the library. How did he find me at Bobkov's, this Novak character? The Devil knows. But he found me alright. What is more, he instructed his agents to tell me to order all the units under my command to join the search for four fugitives. Did you hear that? Who does he think he is, telling me how my units should operate?

He was a sorry major when he retired from the army. We'll show him. We will capture these renegades alright, at all costs."

"Certainly, sir," Pazhari says, sickened by his own obsequiousness. No matter how far the orphaned servant boy has come since he left the Komarovs and fled to St Petersburg, he still ends up grovelling before authority.

Mishenkov retrieves his bottle of rum, pours a small drop for Pazhari and a generous measure for himself, takes a gulp and says, "The agents are saying that the suspects are more dangerous than the Narodnaya Volya revolutionaries. Three men and a woman, filthy *żyds*, I want us to start the search immediately!"

"Absolutely, sir!" the colonel nods.

Usually, at this point Pazhari will leave Mishenkov's quarters and return an hour later with a more sensible proposition to mitigate the general's order. But now, taken aback by Mishenkov's uncharacteristic determination, he blurts out, "But what about training, sir? A manhunt is exhausting, but the soldiers badly need their training. The riflemen are unskilled, the horsemen cannot stay on their horses, and, worst of all, the gunners keep misfiring."

"We will combine the search with a joint exercise for our entire corps. Excellent idea, Pazhari!"

If there is one thing that makes soldiers cringe, gives them a dry mouth, an itchy back and a terrible rash, it is the words "joint exercise". Too late, Pazhari realises his mistake. Now, for the sake of finding four suspects, three of whom are being held in a cell a mere verst away from Mishenkov's office, the general will send out the entire corps to melt in the scorching heat. What can he do? He must find a solution, and quickly.

"Give the order, Pazhari, now!"

"Yes, sir." Pazhari slowly sips his rum.

"Right this minute!"

Even as he is making his way to his officers, which is usually the time when Pazhari comes up with an alternative to Mishenkov's brilliant ideas, nothing springs to his mind on this occasion. One option is to speak candidly with the general, tell him that the Father is their guest and ask him to play along. But Pazhari knows all too well that there are two types of people: those who sanctify the law, and those who follow their own conscience. The former will always win any argument, and the latter will always do the right thing. Mishenkov belongs to the former group, and Pazhari can already hear in his head his superior's reply: "As sad as it may be, old man, it is not up to us to judge right and wrong. If the authorities have decided that Zizek Breshov is a murderer, who are we to help him escape from the law? If we all did as we pleased, following 'our conscience' as they say, or in other words 'our whims', anarchy would prevail."

Pazhari is not a scholar, nor is he an expert on conjecture, and yet he racks his brain for a way to persuade Mishenkov. Completely out of sorts by the time he enters his tent, he glances at the topographical maps on his desk, looks for inspiration from a half-eaten apple rotting on the ground, and listens to the howls of a stray dog. Still, he cannot work out a way to dissuade Mishenkov from complying with Novak's demands.

Finally, he calls in the captain of the guardhouse, Captain Istomin, a strapping officer whom Pazhari has come to trust. He stares into the young man's eyes. "I will understand if you refuse to follow this order. You should know that if it fails, you and your squad will be tried for treason. If it's any consolation, I will stand trial alongside you. You must escort the three detainees to Minsk before the unit returns from the joint exercise. They need to find a man called Zvi-Meir Speismann. Help them find him. The only people who may come near the detainees are your five best men at the garrison. They must give them food, water and medical treatment. Do not touch Patrick Adamsky. Lay him down in the barouche and find him a nurse. Keep the three of them alive and let no-one else know about it. That is all. Will you do it?"

"Yes, sir!" Istomin salutes and leaves.

The next day, with great haste, Lieutenant General Mishenkov orders the joint exercise to begin, leaving immediately thereafter for a few hours in Nesvizh, "to obtain a few authorisations, visit an old friend, take care of budgets and supplies, you understand". He leaves the manoeuvre in Colonel Pazhari's charge, and asks that he receive constant updates on the search, until he returns to take back the reins of command.

Pazhari is on tenterhooks. He does not know how long it will take for Novak to learn of the four outlaws' visit to the camp, so he decides that he must beat him to it, and shortly before leaving for the exercise he sends an urgent missive to the Okhrana's bureaus in Grodno and Minsk. He must throw Novak a bone, Pazhari knows, but not one that is too juicy. He reports that three strange men had passed by the camp; he is unsure if they had a woman with them or not and could not verify their names. One presented himself to the guards as Patrick Breshov, and the other said he was Zizek Adamsky, or something along those lines. In any event, they did not stay for very long or raise the sentries' suspicion.

As Pazhari rides along at the head of the manoeuvre, he is preoccupied by the possibility of a confrontation with Novak. How long will this exercise last? If Mishenkov were asked, he would say until the mission was completed, without bothering to clarify which mission he was referring to and which was the more pressing: capturing the suspects or training his troops. Who remains in the camp? Well, the sentries, a few detainees (three of whom are held in a hidden prison cell), a handful of administrators, sick and wounded soldiers, at least two horses, and several hundred sentinels and spies in the various guard posts, some of which are quite remote and at least one that is manned by a scrawny cantor with a prodigious appetite.

The cantor, by the way, is increasingly convinced that army life is the right life for him. This Oleg he was sent to replace must be a strange man. Why give up such a sweet job? All he is asked to do is sit in one place all day long. There is no shortage of food, although the sardines are long gone and judging by how fast he has been wolfing down the tinned meat, that will last for only a few more hours, and the crackers – how should he say this? – the crackers are clogging internal pathways that need to remain clear. But one should never complain about a full stomach.

And most of all, he should be thankful for the company they have arranged for him. The cantor is not a sap. He knows that Olga is just a blonde scarecrow. When he speaks to her, he knows that his words rebound from a sheet of tarpaulin. And yet her indifference is refreshing; Cantor needn't mince his words or fear a slap in the face or having his teeth broken for upsetting her.

Olga hasn't refused him even once since they met. Cantor lays at her feet rancid cabbage and leftover cucumber. Lucky that there are people in the world like Oleg, who, unhappy with their lot, go off and pursue other fancies. Cantor is happy to take Oleg's place, although someone should come soon to replenish his food supplies, otherwise he will have to return to camp and demand what he is owed. He is not worried for himself, but it is the least he can do for a respectable lady like Olga, who always keeps an eye on him and protects him from the howling wolves at night.

GRODNO

I

At that very moment, Colonel Piotr Novak is heading east from Baranavichy to the town of Grodno. Why Grodno? Well . . .

In the week it took for him to recover from that accursed night in Adamsky's tavern, the public house was converted into a make-shift H.Q. for the secret police and all the drunks who usually haunted the place were kicked out. Once he was able to, Novak left the tavern and headed for the market to stretch his battered leg. For the first time in his life, he paused by the *żyds'* stalls. Leaning on his cane and gritting his teeth, he observed these creatures who have always struck him as primitive and inferior.

He was repelled by their appearance, their strange attire. The bushy beards, the sunken eyes, the way they wet their finger with their tongue as they browse through their mysterious books. There is an entire world outside, and yet they'd rather keep their eyes glued to their boxy script? Damn them. And their foul smell, don't they ever wash? Not for nothing are they surrounded by swarms of pestilent flies.

There is no need to lecture Novak about how all humans are created in God's image. There's no need to tell him that a child can be shaped in any mould. You can raise them to think that sitting indoors and studying all day every day is normal. You can raise them to think that men walking around with sidelocks is normal. You can raise them to think that covering their heads at all times with either a hat or yarmulke is normal. Novak knows all this and more, and yet he thinks they should at least have the decency to blend in, to make even just a minimal attempt to integrate with the rest of society. But precisely because he is aware of his instinctive dislike for Jews, Novak begins to wonder if he might have acted no better than a member of the rabble when he launched into his investigation without a shred of serious reflection. God give him strength, he only met the four foul *żyds* a week ago. The lady of the group murdered his agents, another member of the group crushed his leg, and their toothpick of a companion wouldn't stop singing. The one with the most alarming appearance, the scarred-mouth thug, was silent as a rock. None of them could be described as scholarly. If they had worn plain peasant clothes, they could have easily passed as local farmers. The woman was indeed intriguing, a Jewish Joan of Arc, perhaps, but goddammit what woman behaves like a wild beast? How does she do it? How can she be insolent and arresting at the same time?

As he wandered the busy market, Novak forced himself to stop and observe the *żyds* carefully. He eyed shabby carts piled with a disarray of kitchen utensils and work tools. He was puzzled by the queue at Levinsohn's – their famous pâtissier – and he made a note of the cattle-like etiquette as the line crammed together without complaint. He studied their gestures in conversation – an old lady yelling at a vendor selling vegetables who yelled back just as loudly, only for the pair to embrace and exchange copecks and cucumbers the next moment. There was no space, just a human mass whose every member is compelled to quarrel and complain, as if every transaction must reach climactic dissonance before it can be resolved. Every word in their bizarre language sounds conspiratorial and sickening. Why can't they find a place of their own? Why do they insist on infiltrating a country that doesn't want them?

To his annoyance, Novak's thoughts led him to the same

conclusions over and over again, not a very helpful outcome for his investigation. What did he want? To understand their customs. This is why he paused to observe. And yet his observations have yielded only conjectures that reinforce his starting principles, so perhaps his method is flawed? Perhaps, instead of observing, he should try first-hand experience instead.

Novak had never approached *żyds* before without declaring his rank and status. Every conversation he held with them was for the sole purpose of squeezing out information, which is what he intended to do this time around. He approached the vagrant who had just completed the loud cucumber transaction.

"Hello," Novak greeted him in Polish. The man nodded uncertainly. Immediately, Novak registered the nearby vendors ogling him as one. "How much are they?" Novak asked, picking up a few cucumbers. *"Acht und zwanzig,"* the old man replied, removing a rotten tomato from his stand.

"How much?" Novak repeated, and asked the vendor to write down the figure.

"Acht und zwanzig," the vendor said again, ignoring the request.

Novak said nothing more. The old man's emaciated face was spotted like the face of a ravenous hyena, his speckled hands tended to his vegetables like the hands of a farmer turning soil, his nose was inexplicably bluish and its tip black like the tip of a pencil. Novak took out a rouble coin and slammed it on the scale with a metallic clatter, but the old man did not so much as glance at the money. Novak returned the cucumbers and swept the coin back into his pocket. The vendor's nimble fingers quickly rearranged the cucumbers on the pile.

Novak moved away to queue up for Levinsohn's patisserie. A few peasants further ahead in the queue were chatting with the Jews in a hybrid language of Polish and Yiddish. Novak took this to be an encouraging sign – maybe the Jews here would talk to him. But instead, the queue around him melted away. What was happening? This was the best patisserie in Baranavichy. Everyone said that Levinsohn's cakes were impossible to beat. People waited in this queue around the clock, come rain or come shine. And as soon as Novak arrived, they all vanished?

A strange feeling crept over him: his presence there was unwelcome, he was a stranger in his own country. Worse still, he seemed to know absolutely nothing about the customs of the place. Having always been immersed in the affairs of the Department for Public Security and Order, he had never behaved like a normal citizen before, and the *żyds* were the first to notice it. He did not get up in the morning and go to the same office, he did not return home to the same woman at the end of every day. He lived in the shadows and his face proved it. What did he have to do to be recognised as a normal human being by the local Jews?

Eventually, Levinsohn turned to him and Novak pointed at a slice of plum or cherry cake, he was not sure which. He expected change from his rouble coin, but Levinsohn served him his cake wrapped in paper, shrugged and turned to serve the next customer. Could this be the price of a single slice? It was exorbitant on any scale, the price of an entire meal. The patrons served before him, he seemed to recall, had not paid as much for their slices of the very same cake. But not knowing how to ask the question, and finding the pricing policy incomprehensible, Novak stormed out of the shop. As soon as he had gone, the queue reformed as Jews and locals squeezed in together again, apparently relieved to see the back of him.

Novak was relieved too, to return to observing them at a safe distance. The line that separated him from them was drawn again. He had felt out of place at closer quarters. As an Okhrana commander, his job was to sow fear and suspicion in people's hearts. He knew that an exchange of a few words with any one of the people huddled together in the queue would be all it took for them to pull out a dagger and stab the back of the person in front of them. He could turn them all against each other at the drop of a hat. But in the absence of a concrete threat, they live side by side in peace. All it takes is a nice slice of wild berry cake (he was wrong to think it was plum or cherry; it is a dense confection of blueberries and white mulberry, delectable!), to make the Pole forget that most *żyds* earn twice as much as he does, and that this yarmulke-wearing horde own most of the businesses in town.

On a philosophical level, it could be said that humans are creatures with strictly material needs and wants. All the Poles need is a slice of cake, even one only half as good as the cake that is sliding down his throat at that moment, to make peace with the *żyds*. Luckily for Novak, however, the Poles abhor material concerns more than anything. They always try to show that they are spiritual, divinely inspired. He knows that without the Poles' "values" there would be no violence and, preferable as this might be, without violence Novak would be out of a job. Therefore, all he has to do is ask the Poles for their thoughts on the matter: "What is more important to you – morals or mulberries?", and in just twenty-four hours, Novak could focus the mind of the mob and have them setting fire to half the town's homes. But perhaps there could be another way to infiltrate the ranks of the *żyds*. If he cannot merely observe them, or talk to them as one normal person to another, then, he thought, the only solution is to become one of them. He would need a particularly good lie to cover his identity, and an interpreter of course, preferably a local who knows the *żyds'* customs and is fluent in their conspiratorial language. If Novak were to approach them as one of their own, surely they would open up to him.

But what about his appearance? Well, it is a sorry thing to

admit, but the colonel's face has long been worn and weather-beaten. Once he happened to overhear one of his agents joking with his colleagues that no-one would ever suspect Novak of working with the Okhrana because he looked too much like a *żyd*. And now his decrepit appearance might prove useful. This investigation, he was convinced, would force him to dig very deep. He must mask everything about himself if he wants to find the culprits.

II

Novak retreated from the market, his limp growing more pronounced with every stride. He returned to Adamsky's tavern to find his deputy, Albin Dodek, poring over a map. The north arrow was pointing straight at Dodek's flabby belly, as he puzzled over the symbols on the map as though trying to break a cipher.

"Anything interesting, Dodek?" Novak asked, and his deputy blushed as if caught red-handed.

"Yes, sir, I'm trying to work out which of the nearby villages they might be hiding in."

"And what conclusions have you reached?"

"If they are not in an army camp, which is highly unlikely, they are definitely in one of the villages around here."

His deputy's confident dismissal of the likelihood of the fugitives escaping to an army camp immediately made Novak suspect that this was exactly where they were.

"Have our messengers returned with an answer from General Mishenkov?"

"No, sir, we dispatched them only yesterday, but I did add a note saying that it was very urgent," Dodek said. "I wrote: 'Anyone hiding information about their identity or whereabouts will be considered a full accomplice', or something along those lines."

"But who told you to do that?" demanded Novak. Now the entire region would think that the commander of the Department for Public Security and Order was an idiot. "Send out two agents to Nesvizh immediately," he ordered. "Mishenkov is probably lounging about at Bobkov's. I want the agents to make it clear to Mishenkov that Governor Gurko is involved in this matter, and that I want to take his unit under my command."

"Governor Gurko?" Dodek said, startled. "Yes, sir. Immediately!"

At that moment, they heard a sudden racket coming from upstairs. A man had tried to jump out of the window, and two agents had caught him by the scruff of his neck, only to be pinned down by two more young men and a middle-aged woman, all trying to free their friend. It took Novak a moment to work out exactly what was going on, because he seemed to be watching the unfolding of a cheap comedy sketch: a pile of buffoons sandwiching two of his brainless agents. Dodek calmly explained that "these are *żyds* whom the locals have turned in. We carried out dawn raids on their homes and now they are just making a fuss".

"I don't understand," Novak said, his head in his hands. "How are they related to the investigation?"

"They are *żyds*."

"So are half the residents of this goddamned town."

"Yes, but these *żyds* were reported to us."

"Reported for what?"

"Well, this one, for example," Dodek pointed at the man who had attempted to escape, "they say he was handing out pamphlets."

"And what did the pamphlets say?"

"'Religion is the morphine of the masses', sir."

Novak glanced at a leaflet that looked like the thousands of others he had seen in every corner of the empire. A printed page that socialists circulate to incite the mob.

"But how are the pamphlets linked to our investigation?"

"I don't know, sir, but I'm sure we'll find out. That's our job. This one, though? He just laughs in our faces, the insolent bastard. Do you know what he calls himself? Akaky Akakyevich, as if that's even a name."

"It is a name. Haven't you heard of Gogol?"

"His name is not Gogol, sir, it's Akaky Akakyevich, like I said."

"Never mind, Dodek. Release them and let's get to work."

"Yes," said Dodek without adding the honorific "sir". Novak, who knew every sign of his deputy's discontent, was unfazed. Only a fool needs the approval of another fool.

"Wait a minute," he said, an idea suddenly flashing into his mind. "Bring Akaky over here."

"Yes, sir." Dodek jumped to his feet, glad that his superior had decided to behave sensibly after all.

"And leave us alone," Novak added.

Akaky Akakyevich's head had baby-like bald patches, and his lips were shaped into a parrotfish pucker (or was it the fist to his chin that had done that?), and his pink, unblemished skin made him look almost dainty. If Novak had not known that he was an outlaw, he would have guessed that the man standing in front of him was a footman or butler.

Their conversation may be described as a monologue for two people, or perhaps a one-way dialogue. Either way, Novak did all the talking. He was unstoppable, the words spilling out of his mouth like a verbal avalanche.

"The name Akaky Akakyevich tells me everything I need to know about the gentleman standing in front of me. You, sir, are an arrogant intellectual who has read the glorious works of Gogol and Pushkin, and is convinced that everyone else around him is a dunce. In the case of the overwhelming majority of Okhrana agents, this is not far from the truth. But it so happens that I know Gogol well, and I even know a thing or two about Pushkin, and one day I'd love to discuss *Eugene Onegin* with you, or perhaps the adventures of Chichikov, and maybe even lesser known authors such as Eliza Ozheshko – you must have heard of her, yes? Oh, you haven't? She is a gifted writer living in Grodno, and therefore there is not a chance her name will ever reach the ears of the learned gatherings in St Petersburg. You should know that I myself have issued an order to line the road past her house with straw in order to muffle the clanging of carriage wheels so as not to disturb her peace. Do you know what culture is? Well, you should raise your eyes from your books and look around you. This is culture. You should respect that.

"Perhaps you are surprised, sir, to learn that a senior Okhrana officer concerns himself with things that the wider public might consider trifles. But let me tell you this: if a lady cannot write in peace, for what purpose are we defending the empire? Perhaps a cosmopolite, a superior revolutionary like yourself, believes that policemen are simply fools in uniform. Perhaps Mr Pamphleteer's head is brimming with the ideas that brewed in the mind of that fat, decadent Prussian, Karl Marx, a man who has never worked a single day in his life and was driven by sheer boredom to plan his revolution for the new world. If so, let me ask you this: in the new world of this lazy Prussian, who will spread the roads with straw to let Ozheshko write in peace? Is this something that your revolution has taken into consideration?

"The intentions of Mr Pamphleteer were certainly good. He must have thought to himself: I am sick and tired of being a little Jew, I want to be a man of the world, I want to blend in. But you hate the rest of us so much – what do you call us? Goyim! – you were born hating us, and you cannot reconcile your desire to fit into goy society with the revulsion you feel in our presence. This is why the honourable gentleman is forced to try and change us, to criticise us, to make us more like him. What could be better than socialism, which seeks to eliminate religious and social differences? But then Mr Pamphleteer finds he is left without family on the one hand, and without everyone else on the other. Neither wants anything to do with him. His traditional family disowns him, while the goyim think him no more than a damned intellectual. All he can do is declare himself a revolutionary and hand out leaflets to the illiterate. In the absence of love and encouragement from any other quarter, he is left to embrace 'justice', 'freedom' and 'truth' in the hope that one day the millions who despise him now will lose their blinkers and throw off their shackles – and then they'll skin our Mr Pamphleteer alive in the town square the day they seize power.

"In any event, at this point he has only one way of escaping the pamphleteering imbroglio in which he finds himself. I won't have any trouble finding out your real name. Once that is done, the names of your parents, your wife, children and anyone else with Akaky Akakyevich's blood in his or her veins will also be revealed. If there is one bad apple in the basket, all of the other apples must be inspected immediately. I imagine you do not want to find yourself in Siberia, and you do not want your children to receive a letter telling them about the illness that led to their father's death – not intentionally, God forbid. This is just what usually happens, as I'm sure you understand. The road to Siberia is long and arduous and the terrible conditions in the prisons are a conspicuous disadvantage of the region. And one must concede that the living conditions of convicted criminals can hardly be at the top of the governor's priorities, wouldn't you agree?

"Do not worry, my dear sir. You have not reached the end of your road, and I can see I have your full attention. Perhaps you will be happy to learn that the man before you has no intention of foiling your plans and exposing your contacts. On the contrary. Mr Pamphleteer and the Department for Public Security and Order are actually on the same side. Just imagine, sir, what would happen if there were no more pamphlets. Imagine what would happen if people woke up one morning and discovered that all subversive manifestos had vanished. What would they think? They would think that the regime is oppressive! That there is no freedom of speech! Do you understand me, sir? The government needs resistance. If a minority opposes the government, that must mean that the majority supports it, which is not a bad message to send out. Therefore, the Okhrana has no problem with your leaflets, and they are not the reason why we are here.

"I would like to make a simple proposition: I will give you and your family full immunity, in exchange for which you will assist me in capturing four outlaws who have been rampaging through the district for reasons that are not yet entirely clear. You are hereby requested to accompany me and serve as my interpreter. All I want is to better acquaint myself with your people, not the Marxists of course – I know quite well how to handle them – but the Jews, the people of your birth, that is, before you chose to turn your back on them. You, sir, will help Piotr Novak become one of them.

"Your new undercover name can be Akim, which is close enough to Akaky Akakyevich but more credible, whereas my name should be something that starts with P, perhaps Prokor, the name of a brave officer I once knew in the army. You haven't said a word since the beginning of our conversation, Akaky, that is, Akim. So, what do you think?"

Before the conversation had begun, the pamphleteer had mocked the Okhrana agents when he told them his name was

Akaky Akakyevich, but at that moment he was paralysed with fear. Under his pink skin, Novak detected, this man was no more than a timid baby, small fry, whose only prior displays of courage would have been in fierce ideological debates in some academy or other. And now he had discovered that handing out leaflets, that refuge of cowards, had led him straight into the abyss.

The bald patches on Akim's head were flushing violet, as if Novak's words had stung him and left a rash on his head. His groomed moustache, a sure sign of vanity, fluttered up and down as he gasped, "You can't— Not at all—" His broken sentences sounded to Novak like bursting bubbles. "It's impossible, you could never become one of them – they'd never believe—"

"Exactly!" Novak said, brightly. "That is why I need you."

"But I – who am I? You don't understand – I'm not one of them – my own family doesn't speak to me – I can barely remember the language."

"Excellent!" Novak patted Akim's shoulder. "And now you regret leaving and want to come back. It's a wonderful story. See? We are already making progress."

"But—" Akim squirmed.

"Look, my friend," Novak said, leaning towards him. "My dear Akim, there comes a time when explanations run dry and contradictions no longer matter and the conversation is over. And at that point we must roll up our sleeves and get to work. Who are we? Akim and Prokor. What are we? Jews. Why should they believe us? That remains unclear. But that is why you are here and why you are still alive. Is not that so?"

Novak could not have predicted the immediate and, one should add, exceptional results of his idea to recruit this so-called Akaky Akakyevich. That evening, two men left Adamsky's tavern: Avremaleh and Pinchasaleh Rabinovits, otherwise known as Akim and Prokor. As they walked towards the emptying town square and stripped market stalls, they came across a group of pedlars whose conversation appeared to have drifted away from business and over to gossip. Akim approached them, somewhat apprehensively, and briefly outlined the sad story of Avremaleh and Pinchasaleh. The pedlars listened intently, and Prokor quietly joined the pack. He could tell when Akim had successfully obtained the information he had been sent to get: did they know of a female shochet from the area? Amid the thicket of their strange dialect, Novak identified the name of the town of Grodno and smiled to himself. The recipe he had devised had yielded a hearty casserole indeed.

By the time Akim had finished interrogating the pedlars, Novak knew, even without the help of his interpreter, that they were headed for a town well known to him, where a pleasant office and reliable agents awaited. They would find the butcher's family and discover her motives. It would be interesting to see if she would raise her knife once a dagger was placed against her parents' and brothers' necks. "Good work, Akim," he said to his new, petrified lackey. "We leave tomorrow at first light."

III

There is nothing that Russia prides herself on more than her size, and there is nothing that Russia suffers from more than her size. The empire is a corpulent giantess who cannot see below her stomach or bend down to lace her own boots: she will never know what goes on between the creases of her flab. A Muscovite salt merchant might be called to visit Astrakhan on business and be eager to know that his pregnant wife is well back in Moscow, but any letter he receives will have been sent six months ago. If he replies, his wife will receive his letter six months later. Can he change the past or predict the future? Of course not. It is therefore best that his letters avoid advice on daily matters and instead contain words of affection, inquiries after his children's well-being and health, and words of prayer. These things have always been free from the constraints of time and place.

It is little wonder therefore that the proposal by the Austrian engineer Franz Anton von Gerstner, to connect Russia by railway, was enthusiastically received by Czar Nikolai the First. His advisers did not doubt that this adventure might improve the state of the empire's economy, but they were unconvinced whether the cumbersome Russian giantess could be transformed into a fleet-footed athlete almost overnight. They wondered if tens of thousands of versts of steel could really break through the desolate, intractable expanse, or if the railway would change the character of Russia.

Until then, Yakuts lived with Yakuts in Siberia, and Muscovites lived with Muscovites in Moscow. If the Yakut met the Muscovite, they would have been equally puzzled by the thought that they were subjects of the same empire. Their appearances could not have been more different: one was Turco-Mongol and the other an Eastern European Slav. Their religion was different – despite the Muscovites' attempts at conversion, the Yakuts remained shamanic in faith. And what about their occupations? In one place they were cattlemen and in the other they were clerks and bureaucrats. What could the Yakut and the Muscovite talk about with one another? Well, they might have been able to make a stab at conversation if only they knew each other's language. Would the railway do away with all these differences? It was hard to believe that it would.

In any event, many in government had wondered at the time: why should the Yakut and the Muscovite resemble each other?

This aspiration seemed too far-fetched. Must all relationships be based on a common language, an identical faith and similar occupations? What is wrong with a relationship based purely on selling products, distributing goods or building factories? A wedding between a Yakut man and a Muscovite woman might still be long in coming, but in the meantime, commerce was a realistic prospect, and the railway tracks would multiply opportunities in that regard. Incidentally, before a Yakut and a Muscovite could marry, it would be necessary to build the St Petersburg–Warsaw line first.

When Novak arrives at the busy Baranavichy railway station with his rosy-cheeked comrade-in-arms, the waiting room is packed and an announcement advises that there are delays due to urgent works on the Baranavichy–Slonim line. A muzhik was probably lying on the tracks in an alcohol-induced stupor. This is not a rare occurrence in itself, but instead of running him over, the train driver must have decided to spare his life and braked abruptly, derailing the train and buckling its axles. Now an entire region is paralysed, the passengers are kicking their heels, and no-one knows how long the repairs will take.

At the ticket counter, Novak learns that all trains heading east for Slonim have been cancelled until further notice. As to the question of when the service will resume, the sleepy cashier removes his glasses, rubs his eyes and shrugs. A conductor leaning against the wall next to Novak puffs on his pipe and says, "The way things are run in this country, it will take for ever." Novak sees that the man is expecting to start a conversation. There is nothing better for striking up a conversation than an opening complaint about how the country is run, which soon leads to talk of avarice among the aristocracy, the corruption of bureaucrats, and ends with the defencelessness of the man in the street against the state. What a royal waste of time.

Back at Adamsky's tavern, Novak decides to bypass the accident. They will travel to Slonim on horseback and then take the train to Grodno via Bialystok. The road to Slonim is not short, more than sixty versts of craggy hills, but Novak thinks they should not wait. At the end of their first day of riding, however, he is groaning with pain on account of his leg.

By now anaesthetics are useless. Damn Adamsky for waking up the monster of agony from its slumber. Novak could ask a doctor for morphine once they arrive in Slonim, but it will knock him out and the spectacle of Colonel Piotr Novak muttering nonsense under his blankets is out of the question. He has two choices: either learn to live with the pain or die.

"Need any help?" parrotfish-lips asks him.

The day I need help with my leg from this character, Novak thinks, I will stick a bullet in my head. But when they reach the inn, where they will break their journey, Novak is barely able to dismount from his horse. He is forced to let his butler-like interpreter carry his bag upstairs and sign the register. Novak lies down as soon as he can, but he stays awake for hours, his face buried in the pillow as shame mingles with pain and anger.

When they leave for Slonim on the second day and the interpreter falls asleep in his saddle, Novak can't help but wonder why he keeps chasing after ghosts. His peers frequent sumptuous salons, hobnob with aristocrats and plutocrats, and free up time for their personal affairs by commissioning underlings to do their work for them. And what about him? Is he still trying to please his master, Governor Osip Gurko, or has this investigation turned into a personal vendetta against Adamsky for aggravating his leg? Is he driven by the desire to unearth the motive behind the killings, or by his attraction to their enigmatic perpetrator? Is it even possible to separate the two? What is certain, however, is that Novak would have ridden to Grodno in any event.

On the second day, they manage to cover only a third of the distance they travelled the previous day. Novak needs rest, and the original plan to reach Slonim in two days seems wildly unrealistic. They will have to ride for four, maybe five days. The decision to visit the cradle of the butcher's life was critical: if it proves fruitless, Novak will have lost a vital week in the investigation, and it could be impossible to make up lost time.

Novak finds Akaky Akakyevich intolerable. Heeding authority and honour, detainees tend to curry favour with their jailers so they might have their ear when the need arises, but not Akaky. Sometimes he treats Novak as though he were his patient. "Need any help? Are you hungry? Thirsty?"

"Enough with those questions," Novak says. "I don't need anything from you."

Unperturbed, Akaky starts asking the colonel personal questions, assuming the role of a prying, intrusive interrogator.

Akaky: "So where is your family?"

Novak: "St Petersburg."

Akaky: "And when did you see them last?"

Novak: "A year ago."

Akaky: "Do you miss them?"

Novak: "That is a strange question. I suppose so. But I would let it go if I were you."

Akaky: "Why don't you visit them more often?"

Novak: "Work."

Akaky: "How many children do you have?"

Novak: "Two boys, Ivan and Alexey."

Novak is forced to assert his authority by launching a counter-interrogation.

Novak: "So, where does your family come from?"

Akaky: "Vitebsk, Minsk, Kovne."

Novak: "I don't understand."

Akaky: "Nor do I."

Novak: "And how did you find your way to Marx?"

Akaky: "He found his way to me."

Novak: "What?"

Akaky: "Precisely."

Akaky's laconic answers are too diffuse for Novak to be able to connect the dots. Nonetheless, Akaky is at his disposal, and even if the detainee tries to feign control over the situation, his trembling body gives away his fear.

Yet, regarding this latter point, Novak has made a crude and uncharacteristic mistake. A man who truly fears authority does not poke fun at the secret police by presenting himself as Akaky Akakyevich. There's no guarantee that Novak will indeed force him into submission.

In fact, he does not know that Akaky suffers from chronic arthritis, which torments him with cold shivers and constant tremors. For this reason, he left his home to study medicine in Minsk. His real name is certainly not Avremaleh, and he's never known any Pinchasaleh; his name is Haim-Lazer, and he was not born in Vitebsk, Minsk or Kovne (he's never even set foot in the latter). He is actually a native of the town of Mir. How did he end up circulating Marxist pamphlets? Many years ago, in his anatomy class, he met Minka Abramovich, a Jewish girl who set his head spinning. She seemed so progressive and enlightened, spoke fluent Russian and wore St Petersburg fashions. If she had asked him to join an underground group that hailed the works of some pharaoh, he would have handed out pamphlets lauding the Egyptian monarch. What does he care? And although it was clear from the start that he never stood a chance with her, this did not curb his enthusiasm in the least. He was too old-fashioned for her taste; in other words, he could not completely renounce his Judaism. Indeed, he had quit yeshiva and gone to study medicine, but he had not shed the old world altogether, and had been known occasionally to sneak into a synagogue.

Unlike him, Minka was wild. She kept talking about world revolution, the proletariat and an international uprising. The veins in her high forehead bulged ominously when she gave public speeches. Whenever volunteers were needed to circulate leaflets, she was the first to raise her hand, and he was the second.

After two years, Haim-Lazer left medical school and joined the underground cell under Minka's command. Like other young revolutionaries who tend to forget the personal motivations that originally attracted them to the cause of the rebellion, the ideas and principles became the heart of the matter, even after Minka married a goy and all the more so after she was arrested and sent to Siberia. Years later, Haim-Lazer became the leader of an underground cell and became adept at internal politics, which had always seemed to him to be as corrupt as the government he wanted to overthrow. When he was caught by the secret police in Baranavichy, he did not want to be released that same day. He intended to return to his comrades after a week's incarceration, no, no, after a month's detention, to impress them. That was why he called himself Akaky Akakyevich, and he was surprised when none of the agents recognised the provenance of his alias. When he met Novak he realised that at least this one read something other than police reports, and after listening to the interrogator's speech, he realised that he had become embroiled with a senior Okhranist. A high-ranking secret police officer will not mete out a month's detention, but what the underground calls "an evaporation". And yet, upon hearing about the four suspects that Novak is hunting down, Haim-Lazer decided he has to do whatever is in his powers to disrupt the investigation. The four suspects are not partners in his crime, but they are outlaws, which is enough to make him want to help them.

One thing surprises Haim-Lazer: try as he might, he cannot hate Novak. This is his first substantial encounter with such a senior policeman, a man who stands for everything that is evil in the Czar's decadent reign. After all, the colonel is authorised to comb through the personal letters of any living soul; he can invade any house in the name of national security, drag people from their beds, turn their homes upside down and tear them away from their loved ones. Under the aegis of justice, law and order, he sows chaos in citizen's lives, who, fearful that they might prey on one another in the absence of a central government, allow the imperial chimera to prey on them instead. Unlike others of his rank, however, it seems that Novak believes that he is indeed the protector of public order. His battered body is covered with scars, his cheekbones protrude from his worn-out face, and he shambles about like a broken man. To tell the truth, Novak is as lonely as Haim-Lazer; they are both men who have left home far behind. If Haim-Lazer had to guess whether the person riding next to him was an Okhrana district commander or a troubled Jew like himself, he would have said the latter. Therefore, even though Haim-Lazer wants to see Novak lose, he does not want his defeat to be humiliating.

IV

By the time Akim and Prokor reach Slonim, Novak is a wreck. During the day, the pain in his leg climbed up to his lower back, his saddle sores became a rash, and every stretch of his skin now flourishes a different hue on the red spectrum, becoming almost purple the closer it is to his groin. Novak, one should recall, is close to retirement, and his bones are not as robust as they used to be.

He works out the schedule of the next train to Bialystok and then to Grodno. The train ride does not alleviate any of his pain: the days of riding had already made his bones ache, and the tremor of the train gives them a thorough rattle. He arrives in Grodno exhausted, but on coming out of the train station, Novak draws encouragement from the town's familiar sights: the Neman river encircling the town, the old castle (now an army base), and the spires of St Xavier's that watch over the market. There is a limit to the suffering he can endure. Novak wishes he could make a stop at his local office. The five-day ride on horseback and the taxing journey on the night train have surely earned him the right to rest. But what would happen if someone, even just one Jew, saw him coming out of the Okhrana offices, which are right by the town hall and the market square? How would he continue going about as Pinchasaleh Rabinovits if he had been welcomed by secret agents? And yet, the desire to slip into a pleasant office, crack open a new bottle of slivovitz and change his socks is so overpowering that Novak tries to weave together some justification. Finally, he musters enough strength to accept that, in his pitiful current state, he is ideally suited to infiltrating the Jews at the market. He gives Akim lengthy instructions on how to proceed. First, he should tell their story as credibly as possible, say that they are starving, inquire about the town's slaughterhouses; then ask off-handedly about the female butcher from Grodno, Fanny Schechter, the daughter of Meir-Anschil Schechter.

Everything goes according to plan. Akim quickly strikes up a conversation with a toothless old man oozing the sharp odour of the beetroot and radishes he sells. The vendor listens intently to Akim, and other curious souls begin to gather around them too. Touched by the story of the two lost Jews from Vitebsk, they generously offer them bread, onions and radishes. Novak is famished from the journey and devours the lot, mould and all, waiting for Akim to reach the crux of the matter.

When their audience hears Akim's question about Fanny, Meir-Anschil Schechter's daughter, they quickly huddle for a consultation. "*Die vilde chaya?*" says one. "*Eine barbaren!*" another replies. "*Oistrakht*, fairy tales," the tailor scoffs, and Novak is bursting with curiosity. What the hell are they saying? Goddammit, what a strange language! What kind of tongue is Yiddish, exactly? Second-rate German? Bawdy Bavarian? Refined Prussian?

Akim's face flushes at their comments. Novak tries to catch his eye, but Akim evades him and carries on listening to the crowd. Novak tries to motion him aside to hear the translation, but Akim ignores him. Novak tugs at his jacket. "What are they saying?" he demands and Akim mutters out of the corner of his mouth, "She's not here."

"What do you mean 'she's not here'?" Novak says, horrified. "Where is her family?"

Akim smiles, supposedly in reassurance, but Novak detects a glint of satisfaction in his eyes as he says, "They are all in the afterworld."

"What?" Novak yelps. It is all he can do not to shout. "Are you sure?"

Before Akim can answer him, some of the surrounding Jews start to usher them through the market, past the city's two castles – the old and the new – that overlook the river, and then towards the main synagogue and into a dark, dank hovel, which turns out to be a restaurant. There they are served an odd-looking salad of cucumber with dill, a repulsive, gelatinous dish (probably some kind of fish), meatballs that taste like fried fingernails, and shredded carrot, spicy enough to burn your mouth. Novak forces himself to keep smiling as he tastes these foul foods and thanks everyone, "Dank! Dank!" – a word he picked up from Akim – noticing as he does so that dozens of curious Jews have gathered around him. They stand there, their eyes shining happily as they follow every bite he takes, making it impossible for him to spit anything into a napkin. The odd sip of slivovitz would have made the experience tolerable, or at least it would have refreshed his palate and tempered the flavours, but instead they serve him *yash*, a drink that is somewhere between brandy and rum mixed with cow piss. He empties one glass after another, without stopping, until his heart is aflame.

As soon as dinner is over, they are dragged along an alleyway to a large house with a spacious courtyard. Akaky manages to whisper to Novak, "We have ended up among the Hasidim, they're taking us to the *gute Yid*, the good Jew, the rebbe, great-grandson of Rabbi Alexander Ziskind the Just, author of *The Foundation and Root of Worship*, hailed as a genius by the Vilna Gaon himself. It's a great honour!"

"Lovely," hisses Novak. "But what about Fanny Schechter?"

"I have no idea," Akaky says with a shrug.

The rebbe welcomes them with a warm embrace and tearful eyes, as if they were his own, long-lost sons. Moments later, the synagogue *gabbai* has measured Novak for a kaftan, other hands have placed a fur hat on his head, *tzitzit* sprout underneath his shirt, and everyone dances around him in ecstatic circles. When it is time for prayer at the shtiebel – a shabby, bare and rather damp house of prayer crowded with a motley crew that reminds Novak of the market square – the men crammed around him bend back and forth, right and then left, wrapped in sacred shawls that smell of pickled cabbage. Instead of delighting the high Heavens with melodious sounds in perfect harmony, and purifying the air with incense and perfume, they moan and groan with the ecstasy of bleating sheep.

They shove a prayer book into his hands. One of the rebbe's men stands beside him and helps him follow the angular script, word by word. After prayer they all come up to shake his hand and invite Avremaleh and Pinchasaleh for *tisch*. Novak is desperate for the evening to be over so that he can slide a cup of slivovitz down his throat to wash away the bad taste that lingers in his mouth, before grabbing Akaky Akakyevich by the throat to settle accounts. Yet before they sit down to eat once more, the rabbi gives a speech, wine glass in hand. And Novak finds himself following the others' example, shouting "lechayim" when they shout, drinking when they drink, muttering when they mutter, sitting down when they sit down, singing when they sing, making merry when they make merry and dancing when they dance. He is served different dishes that nonetheless taste exactly like his previous meal, especially the *yash*. This time, however, Novak's stomach is less quarrelsome, so he devours everything, regardless of taste, embracing the mauling of his senses by the hard drink and the heavy dancing.

By nightfall, instead of punching Akaky in the face for making him participate in this farce, Novak happily lies down on a rickety bed in a hut cleared of its inhabitants for his sake. He is at peace. Right now, Fanny Schechter is far from his mind, and he even manages to forget the torturous journey to Grodno. Soon after laying his head on the pillow, he falls fast asleep, still wearing his clothes, his heart uplifted by the echoes of the rabbi's inscrutable speech.

V

Sometimes, the crowing of the rooster awakens a desire for revenge. The sun has not risen yet, but a pair of quarrelling cockerels are pecking at the shreds of Novak's sleep. At moments like these, the colonel regrets that he does not carry a pistol. To his colleagues, he always explains that the Department for Public Security and Order fights a silent war, where any use of firearms would be the mark of failure. "Our cannons are our attentive ears and a good memory," is his favourite quip. But now, as his head explodes and last night's meal inches its way up his gullet, ears and memory are of no use to him.

Just one look at the man snoring by his side reminds Novak of everything he would rather forget. On arriving in Grodno yesterday morning, he was dragged into a feast of fools. They had him drinking gruesome wine at noon, and singing 'Shalom Aleichem' by the night's end. At the shtiebel, a new word for his vocabulary, he swayed in prayer and pretended to read their incomprehensible book. And for what? It turns out that the people he was looking for, Fanny Schechter's relatives, are no longer with us. Novak is beside himself.

He is also beginning to suspect that this Akaky Akakyevich is no innocent lamb. Did he know all along that their arduous journey would end with nothing? If this was his plan from the start, then the pale butler is a knave in parrotfish scales. Very interesting. If Akaky continues to follow his own plans even after Novak's threats of Siberian prisons, then the colonel is facing a worthy opponent.

Novak is well aware that the chain of inferences that has led him to this bed is not without its weaknesses. What's more, the ease with which he was coaxed to attend that feast, the *tisch*, which they held in their honour last night, suggests frivolous,

407

negligent and unprofessional behaviour. And yet, as he remembers the wild joy that clung to those Hasidic men, the attire they made him wear, the food he had to swallow, the dancing that spun his head, he cannot identify a single moment when he'd had an opportunity to escape their clutches. They had simply surrounded him and dragged him along and run next to him and sat him at the table. It is a hard thing to admit, but in their company he had felt a surge of energy – even happiness. They had trampled over his will like a herd of buffalo, and to his surprise, he appeared to welcome the stampede. Even his leg feels a little better, and an entire day is about to go by without him thinking about it once. His slivovitz bottle remains in his pocket, untouched.

Therefore, even though he knows that he must somehow escape and return to Baranavichy, Novak does not protest when two young men enter the hut and invite Akaky and him to the shtiebel. He gets up from his bed and dons the kaftan he was lent the day before. Just look at him now: Colonel Piotr Novak marching arm in arm with three *żyds*, his head adorned with a *spodik* – the tall fur hat – the long black kaftan sliding down his body, a cloth *gartel* around his waist, leaning on his cane on one side and on his "brother", Avremaleh Rabinovits, on the other.

On their way to the shtiebel, Novak notices a few ducks waddling through the courtyards like drunks and cherry trees laden with flaming-red fruit, and he exchanges smiles and warm handshakes with the other Hasidim. Naturally, if Novak's colleagues from the secret police were to encounter him right now, he could explain his behaviour down to the last detail: he has given up on his initial intention of meeting Fanny Schechter's family but he still wants to learn about the *żyd* way of life well enough to pass for one of them. Nothing wrong with that. Yet if he met his colleagues at this very moment, as he enters the

408

rebbe's court surrounded by a crowd swaying in prayer, Novak would probably choose not to mention that his heart is racing with joy.

For lunch, he and Akim are invited to join a family: husband, wife and seven children, four of whom are playing hide-and-seek around Novak. One of the little scamps bumps into a table corner and starts to wail. His mother picks him up and scolds his siblings, the grandmother tries to calm everyone and the father offers him a slice of *lekach* – yet another word added to Novak's vocabulary – and the boy immediately forgets his pain and focuses on the treat, sparking his brothers' jealousy. They too are compensated with some cake and a brief quiet ensues.

Novak never understood what he was supposed to do – with his family, that is. He married of course, as was expected of him, and his wife gave birth to two healthy boys. But this family unit, which he was supposed to commend – where does it go? Who does it fight against? What is it defending? How does it define success? His sons received the best education money could buy. Ivan is already a notary, Alexey is studying engineering in Moscow. His wife Anna is not unhappy either, or so it seems. His entire life, Novak has worked hard to provide and care for them, and if he hadn't risen through the ranks in the army and sent envelopes with bundles of cash each month, they would not have come close to the lives they lead now.

After he had made a great effort to attend his elder son's wedding, Ivan, the groom, had shaken his hand and said "Thank you very much for coming, sir", as if he was just an ordinary guest. And when his younger son left for Moscow, Novak travelled to the big city to make sure everything was in order and left in his hand a year's worth of rent. Alexey had looked at him, embarrassed, and held the notes apprehensively, as if they had been handed to him by a usurer. And even though his son had thanked him profusely, Novak felt that this gesture had set them only further apart.

Now, after watching his hosts' family life, he excuses himself, leaves his translator behind and goes out to take a quick glass of slivovitz. Then he walks alone along the narrow alleyways, slowly drawn to a broad street that leads to the main road and the large synagogue. Before long, he is back at the market square. Passers-by look at him curiously: his limp provokes either repugnance or pity. Willing to risk everything he has achieved up to this point, he walks straight to his office, by the town hall.

VI

Novak's agents are used to his disguises. They have seen him dressed as a beggar or a pimp, as a carter or a concierge, even as a woman. It can be safely assumed that if a civilian walks into the office of the Department for Public Security and Order, paying no attention to the plain-clothes sentries at the gate, this person must be Novak. Once his limp is noted the assumption is confirmed. But for some reason, the Jew approaching the gate is not suspected of being Novak. Even the limp does not stop the guards from barring his path, yelling, "No entrance, *żyd*", and even raising an imaginary stone to throw at him.

Oddly enough, Novak is hurt. He is taken aback by the immediate exemption he has received from basic decorum and his leg smarts as if a real stone has just hit it. He pulls himself together. "Adrian, Nestor, it's me, Novak," and the pair immediately stand to attention. "Yes, sir. Apologies, sir!" They watch in admiration as he walks down the hall, whispering about their revered commander who never fails to surprise them. It is impressive enough that he can pass himself off as a beggar or a pimp, but a *żyd*? The man never rests, and certainly not on his laurels. He becomes completely absorbed in each investigation he works on, treating every wanted outlaw as though they were his first. Even though the colonel has already attained what Ivan and Nestor aspired to have when they joined the Department – the privileges of power – he is still out there, getting his hands dirty.

Whispers of the Jew's true identity precede Novak down the corridors, and everyone he passes bows politely. Once he arrives in his office, he takes off the kaftan and suddenly feels a bitter cold. Being referred to as a *żyd* has touched a sore spot. He sinks into his chair, hurriedly opens a fresh bottle of slivovitz and looks at the army medal for bravery on his desk. He has a sudden urge to close the shutters, lock his door and hide from the world. He usually enjoys watching the market from his second-floor window, wondering how many of the people going about their business – loitering on street corners, listening in taverns, trailing across alleyways, soliciting their neighbours' help – are doing it solely for the benefit of the man on the second floor. But now, sitting in his chair, melancholy lies heavy on his heart. Who is he? What is he? A dirty *żyd*. A worm.

He feels exhausted. He has no interest in the pile of letters on his desk. The envelopes contain nothing but flattery and lies, addressed either to him or by him. He has always believed that, given the opportunity, the rebels and insurgents he pursues would turn this country upside down and wreak havoc. Ignoramuses and imbeciles would replace His Royal Highness the Czar, delinquents and crooks would become army and police officers, while princes and aristocrats would beg for alms in the streets. Total anarchy! But what do they have now? Doesn't this corrupt social order seem more and more like anarchy anyway? What if the law and lawlessness end up becoming the same thing?

What does this pile of envelopes on his desk contain? Betrayal and gossip, half-truths and fiction. One neighbour incriminating another: this one hasn't paid his taxes, that one is lying to the authorities, these ones were seen in the company of socialists, those ones spoke ill of a prince who is close to the Czar. They all contain the line "Please remember that I have faithfully served the Czar", which is immediately followed by: "Regarding another matter, I would like to recommend my son as the perfect candidate for the position of clerk in the civil service." What do they all want? To curry favour, to prove their loyalty, prove their obedience and draw closer to the source of power. He knows all too well that they would join a gang of hoodlums with equal zeal if it held more sway than their monarch.

Suddenly, an idea hits Novak's mind. A thrill of excitement runs through him. He dons the kaftan again, leaps from his chair and limps over to the cabinet, then back to his desk, pacing back and forth. Barely realising what he is saying, he exclaims, "Yes! Of course! That's what I'll do!" and sits back down at his desk. He pulls a blank sheet of paper out of a drawer, dips his pen in the inkwell and smooths back his hair. How should he word it? This will cause a scandal. His letter must be very specific. Governor Osip Gurko must understand the reasons for his resignation. A criticism of the state of the empire should suggest itself between the lines. Novak must make it clear that he can no longer prop up a system that makes citizens live in fear, while the state does everything within its power to turn them against one another, ensuring they remain impoverished and ignorant. But perhaps it is better to be succinct. Perhaps he should write something along the lines of; "I wish to inform you of my resignation from the position of Commander of the Districts of Grodno and Minsk. Sincerely, —" Damn, that letter would leave its mark!

Gurko would be certain to summon him for an urgent meeting.

Gurko: "What is happening, my dear Piotr? Please tell me, we go back a long way."

Novak: "Nothing is happening, sir, I just want to retire."

Gurko: "But why?"

Novak: "There's no need for details. This is my final decision."

And with that, Novak will hold his peace and add nothing further. The mysteriousness of his resignation will lead Gurko to understand that there is something rotten in the Districts of Grodno and Minsk.

But what about the investigation? He is up to his neck in one of the most convoluted mysteries he has ever come across. He would have to explain why he is walking away from the affair that has gripped the entire district. Has he found the killers? If so, why aren't they in chains? Has he ascertained their motives? If so, what are they? This plot has so many loose ends. What would Novak tell Gurko? That he wants to leave this investigation because it makes so little sense, and because the only things that ever make sense about his investigations are also sinister and corrupt? Must he tell Gurko that it is logic itself that is unfair? Will he dare confess to the commander he so admires that he is awed by the bizarre journey these crooked types are on, all the more so, perhaps, because he is ignorant of its purpose? Will he confess that he wants to pull out of the investigation not because he is resigning, but the other way around: he feels it is his duty to resign because he wants to pull out of the investigation?

At this moment, there is a loud knock on his office door, and Novak slips out of the kaftan, opens the shutters, spreads out the pile of letters on his desk and takes out a stamp and a letter opener. Opening the door with the air of one who has been interrupted in the midst of feverish work, he is surprised to see his deputy Albin Dodek standing in the doorway, the bearer of urgent news.

"I searched the whole district for you, sir, and in the end I took the train."

Goddammit, thinks Novak, I risked my leg on that strenuous journey for nothing. This slow, stupid sloth still got here faster than I did.

Dodek continues: "It turns out that, contrary to your opinion, my addition to the end of the letter we sent to Mishenkov has proved useful. I'm referring to 'Anyone withholding information about their identity or whereabouts will be considered an accomplice'. Even though you were angry, I think I had good reason."

This comment could be true, Novak thinks, if it didn't come from someone utterly incapable of reason. The longer Novak is away from Albin Dodek, the more he is surprised when they meet again that this dolt is his deputy.

"In any case, sir," Dodek goes on, "an urgent message has arrived from Colonel Pazhari. He claims that the four we are looking for passed near his camp several days ago, and that one of them is called Patrick Breshov, and another Zizek Adamsky. But since we know one name, Patrick Adamsky, we can surmise what the second name is: Zizek Breshov!"

"Perhaps we can or perhaps we can't," Novak mutters, and returns to the envelopes on his desk.

"I've already made inquiries, sir. It turns out there is only one Zizek Breshov, and he lives in Motal. I bet we will find all the information we need about his accomplices there."

"Motal?" Novak says in surprise.

"Yes, Motal. I sent agents over there."

"You did what?" Novak is horrified.

"Yesterday!" Dodek says, pleased. "They should be there any minute."

"Stop them immediately!" Novak shouts in Dodek's face. "Keep them out of that town!"

"Why? What? Sir?"

"Because I said so," Novak whispers, noticing that his deputy is eyeing him warily, in alarm. "I want to go there and see things for myself," he says, as though this were obvious.

"Certainly, sir, I will tell them to retreat," Dodek says, in a conspiratorial tone.

"Now leave me alone. Let me work."

Dodek takes his time leaving the office, apparently wondering why the conversation they have just had is not considered work.

As soon as his deputy has left, Novak reaches two conclusions. First, this investigation is no longer in his hands. Like a monstrous octopus, this case has stretched its slimy tentacles in all directions. Novak would be hard-pressed to make it go away without anyone noticing. Second, if the culprits' families are indeed found in Motal, Albin Dodek will eclipse Colonel Piotr Novak, who will appear negligent for having failed to apply cold and calculated – perhaps even straightforward – analysis, becoming too personally invested, and for insisting the case is more complex than it actually is. Furthermore, he misjudged Adamsky's loyalty, and then he fell for the cliché that a woman, and a Jewess at that, couldn't possibly be the murderer. But last night, he outdid himself when he played along with the Hasidic feast and drank enough to feel comfortable singing "Shalom Aleichem" at a *tisch*. And now his stupid deputy crosses the names Patrick Breshov and Zizek Adamsky, inquires where Zizek Breshov lives and finds a godforsaken town that had never even occurred to Novak.

Motal. Could it be? When he reviewed all the towns near Pinsk, this name had come up: an isolated place surrounded by black bogs. The home of log merchants and farmers growing potatoes and flax, its residents generally prefer to stay within its bounds and rarely venture further than the markets of Pinsk and Telekhany. They are interested only in trifles: weddings, births and washing clothes in the Yaselda. They pride themselves on the quality of their logs and of their linen, which they consider soft as silk. The last crime in the town was recorded when a drunk muzhik came back from the tavern one night and accidentally entered the wrong house, where he feasted on the pork and buckwheat his wife had left out for him, or so he thought. Appreciative of the fine meal, the likes of which he hadn't tasted in a long time, he removed his boots, planning to slip into the bed of the generous cook and embrace her in gratitude. The moment he encountered a hairy chest instead of luscious curves, however, all hell broke loose. Old scores were settled by brothers, uncles and acquaintances who joined the melee, which had sprung out of a random mistake, as everyone agreed, but whose consequences were inevitable. Could Novak have been so inattentive that he did not realise that the source of the trouble lay in Motal?

True, some of Novak's mistakes reveal a certain superficiality in conducting the investigation. He could have sent other agents to Grodno, couldn't he? He could have gone to Minsk instead of Grodno to search for that Zvi-Meir character, who appears to be the key to the entire affair. The first principle he teaches the district commanders whom Gurko sends to him for training is the commander's location during an investigation. "You cannot choose where you want be; this is something your mission will dictate to you. It's a purely objective consideration." And look at him now. Where are his objective considerations? His curiosity and impulse have taken control of his mind. He didn't even have the patience to wait for the railway tracks to be fixed, and instead set out, as if possessed, on a five-day ride with Akaky Akakyevich. And where did that thread of Fanny Schechter's Grodno origins lead him? Well, to munching on calf's-foot jelly and boot-flavoured meatballs.

He leaves his office still dressed as a Jew, and has the feeling that the clerks are leering at him. Peeking into Dodek's office he sees two pairs of legs comfortably stretched out before his deputy's desk. Noticing Novak, Dodek nods to him. If he wants to know which agents are sitting in Dodek's office, Novak would have to put his head around the door, but he decides not to. As soon as he decides this, he assumes the worst: that from now on, the two agents in Dodek's office will tail him. This is not paranoia. He himself imposed the surveillance doctrine on his agents, which is based on the premise that the Okhrana is not hierarchical but cobweb-like, leaving all of its members equally vulnerable to investigation.

Novak finds Akaky, predictably, in bed. After the required blessing, Avremaleh Rabinovits lunched on egg – an honour reserved for special guests – cucumber salad and lukewarm tea with dry semolina cake for dessert. He then went back to bed to continue his recovery from last night's celebrations and come to grips with his pleasant return to the Jewish fold. Novak pokes Akaky's belly with his cane.

"Get up, we are leaving for Motal."

He is surprised when Akaky smiles in response.

The journey to Motal is short. They board a Baranavichy-bound train in Grodno and, when they arrive, Novak orders the newest carriage and freshest horses. That same evening Akim and Prokor set out for Motal in a barouche spacious enough for five passengers, boasting enormous wheels, copper-coloured spokes and fine leather seats, with a chassis resistant to all manner of shock. As the carriage rolls along, one cannot but admit that this is a fine chassis, dammit, this is what a chassis should be like. Little wonder that the pair arrives in Motal in less than a day.

This time, they do not make their way to the market. Novak

knows that if he repeats this mistake he might end up in a shtiebel, stare at undecipherable script in the afternoon and be gulping insipid cabbage soup by evening. Oh no. This time, he must immediately find the community leader, the rabbi, and make his generous offer discreetly: give up the culprits and we will spare the innocent. The time has come to tighten the strings.

VII

Novak's plan is a resounding success. Even if agents are tailing him, the only thing they can accuse him of is serendipity, that his breakthrough came quite by chance.

Either way, when Akim and Prokor meet with Motal's rabbi, Reb Moishe-Lazer Halperin, and tell him about their grand plans for the town – the building of a new yeshiva and renovation of the mikveh – they could not have imagined that, at that very moment, Mrs Rivkah Keismann would be waiting inside his office. Even if they had, they would not have thought her to be a person of interest to their investigation. But when the rabbi presents the elderly woman and tells them about her ill-fated daughter-in-law, Fanny Keismann, the combination of Fanny's name and the fact of her disappearance beats in Prokor's ears like drums in battle. He has to use every scrap of self-restraint to remain calm. Once Reb Moishe-Lazer Halperin has explained about the disaster that struck the family and told them about the sister and her husband, Zvi-Meir, Prokor is overjoyed. Two birds with one stone: Fanny and Zvi-Meir belong to the same family. Why didn't he work that out himself?

And yet, something in the rabbi's story bothers Novak. Reb Halperin describes the two disappearances, Zvi-Meir's and Fanny's, as completely unrelated incidents, but Novak is sure that the two are connected. After all, the murderess had revealed as much herself, when he gripped her throat.

Novak decides that it is time to meet the Keismann family, who live in the nearby village of Upiravah, and to blockade Motal. When he finally reaches the Keismann home it is almost three weeks since Fanny's departure, and by now not even a stork could leave Motal without Novak's permission. Novak's agents watch admiringly as he tightens the lacing of an invisible, close-fitting corset around the town. He has undercover police waiting on the other bank of the Yaselda, and further south, near the Keismanns' village, a ringleader who will report for duty with his rabble, torches in hand, whenever so instructed. He has at his disposal a small group of soldiers camped out not far from Pinsk, and even several tramps scattered about the black bogs, ready to report on any new information. A crowd of agents and freshly recruited informants infiltrate Motal itself – in the tavern, the restaurant, the market square. One informant could sell cabbages to another without either of them realising who they were.

Novak arrives at the appointment with Mrs Keismann in Upiravah – yet another godforsaken hole – confident that he is about to solve the case. The pieces are lined up on the chessboard just the way he likes them, and even though his four rivals are still at large, their queen included, the rest are held in a clever trap. Let the queen roam free, let her watch her pawns collapse one by one. Let her scurry amid the ruins of her realm. Freedom is not always the mark of triumph, and no-one knows this better than Novak.

There is nothing suspicious in the courtyard of Fanny's home. A few stray chickens, two geese and a vegetable patch. A simple wooden house but quite a large one, and from certain small details, Novak understands that this is a family of some means. And what about the children playing in the courtyard? First of all, it is a good thing they are here. The bargaining position of one's opponents is substantially weakened once children are at stake. And second of all, the bright, penetrating eyes of the eldest daughter remind him of her mother. He will have to inquire about her name.

Reb Moishe-Lazer Halperin ushers them into the house. He has just told Mrs Keismann about their encounter with Fanny and Zvi-Meir, as Akim interprets for Prokor. Now the rabbi asks the old lady to tell them anything that might help them find the two runaways.

"What is she telling him now?" Prokor asks Akim.

"That they've run out of his favourite goat's cheese."

"What does cheese have to do with anything?"

"The rabbi is hungry," explains Akim.

While Reb Moishe-Lazer Halperin pecks at bread and leftover cheese in a corner, the two of them sit before the elderly but surprisingly unwrinkled Mrs Keismann. Her anger appears to be centred in her eyes and the thick eyebrows hanging above them like carobs. It wouldn't surprise them if she were blind, because her eyes remain motionless even when they sit right in front of her. Mrs Keismann appears to be repeating their questions to the walls and then answering herself with mutters and mumbles. Akim translates every word for Prokor.

Question: "You want me to tell you about Zvi-Meir and Fanny?"

Mutter: "They want me to talk about Zvi-Meir and Fanny. Did you hear that?"

Question: "How much time can you spare?"

Mumble: "They think I have time for them, I'm sick of talking."

Question: "What do you know about these two?"

Hiss: "Well, what can anyone know? He is an imbecile and so is she."

Novak, that is, Prokor, is beginning to fidget in his chair and asks Akaky, that is, Akim, to guide the lady with slightly more precise questions. When did they leave? Where did they go? Did they leave a note? Who was the last person to see them? How are the two missing family members related?

Question: "When did they leave, they ask? Who knows when they left?"

Mutter: "And to be honest, who cares? Do I care to count? These two ask many questions. Everyone is here until the day they decide to disappear. Why is it important all of a sudden? They haven't been here for a while. What husband disappears on his wife? Poor Mende, marries a bright yeshiva student and finds out he is an indolent layabout. And Fanny: who ever heard of a bride who sends her mother-in-law to sleep in the courtyard?"

Question: "Where did they go? Do you think they'd tell me where they were going?"

Mumble: "That Zvi-Meir sat at the same table with me for every High Holiday dinner. Never said a single word to me. Philosophised all day long, much ado about nothing, that's what he is. What do I know about the creation of the world, was I there when the world was created? Who am I to talk about Adam and Eve? *Kvatsh mit zozze*, nonsense in gravy. This is your Zvi-Meir. So now, before vanishing, you think he will come to me and tell me where he's going? And Fanny? Even worse. I'm her children's grandmother and she never thought of telling me anything. I'm not asking for much, really. I try to be on everybody's good side, and maybe that's a mistake. What do I get in return? I wait all day long for her to ask my advice: 'Grandma, you have experience of life, I'd like to hear what you think. Grandma, what would you do? Grandma, what was it like for you?' But will she? Never.

She knows everything. So now, when she has this big secret that makes her run away from home, you think she will tell me all her secrets?"

Question: "Did she leave a note?"

Hiss: "What sort of a question is that? Am I a post office? A government bureau? A registrar? Do I walk around the house looking for notes? What do they know? They know nothing. They think that people's lives are like a theatre show. What note? What on earth are they talking about? Can one break someone's heart and leave a note? Destroy a family and say only a few parting words? What can one write, 'Take care of yourselves until I return'? I don't know how such people were raised."

Novak is almost at the end of his tether. He is furious. This shrew had to arrive just when he thought he had the investigation in his pocket. For his part, Akim assumes an angel-like demeanour, and with his rosy skin and fish-like pout, he appears to hang on the old lady's every word. Novak will be damned if Akaky is not pulling a trick or two. Dammit, he has probably warned the grandmother about him. Agitated, Novak grips Akaky's wrist and whispers in his ear: "Listen to me, you idiot, tell her to stop babbling. I want straight answers. Give me each reply in a single sentence."

"What do you want me to say?" Akaky whispers back.

"Tell her these precise words: 'Mrs Keismann, in order to help you, we need you to answer us clearly, in a single sentence.'"

If Novak had only imagined the consequence of his request, he would have chosen his words more carefully.

Question: "To help me?"

Mutter: "They think they are helping me. This Cossack bursts into my house, upsets me, scares my grandchildren, and all for what? To help me! If I needed your help I would have begged the Blessed Holy One to free me from this nightmare they call life.

422

Did I ever ask for anything more than bread, Torah and family? Did I ask for Avremaleh and Pinchasaleh Rabinovits? Did I tell anyone, 'I wish two righteous men would renovate the mikveh'? Let me tell you something: our mikveh is fine as it is. New does not necessarily mean better. What would Natan-Berl's father say if he saw who came to my help? Do you know how I started out in life? We had nothing at home. The well was four versts away. Nothing grew in the bogs. We had to sell our shoes to buy *kartoshkes*. And now you, of all people, you will help me?"

Question: "You ask for a single sentence?"

Hiss: "They want a short answer? Who are they, the sentence police? Tell me, please, when did I start working for someone who tells me how many words I can use? Because if this is the case, I demand full payment for every word I do not say, and believe me, no matter how much money you do or do not have, you will find yourselves out of pocket very quickly. 'A single sentence', they can tell that to their soldiers in the army, the ones with whom they did or didn't eat pork and sang or didn't sing in church, but not to Rivkah Keismann, who is still the master of her own tongue, and whoever tells her one more time 'a single sentence' will find himself out of her house."

Reb Moishe-Lazer Halperin, who has just finished an entire chunk of cheese, though not of the type he likes best, smiles indulgently and says: "I told you that Rivkah Keismann is the best!"

Novak is at his wits' end. He could happily strangle Akaky and shoot the chubby rabbi. If only he had his pistol right now he would have rattled the old lady until she let every last cat out of the bag. His patience is exhausted. If one must have a trained ear in order to appreciate the most innovative composers, then clearly training is needed before listening to Mrs Keismann – a form of preparation that Novak lacks right now.

What is more, Novak has simply had enough. After the blow

to his crushed leg, after meandering across the county, assuming several identities, soliciting informants and enlisting treacherous allies, he feels compelled to flex the muscles of the mighty Department for Public Security and Order. He fancies clenching his fist and delivering a blow that will leave Motal stunned. All he has to do is place the town under curfew and surround this house with police and soldiers. He knows what everyone will say. "See? Even Novak got sick of playing games. See? Even Novak resorts to Cossack methods."

And maybe this is how things should be? Enough disguises: violence instead of subterfuge. True, he used to be an army major with a bright future ahead of him. True, he fought in Pleba and people still talk about his courageous leadership at the Shipka Pass. True, he witnessed the surrender of the great Othman Pasha. But what is he right now? How long can one cling to the past? When was the last time he looked at himself in the mirror and said: "You did well, Novak, you deserve the praise"? Who looks up to him? Albin Dodek and his herd of fools. The major in the world's proudest army has become a shadow of his former self. Mulling this over, Novak thinks that contradicting old habits and imposing a curfew might not be such a bad idea. No-one will be able to keep up appearances anymore and when the games are over and all the cards are on the table, it won't be long before he learns everything he needs to know. And maybe this will free him from the shackles of nostalgia for his army days so that he might finally come to terms with what he has become: a brute, no better than the worst of thugs . . .

Oh, bloody hell, no! There must be another way. If his conclusion is that everything can be resolved by force, then he has devoted the second half of his career to worthless games of the mind and useless manipulations. If he is no better than Dodek, he might as well start misspelling his own letters. If an iron fist

424

is all it takes, why should the Okhrana be a secret service? And what will Governor Gurko say when he hears about Novak's loss of temper? How will the officers who have been trained by Novak react? Curfew? Extortion? Torture? Did they really travel all the way to Minsk to learn what anyone in their profession can do? He has to come up with another plan, even at the cost of losing two more days.

Reb Halperin, who has just swallowed his last mouthful of bread, beams at Akim and Prokor with unabashed delight. "Did you find out everything you wanted to know? Wonderful. We can go back to town for dinner with the local dignitaries."

Akaky looks at Novak, who does not meet his eye but whispers, "Say that we thank them. We will not bother them anymore."

As the two of them start for the door, and the rabbi sweeps the crumbs off the table and hurries after them, the children, who have been playing outside, come running into the house with a terrified woman in tow, and slam the door shut. Novak looks out the window. Dozens of mounted Okhrana agents are galloping towards the house, led by Albin Dodek. What can he be doing, Novak wonders, hoping it's not him that the agents are after. Without a second thought, he ushers the family into a back room.

Dodek and the agents halt at the gate. The deputy slides down from his horse and salutes his commander standing on the veranda.

"Sir!"

"What are you doing, you ass?" Novak could slap him. Dodek has just blown his cover.

"We've come to arrest the family."

"Arrest the family? Who told you to arrest the family?"

Dodek opens the gate and strides towards his commander. The goose retreats with its gander. The deputy climbs the steps and removes the silly bowler hat that makes secret police agents so easy to recognise.

"Things are getting out of hand, sir," Dodek says, breathlessly, without looking at him. "People are talking."

"'People are talking'," Novak says. "What can fools do other than talk?"

"And yet, sir, the situation is serious."

"Who sent you over here?"

"You did, sir."

"I sent you? I told you to wait! Who else is involved in this, Dodek? Who sent you?"

"Gosh, sir, I haven't a clue what you mean by that, sir, everyone's involved in this. The mess with all the dead bodies and all that is no secret. The whole district knows about it. Especially now that Governor Gurko is involved."

"Gurko?" Novak says in bewilderment. "Did Governor Osip Gurko talk to you? Did he tell you to come here?"

"Why would he talk to me, sir?"

"You just mentioned Gurko!"

"No, you did, sir. When you sent the agents to Mishenkov, you told me to say that Gurko is involved."

"Dodek!" Novak bellows. "That was only a threat!"

"How could I know that, sir?"

"So Gurko knows about this whole thing?"

"I have no idea."

"How did you know where to find me? Who followed me?"

"No-one, sir, it was obvious you would be here."

These last words shake Novak. He stares at his deputy, thunderstruck, taking in the full meaning of what he has just heard. Have his cunning methods become predictable? Did the slowest deputy in the armed forces, a man of feeble mind and threadbare brain, just guess Colonel Novak's next move?

"Well. Now what?" Novak says, conceding that he has been caught unprepared.

"It's all organised, sir. We've ordered a curfew. We are in full control of all entrances and exits, sir, the town is blockaded. Now we must arrest the relatives and interrogate them. A brilliant operation, sir, congratulations! Whether Gurko already knows or not, he will definitely be proud."

Stunned, Novak scratches his head. Dodek stares at him as though he is a stranger, or perhaps a suspect, even. Suddenly, Colonel Novak has an idea. He thumps his cane on the ground and pulls a bitter face.

"Oh dear. You have made a serious mistake."

"A mistake, sir?"

"Indeed. You acted too soon. You forgot about Zvi-Meir. He is the key to the entire affair."

"Zvi-Meir?" the deputy asks, confused.

"Enough questions, Dodek! Send an urgent message to the agents tailing Zvi-Meir in Minsk. Tell them to be ready to arrest him."

"Certainly, sir. Zvi-Meir. I hadn't thought of that."

"Thinking is not a part of your job."

"Certainly not, sir."

"What good are the killers without their mastermind?"

"I quite agree, sir."

"Off you go, then."

Novak is relieved to see his deputy instructing the agents. It was lucky that Zvi-Meir came to mind when he did, otherwise Novak would have been caught completely off guard. He has managed to prove yet again that his thick-headed deputy is incapable of thinking creatively, because, like a short blanket,

Dodek's brain is destined to leave the essentials uncovered. To avoid finding himself in this position again, Novak makes a mental note to remember that this investigation is unique. Its twists and turns do not wrap themselves around the fugitives alone; they also grip the investigators by their throats. Is not that so?

MINSK

I

Written and signed in Minsk
By Zvi-Meir Speismann
On the twelfth day in the month of Elul, year 5654

Dear teachers and masters, paragons and friends, the loving and beloved, wise, sagacious and learned in the truths
of the Torah, precious men of wisdom. To my beloved friend
Rabbi Scheinfeld, and to my beloved friend, man of letters,
the erudite Rabbi Kahanah, and to my beloved friend, the
scholarly, pious Rabbi Leibowitz. I turn to you, three wise
men, in peace, as your virtue sustains the world.

The man writing to you is none other than Zvi-Meir
Speismann, the lad you expelled from the Volozhin Yeshiva
eight years ago when he was of the tender age of eighteen.
Fear not, I intend to neither mock nor malign you. My
heart hasn't a drop of bitterness, nor do I gloat over the
final closing of Volozhin's gates. I am no longer the pure,
innocent man I used to be. I, Zvi-Meir Speismann, was
destined to follow the tormented path of the prophets.

I currently reside in Minsk's lower market with neither
a home nor means. My days are numbered, but I could not
be happier. I have found my calling. My heart is alight with
the flames of faith, and my spirit soars to the high Heavens.
My words of truth have spread across Russia. Try as they
might, my persecutors will never uproot the truth that

has clung to so many hearts and won over countless souls. On the contrary, my death will only serve to emphasise the righteousness of my cause and prove the injustice I have endured. Contrary to what our tradition says, justice prevails regardless of whether it has the support of a majority. All that Truth needs is a harbinger, and a harbinger I have been for its cause.

Dear friends, homeless beggars have warned me that mighty legions are on my trail. I do not want to point fingers, but in trying to understand how it came to be that Zvi-Meir Speismann – a meek, obscure thinker, a subaltern scholar – has become a threat to the great Russian Empire, the answer appeared to me, shining with a thousand lights: you, members of the old guard, think my teachings pernicious. Blinded by your sagacity, you have become callous and aloof. Like those who heard the Prophets of Israel, driven by jealousy and knavery you refused to heed my words and cast me away.

In Motal I was an aspiring scholar (if rote and verbal somersaults can be described as "scholarship"). At the cheder the tutor used to call me "the little *chucham*" and sang my praises. My commitment to the Truth, not modesty, compels me to add that my fellow students were fools through no fault of their own. Convinced since infancy that they knew nothing and that their knowledge would have been but one drop from the ocean of the Torah, what reason did they have to study? The children sat staring at the window, waiting for the tutor to give permission to go out to play in the courtyard.

I, for my part, left no book unopened. Against all odds, I was destined to attend Volozhin. If the Chosen People are a light unto the nations, Volozhin is their beacon: the hall of wisdom, temple of learning and font of immaculate argumentation. This academy, I was told, nurtures deep reflection, edifying debate, and even pursuit of the seven sciences: mathematics, geometry, music, astronomy, the natural sciences, theology and philosophy. It was unfathomable: Jewish scholars studying astronomy, proving theorems and hunting butterflies! This dream became reality at Volozhin, towering above all other yeshivas in the Pale of Settlement. Its reputation, beloved friends, extended far and wide to every town and village.

The tutor went to speak to my parents about my astonishing prospects at the famed academy. My mother, Rochaleh Speismann, promptly fainted. My stone-deaf father shrieked, "What happened?", and my mother recovered enough to scold and inform him: "Volozhin, Eliyahu, Volozhin!"

My teachers and masters whose virtue sustains the world: imagine my excitement when my father left me on the train and waved with his handkerchief from the platform. "Do not come back!" he yelled as the train pulled away. I was left to my own devices on Mount Moriah, but unlike Isaac the Patriarch I wasn't bound as a sacrificial offering; I felt I had been blessed by the Angel of God. Now, I knew, my tedious Motal days were over. I wouldn't have to endure slothful classmates intent on hunting insects and shooting craps. I was travelling to enter the house of the wisest among the Jews, who are the wisest of men.

Beloved friends, or should I call you my executioners? Asked by the police and army chiefs who is Zvi-Meir Speismann, you surely described me as haughty and impudent, a menace to the Jews of the Pale of Settlement, spreading lies, inciting rebellion, manipulating the meek and corrupting tender souls. My fellow tramps have been warning me: "Zvi-Meir, beware! Believe it or not, you are pursued by army generals! You have outraged the highest levels in the police! But I know perfectly well the men whom I have infuriated. They raised me and taught me what I took to be pure wisdom but now know is a daydream, a castle in the sky, a leafless tree.

I came to Volozhin at seventeen, and I still remember my first days at the yeshiva as a nightmare. There I was, sitting shoulder to shoulder with great scholars, witnessing their disputes over every jot and tittle, hardly able to tell the difference between one letter and the next. When I would cite a verse they would retort with a quote from the *Chayei Adam* of Avraham Danzig, a line from Eleazar of Worms, and a counter-argument from Rabbi Shmuel Eidels. Then they would pick faults with the *Guide for the Perplexed*, dismiss Abravanel, and land a winning argument from Rabbi Yehudah Shmuel of Regensburg. And there I was, staring incredulously at a page of Talmud, overwhelmed with shame. What had I been doing in Motal? Back then I was a head to foxes and now I was a tail to lions. I had basked in the warmth of the praise of my tutor, who would have been the joke of the yeshiva if he ever got there. As I learned too late, the promise I held in Motal was only in the eyes of fools.

My teachers and masters, for four months, one hundred and twenty sunsets, I sat and said nothing. When spoken to I solemnly nodded and at all other times I was engrossed with holy teachings. "Lift your head up from the page and refute your debater. The Prophets of Israel were not scholars," I was told. Yet, I felt that my faculty of reasoning was still a babe in arms, crawling on its stomach, bleating at night and fumbling for a foothold. Before finishing one tome, I was already on to the next one, and then I reread the former at night. I studied and read under the lantern's light, torturing my eyes. I could not wait for the first term to end on the fifteenth of Av, so I could use the holiday to prepare for the second term. While my colleagues returned to their families, earned a little money, ate chicken thighs and slept in comfortable beds, I stayed behind, lived abstemiously and devoured books.

Reflecting on the commentators' discussions of the Tree of Knowledge, whether it yielded citron, fig, vine or wheat, an idea haunted me relentlessly. I approached Rabbi Scheinfeld, the first member of your troika, hands atremble and legs weak, and feebly asked the venerated master: "How could it be that the injunction against eating from the fruit of the Tree of Knowledge was issued to Adam and Eve before they had tasted it, that is, before they could tell right from wrong?"

Indeed, Rabbi Scheinfeld, my friend, do you remember the innocent question you were so quick to dismiss? Do you recall how you explained to me that many had tackled this conundrum before me, and the greatest and brightest among them had proposed an answer that was right there before me (how could I fail to understand it?). "Knowledge of good and evil" in this sense has nothing to do with virtue, as it denotes the descent of God's immutable truths to the realm of human conduct, where good and bad are determined by whims and passions, for which reason First Man and First Woman were clad with fig leaves, and that is all there is to it.

I nodded in assent, but deep down refused to accept his suggestion. Was he even listening? I did not pose the well-trodden question, which is: why should God deny First Man "knowledge of good and evil", and how could sin earn man the virtue of knowledge? Honourable master, what I set out to know was how could man grasp this prohibition in the first place? Never having seen death, how could he understand the command, "But of the tree of knowledge of good and evil, thou shalt not eat. For in what day so ever thou shalt eat of it, thou shalt die the death"? How could he have fathomed either the prohibition or the punishment it would entail?

I raised the same question with Rabbi Kahanah the erudite, who, to my great surprise, looked at me and muttered: "The Creator never intended to kill man there and then but to make him finite, in other words, make him destined to die." Honourable rabbi, can you even concede that I raised an inescapable perplexity? Is it too much for you to accept that a babe in arms can pose a question worthy of reflection?

I turned to the wise and perfect Rabbi Leibowitz, the first to see the conundrum for what it was and pick at its faults: "Man understood the prohibition full well, as he was told, 'For in what day so ever thou shalt eat of it, thou shalt die the death', that is, you shall cease working, and man knew what work is, for God had placed him in Paradise to toil and preserve it."

My teachers and masters, it took me only a few moments to find the flaws in Rabbi Leibowitz's reply. But before I could answer, Rabbi Scheinfeld came over to scold me: "Speismann, is it you again, with your 'knowledge of good and evil'? Read your Talmud!" No! I wanted to cry, this is not the right answer, but I had no-one to fend for me, and therefore walked away hushed and rebuffed.

I had made up my mind to confront you with this question, three wise men, only once I could formulate it more clearly. I pored over books day and night, not letting the Holy Scripture leave my sight. Time and again I pondered how First Man could understand the prohibition he was under before the "knowledge of good and evil" and before God took him to task. The more I perused those very same verses, and read all commentaries, the hungrier I became for the truth, until it suddenly struck me: "knowledge of good and evil" has nothing to do with the tree and its fruit, be it fig or citron. Knowledge was obtained only once the prohibition was violated. Had he not violated the prohibition, man could not have known what is either good or evil; he could only obey. The tree from which Adam and Eve took the forbidden fruit became the tree of knowledge of good and evil only once they transgressed, not a moment earlier.

Beloved teachers, I cannot describe to you the feelings that overtook me. I collapsed as soon as I let go of my perturbations. I lay on the ground, stupefied, the happiest man alive, spirit without flesh. The Holy Scripture suddenly made perfect sense. Innumerable quandaries were instantly resolved. I kept thinking what else we might learn from this discovery: only once man violated the divine decree he could see there is faith and unfaith, at which point he could choose for the first time between devoutness and heresy. Violation of divine decree is therefore a necessary condition of faith. This is the naked truth. Truth has no need of my knowledge. Two plus two is four with or without Zvi-Meir Speismann.

To me, this discovery was like grinding mountains into powder: only a sinner can be a true believer. If one does not transgress, one is an obsequious dog.

Excited, I expected the greatest minds of our generation, my beloved teachers, to continue the conversation with me. But all they did was grimace and drift from fury to scorn. "Only black can be white," muttered Rabbi Scheinfeld, "and only day can be night," Rabbi Kahanah chuckled, "and only fools can be wise," thundered Rabbi Leibowitz. I could not believe my ears. The troika had disarmed and humiliated me; they left me as easy prey for their disciples. I wanted to die of shame.

Scholars swarmed to throw contradictions at my face: "only a Jew can be a gentile", "only *kartoshkes* are turnips", and so on. At night I pleaded for help from the luminaries of past generations – the Vilna Gaon! Rabbi Yehudah Shmuel of Regensburg! Here I am! – but stalwarts like them, feasting in the afterworld at God's table, could not care less about the novice from Volozhin. Access to my venerated teachers who had seen me suffer day in, day out was denied. If I so much as opened my mouth I was shushed, mocked and abused like an abominable ignoramus. People called me "Motal riffraff" and "King of the Bogs" to my face.

Ostracised, my dears, I knew that my days at the yeshiva were numbered. Indeed, I was not officially expelled, nor was I excommunicated. Nonetheless, we know all too well that denigration and belittlement hurt more than banishment. If I approached colleagues engrossed in debate, before I could open my mouth my debaters would flee. Before long, the single table I could join was the one reserved for the hollow heads who had been admitted to Volozhin thanks only to the donations of their rich fathers.

At that moment it dawned on me that the Volozhin Yeshiva is a marketplace of ideas where one's success depends on one's ability to state the obvious; in other words, it depends on whether one agrees to play by your rules or not. And the three pre-eminent sages that you are, the *gedoylim*, walked around correcting their utterances – guided not by Truth but by whim and caprice. A Turkish bazaar, gentlemen, is what it was. To my mind, Volozhin was about asking any question whatsoever, provided it had rhyme and reason. As it turned out, you presided at Volozhin as sole arbiters of what rhyme and reason might be. Little wonder that meddling became rife, as a wave of leaks and reports to the authorities ultimately led to the locking of its gates.

The day I left the yeshiva was the day I fulfilled the purpose of my studies. I approached Rabbi Leibowitz and took my hat off like a Christian, standing bare-headed before God. I, Zvi-Meir Speismann, went over to the other side to experience heresy first hand, in order to decide on my own if I should follow the Almighty. This was when I vowed to walk in God's path, not the way you understand it, but like an ordinary man; if this means I will be a pedlar then so be it, but I will not bargain with the truth.

I married Mende Schechter, daughter of Meir-Anschil Schechter, a butcher from Grodno. My parents were pleased with this match and the handsome dowry that came with it. Mende was harmless enough – pleasant demeanour, a graceful dimple adorning her chin, innocent eyes, gentle and well-mannered. And although she did not make my heart sing, she was certainly worthy of a promising scholar like myself.

To make a living, I pulled a cart laden with a Jewish home's must-haves: clothes, furniture, kitchen utensils and firewood. But when I offered my wares for sale in the villages, I encountered hesitation and suspicion. Everyone asked, what is a Volozhin student doing with a beggar's cart? My customers considered me too clever to be peddling, and scholars thought me too much of a pedlar to be clever. I had no other choice but to tell my story, and to elaborate on my discoveries to anyone who would listen. You will not believe their reactions. Ears were pricked, hairs stood on end, and the wares offered for sale were completely forgotten. One after the other they advised me to go back to study. When I tried to share my woes with my pregnant wife, she looked at me blankly and dismissed me by saying her head hurt. The next day her head was still sore, and the day after it was spinning, and when our daughter Mirl was born, Mende was tired most of the day. Whenever I tried to raise the subject, she meekly asked me to save the conversation for another time. God Almighty, with whom should a man speak – a donkey?

I will tell you, masters, that if it was not for the children, I would have moved to Minsk nine years ago. But how could I leave my fledglings behind? Night after night I held Yankele in my arms and told him about the Talmud and about the yeshiva he will attend when he grows up. Founded by his father, Rabbi Zvi-Meir Speismann, this academy will be the envy of Volozhin. Rabbi Speismann's yeshiva will teach, first and foremost, intellectual prowess. Anyone memorising verses will be expelled. This is what I told my young son. But the more resplendent and grand my dreams became, the more I found my chores unbearable. There I was, walking the streets, preaching the words of the Torah and cursing the patrons who refused to buy my wares. I took note of the affluence of my brethren who attend synagogue to fulfil commandments taught by rote, without exercising a shred of free thinking. To my eyes they were a horde of insects leaving the wells in search of crumbs.

But how could I complain? Crumbs were our primary concern at home. Mende prattled about the things she bought, who did what and to whom, what people are saying about so-and-so, when did X visit Y, how much tomatoes cost here, and why no-one buys flax there. Who cares? Roaming the realms of the mind, suddenly I would be asked to offer my opinion on a coat she had bought from a neighbour. And if I ever requested peace and quiet, Mende would cover her face with her hands and scuttle around the house like a plucked hen.

My sweet, brilliant children were the apples of my eye. I could, for example, see Yankele sitting in a corner, exploring the contents of a bowl. I would scold him, "Yankele, leave that bowl alone!" and he would return a conspiratorial look and keep at it. The boy, who was not yet three, already understood what took a torturous year at Volozhin for me to realise: transgression is a necessity. Tell me, you who keep the world firm with your virtue, how could you, the wisest of men, fail to understand what is clear as day to an innocent toddler?

I did everything I could for the children, travelling from one village to the next as a measly pedlar, to put bread on their table. Mende's dowry ran out and I had no time left for Torah study. People asked, "Zvi-Meir Speismann, a wise man like yourself, why aren't you at the study hall?" And I would reply with a smile, "There is no Torah without bread. My cart is my study hall." And yet I was mortified. Above all else, I pitied my children. Yankele was about to start attending the cheder, where his spirit would be crushed. Mirl would grow up to be like her mother. How does Mende define a good day? A good bargain on shoes, juicy gossip and gloating at others' misfortunes. All our daughter could learn was that idle talk is all there is to life.

Beloved friends, I could not bear it any longer. My children's eyes filled with shame. I shared with them words of Torah at Sabbath dinner, and left the following evening after the Melaveh Malka dinner that marked the Sabbath's departure. Knocking on doors for a living, what could I possibly share with my clients? They wouldn't buy a single item before slashing my prices to pieces. They'd ask me to come back, the bastards, only once I refused to bargain and turned to leave, as if trade is a muscle-flexing game that only the fittest survive. Looking at them, I realised we were exactly the same: all we cared about was money.

I wished I could separate my calling from my profession. Unfortunately, one's profession never relies on the body alone; it always ends up plundering the riches of the mind. Sitting down at sunset at home, hoping to reflect unperturbed, Mende's prattle would gnaw away at my thoughts. I could not bear the sight of my family dining around me. Greedily chewing on bread, gorging on fat until it dripped down their chins and guzzling soup to the very last drop. I lost my appetite altogether. I did not eat for days, and became a walking skeleton among animals of prey.

My heart skipped a beat every time I saw a bonfire, thinking this might be the burning bush that would summon me to my calling. Yet each time I approached, the people sitting around the fire threw stones to drive me away. In the morning I rose expecting to hear a voice from on high but heard Mende's snores instead. I intended to wait until Mirl grew up and Yankele could think for himself before leaving, but after nine years my life became unbearable. I abandoned the cart and vowed not to return to Motal until my wish was fulfilled: to become a better man and, most of all, a father worthy of his children.

I arrived in Minsk penniless. Good people took me under their wing, letting me spend the night in their home or barn. They refused to let a fellow Jew freeze to death out in the street. When they asked for my story, I told it from beginning to end, at which point they told me that the illustrious yeshiva I had attended had closed down, and told me about Volozhin's history of quarrels and betrayal. I was ashamed, my masters, but not surprised. I vowed to my hosts that a new, magnificent yeshiva would rise, this time on a solid foundation, and asked for a donation to let me lead the rundown local hall of study for a start. They invited me to their academies to share my discoveries and I accepted. But wherever I went, former Volozhinites acted as gatekeepers and denied me access to any dais or hall.

Conceding my defeat, I knew my days were numbered, not seeing a glimmer of hope in this valley of death. Returning to Motal was not an option: it would have broken my children's heart to see their father so defeated and crestfallen. Palestine is a quagmire of hoodlums, and New York, *die goldene medina*, is a bed of thorns. I intended to burn my prayer shawl, taking after the manner of the Mendelssohns, Germany's famed Jewish converts, and then kill myself like those possessed by the dybbuk. Knowing this would play into the hands of my detractors was the only reason I didn't follow through with my plan. I started living on the street and continued spreading my teachings from dawn to dusk. I lost three fingers to frostbite, my lungs almost failed twice, and only the Blessed Holy One sustained me and gave me the strength to continue spreading His word.

Passers-by hollered, "Get a job, you are selling garbage!" I replied only with pure, innocent words. Tell me, what world are we living in, bereft of any truth or spirit, whose dwellers are no better than beasts? Few stopped to listen to my sermons, few threw copecks at my feet, and only my fellow tramps helped me to a bowl of hot soup every day. I did not approach the house of alms and never set foot in a tavern. Beloved teachers, I was all mind, happy and proud of my work.

A few weeks ago I heard that the police were looking for me. "Look out, Zvi-Meir!" a beggar whispered in my ear. "You are being watched." Looking to my right and left, I saw dubious characters on a street corner. I walked over to the square and there they were, hiding in a cloud of cigarette smoke on the stairway to the church. Quietly, I slipped into the cold synagogue, *die kalte Shul*, and saw them pulling out their notepads to make notes.

Who sent them after me? There is no room for doubt. It was the heads of the closed Volozhin Yeshiva. Venerable sages, erudite scholars began fearing the ideas of Zvi-Meir Speismann. They noticed new life, a waft of fresh air reviving the residents of Minsk. The rascal's wise teachings spread by word of mouth, and before long people began to realise that religious faith is conditional upon the freedom of choice. Suddenly they saw Jewish men who agree to wear top hats and suits becoming clerks. Looking at the clock they realise that those Jewish men are working in their offices until late and do not attend synagogue for the evening prayer. And as the word spread the community leaders had no choice but to unite and fight to the death the man they had denounced: me, Zvi-Meir Speismann. But cold water, dear sirs, will not put out the sun.

You sent informants to the police to warn them of the great peril to the empire: Zvi-Meir Speismann, a meek, yet shrewd Jew, who is a tad more discerning than you are. What is more, it was just brought to my knowledge that the army has joined the hunt. I have become the nation's enemy number one. There has been no greater threat to the Czar since Napoleon Bonaparte.

Well, dear sons, your deeds did me justice. I stand before the burning bush I craved, only this time it is not the bush that will go up in flames but the prophet. His body will indeed be consumed, dear disciples, but not his spirit. His name will be on everyone's lips in Motal. He will return to his wife and children on the wings of glory to right the wrong they were served. The tale has reached its end. My work in this world is done. Send my love to the members of my people whom I have consecrated and to my family, whom I have loved more than anything.

Yours sincerely,
Zvi-Meir Speismann
A simple man
Minsk, year 5654

II

Their travels along the road from the barracks to Minsk with a military escort are very different from the wayfarers' previous journey. First, only three of them remain. Shleiml Cantor's whereabouts are unknown. Second, this time they are taking the main road, calmly and confidently. The sleepy passengers in the carts that pass them tremble with fear as soon as they recognise the approaching caravan. Innocent travellers look away like culprits, troublemakers bow their heads submissively. Everyone tenses at the sight of them and breathes a sigh of relief when their convoy moves on.

The summer heat makes one discover new parts of one's body, parts that would have been ignored had they not become moist and sticky. On the first night, they stop for several hours in a field of sugar beet. The garrison commander, Captain Istomin, leaves two guards to watch over the barouche and permits the other soldiers to take a nap on the ground. The repose is too brief, the horses are tired, and the captain tells the two women in the barouche, Fanny and the nurse, to cover their injured passenger with a blanket. Only one of them obliges, and Istomin is taken aback by the other woman's indifference. He gives her an authoritative glare, which she counters with her predatory wolf's eyes. He wonders whether he should assert his military rank, but, on further reflection, he decides that she might just refuse and humiliate him.

Fanny's eyes follow Captain Istomin's sturdy back as it walks away from the carriage, and then glance down at the nurse's uniform she is wearing. She has lost track of the identities she has assumed over the course of this journey.

One might suppose she feels guilty for the precarious position in which she now finds herself. Had she not left Motal at two hours past midnight, one family (albeit a family of thieves) would still be alive. Two agents, family men, would have also returned home. And the two men by her side – one suspended between the world of the living and the world of the dead, the other between the past and the present – would have stayed put, the former in a shoddy tavern, the latter in a boat, and neither would ever have risked an encounter with the gallows. She would have gone on with her life, Mende would have recovered, and Zvi-Meir Speismann – well, perhaps being Zvi-Meir Speismann is sufficient punishment in itself.

And yet, even when that detective gripped her neck in the dead of the night, his fruity breath on her face, she did not consider going back to Motal. If she makes it to Minsk, she is sure to meet with the man from the Okhrana again, but the thought of hiding from him doesn't cross her mind. It has been a while since she has known whether she is running away from her pursuers or rushing towards them.

The nurse looks at Fanny reprovingly. Some women are infuriated by other women's indolence. Seeing little difference, if any, between a world where such women exist and a world where they do not, they ask, "Well, is this sloth useful in any way?" And since they consider existence and usefulness one and the same, they conclude that a lack of usefulness means they do not exist. Every simple action – covering a wounded man with a blanket, for one – becomes an exhibition for them. The nurse beside Fanny shakes out the blankets over the side of the wagon, folds two of them four times and lays them on different parts of Adamsky's body. Then she unfolds the blankets, spreads them over him again, smoothing out the folds, and sighs. Then she rubs oil and ointments on his injured body, busily administers painkillers and herbal concoctions, and emphasises Fanny's idleness all the more.

Fanny starts to feel as though everyone is against her: detectives, soldiers, sentries, law-enforcement officers, hangmen, judges. Even her travel companions. If Adamsky were healthy he would not have been able to control himself. And Zizek: he has taken nothing but blows on her behalf from the moment he joined her journey. And her family? Natan-Berl must be fuming. Returning home in the evening he probably ignores her place on the bench at the dining table. He sits down to eat his dinner, plays with the children and goes to bed. If their mother's name is mentioned, he turns away as if he has heard a word in a foreign language. In his eyes she does not exist if she is not there. He will say his piece only when she returns. Gavriellah, her eldest, cannot replace her mother, no matter how sensible she might be. Her other children, dear God, must be at a loss to know how to deal with their resentment. Whereas Rivkah Keismann must be elated, surely.

Fanny remembers how she used to run her fingers through Elisheva's hair every evening, tuck the blankets over David's feet, and slip into her bed, feeling in her bones that disaster was imminent. Life cannot remain so peaceful for long, this much she knows, and danger is never far from home. Her world – the tranquil, serene, wonderful world she aches to rejoin – was founded on injustice, to which she was an accomplice. Her well-ordered life played dare with justice as she kept turning a blind eye to the catastrophes on her doorstep. "Not now, Fannychka, not now, Mamme is tired."

And so she shut herself up in her home, closed the shutters and locked the door. She was perfectly satisfied in her kingdom, thanking the Creator for her healthy children and husband. She was grateful for every breath her Mishka drew, overjoyed for every word of Hebrew that Gavriellah learned. Doubtless, the tragedies that befell her neighbours must have happened for a reason. Her mother had taught her that. Carelessness, negligence, transgression; in hindsight, any disaster could have been predicted. And the past is a prophecy that conceals the bitter truth: Fanny has control over nothing. Fannychka cannot control a damned thing. "Not now, Fannychka, Mamme is tired."

And you, Fanny Keismann, your ruin was also predicted. Were they right? For years, Mende hinted that the townspeople were sneering at Fanny's decision to live among the village goyim. Her sister kept telling her the town wanted the Keismanns to return to the fold: those who sleep with dogs should not be surprised if . . . But Fanny did not repay her sister in kind. She did not tell Mende what people were saying about her husband, that Zvi-Meir Speismann was a buffoon posing as a genius, a man who should learn a trade instead of pretending to be the nation's leader.

Once Zvi-Meir had abandoned her sister, however, it was nigh-on impossible to ignore the slander. Fanny was forced to hear the insults that circulated, especially those by other women. What else could be expected of such a couple, they said. At first, they blamed Zvi-Meir for being a hopeless failure in the guise of a tzaddik. Then, in due course, they began to name Mende's faults, one by one. After all, a vigilant, firm and responsible wife does not let her household fall apart. They blamed her for her own predicament, for being a husbandless wife, as if she were responsible for Zvi-Meir's flight. Fanny wanted to tear out her hair when this calumny reached her ears.

Then it was too late. Mende almost drowned and was rescued from the river by Zizek, the man believed by all to be the village fool, who is now sitting by her side, holding the hand of his battered whoremaster of a friend.

Of course, a stern lecture awaits her at the gates of Motal. She will definitely be scolded for the path she has taken. How could two wrongs yield justice for her sister? A delegation of rabbis could have brought back Zvi-Meir without leaving a trail of dead bodies behind them. A letter from his parents might have gone much further than Fanny's hobnobbing with hoodlums. Why did you look for adventure, Fanny Keismann? If that was all you wanted, you shouldn't have pleaded the cause of justice in vain. There are hundreds of women like your sister. Why don't you track down every wayward husband in Grodno County? You could at least confess that you have been acting out of self-interest: after all, the world will not mend its ways thanks to you. If you really cared so much about rescuing your sister, you could have taken a different path. And if you were guided by another cause, now is the time to admit it. In short, what is it?

She doesn't know. The one thing she knows for certain is that it is too late to turn back.

III

By the end of the third day of their journey, they can see the lights of Minsk shimmering in the distance. Nonetheless, the garrison commander orders his troops to make camp again. Fanny is surprised to see that they are not staying in a tavern after such a long journey, with aching backs, dusty beards, sooty faces and parched throats. The soldiers' encounter with the hard ground does nothing to improve their morale.

They eat the few vegetables they have left, courgettes mostly, and a few bitter, limp cabbages they gathered as they marched across fields. The soldiers sit apart from the three companions, and it doesn't take long for their group to emit drunken laughter and pipe smoke. A hussar humbly approaches the Father and invites him to join them. Zizek refuses, and the soldier kisses his hand and shoves dried sausage, tobacco and crackers into the pockets of his shirt.

The nurse prepares one of the tents for their wounded friend and motions to Zizek and Fanny to stay in the other tent. Zizek, however, will not leave Adamsky, and sleeping by herself seems like a bad idea to Fanny. She looks around, uneasily, hoping to catch Zizek's attention. His unshaven face is sunburned, his scarred mouth is drooling, and his eyes glisten in the lantern's weak light.

"Please, Mrs Keismann," he says, "let's stay with them."

Fanny sighs with relief and enters the small, cramped tent. The odours of rum and urine blend with the smell of old bandages and antiseptic. Zizek hands her a piece of cheese and breaks a cracker with his teeth for them to share. They munch their crackers, then silence falls and only the beating of their hearts remains. A strange sense of kinship seeps into Fanny's beleaguered body, and emotion overwhelms her. Who would have believed she would make it this far?

"Zizek Breshov," she whispers, "why did you come with me?"

"I'm sorry, Mrs Keismann," he says at once, without looking at her, as if this sentence has been ready in his throat for a long time, "but you came to me."

"Many people came to you, yet you obliged only me."

"Many came?" He coughs heavily. "I'm sorry to say this, Mrs Keismann, but no-one else came. Only you."

Before she falls asleep, he sighs and mutters, "You and him."

IV

They wake in the morning to discover that they have camped right on the edge of the city. The garrison commander knows that if a sniper was stationed in one of the nearby houses, they would have been an easy target. Zizek muses that if the city had walls and a sentry had pissed from one of the watchtowers, they would have all got wet. Adamsky is imagining the courtyard of his and

Ada's home: her misshapen face beaming, her buxom chest inviting beneath her apron. Two chickens are pecking at grains, and clothes in different sizes, from infant to old-timer, are waving in the last breeze of the summer. Each man to his own thoughts.

The soldiers are exhausted. The hussars' faces are haggard, and dust fills the wrinkles in their faces. When the garrison commander orders them to fold up the tents and move out, they look at one another with disbelief.

Their entry into the city is smooth. Fanny thinks they would have been welcomed with the same indifference even if they'd been wearing Ottoman uniforms. A few clerks cackle like roosters by the station. Drowsy beggars slowly awaken and watch them pass with unease, as if they were trespassing on the soldiers' space. Labourers arrive in the city hoping to be hired for the day. Fanny notices many Jews among them.

It would make sense for the commander to leave them in a tavern while the soldiers search for Zvi-Meir Speismann. But that is not how it works. As time passes, Fanny realises that they are aimlessly roaming the streets. Every now and again, two horsemen break away from the group and another pair joins them. This ruse, she surmises, is a precaution to ensure they are not being followed.

They start their search in the city centre. Fanny stares, wide-eyed, through the barouche window. She sees tall buildings, offices and factories, a theatre sign, and then another, and a café on every other corner. When do they ever work here in Minsk? And what is this – a horse-drawn omnibus? Good gracious! And this damp odour, could it be that homes here have running water? And the buildings, so grand, one floor wasn't good enough for them? Must they have a view of . . . what is that? Such an impressive bridge!

The Jews here look different, too, with their shiny shoes,

groomed beards and fancy caps. Good God, some of them are adorned with mink hats and others sport bowler hats like goyim. No-one would dare walk around Motal looking like that. Look, that man just pulled out a gold watch from his coat, and right behind him a bunch of Jews are sitting and joking with university students. Would one have to actually ask people about their denomination in order to know what it is?

They steer clear of the upper market square, which is overlooked by a palace – the governor's probably – and cross a large river that must be the Svislach, heading east. When there are no longer any other carriages in sight and potholes multiply and the roads become narrow, they know they have reached the slums, known here as Minsk's "swamp", *die Blotte*, the Jewish neighbourhood. Fanny is surprised at the squalor and misery around her. In Minsk, they had told her, there are more soup kitchens than poor people. All a hungry man needs to do is turn his head and he will find a charity: Saviour of the Meek, Acts of Kindness, Charitable Dwelling, Tent of Israel . . . But the sight that Fanny sees from the window of her barouche is quite different: Jews with bent backs, shrouded in penury and weighed down by hunger. They look just like the crowds in Motal and Grodno, but perhaps it is their poverty that makes them so indistinguishable. Two elderly women are fighting over a customer on a street corner, each of them holding a basket of shrivelled cucumbers. One is yelling at the other: "You've already sold two today, now it's my turn!" and her friend replies, "There are no queues here, Mrs Gurevits, this is a marketplace!"

After another tour of synagogues, Captain Istomin stops the search party near a conclave of locals, who do not seem to have noticed the strange procession of approaching soldiers. Captain Istomin dismounts and walks over to the barouche. "Well," he growls at Fanny and Zizek, "hurry up, get out and ask about your man. We'll keep close by." With their sunken eyes and dazed expressions, Fanny and Zizek appear to have forgotten why they are there. "Go on," the captain says. "You don't want us to talk to them, do you? They'll run away crying 'Gevalt!' and rouse the entire city." Oddly enough, Fanny and Zizek still do not move. "These are *your* people!" the officer says loudly, and the huddled Jews raise their heads as one.

Istomin realises he is attracting unwanted attention and lowers his voice to a whisper. "Look, here's the deal: no-one in our army can talk to any of your people without provoking hatred and suspicion. That is how things stand in Russia. That's a fact. How will your story end? I do not know. But Colonel Pazhari has assigned this mission to me and I intend to follow it through. Now, kindly get out of the barouche and talk to these people, before they start a riot."

The captain's words make sense. Fanny and Zizek emerge from the carriage. The group of Jews stand firm, clinging to one another as if they are already under arrest. A few of them briefly raise their heads, and when Fanny and Zizek draw closer, they shove their hands into their pockets and tighten their kaftan belts.

"*Sholem Aleichem*," Fanny begins, "*a gute morgen*." The group step back as one, stumbling against each other as they retreat. If the garrison commander had approached them they would have known how to react. But a goy lady with fair hair and burning eyes who marches across the street and speaks fluent Yiddish? They've never seen such a mongrel in their life.

"*Wart a minut! Halt!* Wait a minute," Fanny yells, and they turn to look at her, embarrassed. "We need to ask you something."

"*Fragen?*" one of them repeats, nervously twiddling his side-locks. "Ask a question? Nobody asks questions with soldiers backing them up. Their rifles are enough."

Fanny tries to reassure them.

"You have nothing to worry about. They're on our side."

An old man bursts out laughing. "You are either a *meshugene*, completely mad, or a liar," he says. "The army is never on our side." He adds in a whisper, "The army is for pigs. And what makes you think that we are on the same side as you?"

"I'm sorry, but we come in peace," Zizek Breshov says. Although he speaks in Polish, he accompanies his words with calming gestures, and the group appears to understand him.

"Please listen," he says, "we mean no harm. We are looking for Zvi-Meir Speismann. That is all. Tell us where he is and we'll be on our way."

The men sigh with relief. "Zvi-Meir Speismann? Of course, Zvi-Meir Speismann. Who else but Zvi-Meir Speismann?" They repeat the name over and over again. The oldest among them, whose eyes seem to fill half his face, explains: "He's a madman, a *meshugener*, debaucher, miscreant, *shkotz*. You've never seen anyone poorer in your life, it's frightening. He lives in the street with rats for neighbours. He keeps saying he's one of the *gedoylim*, but everyone knows that he's no more than a sparrow-fart. His nose is always pointed at the heavens, intolerably arrogant he is, and he spares no-one his lectures. He is full of bitterness for the great Torah scholars, convinced that the illustrious Volozhin Yeshiva is a den of idiots. He keeps repeating an inane phrase like a prophecy – "faith is sin", or the other way around, no-one can remember. He bases his entire thesis on the story of the Garden of Eden, and not a single soul has managed to understand what it is that he wants to say. He spends his days chasing after married women, drinking *yash*, and ending up in a tavern every so often. So, it's Zvi-Meir Speismann you want? Please! Go to the lower market and inquire after him in the alleyways off Rakovias Street. It won't be long before you see him in all his glory. He's the one you're after? Why didn't you say so? You can have him!"

For some reason, Fanny feels a sudden pity for her brother-in-law. She of all people should have been glad to learn that Zvi-Meir is considered a fool. But right now, by God, she would rather save him from the herd of snitches that has gathered around her. As soon as they realised they wouldn't be in danger if they talked about Zvi-Meir Speismann, they'd yapped like there was no tomorrow. They never thought to inquire about the woman interrogating them, or the man speaking Polish, not to mention their military escort. This group simply gave him away without batting an eyelash.

"Go to the lower market," the old man reiterates, "and you are bound to find this Speismann character." The others nod along with his every word, clearly proud to have this man speaking on their behalf.

While the old man relishes the admiring looks of his friends and enjoys their approval of his fine words, Zizek notices Fanny's hand sliding towards her thigh, and he hastily grabs it and pulls it back. Fanny is exhausted, which might explain her rash action; until now, she has never dared to pull the knife on one of her own. Granted, she didn't flinch when she slew the family of bandits, or when she slit the agents' throats so swiftly, and if she'd had to pull her knife on the soldiers in the camp she would have done so at the drop of a hat. But now she feels the need to protect Zvi-Meir Speismann from her own people, a pack of wolves that has just feasted on his carcass. The old man's words have struck a chord because they are true. He had said, "What makes you think we are on the same side?" Indeed, she is far from certain that they are on the same side, and if she's not on their side, whose side is she on? This is why her hand reached for the scabbard on her thigh. If it hadn't been for Zizek, who knows how this encounter would have ended.

"I'm sorry, thank you," says Zizek, and drags her away.

At the lower market, of all places, where bribes are usually effective, they hear conflicting reports regarding Zvi-Meir's whereabouts. The finger of a potato vendor points them in the direction of a small synagogue near the cemetery. Another finger, a balding beggar's, sends them over to a soup kitchen run by Saviours of the Meek. A *luftmensch* they come across claims he only arrived in town yesterday from Vitebsk and knows nothing about what goes on in the city. And a boy with a bundle of rags says he has never heard of anyone called Zvi-Meir Speismann. The money they offer in exchange for information doesn't help; perhaps it only serves to increase the confusion. They attract a herd of beggars, each attempting to prove that the information he has merits a reward. It is only after making several tours around the market that they notice a beggar standing with a few drunks on the corner of a nearby street (if a row of wooden huts can be called a street), imploring passers-by: "Come and hear the words of a simple man, Zvi-Meir Speismann, who has little by way of fortune, but from whose mouth the truth flows."

Fanny and Zizek approach the self-declared prophet. Hair as lank as drooping stalks falls over his face and hides his eyes, but Fanny can clearly recognise the voice of her brother-in-law, the man who destroyed her sister's life. Contrary to how she remembers it, his voice is free from sarcasm and conceit, from a wish to remonstrate and condescend. "Come and hear the words of a simple man," he invites them, and Fanny notices a half-open bag on the ground beside him, containing a thin blanket, a few cabbage leaves and a piece of stale bread.

Fanny approaches Zvi-Meir. She faces a perspiring prophet in tatters, wearing torn shoes and reeking of onion. His left hand is missing three fingers. Zizek stays back, not wanting to intrude on a family affair that does not concern him.

"Come close and listen!" Zvi-Meir calls to Fanny, his head bowed. "Fear not, I am a simple man, Zvi-Meir Speismann is my name. Ask anyone in Minsk and they will tell you who I am. You can invite your husband, too, dear lady. He needn't fear my words, their wisdom speaks for itself."

"Zvi-Meir," Fanny begins, unable to make out his eyes through his long hair.

"Yes, Zvi-Meir is my name, you can ask anyone. In public people will tell you I am a fool, but ask them in private and they will tell you about my virtues. By God, madam, they sent the Imperial Army after me. And who am I? My name is of no consequence. I am a simple person, just like yourself. I don't ask for anything."

"Zvi-Meir," she tries again, her voice trembling.

"I am indeed Zvi-Meir, my dear, I can hear apprehension in your voice." He extends his mutilated hand towards her, stretching out a finger and a thumb. "Everybody knows that you should stay away from Zvi-Meir. His words are dangerous and the *gedoylim* disapprove of him. And yet, just like you, everyone comes to listen. And why? Because the truth has no need for approval; the truth has no need for gullible herds. Lies can be spread among the masses, but the truth touches the hearts of individual souls. If you have a soul that craves wisdom, then one of these days you will find yourself here, at Zvi-Meir Speismann's hall of learning."

"Zvi-Meir, it's me, Fanny Keismann."

Good God! The first flash of his gaze startles her. Behind his crust of poverty and his filthy stalks of hair, there burns a pair of bright green, zealous eyes. His face is handsome, although his smile reveals several missing teeth.

"Fanny Keismann?" he whispers, tears welling up in his eyes.

"Is Mende here too? And my babies, Mirl and Yankele? How I miss them, oh my, oh can it be? Has my reputation reached as far as Motal? Do I hold sway in the district of Kobryn and in Grodno County?"

Fanny says nothing. Oddly enough, she is touched by his words.

Suddenly, they hear a commotion from a nearby rooftop. A boy's voice, shouting, "Zvi-Meir Speismann! Run for your life! The soldiers are here!" The prophet raises his head and sees, over Fanny's shoulder, Captain Istomin and his soldiers coming towards him. A broad smile stretches across his broken face and he begins to rock backwards and forwards in prayer.

"At long last, Fanny Keismann," he whispers in a trembling voice. "My children will finally have a father they can be proud of. Tell them how soldiers came to take their father away. Tell them how their father shook the world with the truths he taught. They must know that everything I did was for their sake, and that even if they suffer, it will not have been in vain. And kiss Mende, my beloved, who must think that I have aggrieved her for no reason. She probably thinks that I haunted bordellos, or went in search of fame and fortune. By God, Fanny, it would have been so much easier to explain my decision if I had opened a match factory. It would have been so much easier to convince them of my love if I had tried to support them through trade. But all I asked for my family was wisdom and integrity. You must tell her how her husband became the terror of the corrupt and the senseless. Will you?"

Captain Istomin approaches and Zvi-Meir stretches out his wrists to be handcuffed. "I fear nothing," declares the prophet. "I am prepared to pay the price for justice."

"Come on!" the officer says to Fanny in Polish. "We have to go! Did you get what you wanted from this good-for-nothing?"

"I need just a few more minutes," Fanny replies.

Zvi-Meir shoves his hands back into Captain Istomin's face, begging for handcuffs. "Don't try to defend me, Fanny Keismann! I've been waiting for them to come. By God, I've been waiting for them for years."

"Tell him to get his filthy hands out of my face," growls the garrison commander.

"Zvi-Meir," Fanny turns back to her brother-in-law, "I came all this way to get you to sign a writ of divorce. You are coming with me to the head of the rabbinical court in Minsk, and in his presence, you will sign a writ of divorce from my sister."

"Divorce?" Zvi-Meir mumbles. "What do you mean 'divorce'?"

"A gett, Zvi-Meir, you will sign a gett."

Zvi-Meir rummages in his nose but comes up with nothing. He tilts his head and stands on one leg as if trying to drain his ear. "I don't understand." He raises his voice as though addressing a crowd. "A minute before I am hanged in the city square, you want me to sign a gett to divorce your sister?"

"No-one is about to hang you, Zvi-Meir Speismann," Fanny murmurs.

"Fanny Keismann!" roars the prophet. "Do you not see the military force that surrounds me? Has a squad of half a dozen hussars gathered in the lower market for no reason? Who do you think sent them?"

"I did, Zvi-Meir," she says. "I sent them."

"You?" the prophet chuckles. "Since when did you become a general in the Czar's army?"

"Zvi-Meir," Fanny is pleading now. "Come with me and sign the gett."

"A gett?" he thunders. "What's that got to do with anything? I love my children, and no wife is more devoted than Mende Speismann. I would give up my life for their sake!"

460

"Zvi-Meir!" She grabs him by the arm. "Get yourself into the barouche so we can go to the rabbi. Otherwise, you are coming back to Motal with me."

"Motal?" His eyes glisten and his voice grows soft.

He sinks to the ground and hides his face in his hands. His shoulders quiver. He starts to cry. Raising his head a little, he inspects his maimed hand. "How can I go back to Motal?" he asks his palms. "My children can't see me like this, a certified failure, a penniless beggar, the joke of the city."

"Come on, Zvi-Meir." Curious faces gather around them as she tries to stand him up.

Zvi-Meir's hair falls forward, covering his wet face, and he starts mumbling. "Why would God lay down prohibitions for those who cannot grasp them? Adam reflected on the prohibition and failed to grasp its magnitude. What is this like? This is like seeing a line drawn on the ground separating nothing from nothing and being told, 'Do not cross this line.'"

Standing over Zvi-Meir, Fanny begins to feel uncomfortable. More and more people are gathering around the strange scene, eager to solve the mystery: why has such a menacing army detail been called in to capture a trembling leaf? Vagrants and merchants, old people and children flock to them, all curious to see what will become of the wretched Zvi-Meir.

Captain Istomin walks up to her again. "See what you've done? This racket is about to spread to other neighbourhoods." With a hand on the hilt of his sword, he turns to Zvi-Meir. "Get up!" he orders, and the prophet lurches forwards with outstretched arms, begging for handcuffs again. "Behold, House of Israel!" Zvi-Meir yells. "Here I am, Zvi-Meir Speismann, enemy of the nation, whose wisdom threatens the *gedoylim* to the point where they have called in the Czar's army to arrest me for committing the crime of striving for truth and justice!"

"Zvi-Meir," says Fanny, grimly, "come with us to sign the writ of divorce."

"They want me to divorce the truth, gentlemen! They want me to sign a false confession! Beloved teachers and masters, I will never sign this piece of paper! I will never part with justice!"

The crowd gathered around them is growing larger by the minute. Curiosity is at fever pitch. People have begun nosing around the barouche and speculation abounds. The horses' path through the crowd is blocked, and Captain Istomin draws his sword and orders the crowd to retreat. His five hussars, all unaccustomed to handling civil disorder, follow suit.

And then, at that moment, several members of the crowd sweep off their black kaftans, and Fanny realises she is surrounded by undercover detectives, true blue secret agents to challenge Captain Istomin and his hussars. They have placed snipers on rooftops, blocked all the surrounding streets and alleyways and locked the crowds in an airtight trap. They drag the hussars from their horses in the blink of an eye, and not one, not two, but three officers leap into the carriage, pinning down the patient and his nurse. Captain Istomin manages to draw his pistol, but five more agents restrain and disarm him. Not a single shot was fired, not a single tooth was lost, and no noses were punched in the process.

As for Fanny and Zizek, no-one comes near them. More than twenty police surround them and their commander orders Fanny to take out the blade hidden under her skirts and lay it on the ground. His intelligence was accurate, and now more than twenty bullets lie in wait in the surrounding gun barrels, in case either Fanny or Zizek, and especially Fanny, makes a suspicious gesture. She pulls out the knife and puts it on the ground, Zizek raises his arms in surrender, and four thugs step forward and club him in the stomach. Fanny turns in his direction, but, anticipating her move, one of the brutes sends a fist flying into her right cheek. As she falls to the ground, just before she loses consciousness, Fanny senses the blow's might, which unleashes first a kind of metallic pain, then a sense of humiliation, and then finally an epiphany. She has been expecting this punch her entire life without realising it, and now that it has arrived, as four men rush to cuff her arms and legs, she feels enormously relieved.

A moment later, uniformed police in their fancy caps pop up out of nowhere. Apparently, this is a complex operation involving more than two hundred men. Their commander instructs his deputy to send an urgent message to Motal: "Inspector Novak, we have arrested the suspects: woman, man, Adamsky and Zvi-Meir Speismann. Detail from Mishenkov's unit led by Captain Istomin also taken in for questioning. Suspect described as 'toothpick' still missing, will be tracked soon. Convoy to arrive in Motal in three days." Then the commander lights his pipe and barks, "To the railway station, let's go!"

MOTAL

I

On the umpteenth morning of his service, Corporal Shleiml Cantor is woken for duty for by an irritating fly that rests on the tip of his nose, and realises that he is hungry.

The previous evening was something special. There was one last bottle of *yash* left, a sleeve of fine sausage (kosher of course), half a loaf of bread, three crackers and an apple. Cantor worked out that if he ate half of that he would be full, which is indeed what transpired. And yet he could not stop thinking about the half-meal that remained ...

Now that the fly is shooed away and the food crate is open, he is about to invite Olga – "Shall we eat?" – but there is no food left. Cantor looks over at his companion, embarrassed. He has been caught off guard. She stares back at him, her arms folded and her mouth askew. It's bad enough that he had to replace Oleg in such a forlorn corner of the camp, not to mention the unbearable heat he has to endure, but are the guard and his companion expected to live on fresh air alone? What good is a sentry if his body is trembling with weakness? If Cantor is to regain his strength, he must have something to eat as soon as possible. Without stopping to consider his duty, the cantor rises, stretches his limbs and leaves his post, pulling Olga along with him. Unaccustomed to movement, she falls apart. But Cantor is not one to turn his back on disadvantage or disability. He takes his beloved in his arms like a bridegroom and sets off for the camp to replenish his supplies.

Alas, neither Cantor's sense of direction nor his faculty of reasoning is his forte. He remembers that, when he first came to Oleg's guard post, he walked in the direction of the sun. Therefore, he surmises, he should walk in the sun's direction in order to return, and he cheerfully sets off in the wrong direction. What will the soldiers say when they see him again, after all this time? What will they say when they see that he does not return alone, but with a companion?

After half a day's march "towards camp", Cantor arrives at a small shack that might be described as a bar. The corporal enters the place holding Olga, and immediately notices a certain attitude of deference towards him. The men would never dare abuse him to their heart's content, he thinks, because now he is wearing the uniform of the Czar's army. He sits Olga in a chair next to him, slaps the table and calls out, "Can't a corporal and a lady get a drink around here?"

The roars of laughter that follow are heard all the way to Nesvizh, perhaps even as far as Baranavichy, if one has the sharp hearing of an owl. But ordinary passers-by have no need of superhuman senses to realise that something is up at the local bar and they flock to enjoy the show of an ass of a Jew with a clipped beard and shorn sidelocks posing as a soldier, married to a wooden plank, issuing orders to everyone around him.

Needless to say, they sit down with him, listen to his stories and let him run up a heavy debt in a card game he was sure he could win. Once he realises that his uniform will not extract him from this one, he offers to repay his debt by singing "Adon Olam", or by ceasing to sing it. His debtors, however, prefer to give him a thorough beating.

What is Shleiml left with? No food, no drink, and very few teeth. He is saved only by the passage of time, for the simple reason that at some point the muzhiks drift away to their homes and let him be. Shleiml Cantor leaves the bar with a hardly a spot on his body unbruised, wearing neither uniform nor insignia, but with no hard feelings either. Sometimes you're up and sometimes you're down, and right now he's down. So what? At least he has Olga, even if she is pretty battered and bruised herself.

At dawn, a rickety wagon carrying potatoes drives past him. The cantor gathers Olga in his arms, mounts the wagon and the couple reaches the nearby town not long after. Those who are quick to conclude that good souls are an extinct species should feel ashamed, heretics that they are. To wit, as they approach Baranavichy the wagon's driver yells at Cantor, "Now get out, you wretch!" and throws a quarter of a loaf of bread after him. Shleiml thanks the farmer for his free ride, and marches on towards Baranavichy. But alas, Baranavichy is no place to be if you are the local cantor's rival, let alone if you are one of four murder suspects in a town swarming with secret agents, all on high alert for your arrival.

Naively enough, Cantor does not consider himself to be linked to the murders in question. More fearful of his professional nemesis than the law, he avoids the synagogue and enters a local tavern on the main street in the hope of an encounter with Lady Luck. This time, he isn't punched. Instead, he is surprised to encounter eyes registering his resemblance to the facial composite on the "wanted" notices pasted all over town. Before an hour goes by, he is handcuffed and on his way to meet Inspector Novak in Motal, his hands still clasping two broken planks and a sheet of tarpaulin.

II

There are moments in the life of a nation, thinks Colonel Novak, which portend its demise. The end always begins with something small, a trifle, which would have gone away had it been taken care of promptly. And yet, once it has taken root, it is almost impossible to eradicate, as its tendrils reach into the remotest corners of the empire.

The military and the police, those hallmarks of state rule, are supposed to be on the same side: the former fighting against threats from without, the latter fighting threats from within. Now they are flexing their mighty muscles at one another in a tense confrontation. Clearly, the army has been trying to shield the four suspects, and there is no doubt that Colonel Pazhari lied through his teeth in his report about "Zizek Adamsky" and "Patrick Breshov". What is more, Novak has now conducted a thorough inquiry into David Pazhari's true descent. Why? Well, surprisingly enough, no-one had ever thought to try it before him. In order to have a nephew, Count Alexander Pazhari would have to have a sibling, and indeed he has: a sister. Except not a single soul in St Petersburg ever recalls having seen the sister, who is well known in many circles, pregnant. Drunk? Absolutely. Making an exhibition of herself with a friend named Dushinka? On occasion. Committing adultery? Careful now, her husband doesn't suspect a thing. But pregnant? Oh no, not even St Petersburg corsets could have hidden it if she was. Therefore, Count Alexander Pazhari of St Petersburg should be put under surveillance, because for some reason he has never bothered to deny this bogus family connection with the illustrious officer. Truth be told, it was thanks to this discovery that the entire affair came to light. At long last, the whole chain of events related to this case leads to a powerful and influential man from the capital.

This is the only plausible explanation for the decision of a fake nobleman who has become a senior army officer to put his life on the line for four murder suspects. It also serves to explain why Captain Istomin, an impressive officer with an impeccable record, did the same.

Based on this, it can be assumed that Alexander Pazhari is a decadent count who for some reason is unhappy with his lot. On some whim or other, he recruited several henchmen to stir up disorder in Kobryn District. What is surprising about his plan is that he managed to recruit Jews for his scheme, despite their usual caution, which suggests that he must have made them an offer they could not refuse. There are people, among them fools and intellectuals, who believe that the *żyds* are plotting to take over the world. Novak will be bitterly disappointed if his investigation ends up supporting the prejudices of those buffoons and geniuses. Unfortunately, for now he has no other theory, but the theory he doesn't have preoccupies him far more than the one that he does. Has he missed something? He cannot tell. Still, it is safe to say that everyone mixed up in this affair knew that the Okhrana was pursuing them, and yet they were not deterred. This is exactly what the end of a nation looks like, when people no longer think that the law is synonymous with justice.

But why should he be surprised? All he needs to do is take a look at his own men. He is surrounded by a pack of idiots. Thankfully Albin Dodek is at least not a drunk, but the rest of them reek of vodka and do not even try to hide it with fruit liqueur. They burn their stomachs with cheap kvass and then go out to make night arrests. They are incapable of any manner of thought, reflection or meditation. Being told to "bring in so-and-so", they go and do it, no questions asked. Yet another sign of the nation's demise: oafs filling the ranks of its police and security forces.

And what about the commander-in-chief, His Excellency

Field Marshal Gurko, the celebrated governor? Why the hell did Gurko entrust him with this pestiferous role in the first place? Why hasn't he invited Novak for a private audience in so many years? When Gurko had convinced him to accept the job, he had told him, "Piotr, I need you here. You know why." And he did know, at least he thought he knew. But now, Mr Governor, dammit, I don't understand a thing. Where is the respect that was promised me? Not the respect that derives from status or pay, but respect for one's profession? All I am is a soldier, Field Marshal Gurko, all I ever wanted to be was a soldier. I always faced other armed soldiers, just like me. I faced forces that were organised just like my own. With flags flying just like mine. But as soon as I was hurled from a horse and crushed my leg, I became little more than a sewer rat.

Now my enemies have inferior firepower, their forces are in disarray, and, lacking any kind of banner, they hold fast to some trenchant belief or other instead. How did this come about? Did you imagine that you were sending me to a different battlefield? Or did you already know, back when you invited me to your office and buttered me up with flattery, noticing my limp, that a disabled man like me is only fit for lurking in the empire's sewers? Is it perhaps true, Mr Gurko, honourable Governor, that you have not invited me to your office because you can't look a rat in the eye? There's another sign for the nation's imminent downfall: the commander of the investigation is on the brink of going mad.

"Sir." Dodek makes him start. "He's ready."

"He's ready?" Novak says, trying to keep up. "Who is ready?"

III

When Novak realises that his honourable guest is Shleiml Cantor, his morale finally collapses and he drops his cane. Thus far, he has learned nothing new from any of the interviews he has conducted in Motal, including the "conversation" with that mute recluse, Natan-Berl, and the monologue of the infinitely loquacious Rivkah Keismann.

Novak has no intention of asking the local townsmen about Colonel David Pazhari, and clearly it would be pointless to ask them about Count Alexander Pazhari, of whom they have never heard. In fact, it is doubtful whether any Motalite has ever met a Russian nobleman. As soon as they hear the name "St Petersburg" they flap their arms about as if they are drowning. They find the very mention of the capital abhorrent; to their ears, it sounds like a word in a fancy language they do not understand.

However, he can't complain about the locals – Jews or gentiles – who are cooperating without protest. Reports stream in detailing matters Novak could not care less about: tax evasion, suspected insurrection, defections and God knows what else. They have even snitched on the local adulterers, down to the very last one. This has created a paradox: the residents, wishing for the curfew to lift and the Okhrana agents to leave, have been falling over themselves to give Novak information that only convinces him of the necessity of the secret police's presence in the town. Motal, it turns out, is not as innocent as it first appeared. There is solid evidence for the presence of Palestine dreamers, and even the odd communist pamphlet has been sighted. The townsmen disclose this information under the assumption that the Department for Public Security and Order is in Motal to take care of a specific issue that the curfew should resolve. None of the residents imagines that the blockade is an end in and of itself and that the Okhrana has quite different concerns on its mind.

Reb Moishe-Lazer Halperin is especially diligent and is proving to be a great help. Indeed, at first he was hurt and reticent. He had treated Akim and Prokor as though they were his own sons. Other towns had driven them away, but he had generously opened the doors of his congregation to them. And how did they repay him? They sowed false hopes in his heart, then took off their disguises and pulled out their identification papers. Shame on them, the villains. What a disgrace.

It did not take long for the rabbi to realise, however, that as a public figure he does not have the luxury of yielding to his private emotions. He must protect his community and make amends for his mistakes. As it happens, Novak has appointed him as the townsmen's representative to the authorities. The rabbi goes from house to house, pleads with his congregants to answer questions, tells them about recent developments and then goes back to Prokor, that is, Piotr Novak, and tells him everything he knows.

If only a week ago someone had told Colonel Piotr Novak, the Okhrana commander of the north-western districts, that he would interview Yoshke-Mendel the store owner, interrogate Schneider the tailor, press Liedermann the cobbler for answers, probe Grossman the handkerchief vendor, rattle Blumenkrantz the pâtissier, sweet-talk Isaac Holz the lumber merchant, whisper in the ear of Mordecai Schatz the book-cart owner, and even yell at Simcha-Zissel Resnick the butcher (who won't stop talking about Mende Speismann's lust for fresh meat, for some reason) – Novak would have told them that they were mad. He does not trouble himself with such useless interrogations. That's what Dodek is for, even if his deputy is a specialist in keeping the chaff and throwing away the grain. And yet, despite talking with so many locals, Novak cannot put the pieces together to form a cohesive picture, and he certainly cannot link it with the count, His Highness Alexander Pazhari of St Petersburg.

Only two families in the town refuse to talk to Novak, and remain indifferent to threats or intimidation. Reb Moishe-Lazer Halperin pleaded their defence and begged the inspector not to demolish their homes. "These are two stubborn families," he explained, "and they know nothing in any case."

"How can they know nothing?" Novak said, furiously. "They are the Berkovits and the Avramson families! Their sons are my suspects!"

"True," the rabbi touched his forehead and heart, "but the families lost all contact with Pesach Avramson and Yoshke Berkovits when the boys were twelve."

"How is that possible?" Novak asked, and immediately regretted the question, which prompted a thirty-minute lecture from the rabbi.

It is hard to recall every detail of the rabbi's outpouring, but the gist of it is that, long ago, a terrible tragedy took place. The authorities tore Jewish boys away from their homes. No family would volunteer its progeny, forcing community leaders to decide who to part with. Could there be a more thankless task? After many calculations, they announced their decision in good faith and without prejudice. "If my children had been the ones chosen to go," the rabbi ran his hand through his tousled beard, "wouldn't I have given them up? Let me put it this way, dear sir, even though you are not well versed in the Old Testament: did Abraham not give up Isaac? This is all there is to it.

"Well," the rabbi continued, "these two families refused to accept the community's decision. We spared nothing in our attempt to be reconciled with them. But they would never forgive and forget. You should know this, Inspector Novak: every Jew is like a link in a chain, we are all connected by an unbreakable bond. Zizek Breshov and Patrick Adamsky are links that fell out of the chain. Their families made things worse by choosing to deny that this bond exists at all. Of course, one should not be judged in one's hour of sorrow, but in this case, sorrow threatened to undo the very fabric of the community."

In one of his few lapses of judgment, Novak loses control. He takes four agents and breaks into the Berkovits household. The father, of course, has long been dead, and only one brother still lives with the mother. Novak orders two agents to interrogate the mother in front of her son to extract information from her, but to his surprise, this yields nothing whatsoever. Never mind the fact that they get next to no information out of the son, even when he is forced to watch as his mother is pinned down by two Cossacks, but the old lady herself remains quite unruffled. She is beyond fear, Novak thinks to himself. This woman is nothing but wrinkles; life has already squeezed her down to her last drop, nothing more can be wrung from her now.

It suddenly dawned on Novak that when the state completely crushes its citizens, it only makes them immune to threats. A state seeking to secure absolute control over its citizens must leave them something precious, a modicum of freedom to cling to. He orders his men to leave the Berkovits house at once, and does not bother to go to the Avramsons'.

As the operation drags on, Novak orders his temporary head-quarters to be set up in a house near the synagogue, leaving only one room to the family living there, the Weitzmanns. Once Novak is settled, the town's residents are called in for questioning one by one, and interrogated in the courtyard. Akaky Akakyevich, formerly known as Akim and now going by his birth name, Haim-Lazer, serves as Novak's interpreter. The inspector knows that once he has questioned everyone else, it will be his interpreter's turn for a grilling. Something about Haim-Lazer's frequent smiles, grimaces and teasing gives Novak the feeling of being in the hands of someone who is anything but submissive and who might even turn out to be dangerous.

"What do you think?" Novak asks him after they have questioned Mikhail Andreyevich, the driver of the wagon that took Fanny out of Motal on the night of her escape. Not only was Mikhail's testimony completely useless, he kept coughing up phlegm and didn't trouble to keep it in his mouth.

"This is hilarious," the interpreter chortles.

"What's hilarious about five dead bodies?" Novak demands.

"Nothing," Haim-Lazer says quickly, seeming to recall that he is not free from danger himself. "I mean, these people have no idea, they live like their ancestors did a century ago."

"Why don't you give them one of your pamphlets," Novak suggests, but he knows that there is something to his interpreter's observation. This obsolete way of life, here in Motal, is doomed to disappear. He will gain nothing by questioning these crackpots.

"When all of this is over, I will leave for New York," Haim-Lazer says unexpectedly.

"New York?" Novak says. "How does that fit in with your socialist ideas?"

"It doesn't," replies Haim-Lazer, "but this place is doomed."

Novak decides to stop questioning the local residents. The rest of the investigation is not faring too badly, overall. Colonel Pazhari has been summoned to Motal to "testify" about the suspects' whereabouts. Novak does not want to arrest the colonel with an armed unit right behind him, which is why he prefers to meet Pazhari when the suspicions against him are still not official. The colonel will arrive in Motal cocksure, only to find himself in chains.

All residents are under curfew. No-one can either enter or leave. It goes without saying that the local muzhiks are allowed to go about their daily affairs – there is no point in punishing innocent peasants – but they, too, are subjected to inspections of their papers and searches of their wagons. The families in the eye of the storm, Keismann and Speismann, are under constant pressure. All that remains for him to do is to seize his suspects in Minsk.

So it is little wonder that, when the suspect is brought to Novak, and he realises it is Shleiml Cantor, he sighs with despair. What can he get out of this toothpick, goddammit? Of what use is this hare-brained, imbecile, drunk cantor? What can he do with the compulsive gambler he saved from being lynched at Adamsky's tavern, who proceeded to piss the bed next to Fanny's later that night?

As the toothpick is told to sit down, he immediately demands food: for himself and for the lady. What lady? Novak wonders, but then he realises that Cantor's putative companion is made up of two broken planks and a sheet of tarpaulin. Novak begins to feel embarrassed, surrounded as he is by his agents. Such an interrogation risks blemishing his reputation.

"Lock him up," Novak orders. "He's useless."

"That is no way to speak to a soldier," Cantor says, very seriously, and the Okhrana detectives in the room burst out laughing.

"Take him!" Novak raises his voice. "And throw away those damned planks."

What happens next, Novak could not have anticipated. Some men have a family – wife and children – whom they embrace every day. And then there are people like Shleiml Cantor, who have two wooden planks and a sack that mean the world to them. They were destined not to grow up under the wings of a soothing mother and a comforting father. As far as they can remember, they experienced the touch of skin against skin only when copecks were transferred from one hand to another, if they were lucky, but more often when they took slaps and punches. Then one day, Cantor was sent to a guard post where he met a pleasant damsel. Is she the prettiest lady he's ever set eyes on? Is she the most talkative? Certainly not. But who is Shleiml Cantor to expect the best? So he threw in his lot with her. And although he is certainly used to losing, Olga is one thing he is not prepared to lose, which is why he falls to his knees and starts weeping. "Olga!" Sobbing, mouth drooling, nose dripping, eyes swollen and shoulders trembling, he cries, "Olga!"

Naturally, Shleiml's little scene makes the audience roar all the louder. There is nothing funnier than a man who has fallen as low as a man can. One is almost compelled to laugh, otherwise one might imagine oneself in his place. Everyone is laughing except for Novak, who for some reason is moved by the cantor's tears. He, Novak, could not cry like that even if he wanted to. He, Novak, could not rejoice like his Hasidic hosts in Grodno. There's no such drama in his life, for better or worse. He is like an abandoned, ransacked house without furniture, window frames or floorboards; a bare framework supported by old foundations. So even this matchstick has an advantage over him, albeit one that amounts to no more than two planks and a sheet of tarpaulin. Dammit, Novak, are you losing your mind? He orders his agents to let Cantor reunite with his bride.

A messenger enters the room holding a telegram. Novak anxiously scans it and smiles, a smile that dispels all of his former doubts. It is the smile of success.

"The four suspects have been apprehended in Minsk," he informs his agents. "Fanny Keismann, Zizek Breshov, Patrick Adamsky and Zvi-Meir Speismann."

The room resounds with applause, handshakes and back-slapping, and Dodek looks at Novak in amazement.

"You've done it, sir," he says, clapping him on the shoulder. Novak says nothing, but thumps his cane on the floor.

"Well done," whispers Shleiml Cantor. "That Zvi-Meir will pay for his deeds at long last."

"His deeds?" Novak straightens his back and leans on his cane, all ears. "What do you know about Zvi-Meir's deeds?"

"Well," Cantor stutters, "he's quite a rascal, isn't he, Olga?"

"Release him," Novak orders, "and leave us alone."

IV

Novak's keen senses lead him to assume that what the human toothpick is saying can be either worthless or priceless. But it does not occur to him that Cantor's account will turn out to be of tremendous value precisely because it is worthless.

He has no need of Haim-Lazer right now as the toothpick speaks Polish, at least. Novak leads Cantor down to the Yaselda. How long does their conversation last? Not very. Novak begins by asking about his links with the gang, and the toothpick is horrified by his suggestion. As far as Cantor is concerned, there is no link at all. They found him on the road and took advantage of his naivety. What business does he have with them? Their relationship is like the one between people and the weather. When the former is present the latter always appears, but this does not prove cause and effect. This metaphor surprises Novak. Although far from perfect, it is not something you'd expect from a complete imbecile.

"Still," Novak presses, "how do you know Zvi-Meir?"

"Zvi-Meir?" the toothpick says. "Obviously, I don't know him at all."

"And yet you observed that he is a rascal," Novak says.

"A rascal through and through," the cantor affirms. "Fanny is right to be chasing after him."

"Fanny?"

"I think this is her name, is not that so?"

Strange, thinks Novak, "is not that so?" is my phrase. Is there more to this wretch than meets the eye, and especially more than meets the nostrils?

"Why is she chasing after him?" Novak asks.

Cantor repeats the whole story he heard at the barracks. In short, Zvi-Meir, a villain of the first order, left his wife and children and ran away to Minsk. Fanny, the woman whom the honourable gentleman is pursuing, went after him to get a writ of divorce and save her sister from a life of solitude. And therefore he, the cantor, is completely unrelated to the whole plot. If being poor amounts to conspiracy, why hasn't the honourable gentleman arrested every single citizen of the empire? Either way, there must be—

"That's enough!" Novak interrupts him, and the toothpick stops talking and stands as straight as a birch tree. "Now go away!"

The cantor turns this way and that, walks in circles, and finally chooses a random direction. He could be shot for breaking the curfew, Novak thinks, and yet he does not call him back. Standing on the town's empty main street, the inspector looks around. He can sense the townspeople peering at him through the closed shutters, Hasidim mocking him from rooftops, black crows ready to peck at his eyes.

He sets off in the direction of the Jewish cemetery, then towards the road out of Motal. A writ of divorce? Is this what all the drama is about? Is the entire Okhrana on high alert because of this ridiculous story? Impossible. Women do not leave their homes with knives on their thighs in the middle of the night to teach a wayward brother-in-law a lesson. What is more, there is nothing in this story to explain the other details of the investigation. Why did the army join her cause? Why did complete strangers come to her help? How has this affair reached as far as His Highness Count Alexander Pazhari? The divorce story must be a red herring.

Or maybe . . . maybe there really is a very simple explanation. A woman set out to help her unhappy sister and defended herself with a butcher's knife. Yet, even if this is indeed the true course of events, how did it lead to this point? Again, why did all these strangers help her? How could such a trivial matter lead the empire's two most loyal forces to a head-on confrontation? There must be more to it than this. There must be.

The more Novak is trying to come to grips with the tale he has just been told, the more his heart tells him that he has let himself be fooled. There is nothing profound about this business. The story is embarrassingly straightforward. Fanny paid Zizek to join her, and after they had the run-in with the family of thieves, they became frightened and turned to Zizek's old army friend, Patrick Adamsky, for help. Then the debacle deteriorated into a blood-bath, and they were forced to seek refuge in the army camp. They must have used old contacts with David Pazhari or one of the senior officers and managed to have the garrison escort them to Minsk. Mishenkov will be putting his boots up in Nesvizh as usual, Alexander Pazhari will walk away free for lack of evidence, and what is left for Novak? Wild delusions about a revolution.

Novak looks up. Clouds crowd the autumnal skies. Pine needles prick the wind. In a week, maybe two, the rains will start falling and the entire region will become a bog. He wanders down to the Yaselda and stands on the riverbank. What does it take for a man to walk on water? If he took a confident step, could he avoid drowning? What does it take for a man to drown in a river? If he dunked his head underwater, would his nostrils open? That would make one hell of a resignation letter.

In the distance, Novak hears the sound of galloping hooves, and turns towards the forest on the opposite shore. Could the suspects have already arrived from Minsk? Realising that the procession is making its way towards him, he quickly climbs up the bank to take a better look. The riders unharness the horses from their carriages and urge the animals to enter the river. Dammit, these are skilled horsemen. The horses' heads bob above the water as they advance towards midstream, until they finally swim across to the other shore with their riders. Novak's surprise vanishes once he recognises the new guests.

A grey-haired man with a bushy, extravagant moustache dismounts from his stallion. His uniform, the sumptuous attire of a high-ranking general, is awe-inspiring. His boots are laced all the way up to his knees, the hilt of his sword glimmers above its scabbard, and the butt of his gun is gilded. Now there's a proud Russian, Novak thinks. There's a fearless face, the moustache of a warrior, the gaze of a leader, the uniform of a count, a clean-shaven chin (how long has it been since Novak last shaved? He must look like a miserable old vagabond). There you go, Piotr, this man is everything you could have been.

"Your Excellency," he says to Governor Osip Gurko.

"Your Excellency?" Gurko barks, ruffling Novak's hair as if they were two humble soldiers. "You and I swam through shit together."

"Indeed, Your Excellency," Novak says, smiling, "and yet, your rank obliges."

"Rank my ass! Novak, old man, give me a hug. It's been years! You know how badly I've wanted to visit! I keep saying to Arkady," he says, turning to one of the horsemen whose name must be Arkady, "'we must visit Novak.' But work, m'dear fellow, as you of all people should know, forces us to keep our noses to the grindstone."

"Quite," Novak says, nodding.

"So, what have you been up to?"

"Not much."

"Not much?" Gurko laughs. "Did you hear that, Arkady? I wish everyone else would do as little as he does. And how's your leg, old man?" Gurko thumps him on the shoulder. "Is it any better?"

"It's getting worse," Novak says, his smile vanishing, and Gurko roars with laughter again. "Did you hear that, Arkady? It's getting worse!"

Novak has always detested Gurko's habit of repeating everything he says to everyone else present. He notices that the one called Arkady does not even raise his head. Arkady must have also grown accustomed to being used as a rhetorical device.

"Did you come to welcome us?" Gurko asks.

"Yes, sir," Novak lies, wondering who has brought Gurko into the matter. The obvious answer would be Dodek, but that would entail wit that this witless creature doesn't have.

"Let us walk a little," Gurko says, removing his cap. "I'd like a word." Novak follows him. They walk along the riverbank and Gurko stops by a bare sweet-cherry tree and inspects its branches. Standing next to him, Novak suddenly notices how deep the wrinkles in Gurko's face have become. He's grown old, dammit. The hands that emerge from the governor's uniform sleeves are shrivelled and pale, as if they have just shed their skin, like a snake.

"Your name keeps coming up, Novak," says Gurko. "Did you know that a major reorganisation is planned for this region? We will need new governors, mayors; not today or tomorrow, to be sure, but you know, when the day comes . . . in due course. Your Anna will be very pleased, and so will the boys."

"Yes, Your Excellency, thank you." Novak bows his head. "My Anna will certainly be pleased."

"Is anything the matter, Novak? You seem a bit downcast."

"Everything's fine."

"I thought you would be happy to hear this."

"Very happy, Your Excellency."

Gurko sighs. "Well, old man, do you want to tell me what's been going on here?"

Novak knows that the moment of truth has arrived. He would like to say, "It's nothing, Your Highness, this affair proved to be much less serious than we originally thought. A Jewess went out of her mind, that's all." Yet even this one sentence would be false, because Novak cannot deny his admiration for the main suspect, Fanny Keismann. Can he separate his feelings from the conclusions of the investigation? Who is he trying to deceive? How much power does he really have? If he dares to shares his version of the story, he will face ridicule. "He's lost his mind," people will say, "nothing about his version corresponds with the evidence." Could it be that the entire army had mobilised because of a writ of divorce? A colonel disobeyed orders so he could hunt down a runaway husband? The honourable Count Alexander Pazhari lied to rescue a Jewish woman from loneliness? Did the governor take the trouble to come all this way only to make a fool of himself? Gurko's presence alone requires the construction of a story that he can take back to St Petersburg.

At this point, Novak realises that he is powerless. He has control over nothing. No matter what he says, the only version endorsed will be, by necessity, the version deemed most beneficial to the powerful and the influential. Count Gurko will return to St Petersburg a hero, the Okhrana agents will once again prove the efficiency of the secret police, Novak will keep his job and may even get an appointment in the civil service (a mayor? He never imagined himself without a uniform). The suspects and their accomplices will pay the price either at the gallows or in Siberia, and the local mob will vent their feelings by staging a small pogrom. As far as the authorities are concerned, there is only one way to bring this story to a satisfactory conclusion.

"Well, m'dear fellow?"

Novak delivers the goods. Gurko did not expect such a windfall. As Novak's story builds, he notices satisfaction spreading across Gurko's face. This is what the inspector tells the governor: Count Alexander Pazhari, nominated to be the Czar's closest adviser, and, according to some, already serving in this capacity short of an official appointment, has been lying for years about family ties with a senior army officer, Colonel David Pazhari. The precise nature of the relationship between the two men is still unclear, but what *is* clear is that Count Alexander Pazhari has at his disposal a formidable military force that he can use at will. While he is still deciding to what end he should put this unit, the count has been sending agitators to circulate the radical views of a *żyd* from Minsk named Zvi-Meir Speismann. The precise nature of Speismann's activities is yet to be ascertained, but what is already known is that his followers are prepared to slit the throat of anyone who refuses to adhere to his teachings. The cases at hand – and there must certainly be others they don't yet know about – were committed by Zizek Breshov and Patrick Adamsky, two former Jews – what else? – who have left a bloody trail behind them. Every once in a while, Count Alexander Pazhari dispatches, by means of Colonel David Pazhari, a small troop of soldiers to help them carry out their misdeeds. The garrison that escorted them to Minsk, for example, was sent to secure a secret meeting with their leader, Zvi-Meir Speismann. It is reasonable to suspect that Count Alexander Pazhari is waiting for the opportune moment to put his private unit to good use, at which point five

486

dead bodies will seem like a trifle. "We are on the brink of disaster," Novak concludes. "A fifth column made up of our finest men is on the rise, high-ranking noblemen from St Petersburg, advisers to the Czar, are raising private armies under our very noses. Would you believe it?"

"Believe it?" Gurko's massive moustache quivers. "These Petersburgians are all snakes, the lot of them. If it were up to me, I'd have them all before a firing squad."

"Well, that is where things stand."

As Gurko mulls this over, every strand of moustache that his fingers stroke seems to outline a new thought. "But what about the woman?" he asks, and Novak reddens with embarrassment. Who the hell has been keeping the governor informed of every detail of the investigation?

"Oh, her? She's of no importance. Led astray. An innocent lamb."

"But I heard that she is good friends with her knife."

"W-well," Novak stutters, "that is what we thought at the beginning . . . I mean . . . being a butcher . . . it seemed to make sense. But when it comes to it, there is no doubt that the men are the culprits."

"I want her too, Novak."

"Certainly, Your Excellency, we have no intention of releasing her."

"I am not talking about releasing anyone. I want them all hanging from a noose, no ifs or buts."

"There won't be any."

"Excellent. I'm sick of them! These *żyds*, they are not Russian."

"Of course not."

"They are not like us."

"How could they be like us?"

"They stink and live on top of each other like vermin. They are uncultured."

"I quite agree."

"Take a long look at us, how far we have come. A proud nation. People are finally holding their heads up high. We did not fight in vain, Novak. You did not lose your leg for nothing."

"Of course not." Novak bows his head.

"Why don't they go somewhere else? Aren't there other countries in the world?"

"I don't know, sir, maybe they're too comfortable here."

"Quite so, that is exactly the problem. This whole affair comes at an excellent time. It will prove to people that there is only one answer."

"Of course, Your Excellency."

V

Motal has been transformed into Okhrana-berg. It looks like a police academy or a barracks. This is surprising, since the curfew does not apply to half its population – the gentiles – who for some reason have not rushed to take over businesses and make a quick profit now that the Jews are absent. The market is shut and few people leave their homes. Motal is desolate. Without its Jews it is like a creature paralysed.

Agents enter homes and leave carrying *kartoshkes* and bottles of *yash*. Every now and again they take a golden candlestick, which the hosts complement with its matching partner, whatever it takes to make the agents leave.

Reb Moishe-Lazer Halperin passes between his congregants' homes. He is the only Jew permitted to ignore the curfew on Prokor's, that is Piotr Novak's, orders. The rabbi expects to be welcomed as usual: the table set, a loaf of bread ready to be served and eyes hungry for his every word. But now, their faces, good grief, their faces are so grim. Disaster is about to strike the town; they can all sense the impending doom.

It didn't take much for everyone to piece together the story. Without any experience in murder investigations, they linked Zvi-Meir Speismann's disappearance with Fanny Keismann's unpredictable nature and background in ritual slaughter, and came up with the solution for one of the most complex episodes in the history of the Russian Empire. "If only she had stayed put, none of this would have happened. And what good has come of it? She disgraced her family, leaving her home after midnight, God knows why, like a moonstruck spinster."

Fearing Rivkah Keismann's accusatory gaze, the rabbi has been steering clear of the Keismann household, where Mende has settled in with her children. Rivkah Keismann blames the rabbi for everything. If he hadn't been duped by Akim and Prokor, Avremaleh and Pinchasaleh Rabinovits – names that are obviously false – the town would not have been put under siege. Rivkah did not ask for much from the rabbi. All she wanted was for her son to unite with his wife's sister. And what did she get instead? A sword at her neck. How can she leave this world? God help her, she would have been better off dead.

People say: Rivkah Keismann is a strong woman.

The truth is: Rivkah Keismann is on the verge of collapse. Her son sits at the dining table from dawn to dusk, his head in his hands. He cannot tend to his flock, he is not allowed to mend the fences. He cannot even go out to empty his bowels without permission. Every now and again he chews a piece of bread, without cheese, looking as if at any given moment he might hurl the table at the wall and confront the agents outside. All this time Rivkah sits opposite him and does not budge. She is afraid that as soon as she takes her eyes off him, he will do something that they will all regret.

And what about the children? God help her. Unmanageable, wild, just like their mother. Most little ones wet themselves as soon as they hear the word "police". But these children? They slip away from the house, crawl under fences, hide in bushes. They think this entire affair is a funny game. Forget about the younger ones, they'll be fine as long as they don't hurt themselves. Not even the most brutal of soldiers would treat a child like a criminal. But Gavriellah, the eldest? She's eight years old already. "Grown girls" like her can be accused of conspiracy. And true enough, she disappears for hours on end. Where does she go? No one has any idea.

"Natan-Berl, where is Gavriellah?"

"Mmmm . . . ummm . . . Gavriellah? She'll be fine."

People say: Rivkah Keismann is a bitter woman.

The truth is, Rivkah Keismann was right all along. Fanny Keismann was nothing but trouble, and now everyone can see the outcome. Rivkah should probably have put her foot down from the very beginning, but she always tries to please everyone. Perhaps this is all her fault.

Mende Speismann locks herself away in her room. She is fuming. How could her younger sister humiliate her so publicly? Good God! Wasn't Mende managing just fine, even without Zvi-Meir Speismann by her side? Did Mende behave like those miserable women who send a grovelling advertisement to *Hamagid*? Did she allow her name to appear below any newspaper headline that reads "Lost" or "Help"? Did she ask the entire world to take an interest in her private affairs?

Now her name will be known to all, read not in advertisements but in the news sections; not only in *Hamagid* but also in *Ha-Melitz* and in other newspapers, too. What did Mende do to her younger sister to deserve this torture? Is Fanny that jealous?

Mende is not one to return the offences she receives. She

certainly does not seek retaliation at the children's expense. There is only one thing on her mind right now: making sure that no child leaves the courtyard. Natan-Berl is immovable. Rivkah Keismann is with her in spirit but her flesh lacks the energy to chase after anyone. So Mende finds herself watching over her two fledglings and Fanny's five jewels like a hawk.

Only Gavriellah escapes Mende's watchful eye. In fact, even if Mende searched beyond the courtyard she would never have found her niece. Gavriellah has started spending long hours away from home and no-one in Motal could ever guess where. The place is quite central, in fact, just a quarter of a verst from Motal's main square. And yet no-one has noticed her. Did she find a hiding place in an abandoned stork's nest? If not, where is she?

Like the other children, Gavriellah has collected bits and pieces of the story here and there. But, unlike them, she has understood exactly what the details mean and striven to learn as much as she can about Zizek, her mother's accomplice. She has found herself siding with the Berkovits and Avramson families and begun to feel a strong resentment for everyone else.

Leah Berkovits, a cantankerous old lady at the best of times, could not believe her eyes when she opened her door and found an eight-year-old child on her doorstep.

"What are you doing here, brat?" she screeched, mistaking Gavriellah for a boy, since the old lady's eyesight – how should we put this – has seen better days.

"I have come to stay with you," Gavriellah replied, and she did just that.

What did Gavriellah talk about with Leah? Not much. Like the Keismanns, the Berkovitses are not big talkers. What did they do, then? Well, they did what most other Motal residents do. They sat down, stood up, cleaned, ate, knitted, read, day-dreamed, dozed off, waited. They definitely did something, that's for sure.

After all, neither the old lady nor her son slammed the door in Gavriellah's face as they have always done with everyone else. What is more, they let her call Leah Berkovits "Babushka". And not only that, they let her stroke Leah's rugged face, a face through which tears have dug indelible furrows.

"I have come to stay with you," Gavriellah told them, and they let her in.

VI

When Fanny wakes up, her right cheek is still burning where it met with a fist. In fact, her whole face is in pain. Her jaw creaks. Has she lost a tooth? Her nose is numb. Is it broken? The crown of her head feels like someone is pulling it upwards. Has she been drugged? She has no way of knowing.

Wouldn't she rather be the owner of an unbattered face? Of course she would. Yet right now, she feels certain that a person who has never been punched in the face must know nothing about life. The blow she sustained not only aggrieved her face; it shook her to the core. The loss of control was absolute. She was entirely at the mercy of the brute who punched her, who could have struck her other cheek if he'd wanted to. But his single jab was perfectly accurate, a necessary conclusion to her journey.

Her head is sore. She has been travelling for many hours in a rickety wagon and the driver has not missed a single pothole. Her body is shackled in an uncomfortable position, and she is crammed in with three men. One is unconscious, still tended by a nurse. What is he dreaming about? Who's to know? The second has a face that has not looked this serene in many years. Still holding Adamsky's hand, it is unclear if he is alive or dead.

Whereas the third, well, this is not exactly what Zvi-Meir Speismann had in mind when he heard that both the army and the police were on his trail. His eyes are locked on the floor of the wagon and his lips are mumbling meaningless prattle.

Fanny sees another wagon further up ahead, carrying Captain Istomin and the five sturdy hussars. From what she has heard, nothing in the history of the excellent garrison commander could have predicted that he would one day face accusations of disobedience and mutiny. Now, of course, none of the many brave acts he has performed for the empire's sake will stand in his credit. People are mistaken when they think that good citizenship will earn them immunity. All it takes is for someone to swim just once against the stream for them to find themselves standing before a firing squad, shoulder to shoulder with criminals and traitors.

Two horses nicker behind her. One is grey with a black mane, and the dip in his back shows that he has been around for many years. He is ageless. There's not a war he hasn't been in. The second is a colt who won't stop swishing his tail. On the night she left, when Fanny crossed the Yaselda and realised that Zizek had prepared horses and a cart for them, it dawned on her that this journey was not just about her. Now she is proud of the riff-raff she has gathered around her, the types that townspeople would point at and say: "See them? They're exactly what we're not." Well, this is her army. And although none of them would admit it, she knows that whatever powerful thing it is that unites this divided, battered crew, it has made waves throughout the entire empire.

Is she of sound mind or insane? She could not care less. She is flooded by countless emotions, but regret isn't one of them. Every prospect is clear to her, even that of losing her children, and yet she doesn't wish she could go back in time and do things differently. They must be taking her to meet that inspector.

Despite her unquestionable inferiority, this time he will have to talk to her face to face, in daylight, and not while gripping her throat. This meeting, she feels, is of paramount importance. She knew they would meet again after the night at Adamsky's tavern. What will she tell him? She doesn't know. But this time she will face him like his equal, even if her knife is no longer with her. He strikes her as the only person in the empire she can talk to.

She doesn't expect to exchange a word with her brethren in Motal. She knows all too well that almost every single one of them will be convinced that she is out of her mind. The town community is hell incarnate, of this she is sure. Each of the townsfolk hovers somewhere between individuality and conformity, trying his best to think like everyone else. They will never be independent. They look upon any form of liberty as a form of rebellion; any uniqueness as deviance. Is there anything they will not say about her? Good grief, she should expect the worst. But Natan-Berl won't believe them, nor will Gavriellah. And the little ones will not abandon her, however angry they are. She might very well be crazy, but she knows she will see them again very soon.

"Where are they taking us?" Zvi-Meir hisses a surprising question amid his barrage of gibberish.

Fanny says nothing and looks at Zizek, whose eyes join Zvi-Meir's question. "Home," Fanny replies. "Where else?"

VII

Kindness is not necessarily accompanied by courage. If it were, could we distinguish one from the other? Kindness reveals itself in any manner of ways and sometimes, when it is uncoupled from courage, people do not recognise it.

People who see the world in black and white might argue that the Motalers' welcome of the procession from Minsk was unkind. To wit, for the first time since they came under curfew, the residents opened their shutters and hurled a range of missiles at Fanny's wagon: wood chips, apple peel and all manner of rotting vegetables. Before passing judgment, however, one should stop to consider the following. What would you do after a week-long curfew? What would you do if the lives of your children were at stake? First, you would begin by looking for the cause. Well, there's no question on that score: Fanny Keismann has dragged the entire town into this mess. Second, you would imagine that you'll breathe a sigh of relief when Fanny's fiasco is resolved and the Okhrana's agents have left town. Third, you would want to demonstrate your allegiance to the authorities: both to set your-self apart from those responsible for this fine kettle of fish, and to make sure the police have no reason to stay any longer. In short, with all that in mind, who wouldn't throw rotten tomatoes at Fanny?

Nonetheless, we must add, the rough welcome of the prison-ers' wagon could have been far worse. The townspeople could have thrown stones at the offenders; instead, they pelted them with apple peel and twigs. They could have hurled insults at the ringleader; instead, they whispered their rebukes behind closed doors. In any other place, the prisoners would have arrived at their destination with swollen faces and clothes wet with rotten egg yolk. Whereas here, two of the five hussars picked up the apple peel that hit them and ate it. Such are Motal's Jews: like no other.

Take Mina Gorfinkel for example. Some people say that Yoshke Berkovits was in love with her before he was snatched from his bed. Some can still recount how he floated on air after seeing her at the market square. Others still will swear that he has dreamed his entire life of the day when he would see her again. No-one can confirm whether any of this is true or not. In any event, close to fifty years had gone by since the Berkovits family's tragedy, and Mina Gorfinkel obviously did not sit and wait for Yoshke. She married at fifteen and became a grandmother twenty-five years later. But when the procession drove past her house, she opened the shutters and took a peek at the detainees. "Who are they?" her sons asked. She could have answered "criminals, crooks" like everyone else, but instead she closed the shutters and said nothing.

At the Weitzmann house, now transformed into makeshift headquarters, Colonel Piotr Novak and the rest of the top brass are waiting. The governor, Field Marshal Osip Gurko, is sitting behind the desk, anxious to return to Minsk with clear-cut proof of a murder plot against the Czar. Colonel Piotr Novak is standing next to Gurko, tense, waiting for the outlaws to arrive. Albin Dodek and Haim-Lazer are just behind him. Neither man is pleased to be so close to the other. Haim-Lazer feels that he is on the wrong side of the barricade, a collaborator with the corrupt regime, whereas Dodek is unhappy at being forced to collaborate with a prisoner. Sitting across the desk with his back to the door is another surprising figure: Colonel David Pazhari. For now, he thinks he has come to join the investigators, but he is soon to join the suspects.

"A great honour, sir," Novak says to Pazhari when they meet. "It's not every day you meet the future chancellor's nephew," he adds, waiting for his reaction. Pazhari nods but cannot look the inspector in the eye. Novak assumes that Pazhari is experiencing a pang of conscience, but in truth the colonel is taken aback by the inspector's gaunt face and frail posture. At the Shipka Pass, he had encountered a well-built colonel, whereas the man before him now reminds him of a house of cards – extract one and the entire edifice will come tumbling down.

Although he knows this is probably a bad idea, Pazhari feels he cannot repeat the mistake he made at the Shipka Pass. He takes Novak aside and looks directly into the inspector's eyes. "Voivode," he whispers in his ear, "we fought together at the Shipka."

Novak's face lights up. A long time has passed since someone has called him "Voivode" – Commander.

"Did we?" He tries to hide his excitement. So there is a man in the room other than Gurko who has seen the true Novak. A man who knows that whatever takes place in the room now will not be what Piotr Novak would have planned. A man who knows the difference between Albin Dodek and Piotr Novak.

"Some battle," Novak raises his voice, wanting his agents to hear a conversation between two veterans, to show them what true courage looks like.

"I wanted to tell you that . . ." Pazhari lowers his voice, "I rode by your side when . . ."

Many things can be said about Novak, but slowness of mind is not one of them.

"For years I regretted not . . ."

"You have nothing to regret," Novak says, with a grin. "The Turks fared worse than my leg, didn't they?"

But this exchange leaves Novak feeling deeply troubled. On the one hand, the man here has seen him leading a cavalry regiment into battle. On the other hand, the same man saw him crawling on the ground like a lizard. This contrast – how should he put this – begs for reconciliation.

Gurko touches the inspector's shoulder. "Is everything alright, my friend?"

Novak replies with a confident smile, "Perfectly, Your Excellency."

When the prisoners are brought into headquarters, Pazhari turns pale at the sight of Captain Istomin in handcuffs. He signals to Novak that he wants to have a word before things get out of hand. The commander of the investigation nods and gets to his feet, but Albin Dodek winks at four of the agents and they step forward and disarm the colonel. Startled, Pazhari does not resist. Stripped of his sword and pistol, he goes back to being David from the orphanage. When they stand him next to Captain Istomin he hears in his head, "David, *mon chéri*, my sweet, my jewel, *petit*", and starts looking for a way to escape. Strangely enough, he is relieved that the men who were his allies until a moment ago have now transformed into his bitter enemies.

At this point, Novak is no longer surprised by anything. Clearly, these decisions are no longer in his hands, even though he cannot say in whose hands they might be instead. As he bows his head to Pazhari, the colonel understands that he has reached the end of his road.

From right to left, the suspects standing in the office are: Colonel David Pazhari, Captain Istomin, five hussars, Zizek Breshov, Fanny Keismann, Zvi-Meir Speismann, Captain Adamsky (lying on a stretcher), and for lack of space the matchstick Shleiml Cantor squeezes in behind them, holding two planks. No-one would notice if he left the room with Olga, and yet he stays put.

"Well, Colonel Novak," Field Marshal Osip Gurko calls to him, "shall we begin?"

Novak knows that whoever he questions first will provide the evidence that the people on the other side of the desk want to hear. He can easily trap Pazhari with the imaginary blood relation he never denied, accuse Captain Istomin and the hussars of treason, put the feeble-minded Zizek Breshov on the spot, produce several eyewitnesses to testify against Adamsky and present his own crushed leg as supporting evidence. As for Shleiml Cantor, well, this fount of information requires no further encouragement.

Any of these men would yield the desirable outcome, but he chooses to start with Fanny. He knows that he is the only man present, including Gurko, who is capable of confronting her. This is the moment he has been waiting for his entire career.

"Now, Mrs Keismann," he begins in an impressive tone, "please identify the people standing here and describe the nature of your relationship with them."

Fanny says nothing. This is an awkward moment. Novak decides he must refine his question.

"Oh bother," Gurko suddenly stands up, "time is pressing. I have to be in Minsk the day after tomorrow. Give them their goddamned confessions, for God's sake, and let them sign them."

"Confessions?" Novak says, blankly. "What confessions?"

"Here." His deputy Albin Dodek hands him the papers. Novak looks around, in terror. Any moment now – he can feel it – he too will join the shackled prisoners.

"Your Excellency," Novak mutters. "What about the trial?"

"Trial?" Gurko asks, surprised. "And how long will that take? Do you think that in emergencies, when grave danger looms over the empire, we can afford to wait for trials to end?"

"All the same," Novak says. "The trial is . . ." He cannot complete his sentence. The trial is . . . what? Goddammit, what is he trying to say? He doesn't know. And yet, the trial is important, perhaps it is the most important thing of all.

"The trial might expose more accomplices," Novak says finally, "other cells."

"This is precisely your job, my dear Novak." The tone of Gurko's voice has changed. "We have not finished here, oh no. But right now, what we are looking for is deterrence."

Novak is silent. He feels that his life is hanging by a thread. His trial has been cancelled against his wish. It can't possibly end this way, without a trial.

Suddenly Fanny steps forward. Her wolf-like eyes consume the hearts of all men present. Each of them feels that they have been served a piece of death, a fragment of the End. She throws the document she has just been handed, her so-called confession, to the floor and says calmly, "I am not signing anything until I have seen my children."

Novak is pleased. Now his colleagues, and Gurko most of all, will begin to understand just how complicated this investigation really is. They thought they could bury the case with fabricated confessions. Well, not with a woman like this.

"She can have her wish," Gurko says and adds to Novak, "we'll forge her signature. Are the gallows ready?"

"Gallows?" Novak chokes, flabbergasted.

He turns to the window and sees that five gallows have indeed sprouted in the market square overnight. How did he miss them? They stand before him like ancient trees, defiant. Who gave the order to erect them?

Pazhari steps forward and stands next to Fanny. "You can't kill him." He points at Zizek Breshov. "He is the Father."

"The father," Gurko echoes. "Whose father?"

"He has no children," Dodek says. "We checked."

Novak feels the blood drain from his face. His head swims. The Father! How could he have missed it? The Berkovits family, he's such an idiot! Yoshke Berkovits who became Zizek Breshov, there is not a single soldier who doesn't know his story. That's why they were helped at the camp. For crying out loud, this is not a conspiracy at all, but a code of love and honour, a code that he himself used to follow.

Novak turns to Gurko. "Sir," he begins – a strange way to address a count. "We must remember we are standing before Yoshke Berkovits, who is none other than the Father, General Radzetsky's adjutant. We shouldn't rush the decision."

"I don't know who 'the Father' is," Gurko chuckles. "But General Radzetsky was an idiot."

Novak turns red. He has never been humiliated like this in front of his men before, and Gurko leans towards him and whispers in his ear, "You know, my friend, we can always set up a sixth gallows out there." He sniffs at Novak, and screws up his face, as if Novak is nothing more than a drunken beggar, then camouflages his disgust with a broad smile, from one tip of his magnificent moustache to the other.

"And what about them?" Dodek jerks his head towards Pazhari and his soldiers.

"They should be escorted back to the camp," Novak says, "and face a court-martial."

"No need," Gurko says, "they can face a court-martial right here. Do you have anything to say in your defence?" he asks, turning to Pazhari.

The colonel lowers his eyes. Novak is stunned.

"Excellent," says Gurko. "You are all hereby sentenced to death by firing squad, like the traitors that you are."

Novak cannot believe his ears. Everything is happening so fast that he can't even utter a single word before Colonel Pazhari, Captain Istomin and the five hussars are led out to the wall of a neighbouring old, black house with a low roof. The firing-squad commander yells something, Novak's mind is wrapped in darkness, and gun blasts cut through the air. Peering through the window, Novak sees seven soldiers, including the colonel, lying on the ground in pools of blood.

"You've done a wonderful job, dear Novak." Gurko pats Novak's shoulder. "I'm off to Minsk. Send me a report after the hangings."

"Certainly, Your Excellency," Dodek replies in place of the dumbfounded Novak, and Gurko marches smartly away.

Novak leaves the house and limps over to Pazhari. On th

hand, there's a man lying on the ground who has seen him leading a cavalry regiment into battle. On the other hand, there's a man lying on the ground who has seen him crawling like a lizard. How can these opposites be reconciled? There's the end of an era for you: an era of irresolution.

VIII

If a twig does not want to be washed down a river, what should it do? It can ask, or even beg the stream not to carry it away. But the river itself has no say. Being a river it flows relentlessly, and it is one and the same whether it sweeps along a twig or a baby squirrel in the process.

Such is the situation in Novak's makeshift office. The moment Field Marshal Gurko leaves the room there is no stopping the onrush. Like the flow of a river, the Okhrana agents cannot turn against their own nature, and after honouring the five remaining condemned prisoners with punches and kicks, they go out to gather spectators for the hangings.

In less than two hours, the market square is packed with the residents of Motal and its environs. The agents storm one house after another, dragging out women and children, leaving only to gentiles the choice of whether or not to follow them. Yoshke Mendel is standing beside his shop mumbling "many thanks" out of habit. Simcha-Zissel Resnick, having been dragged away from the shop that is also his home, has left his wife and children in hiding. Two informants notice that he is without his family and ask him where they are. His first stutter earns him a slap in the face, his second stutter costs him the contents of his pockets, and his tears prompt the agents to break into his house, kick his wife and children over to the square and turn his shed upside down in search of his finest meat.

Reb Moishe-Lazer Halperin goes from house to house and pleads with the inhabitants to come out. "Haven't you heard what happened to Simcha-Zissel?" he asks. "Don't try to be clever. Soon we will put all of this behind us, with God's help."

Gathering together in the market square raises everyone's morale. Blumenkrantz winks at Schneider, Grossman teases Isaac Holz, asking whether he sold them the wood for the scaffolds. After spending a week under curfew, isolated in their homes, they stand together to face a single fate. Being a tightly knit community, they know that police officers and agents cannot infiltrate their ranks, which is reassuring. After a while, the children run out of patience and start playing hide-and-seek. Their parents are their hiding places, and the little ones roam free, laughing and shrieking with joy. They are in a festive mood. There's nothing wrong with that. What else can their parents do – tell them the truth?

Two barouches make their way through the crowd, escorted by the secret police agents. The nosiest people by the carriages peer inside and report their findings to the rest. In one carriage sits poor Mende Speismann. What her sister has done to her is abominable. Fanny has publicly humiliated her, brought her good name into disrepute and turned her into the joke of the town. There is not a single household in Kobryn District and Grodno County that hasn't heard about Mende Speismann's misery. Now she is holding her two children close, unaware that she, Yankele and Mirl are about to see Zvi-Meir for the first time in a year, under mortifying circumstances.

In the second carriage sits Natan-Berl. A mighty bear in handcuffs who keeps his head bowed. His mother, Rivkah Keismann, is sobbing by his side. This is not how a bubbe should end her days. She would have been better off dead. She draws her strength from the need to protect her grandchildren, even though the eldest has disappeared. The last she saw of Gavriellah was yesterday, and she is worried sick. What a rebellious little girl. But how could she not be? She is taking after her mother, if this daughter-in-law of hers can be called a mother at all. What woman would do such a thing to her children?

The carriages drive past Rochaleh Speismann, Zvi-Meir's mother. Catching a glimpse of Mende's face, she raises her eyes to the heavens: "Blessed Holy One, I have toiled my whole life, and for what? If You reserved one act of grace for an entire lifetime, You should use it now: save the meek! Rescue my son from the hand of the gentiles and spare my grandchildren." Eliyahu Speismann also tries to look up, but his bent back only permits him to see right in front of him. In his attempt, his gaze rests upon the five sets of gallows and the stool beneath each noose.

IX

The execution has not been planned well. The scaffolds have been built too close to the Weitzmanns' house, where the condemned prisoners are held. The quintet has little time to reflect on their last moments, and the mob has no space in which to cheer and jeer. Instead of being led through the crowd, the guards and prisoners advance down a side street. Those who blink at the wrong moment because of the blinding sunlight miss the procession altogether and by the time they reopen their eyes, they find that the prisoners are already tied to the poles.

Novak stands to one side and observes the unfolding of events. He has no wish to participate in the execution proceedings and he has no power to stop them. He watches Dodek scurrying back and forth, brandishing papers. There can be no doubt now: someone who is not Novak is running the show. The hangmen are obviously rookies. It would surprise him if they knew how to tie a noose. There's the beginning of a new era: everything must be done with haste while patience is considered the Devil's work.

This general state of carelessness gives the condemned companions more time to accept their hour of reckoning. There's neither pomp nor circumstance. The hangmen put the rope around their necks with the indifference of tailors taking measurements for new clothes. The stools on which the prisoners stand have been carried out from various houses, each is of a different height and colour. A circus, that's what this execution is.

Of the five, Shleiml Cantor is the only one to lose his composure when the noose is tightened around his neck.

He tries singing "Adon Olam", yells "Help!" at Olga and then turns to the crowd. "This is the Father!" he shouts, pointing at Zizek Breshov. "The Father!"

A subdued Zvi-Meir Speismann does not scan the crowd for his wife and children. Before his capture, he had finished putting together what was to be his final sermon. It was tremendous, a speech not to be forgotten, words that were to enter the annals of history. But now his lips are sealed, and his one hand feels the empty space left by the three missing fingers of the other.

Patrick Adamsky requires special treatment. Half-conscious, he can only stand if he is supported on both sides, but he protests – can't they see that Ada is trying to rock their baby to sleep in her arms? Shush, quiet please! People are pigs.

Zizek Breshov stares at the crowd. Does he really? Well, his eyes are open. His tongue feels the scar in his mouth, and, wishing he could smoke, he is reminded of the tobacco box he was robbed of on the road to Telekhany. This scene should frighten

Zizek to the point of petrification. But the truth is that he hasn't felt this tranquil for a very long time. When the child Yoshke Berkovits rode into that accursed night with Leib Stein the abductor and his pack of thugs, he knew that a chasm had opened up between him and Motal. On one side of the abyss he stood together with the Avramson brothers, while on its other side stood, well, everything else. One is born into the bosom of one's family. A baby utters a word and immediately seeks its parents' approval. It stands on its feet and looks to them for reassurance. From morning until evening, it is told that it means the world to them. Then one fine day the world sacrifices the boy to Moloch. His parents go into mourning, the congregation feels as if a piece of its own flesh has been torn away, but the world keeps turning. Overnight, the boy comes to learn that his own world and the big wide world are not one and the same. He is left hanging like a loose bandage on a wound, waiting to be ripped off.

And now Zizek turns his calm, blue eyes to the square and recognises twelve-year-old Mina Gorfinkel in the crowd. She holds the tips of her hair and twists her braids, holding in her hand a rag doll her mother had made for her. Mina's older brothers tease her, and Yoshke wants to help her but fears their reaction. His bones are on fire as she passes by and he knows he will never let her down. His family will finally overcome penury, once he becomes a revered scholar who will make Mina proud. He aches to approach her but worries that his tongue will fail him. Then she is gone. Oh well. They have their entire lives ahead of them. The world will bring them together, one step at a time, and Motal will celebrate their unification in holy matrimony.

X

In the absence of speeches or requests for final words (good grief, the hangmen's faces aren't even covered), it is not entirely clear when the time has come to kick away the stools and put an end to the matter. Since no specific time has been designated for the execution, no-one can be certain whether or not it is running late. There is a rumour that they want a painter or a photographer to capture the event, but no-one knows for sure.

Even the spectators' behaviour is unconventional. Where are the tomatoes, the torches, the abuse? They stand with gaping mouths as if they are watching an auction of diamonds they'll never be able to afford. Novak stands amid the crowd, helpless, focusing on the only thing that gives him consolation: Fanny Keismann.

Fanny is not searching for an opportunity to strike. There's no shortage of daggers, some of them are even within her reach, but she does not want her children to witness a gory escape attempt that is doomed to fail. Caught off-guard by the unexpectedly fast turn of events, Fanny's hopes of a last-minute reprieve are slowly evaporating.

She spots Natan-Berl's hairy arm in one of the barouches. Now his face turns the other way, and she prays to God that the tiny hand she can see on his chest isn't . . . yes, it is Elisheva's. Her youngest daughter is sitting in her husband's lap, pulling at his shirt. Natan-Berl is pointing at the window opposite Fanny to distract the toddler, who points too and laughs.

In vain Fanny tries to catch Natan-Berl's gaze. Now he is entertaining Mishka, David and Shmulke with a strange game he has just made up involving his handcuffs. The three boys are bent over the irons, trying to prise them off his wrists. The agents let them play. Natan-Berl will do anything to prevent his children from seeing their mother on the gallows.

A heavy lump lodges itself in Fanny's throat. Her husband is behaving most sensibly. No child should see their mother like this. But brave as she might be, she needs their attention right now. In defiance of anything that might be considered for the good of the children, she screams with a mad despair: "Mishka! Elisheva! David! Shmulke! Gavriellah!"

The crowd falls deathly silent. All eyes are turned to the carriage carrying the Keismann family. The children anxiously look through its window. Are they dreaming or did they just hear their mother's voice? She calls again: "Mishka! Elisheva! David! Shmulke! Gavriellah!"

Natan-Berl stares at her, utterly wretched. His face is seething with rage and his fists are clenched. She sends him a pleading look. Something, God knows what, compelled her to vanish into the night at two hours past midnight. Why her, of all people? He does not know. And now, disregarding all reason, she has to hear herself calling out to her children. She has to see them see her. Is she wrong? She must be. But Natan-Berl is used to her mistakes.

The commotion that ensues signals to the powers that be that they had better draw the proceedings to a close. One of the boys tries to break out of the barouche, as police officers struggle to keep his two daredevil brothers from leaping out of the window. Deafening screams of "Mamme, Mamme!" are met with "Mishka! Elisheva! Mamme is here! Where is Gavriellah?" Natan-Berl tries to calm them down. His children, however, crush his face in their attempts to escape from the carriage, at which point one of the policemen goes one step too far. As Mishka squeezes himself out of a window, the officer grabs him by the throat and slaps his face. The crowd holds its breath. Shocked, Mishka looks around, trembling. Realising that the entire town is watching him, the boy breaks into heart-wrenching cries, "Mamme! Mamaleh!" Fanny bites her tongue as Natan-Berl tears his shirt in a wild

508

attempt to break free from his shackles. The other officers reach for their guns, the situation is getting out of hand.

Fanny looks at the crowd. Now! Now is the moment! Her mind calls to the people. There are thirty policemen and maybe ten more agents but there are more than a thousand of you, dammit. No-one budges. Ashamed, the people in the square look at one another meekly, standing in the sunlight like a herd without its shepherd. The odd man might sneak a furious look at the officers, but otherwise his face remains dull and his posture submissive. When the noose is placed around Fanny's neck she hears, "Not now, Fannychka, not now. Mamme is tired," and knows that not only is her mother tired, but the entire world is tired. The crowd caves in under the weight of exhaustion and terror. Despite their enormous collective power, they are weaker and meeker than one man. Could it be that fear is not just an emotion that overtakes them, but rather a choice, a deliberate choice that prevails over everything?

As the rope cuts into her neck, Fanny tries to ignore her resentment and focus on her children. But she finds it impossible to suppress her loathing for the human backdrop in the square. Her blood is boiling. As long as they can open their shops the next day, they will continue to stand docilely at public hangings. Not more than a day will pass before sounds of bargaining over radishes and haberdashery will rise again from the market. They will tell her story between a purchase and a sale. "A deranged woman," they will say, "since childhood" – adding a word about her companions, "drifters and renegades". Indeed, it is a fact: those who don't resist don't get hurt, and those who don't look for trouble don't find it. And Fanny Keismann? No-one asked a mother to leave her home at two hours past midnight.

And yet, the execution does not grant the townspeople the relief they were hoping for. The first to be pushed from their stool is Shleiml Cantor. But, being such a lightweight, the matchstick's neck does not break, and although the rope tightens around his trachea, he remains alive. He jerks his head, left and right, explaining the mistake to his hangmen. "Wait a minute, take me down here, wait, there's something wrong with the rope, just a second, it's strangling me, listen a minute, sir, Olga! Wait, you don't understand, I wasn't even— They took me— Why so tight with the rope?" Slowly, the verbal flux subsides. "What . . . just a second . . . this is wrong . . . Olga . . . the rope . . ."

The second in line is Patrick Adamsky. In spite of his stupor, his legs refuse to leave the stool. The hangmen kick it and move back quickly, having heard from several different people the stories about torn earlobes and gouged-out eyes. Mustering a hidden strength, Adamsky clings to the stool, imagining that his children are jumping on him and hugging his neck. What a joy! Ada, standing beside him, watching, is beaming. The house is warm and fragrant, and soon they will sit down to eat. One of his children goes too far. Adamsky loses his breath. Wait a minute, this isn't his boy. Who broke into his house? People are pigs, goddammit, they never leave him be.

The third to be pushed from the stool is Zvi-Meir Speismann, refusing to the end to sign his gett. His three missing fingers allow him to remove a hand from his cuffs, and he manages to grab hold of his hangman's uniform. "Severing the marital bond?" he says to the executioner. "What for? I will never give her a gett! Never!" he yelps through his blanket of hair.

The fourth to follow is Zizek Breshov. The executioners appear to have forgotten how tall and broad he is. As soon as they kick the stool away, his feet land flat on the ground. With no other choice, three agents try to pull at his noose in order to asphyxiate him instead of breaking his neck. Zizek's eyes glisten as his tongue licks his scar. He hasn't been to Motal's market square since he was twelve, but nothing has changed. Then as now, people stood in the square yelling, "Thieves is what you are!" Then, as now, they whined and moaned, "Killers!" His return is not an attempt to heal the rift; it is his final breakaway.

As a boy he was torn not only from his hometown but also from its language. He'd forgotten hordes of words. When Rabbi Schneerson from the Society for the Resurrection of the Dead delivered his mother's letters to the army camp, Zizek never understood why she addressed him as "my boy", who is *meine zisalle*, and how come "Mamaleh is here", why does she claim that her heart burns with longing for him? He read the words over and over, and felt guilty: what child does not understand his mother tongue? He thought about writing back but never knew what he should write. He did not send her a single letter.

Fanny Keismann is fifth. Now, for some reason, everyone is looking the other way. She is not as skinny as Cantor and not as tall as Zizek. Her hands are bound and her legs cannot cling to the stool. There will be no need to make any adjustments here. One kick to the stool and her neck will break. Off you go. But then a strange smell starts to rise. Is someone cooking potatoes? This is hardly the moment. Oh no. Something is burning. Good God! A pitch-black cloud is billowing from the direction of the Yaselda and sulphur is raining down from the sky. The hangmen let go of the ropes, and Dodek screams at his agents to draw their weapons as Novak watches an incendiary monster spitting fire in all directions.

Stupendous flames rise instantly, setting an entire street ablaze. Sounds of explosions come from the burning houses as thick smoke escapes from them like a demon. "The synagogue!" yells Reb Moishe-Lazer Halperin and runs towards the inferno. But before he can cross the square the roof of the *beit midrash* crashes into the heart of the conflagration. The crowd disperses in a panic. One man yells, "To the river!", another, "To the well!", and a third recalls that Motal has a fire-fighting wagon. The heat closes in on the crowd, defiant of the brave few who try to come near it with buckets of water. Parents shield their children, covering their faces with clothes they have shed, and they all flee. Even the agents and police officers, including the ad hoc hangmen, run for their lives. Only one of them refuses to give up, the one who answers to the name of Albin Dodek. His commander Piotr Novak is standing close by.

"Come on!" Dodek pleads with Novak, burying his scorched face in his shirt. "Help me, we must make sure that the five of them are dead!"

Novak does not move.

"The law is the law," Dodek screams. "Help me!"

"Righto! Pull the first rope," Novak yells, approaching his deputy. And as Albin Dodek takes the rope that is still attached to Shleiml Cantor, Novak draws his sword and impales his deputy's heart until the blade protrudes from Dodek's beefy back.

"What conclusion would you write in your notepad now?" he asks his deputy, who stares back at him with a glazed expression, as he sinks to his knees.

THE YASELDA RIVER

August 13, 1894
To
The Governor of Poland, Field Marshal Osip Gurko

Your Highness,
Please be advised that the investigation in the town of
Motal has been completed. On your orders, the five suspects were put to death by hanging and the verdicts were
delivered to their families. Although all suspects, including
Zvi-Meir Speismann, are pawns of little consequence, the
trail leads to St Petersburg's upper echelons, and to Count
Alexander Pazhari in particular. At present the cause of the
uprising and its final goal remain unknown, but the main
thrust of the investigation will now shift to the capital.

The army rebels were executed by a firing squad. Two of
them were officers, one of whom held the rank of colonel.
The possibility of Major General Mishenkov's involvement
in the affair should not be excluded. Throughout the investigation the camp commander was in Nesvizh, visiting
the adviser Bobkov. The nature of the adviser's ties with the
Radziwills calls for further investigation.

A fire broke out shortly after the executions, and its
flames consumed the synagogue and half the town's main
street. The cause does not appear to have been arson. As
is well known, infernal heat and low-quality wood tend to

favour the spread of fire. Nonetheless, there were no casualties and in due course the local assessor will report on the completion of the renovation works. Naturally, all expenses will be paid by the Jewish community.

The residents of Motal seem to have learned their lesson, but the Okhrana will increase surveillance around the black marshes of Polesia.

To conclude, a violent assault on the citizens' security was foiled. It is believed, however, that the enemy we face is still lurking in the shadows and keeping his motives well hidden. It should come as no surprise if additional pockets of resistance are encountered.

Sincerely,

Colonel Piotr Novak

Commander of Grodno and Minsk Counties

The official letter Novak drafts clarifies one key feature of the investigation. Take the truth, turn it upside down, and you will come up with something Gurko wants to hear. In order to please his master Novak must reverse the course of events. Had he wanted to submit an honest report, however, he would have written more or less as follows:

Although the five suspects were executed, none of them died. True, Shleiml Cantor lost consciousness as the rope around his neck tightened and he had a brief encounter with the Angel of Death. But if you saw him now, you wouldn't believe that only a week ago he was tied to a scaffold. He sits in Fanny Keismann's house freely gorging himself on cheeses, but this time, he is not *schnorring* but making a living. And no, his job is not cheese-tasting. Shleiml Cantor has a real job: he has replaced Adamsky's nurse and has become the Jew-hater's caretaker. What is more, since the Keismanns never attend the Motal shul, the cantor sings to them constantly to make up for the prayers they miss.

The upshot of this is, well, rather problematic. For if Shleiml Cantor is staying at the Keismann household and is charged with caring for the anti-Semitic captain, this means that Adamsky must be staying close to Fanny's home, which sounds absurd. Well, is a hut in the Keismanns' courtyard close enough? Impossible. Is it the same hut where Rivkah Keismann once lived? Precisely! How on earth did Fanny agree to this? Well, it is easy for one to agree with one's own ideas. And so Fanny has chosen to take into her ark a fine pair: a drunken vagabond and a battered tavern owner. God help them all. And didn't Natan-Berl object? Well, Natan-Berl considers himself lucky that these are the only problems he has now.

Should we surmise that all five of the condemned partners in crime have reunited at the Keismann home? This is a strange question. Doesn't Zvi-Meir have a home of his own? Why, then, should he dwell among the Keismanns? When he was removed from the scaffold, Zvi-Meir showed up at his parents' home without saying a word. A week has passed and he has still not mentioned the Volozhin Yeshiva, nor has he uttered the names Adam and Eve, and he no longer maintains that sin is the pinnacle of faith. He looks for work from sunrise till sundown. Meanwhile, on Mende's orders, he has cleaned up the courtyard, sowed vegetable seeds and travelled with their son Yankele all the way to Pinsk to buy cheap manure. Yesterday he asked the local tutor, the melamed, to refer to him young students in the afternoon hours, promising that he will teach them according to tradition and not according to his own "method". He hugs his children every evening, and begs his wife to let him into her bed. Mende Speismann shows him no mercy, God help her, but promises that everything will be back to the way it was once he finds them a house of their own. What's fair is fair.

Zizek is not staying with the Keismanns either. As soon as he parted with the noose, he marched straight to his home, the Yaselda river. He took off his clothes, swam across the mild stream and found his boat exactly where he had left it. The first thing he did was place a full barrel of rum on board, and then he went back to rowing between the banks. His first customer came yesterday and offered to pay him the fare, but Zizek ignored the outstretched hand and rowed him over to the other side.

And Natan-Berl? Ever since his wife's return, he has tried to work out what he should say to her, but whenever the moment arrives he says nothing. Can he convince her not to repeat this deed ever again? Of course not. Does she admit to her own recklessness? Of course she does. Has she learned her lesson? She has, and yet, if the need should arise she will certainly leave again. Can anyone say anything to this woman? Natan-Berl is not one to back down easily, and so after a prolonged silence he declared: "My mother is not going back to the hut in the yard. That's the end of it. Full stop."

"Alright," Fanny replied, and not another word was said.

It is not at all clear whether Natan-Berl's declaration follows from a years-long protest against the mistreatment of his mother, or an attempt to show Fanny who wears the trousers in their home. Either way, Rivkah Keismann is finally experiencing the bliss she deserves in her ripe old age. Initially she hesitated to return to her son and daughter-in-law's madhouse. On the one hand, she is not young anymore and would like to leave this world sooner rather than later. On the other hand, how can she leave them all in such a terrible state? The house is filthy and the grandchildren are undisciplined. Until now she has tried to keep everyone happy, which was a mistake. Enough is enough! She will show them how to run a household. Her daughter-in-law has much to learn. Indeed, Rivkah Keismann is not particularly educated, but she does have experience in abundance. "Mishka, don't walk barefoot around the house! David, wipe up the water you just spilled! Shmulke, help your grandmother clean the house! Elisheva, little ones can be helpful too! And Gavriellah – where has she disappeared to again? God help me, I'm raising puppies, not children. Just look at my life. I would be better off dead."

What about the executed soldiers, led by Colonel David Pazhari? Novak cannot decide if they were rebels or traitors. But there comes a moment in a soldier's life, any soldier's, when justice and the orders he receives clash. Novak knows that this is never easy, trust him. After all, the first thing a soldier is taught is to believe that orders and justice are one and the same. But once confronted with this dilemma, the soldier knows that opposing what his heart commands would make him a coward. For it is not only death that claims its victims, and charging at the enemy is not the only measure of courage. A just heart can also raise an army of its own, and fighting in its cause can be just as fatal.

As for the fire – or should we call it the arson? It is hard to say. Novak knows that not every resident of Motal attended the hangings. No matter. Everyone in Motal knows exactly who was absent. First and foremost, the Berkovits and Avramson families. When the police went from house to house and forced residents to attend the execution, they skipped both families. What could they have done? Slapped Leah Berkovits' face? Twisted Mirka Avramson's arm? The two old ladies would have looked at them with contempt and remained sitting. "Who are you to tell us what to do? You've already robbed us of our loved ones. Are you threatening an immovable rock with fists? Be our guests!"

Speaking of the Berkovits and Avramson families, Fanny's cry of "Where is Gavriellah?" should not be forgotten. At least three informants reported to Novak that they saw a girl of about eight or nine entering the Berkovits household during curfew. Put two and two together and you will end up with a plausible conclusion: volatile revenge meets the Keismann spark.

Another factor that should be taken into account is the fire's path. The blaze broke out in a house on the main street, not far from the Berkovits residence, and progressed directly towards the synagogue. While many of the nearby houses indeed burned down, other homes that were equally close were unscathed. The fire followed a precise path towards shul, as if someone had doused one house after another with something flammable, but skipped the homes of the local Poles. Can Novak be sure of this? It doesn't matter. He has no solid evidence either way.

The Jews of Motal, however, are convinced that the fire was set by a rabble who came to town to start a pogrom. After all, the havoc wreaked on them in the past week can only be a sign of the authorities' torturous persecution: one Jewess went astray and suddenly all *żyds* are barbaric murderers. This is all the muzhiks need to light up their imagination. They have no need for evidence before they burn and pillage. Where did they come from? There's no shortage of possibilities. What did they want? Jewish blood and children's tears.

The day after the fire, the townspeople went to the square to appraise the damage to the synagogue and calculate the cost of renovations. Reb Moishe-Lazer Halperin placed a *pushke* for donations at the heart of the square and people flocked to leave money in the cup. This gesture must have ignited a miraculous spark: in an instant, pedlars sprang out of nowhere with carts crammed with vegetables and fruits. They were followed by wagons packed with goods, which reminded everyone that not only is the Sabbath approaching, but also the Yamim Noraim, the holiest days of the year, are nigh. A few shops opened. Fish for the Sabbath will not fall from the sky, will it?

The people of Motal and the Keismanns seem to have nothing in common. The village Jews are in the village, and the Motalers are in Motal. The Speismanns and the Keismanns have not renewed their relationship either. Mende will never forgive her sister for what she has done to her, and she keeps explaining to Zvi-Meir how unfortunate, how desperate a wife must be to leave her home at two hours past midnight. Zvi-Meir, for his part, sits across from his wife, browsing through an issue of *Hamagid* with the two digits that remain on his left hand. These pages, Speismann knows, will not print his name ever again. His sagacity will not make any waves either. But, hand on heart, can this even be called a proper newspaper? Such low standards, such prolixity, the folly and whims of exhibitionists eager to become famous. Just look at this advert: "The voice of a merry and contented wife", who would like to thank the Blessed Holy One for having kindly and graciously given her a roof over her head and two darling children. For heaven's sake, is this a way to write? This newspaper is only good for wrapping fish. Shame on anyone whose name makes its way into these pages.

The previous night, after evening prayer, the Speismanns were seen arguing in the street, and not about the Torah either. Mende said something and Zvi-Meir clapped his hands over his ears. Mende kept on babbling, and Zvi-Meir lost his patience and roared, "Quiet, you hen! Enough with your nonsense!" What happened there? No-one knows. But judging by the angry tone, the epithet "hen" should not be taken for an affectionate pet name.

This is what Novak would have written, more or less, had he wanted to tell the truth about the investigation, and then he would have added:

To conclude, Field Marshal Osip Gurko, celebrated Governor of Poland, there has been no violent attack on the citizens' personal security. The threat we face is indeed hidden from us, but only because we refuse to see the world as it truly is.

Yours unfaithfully,

Piotr

Novak and his interpreter, Haim-Lazer, stand at the entrance to the village of Upiravah, some seven versts away from Motal. Before returning to St Petersburg, Novak wants to talk to Fanny Keismann one last time. He has no need of an interpreter anymore and so he asks Haim-Lazer to wait by the carriage.

"It's so peaceful here," Haim-Lazer observes. "Life in Motal seems to be slowly returning to its old course."

"If that is what you think," Novak says as he limps away, "then you've learned nothing."

"Are you leaving me here unsupervised?" Haim-Lazer calls after him.

"I live in hope that I won't have to see you when I return."

From a distance, the Keismann home looks like the neighbouring houses, but as Novak approaches, he notices that it has been extended at the rear. A few chickens wander in the yard, geese stretch their necks out at him, and a one-eyed sheep dog alerts its master to Novak's arrival. Natan-Berl appears in the doorway, holding his youngest daughter, Elisheva, in his arms. The bear recognises Novak and tries to read his face. Before long he understands that it's not him the inspector has come to speak to and he mumbles a few words into the house.

Fanny comes to the door, accompanied by Gavriellah. Natan-Berl asks her to go back inside, but she takes the hand of her eldest and walks over to the gate. Novak cannot stop staring at the girl's eyes – they are unmistakably her mother's – and advances towards them along the fence with the help of his cane until he reaches the gate.

"Would you like to come in?" Fanny asks.

"No," Novak says, surprised. "No."

"I was expecting your visit," she says.

Novak is silent.

"Have you come to arrest me?" she asks, staring at him intently.

Noticing the movement of her left hand he readies his cane, just in case.

"No." Novak says, looking at her gravely. "I have no intention of harming you, and I hope this is mutual, yes?"

Without warning, Fanny pulls out the knife and hands it to

him. Stunned, the inspector looks at the tiny blade she has just placed in his palm. He cannot believe that something so small has slit so many throats with such precision.

"So why are you here?" she asks, scanning his melancholy face.

What does she see? He would have liked to ask her. A coward? A wretch? A drunk? A decent man?

"I have come to warn you," he says. He bows and returns the knife to her. He expects the obvious questions: "Warn against what? Against whom?" But Fanny simply nods. Understood.

Novak turns and walks away, ambling hesitantly, his cane barely supporting his weight. Fanny's gaze follows him, her hand still holding the knife tightly. She can neither throw it away nor strap it back on her thigh. She glances down at Gavriellah, who looks back pleadingly, and she hands over to her eldest child the inheritance she had received from her father. Gavriellah's eyes glisten with pride, and Fanny smiles back, suppressing tears.

The Polesian expanses are crisp, the birch trees rise up straight into the sky and the storks survey the bright fields. Underneath it all the black marshes seethe as their putrid waters flow into the rivers. Distant clouds herald the arrival of autumn rainfall, after which everything will be covered in snow. The rains of the Flood started falling many aeons ago, Fanny knows, and they continue to fall now. The world is on the verge of catastrophe, and what has happened in the last few weeks is nothing compared to what is yet to come. Still, no-one rushes into the ark while the soil is yet to be submerged, and a slow decline is still unfelt. There's always time for a miracle, isn't there?

On his way north towards Telekhany, Novak rides through Motal and witnesses a strange scene. By the riverbank, Zizek is sitting in his boat, minding his own business, nestling a cup of rum in his hands. Two horses are standing there: one with a sway back, the other swishing its tail. And although they are not tethered, they calmly chew their hay. A very old, haggard lady is making her way toward the riverbank, a fair distance from Zizek. Novak cannot tell who she is at first, but as she draws closer, he recognises the wrinkled face of Leah Berkovits.

The young steed neighs, his older friend grunts, and the scar-mouthed hulk notices the elderly woman approaching. One would assume that Zizek would jump to his feet with alacrity. After all, he has been waiting to see her for years. But lo and behold, he does not go out of his way. He places his cup on the seat and helps the old woman into his boat. She, for her part, says nothing and merely sits across from the burly man. There's no *"meine zisalle"*, no "my boy", and no "Mamaleh is here".

Zizek rows across the still water with a placid face. When they reach the middle of the river, he stops the boat as he does with all his passengers. He offers her rum from the barrel. The old lady grimaces but then she thinks better of it, snatches the cup with her sinewy hand, and downs the drink in a single gulp. Zizek nods and continues to row towards the opposite bank.

THE END

YANIV ICZKOVITS is an award-winning author and was formerly a lecturer in philosophy at the University of Tel Aviv. His previous works include *Pulse* (2007), *Adam and Sophie* (2009) and *Wittgenstein's Ethical Thought*, based on his academic work, in 2012. In 2002, he was an inaugural signatory of the "combatants' letter", in which hundreds of Israeli soldiers affirmed their refusal to fight in the occupied territories, and he spent a month in military prison as a result. *The Slaughterman's Daughter* is his third novel and won the Ramat Gan Prize and the Agnon Prize in 2015, the first time the prize had been awarded in ten years. It was also shortlisted for the Sapir Prize. Yaniv Iczkovits previously held a postdoctoral fellowship at Columbia University and lives with his family in Tel Aviv.

ORR SCHARF teaches cultural studies and translation theory at the University of Haifa. He is the author of *Thinking in Translation: Scripture and Redemption in the Thought of Franz Rosenzweig* (De Gruyter, 2019). *The Slaughterman's Daughter* is his first literary translation.